LIMIT
OF VISION

LIMIT
OF VISION

Linda Nagata

A TOM DOHERTY ASSOCIATES BOOK
NEW YORK

This is a work of fiction. All the characters and events portrayed in this book are either products of the author's imagination or are used fictitiously.

LIMIT OF VISION

Edited by Patrick Nielsen Hayden

A Tor Book
Published by Tom Doherty Associates, LLC
175 Fifth Avenue
New York, NY 10010

www.tor.com

Tor® is a registered trademark of Tom Doherty Associates, LLC.

ISBN: 0-765-34211-1
Library of Congress Catalog Card Number: 00-048808

First edition: March 2001
First mass market edition: July 2002

Printed in the United States of America

0 9 8 7 6 5 4 3 2 1

ACKNOWLEDGMENTS

Limit of Vision was a long time in the making, and many people helped along the way. Thanks are due to Mark O. Martin, who suggested *Agrobacterium tumefaciens*, blue-green light, and other delectables. To Howard Morhaim, for putting up with me when I dumped the original manuscript and started over. To Sean Stewart, Kathleen Ann Goonan, and Wil McCarthy, for reading the story-in-progress and offering invaluable suggestions. To Thuy Da Lam, for providing Vietnamese phrases and vetting the manuscript for cultural flaws. (Any remaining errors are my own.) And to my husband, Ron, whose confidence in me always far exceeds my own.

LIMIT
OF VISION

CHAPTER 1

The age had its own momentum. Virgil Copeland could sense it. Even here, now, as he waited anxiously for Gabrielle, it tugged at him, whispering there was no going back.

He stood watch by the glass doors of the Waimanalo retreat center, willing Gabrielle's car to appear at the end of the circular driveway. He imagined it gliding into sight around the bank of lush tropical foliage—heliconia and gardenias, ornamental ginger and potted orchids—their flowers bright in the muted light beneath heavy gray clouds.

But Gabrielle's car did not appear. She didn't call. All afternoon she had failed to respond to Virgil's increasingly frantic messages. He couldn't understand it. She had never been out of contact before.

Randall Panwar stopped his restless pacing, to join Virgil in his watch. "She should have been here hours ago. Something's happened to her. It has to be."

Virgil didn't want to admit it. He touched his forehead, letting his fingertips slide across the tiny silicon shells of his implanted LOVs. They felt like glassy flecks of sand: hard and smooth and utterly illegal.

"Don't do that," Panwar said softly. "Don't call attention to them."

Virgil froze. Then he lowered his hand, forcing himself to breathe deeply, evenly. He had to keep control. With the LOVs enhancing his moods, it would be easy to slide into an irrational panic. Panwar was susceptible too. "You're doing all right, aren't you?" Virgil asked.

Panwar looked at him sharply, his eyes framed by the single narrow wraparound lens of his farsights. Points of data glinted on the interactive screen.

Panwar had always been more volatile than either Virgil or Gabrielle, and yet he handled his LOVs best. The cascading mood swings that Virgil feared rarely troubled him. "I'm worried," Panwar said. "But I'm not gone. You?"

"I'll let you know."

Panwar nodded. "I've got sedatives, if you need them."

"I don't."

"I'll try to message her again."

He bowed his head, raising his hand to touch his farsights, as if he had to shade out the external world to see the display. He'd had the same odd mannerism since Virgil had met him—eight years ago now—when they'd been assigned to share a frosh dorm room, shoved together because they'd both graduated from technical high schools, and because they were both sixteen.

Panwar's dark brown hair displayed a ruddy Irish tinge, courtesy of his mother. By contrast his luminous black eyes were a pure gift of his father. Ancient India in a glance. At six-three he was several inches taller than Virgil, with the lean, half-wasted build of a starving student out of some nineteenth-century Russian novel. Not that he had ever wanted for money—his parents were both computer barons, and all that he had ever lacked was time. Then again, it would take an infinite amount of time to satisfy his curiosities.

He looked up. A short, sharp shake of his head conveyed his lack of success. "Let's drive by her place when we get out of here." His own implanted LOVs glittered like tiny blue-green diamonds, scattered across his forehead, just beneath his hairline. Like Gabrielle, he passed them off as a subtle touch of fashionable glitter.

Virgil's LOVs were hidden by the corded strands of his Egyptian-wrapped hair, and could be seen only when he pulled the tresses back into a ponytail. "Maybe she just fell asleep," he muttered.

"Not Gabrielle."

Virgil glanced across the lobby to the half-open door of the conference room, where the droning voice of a presenter could be heard, describing in excruciating detail the numbers obtained in a recent experiment. It was the sixth project review to be laid before the senior staff of Equatorial Systems in a session that had already run three hours. The LOV project was up next, the seventh and last appeal to be laid before a brain-fried audience charged with recommending funding for the coming year.

Gabrielle *always* did the presenting. The execs loved her. She was a control freak who made you happy to follow along.

"Maybe she lost her farsights," Virgil suggested without belief.

"She would have called us on a public link. Maybe she found a new boyfriend, got distracted."

"That's not it."

It was Virgil's private theory that in a world of six and a half billion people, only the hopelessly driven obsessive could outhustle the masses of the sane—those who insisted on rounded lives, filled out with steady lovers, concerts, vacations, hobbies, pets, and even children. Sane people could not begin to compete with the crazies who lived and breathed their work, who fell asleep long after midnight with their farsights still on, only to waken at dawn and check results before coffee.

Gabrielle had never been one of the sane.

So why hadn't she called?

Because something had stopped her. Something bad. Maybe a car accident? But if that were it, they should have heard by now.

Virgil's gaze scanned the field of his own farsights, searching for Gabrielle's icon, hoping to find it undiscovered on his screen.

Nothing.

Panwar was pacing again, back and forth before the lobby doors. Virgil said, "You're going to have to do it."

Panwar whirled on him. "God, no. It's five-thirty on a Sunday afternoon. Half the execs are asleep, and the other half want to get drunk. They emphatically *do not* want to listen to *me*."

"We haven't got a choice."

"You could do it," Panwar said. "You *should* do it. It's your fault anyway Nash stuck us in this time slot. If you'd turned in the monthly report when it was due—"

"Remember my career-day talk?"

Panwar winced. "Oh, Christ. I forgot." Then he added, "You

always were a jackass. All right. I'll give the presentation. But the instant Gabrielle walks through that door, *she* takes over at the podium."

Virgil skulked in the conference-room doorway, as much to make it awkward for anyone to leave early as to hear what Panwar had to say. The LOV project always confused the new execs, stirring up uncomfortable questions like: What's it for? Where's it going? Have any market studies been done?

The project was the problem child in the EquaSys family, refusing to stay on a convenient track to market glory. It was Panwar's job to make the execs love it anyway.

Or rather, it was Gabrielle's job. Panwar was only subbing.

"... *At the heart of the LOV project are the artificial neurons called asterids. Conceived as a medical device to stabilize patients with an unbalanced brain chemistry . . .*"

Virgil scowled. Wasn't Panwar's passion supposed to illuminate his voice, or something? Why had this sounded so much better when they'd rehearsed it with Gabrielle?

"*Test animals used in this phase of development began to exhibit enhanced intelligence as measured on behavioral tests, though never for long. The cells tended to reproduce as small tumors of intense activity. Within an average sixty days postimplantation, every test animal died as some vital, brain-regulated function ceased to work.*"

Not that Panwar was a bad speaker. He was earnest and quick, and obviously fascinated by his subject, but he wasn't Gabrielle. The rising murmur of whispered conversations among the execs could not be a good sign.

"*The tumor problem was eliminated by making asterid reproduction dependent on two amino acids not normally found in nature. Nopaline is required for normal metabolism, while nopaline with octopine is needed before the asterids can reproduce.*"

Virgil shook his head. Nopaline, octopine, what-a-pine? The nomenclature would have been music coming from Gabrielle's mouth, but from Panwar it was just noise. Virgil glanced wistfully at the lobby door. Still no Gabrielle.

"*In the third phase of development, the asterids were completely re-designed once again. No longer did they exist as single cells. Instead, a colony of asterids was housed within a transparent silicate shell, permitting easy optical communication. In effect, EquaSys had created the first artificial life-form, a symbiotic species affectionately known as LOVs—an acronym for Limit of Vision, because in size LOVs are just at the boundary of what the human eye can easily see."*

A new species. To Virgil, the idea still had a magical ring. It was the lure that had drawn him into the project, but to the execs it was old news.

"When implanted on the scalps of test animals, the asterids within each shell formed an artificial nerve, able to reach through a micropore in the skull and past the tough triple layer of the meninges to touch the tissue of the brain. To the surprise of the development team, the LOV implants soon began to communicate with one another, and once again, long-term behavioral effects were observed in test animals. They became smarter, but this time without the development of tumors, or failures in vital functions."

The momentum of discovery had taken over the project. Virgil had not been part of it then, but he still felt a stir of excitement.

"The original medical application was expanded, for it became apparent that the LOVs might be developed into an artificial or even an auxiliary brain.

"Then came the Van Nuys incident."

EquaSys had not been involved in that debacle, but the company had been caught in the fallout, when the U.S. government agreed to a two-year moratorium on the development of all artificial life-forms. One of the witnesses in favor had been the original LOV project director. To Summer Goforth, Van Nuys was a wake-up call. She'd publicly renounced her work, and the work of everyone else involved in developing artificial life-forms. Virgil had been brought on board to take Summer Goforth's place.

"In a compromise settlement EquaSys agreed to abandon animal testing and to export the LOVs to a secure facility aboard the Hammer, *the newest platform in low-earth-orbit. From such a venue, the LOVs could not possibly 'escape into the environment,' as happened in Van Nuys."*

The LOVs had been so easy to contain. That's what made them safe.

"Since then our research has been limited to remote manipulation, but that could soon change. The two-year moratorium will expire this June 30. At that time EquaSys will be free to exploit an unparalleled technology that could ultimately touch every aspect of our lives. . . ."

All that and more, Virgil thought, for if the LOVs could be legally brought Earth-side, then no one need ever know about the LOVs the three of them had smuggled off the orbital during the moratorium period. He still could not quite believe they had done it, and yet . . . he could not imagine *not* doing it. Not anymore.

It had been worth the risk. Even if they were found out, it had been worth it. The LOVs were a gift. Virgil could no longer imagine life without them.

The original studies suggested the LOVs could enhance the intelligence of test animals, but Virgil knew from personal experience that in humans the LOVs enhanced *emotion*. If he wanted to lift his confidence, his LOVs could make it real. If he sought to push his mind into a coolly analytical zone, he need only focus and the LOVs would amplify his mood. Fearlessness, calm, or good cheer, the LOVs could augment each one. But best of all—priceless—were those hours when the LOVs were persuaded to plunge him into a creative fervor, where intuitive, electric thoughts cascaded into being, and time and hunger and deadlines and disappointments no longer mattered. With the LOVs, Virgil could place himself in that space by an act of will.

"All of our research to date," Panwar said, concluding his historical summary, *"has shown without doubt, that LOVs are perfectly safe."*

An icon winked into existence on the screen of Virgil's farsights—but it was not from Gabrielle. He felt a stir of fear as he recognized the symbol used by EquaSys security. He forced himself to take a calming breath before he whispered, *"Link."*

His farsights executed the command, and the grim face of the security chief resolved within his screen. Beside it appeared a head-and-shoulders image of Dr. Nash Chou, the research director and Virgil's immediate boss. Nash had hired Virgil to handle the LOV program. Now he turned around in his seat at the head of the conference table, a portly man in a neat business suit, his round face looking puzzled as he gazed back at Virgil.

"Dr. Chou," the security chief said. "There's been an incident in Dr. Copeland's lab."

A cleaning robot had found Gabrielle. The little cindy had gone into the project suite just after five, tending to the carpets in the hallway and offices before entering the common room. At five-nineteen it contacted security, reporting that its air-quality sensors had detected the presence of noxious or hazardous airborne vapors.

Security discovered her body at five-thirty-two.

"Oh, God, no," someone said. "It can't be true."

"Virg?"

That was Panwar. He sounded like a kid again, sixteen years old and scared.

Virgil sat hunched on a sofa in the retreat center's lobby, his face in his hands. "God, my chest hurts."

Panwar's hand closed awkwardly on his shoulder. "Hold on to yourself, Virg. Don't lose it. We still have to get there. Find out what happened."

Virgil nodded. They'd driven over together from Honolulu. Significantly, Gabrielle had declined to carpool. She'd been in a hurry Saturday, when Virgil had called. *You two go ahead. I've got some business to take care of, so I might be a few minutes late.*

So. Time to head back, then. He started to rise.

"No, wait here," Panwar said. "I'll get your car."

"Get it tomorrow," Nash Chou interrupted from somewhere nearby. His voice was soothing, fatherly. "It's getting dark, and neither of you is in any shape to drive."

So Nash drove them back in the rain. Virgil sat in the shotgun seat, his head bowed against his hand, drowning slowly in a grief that seemed to have nothing to do with feedback from the LOVs. *How?* he wondered. *Why?* He was dimly aware of Nash behind the wheel of the Mercedes. The windshield wipers were on. Veils of rain pattered against the glass as the car accelerated into heavy traffic on the freeway.

A light started blinking, somewhere close to Virgil's eye. Its insistent optical bleating tugged at his consciousness, teased him, forced him to look at it.

It was Panwar's icon—an infinity sign made to look like a twisted lane of black space containing thousands of stars, set against a powder blue background. Why was it there on the screen of his farsights? Panwar was only a couple of feet away, behind him in the backseat.

Still, it was easier to accept the link than to turn around. He tapped a quick code with his fingers, stimulating the microchips embedded in his fingertips to emit faint radio signals, detectable by his farsights.

Panwar's face replaced the glittery icon. He looked wary, almost defensive as his gaze fixed on Virgil, but he didn't speak. Instead, typed text in bright white letters appeared in Virgil's field of view:

→ Don't say a word! Understand me? Don't let Nash know we're talking.

Virgil stared at the message, trying to make sense of it, until a new couplet replaced the original sentences:

→ Virg? You understand?

Without looking up or lowering the hand that shaded his farsights, Virgil dipped his head in a slight nod. More words arrived:

→ Pull yourself together, man, because you are scaring the shit out of me!!!

Virgil started to open his mouth.

→ No! Don't talk!!! Listen to me, and try to remember what's at stake. Gabrielle's dead. I can't believe it either, but we can't bring her back. We're not that far along yet.

Virgil squeezed his eyes shut, wondering if they ever would have the power to heal death. The human body was a machine; he knew that. He had looked deep into its workings, all the way down to the level of cellular mechanics, and there was no other way to interpret the processes there than as the workings of an intricate, beautiful, and delicate machine.

Machines, though, could be repaired. They could be rebuilt, copied, and improved—and sometimes it seemed inevitable that all of that would soon be possible for the human machine too.

But not soon enough for Gabrielle.

When Virgil looked again, new words had replaced the old ones on his farsights:

→ Remember the LOvs, Virg. HER LOvs. The coroner could find them.

Panwar had found the arrow to pierce Virgil's confusion. He sat up. His hand fell to his side. Every communication their farsights handled was encrypted and passed through anonymous servers, protecting them from pirate spammers and data thieves. Most farsights worked that way, producing messages that were untraceable and unreadable except by their intended recipients. Virgil felt grateful for that security as he scanned Panwar's next message.

→ You see it now, don't you, Virg? EVERYTHING is at stake.

Nash glanced over at Virgil, his hairless brow furrowed in concern. "Better now, son?"

Virgil said: "I think so." His voice was hoarse and thick with grief, but he was thinking again.

"It's an unimaginable thing," Nash said. "I can't tell you how sorry I am."

Virgil's hand rose again to his forehead, this time to touch the tiny glass shells of his implanted LOvs.

More words appeared in his field of view:

→ Answer him.

Virgil shook his head. *Unimaginable.* He turned to Nash. "What was she doing there? That's what I can't figure out."

"She wasn't scheduled to be in?"

"No. We had all agreed to take the weekend off. She was supposed to meet us at the retreat."

"Maybe she had a private experiment under way," Panwar said, his voice low, angry, coming from the blackness of the backseat.

Nash frowned. "Was competition a problem?"

It took a moment for Virgil to understand what he was asking. "God, no! We got along fine."

"That's right," Panwar said. "Of course there was competition. There always is at this level, but we understood one another."

Nash spoke delicately: "Gabrielle had been working hard. All of you had. I've seen your logs. You're all utterly dedicated to your work. Sometimes that's good, but sometimes . . . it inflates the importance of what you're doing. Had there been any . . . setbacks recently? Something that might have . . . disturbed her? Disappointed her? Nothing was mentioned in your last report, I know, but . . ." He let his question trail off.

Virgil stared at the rain shooting down through the headlights, momentarily hating Nash for asking such a thing. "She was happy," he said, each syllable crisp. "There were no setbacks. And if there were, she would have handled them. She was tough, Nash. Smart." *Beautiful*. Virgil could almost taste her skin; feel its softness beneath his lips.

Never again.

"Sorry," Nash said. "I had to ask."

Virgil turned to look out the side window at traffic flowing in parallel lanes and the black wall of rain forest beyond it. On the screen of his farsights, Panwar nodded.

→ Good man. Now think.

Virgil didn't want to. But Panwar was right, damn him. If Gabrielle's implanted LOVs were discovered, they could lose everything. Their jobs. Their freedom.

Their own LOV implants.

That frightened him most of all. The implants were part of him now. Taking them away would be like taking away part of his mind—

Focus!

Keeping his right hand low against his thigh, Virgil started tapping codes, trying to remember the procedure for sending typed messages. His ROSA—his ROving Silicon Agent—appeared on-screen, ready to help him. A ROSA was an artificial intelligence program personalized for its user. Virgil's ROSA appeared as a tiny, idealized woman of ancient Greece, her tawny face framed in iridescent hair. He called it Iris.

Iris whispered questions. Virgil tapped his responses, and a keyboard display appeared. After that it was easy. All he had to do was gaze at a letter. Iris would place it on a working line. With three or four letters in place the ROSA could usually guess the remainder of the word. Sometimes it took only one or two.

He typed:

The only danger—if they find her Lovs.

The answer came back immediately.

→ Exactly.

Will coroner ask questions? Should assume body jewelry.

→ Maybe. Maybe not. But if Nash looks close, he'll know.

Virgil gave a slight, negative shake of his head and typed:

Squeamish. Won't look close.

→ Bet your life?

Virgil sighed, pressing his head against the cold glass of the side window. It came to exactly that, didn't it? Gabrielle was gone, and all they could do now was try to save themselves.

WHAT HAPPENED TO HER???

→ Later!!! Now, Lovs! Have to extract, before body's removed.

  How?

HER body, Virgil reminded, sending the little gibe without really thinking.

Panwar glared at the words. Then his eyes darted as he composed a retort.

→ Fuck you V. Think I don't care?

Virgil leaned against the seat back, trying to slow the beating of his heart. Her skin had been like cinnamon cream; her breasts were smooth and full, the nipples honey brown.

"You were very close to her, weren't you?" Nash asked, his voice low, and a touch embarrassed. He cleared his throat. "I wouldn't ask this, except . . . the investigation. They'll want to know. Were you . . . lovers?"

Virgil shook his head. Then he shrugged. In a choked voice he answered, "Sometimes."

Panwar's image displayed comical surprise. Then the expression vanished like hail on a hot street. His black eyes radiated a terrible anger. Aloud he said, "I didn't know."

In typeface he added,

→ You bastard.

She wanted it private.

→ You used Lovs?

Virgil stared straight ahead, not wanting to answer, not wanting to remember what was lost, but Panwar wouldn't let it rest.

→ Answer me!

Yes then! Yes, yes, yes! Her LOVs had spoken to his in a closed loop of enhanced emotion. Never had he felt more connected with another human being.

No response came from Panwar, not right away. He brooded as they descended into the city. A few minutes later, Nash took the off-ramp to H-1. Traffic was almost bumper-to-bumper, but it hadn't come to a stop yet. Virgil watched the skyscrapers slide by until they reached the exit to downtown. The EquaSys building was only a few blocks from the waterfront. Virgil looked for it, picking it out from the surrounding towers. Gabrielle would be there.

New words printed themselves across his field of view:

→ Only one thing matters now, Virgil Copeland. If anyone discovers Gabrielle's LOVs, both of us are good as dead. Remember that! And don't fuck up.

Virgil didn't answer. Nash stopped at the security gate to the underground garage. The guard stepped out of his booth to scan their faces. Virgil ignored the formalities. At the bottom of the ramp, parked beside the elevator bank, were two squad cars and a coroner's white van.

CHAPTER 2

In the fish market at Can Tho a two-foot river carp lay on the chopping block while a diminutive housekeeper argued with the knife-wielding saleswoman for a better price. It was a common scene in the Mekong Delta of southern Vietnam, but it still made good video. Ela Suvanatat was using her farsights to record surreptitiously the early-morning dispute when the icon of her job broker appeared on the net goggles' interactive screen.

Ela caught her breath, certain this link would be about the

article she had prepared for *Nine Dragon Daily*. For two years, she had worked as a freelance producer, creating video articles for regional magazines. Her job broker was supposed to find her new assignments, but things had been slow lately. Ominously slow. *Let this be good news*, Ela thought. *Please*. She couldn't help totting up in her mind the change left on her debit cards. Not enough to eat tonight, at least if she expected to pay for her room. She would have to start selling equipment soon.

She turned away from the market's gossiping heart, looking for a place quiet enough for conversation. She found it in a few inches of free space at a wooden railing that overlooked a canal. Her intrusion earned her an angry stare from a young woman who squatted there, selling frog-meat filets, but Ela ignored her. As a foreigner, she was used to stares.

Ela was half-Thai and half some unknown European vintage that had boosted her height past five-seven. At nineteen she could be described as lithe as a dancer—or freakishly tall and skinny, depending on one's idea of beauty. It was easy to guess which view the frog woman held.

Looking out over the water, Ela tapped a code with her thumb and fingers, using her implanted microchips to accept the link. Joanie's image appeared on Ela's screen, head and shoulders only, overlaid against the bustle of wooden boats plying the canal. "Joanie? Did you hear from *Nine Dragon*? Did they like the article?"

Joanie was a pale, blunt-faced Chinese woman who always dressed in black. "Ela! Oh yes. They liked the article a lot. . . ."

"But they didn't buy it."

"They didn't buy it," Joanie agreed. "The editor feels your work is too . . . *sophisticated* for the market he serves."

Ela's hands squeezed the fish-slippery railing. "Sophisticated? What is that supposed to mean? That my work assumes too much from the viewer? Or it's just boring?"

"No, Ela, no. This is not criticism. Your work is wonderful. Passionate. Both in image and in voice. But not everyone has the benefit of your education."

Ela shook her head. She had gotten her education free off the net from corporate-sponsored schools. She'd learned fluent

English by reading and listening to pirated books and magazines. Now her work was too intellectual and passionate for an affluent regional magazine? The journalism prize that had bought her passage out of Bangkok suddenly seemed a joke. She was supposed to be smart, so why was she always broke?

"All right," Ela said, her voice low and very controlled. "You're saying I need to adopt a simpler style."

"No. Your style is beautiful, just as it is. And besides . . . viewers always know when you're talking down to them."

"Then what *are* you saying? That I can't produce a dumb enough vid for the big markets?"

"You're too bright for them, Ela. There's a lot more fluff than substance in the world. You've just never been good with the fluff."

Ela's throat felt dry despite the humid air. "I did the piece on spec, Joanie. Can't you market it somewhere else?"

"Well of course I'm trying. . . ."

"But you don't think it will sell."

"This is not the end," Joanie said. "It's not our last shot. The Coastal Society article is still open after all, and you're perfect for it. The editor wants you to do it."

Ela turned her back to the railing, meeting again the glare of the frog woman. She returned it in full measure.

The Coastal Society was an environmental charity looking for a propaganda article on the impact of overfishing on the coastline of the Mekong Delta. To Ela, it was the literary equivalent of burger-flipping, only for less money. She had twice refused the assignment already. "That article's still open because there's no one else in this miserable shit-swamp of a country who would consider doing it at the fee they're offering!"

Joanie looked apologetic. "It's all I've got right now."

Ela made a fist at the frog woman and won some small satisfaction when she looked away.

If she accepted this project, it would mean a two-day trip to the coast. She would need to hire a boat and rent diving equipment. Along the way there might be bribes, or "taxes" to pay, so that by the time she got back to Can Tho there would be little money left. Certainly not enough to get her out of the country. But if she didn't take the project, she wasn't going to eat.

"Ela? I need to let them know."

"Did you know I used to be good at telling fortunes?"

"Say yes, Ela. You have no real choice."

"All right," she said bitterly. "I'll take it."

By noon she was on the river, the sole passenger aboard a sleek little fiberglass boat with a sky-blue hull and rails painted red to match the red eyes on its prow. Ela sat on a wooden locker, in the pool of shade beneath the boat's canopy, watching the captain thread a careful path through a loose fleet of long, wooden farm boats returning home from the dawn market. Swaddled figures sat in their sterns, hiding from the sun beneath conical hats.

Noon was a bad time to be moving about. Sweat shone on the captain's neck and in dark streaks on his green-silk shirt. His vessel's new paint stank in the heat. Captain Cameron Quang was a businessman. That's how he'd introduced himself. He claimed to have an appointment at one of the offshore fish farms, and he'd been happy to take Ela along for a small fee. Now she listened to the soft hum of the fuel-cell engine and wondered again what sort of business might require a small, fast, and nearly silent boat.

Standing on the dock in Can Tho, she had listened to her ROSA's assessment of the captain, delivered in a whispery voice through the earpiece of her farsights: *The subject is confirmed with ninety-one percent accuracy as Kam Ho Kwock, also known as Cameron Quang. Age twenty three. Education, Certificate of University proficiency. Profession, independent merchant. No criminal record. Business associates include . . .*

Ela's ROSA was housed on a high-security server in Sydney— and thank god that account was paid up through the end of the year. She had named the ROSA Kathang, after the Thai mountain salamander, and given it that creature's form. It crawled around the screen of her farsights, a tiny icon with shiny brown skin and a bright orange dorsal stripe and tail: cryptic coloring that let it hide in the light.

After the formal briefing, Kathang had added another assessment, this one generated by the fortune-telling program Ela had used in Bangkok: *This one is too clever for violence, but his loyalty will follow the money, and not his word.* Ela had considered this carefully, for she would not be paying him much. She remembered Sawong's endless lectures and the way the aging transvestite's graceful hands would move as he spoke, as if shaping pictures in the air: "Think of each customer as a game piece placed upon a playing board. See their position, understand the board, and you will know their next best move. Do not concern yourself with the influence of luck. Luck is a fiction of the Chinese. We are humble fortune-tellers. Nothing extraordinary will ever happen to the people we serve."

In the end Ela accepted the risk and registered her plans with Joanie Liu, telling herself it would be easy to do worse.

A s Can Tho slipped farther behind, the boat traffic thinned, and the afternoon grew quiet. The sleepy hum of the electric engines became a bass note complemented by the finer tones of water rippling from the bow. The sound of the water made Ela aware of a growing thirst. The sight of dense stands of mangroves planted along the shore made her long for real shade. The little boat's canopy seemed made only to hold the heat in. She breathed lightly, unwilling to draw the steamy air too deeply inside her. She knew it must be full of living things.

The captain tensed as a dark patch appeared at the upper edge of his console's sonar screen. The submerged object was several feet below the surface of the muddy water—too deep to be a navigational hazard. Still, it brought a scowl to his face. "Another one?" Ela asked.

As the boat slipped downriver, the image glided down from the top of the screen. The captain sighed in a world-weary way. "Nevah enough land to bury them all," he observed in his grand Southern American drawl, customized with just a trace of a Vietnamese accent. He did not look at Ela as he spoke, though behind his lightly tinted farsights he seemed confident of her attention.

Now he reached for a watertight box mounted to one side of

the console, unsealing it for the third time since leaving Can Tho. Out came another packet of firecrackers. Ela got ready to plug her ears.

As the dark patch neared the bottom of the screen, it took on the eerie outlines of a human form.

The captain toggled a switch, firing up an electric match. He used it to light the main fuse on the packet of firecrackers, then he pitched them into the air just as the boat slid by the patch of haunted water.

Ela jammed her fingers in her ears as the crackers rattled their threat to all malicious spirits. Fragments of red paper rained down upon the water as the scent of gunpowder filled her nostrils. She looked over the side, but the body remained invisible beneath the muddy current.

The captain nodded at her. "You can nevah see them. Without sonar, theah's no way to know if ghosts are about. The fishin' is bettah now. No doubt."

Ela watched the riverbank slip past. Tall levees had been built to combat the rising level of the ocean. They'd been planted with mangrove stands that leaned out into the river, their submerged roots a rich nursery for aquatic life. But as the boat drew closer to the coast, the mangroves began to thin. Red circles of cut wood gleamed among the leaves. Some still bled sap. Farther along, the thickets had been reduced to a clutter of stumps, leaning like dizzy fighters struggling for balance in the mud. Within a few hundred yards, sedges and salt-tolerant grasses laid claim to the ruined bank.

With the mangrove gone, Ela could see beyond the river for the first time since leaving Can Tho. The brilliant green carpet of the inland rice paddies had been replaced by a brassy patchwork of fish and shrimp ponds, one after another across the flat landscape until they faded into haze.

The captain popped the top of a Coca-Cola. "We'ah nearin' the Eastern Sea," he explained. "Thea's salt in the water, so the rice won't grow, but shrimp grow here. Tilapia fish too."

Concrete tombs dotted the narrow levees that separated the ponds. Close to the river, a group of children worked with small nets to strain tiny fingerlings, which they placed on racks above a smoky fire. At first glance, Ela thought they were all wearing wraparound sunglasses. Then she realized each child had a set of farsights. It seemed very strange, for their clothes were faded and worn. They did not look as if they could afford such things.

The captain's gaze grew fierce as he studied the kids. "No one watches them," he muttered. A hard V had formed between his eyes. "They should not be heah." He reached for another pack of firecrackers, though no submerged burial had appeared on the sonar. He lit the pack and tossed it in the air. Ela hunched against the noise. Onshore, a couple of boys paused in their work to jeer at the passing boat, but most of the ragged children did not even bother to glance up from their labor. The captain was right: There were no adults in sight.

"What was that for?" Ela asked. "What's your problem with these kids?" She looked to the captain for an answer, but he only stared straight ahead as if he had not heard her speak. Puzzled, she looked again at the laboring children.

"They ah *Roi Nuoc*," the captain said reluctantly. "A cult of the farsights." He tapped his temple. "You unduh-stand?"

"A youth cult?"

He nodded. "They hav' been bewitched."

CHAPTER 3

A security officer escorted Virgil Copeland, Randall Panwar, and Nash Chou to the LOV project suite, where they were met by a detective named Mitchell Kanaha. He was a lightly built officer with faded brown hair, his eyes invisible behind opaqued farsights the same brassy color as his skin. Virgil had no doubt that a ROSA was at work behind the lens, drawing up an assessment of their emotional states from the telltales of their expressions and the temperatures of their skins. Were they sufficiently shocked? Sufficiently grieved? Or could a trace of guilt be read into the precise period of time they held his gaze? Virgil imagined himself to be suddenly transparent.

Nash recognized his vulnerability and took hold of the situation, relieving Virgil of the need to speak. "Have you determined what happened? And when?" he asked as they huddled in the suite's short hallway between bulletin boards cluttered with announcements, ads, and joke pictures. All three office doors stood open.

Kanaha said, "When it happened is easy. The M.E. puts time of death at no more than an hour before the report was made."

Virgil blanched. "Then if the cindy had come in . . ."

"Just a little earlier, yes, it might have been possible to save her. She was probably unconscious for several hours before death. Certainly she was dehydrated."

Virgil had never thought to look for her in the lab. Why should he? If she'd been in the lab, she would have been in easy reach of a link. He turned to look for Panwar and spotted him ducking out of his office, his right hand deep in the pocket of his trousers.

"I just don't understand it," Nash said. "She wasn't sick. In fact, she was in perfect health. Right, Virgil?"

Virgil started, tearing his confused gaze away from Panwar. "Huh? Oh. Right. Of course. She exercised every day, and almost never got sick. She was perfect . . . that way." *Beautiful.* A beautiful, intricate, self-aware organic machine, an exquisite dance of biochemistry, stopped now. Broken.

"No sign of violence?" Panwar asked as he moved close to Virgil.

"No external signs at all," Kanaha confirmed. "Toxicology will have to tell us what happened."

Nash frowned, puzzling over this. Virgil closed his eyes, waiting for Nash to catch on. He didn't disappoint. "Oh. You're thinking some sort of . . . recreational drug?"

"It's the most common means for stopping the heart of a healthy young woman."

Virgil stared at the floor, biting the inside of his lip. Let

Kanaha believe that! Let him believe that Gabrielle's long unconscious period had allowed the drug residue in her body to drop to undetectable levels.

"Of course," Kanaha said, "we've found no supporting evidence. No needles, skin patches, vials, powder packs, anywhere on her, or anywhere in the suite."

"I never knew her to use illegal drugs," Panwar said. "Then again, I did not share her private life." He laid a companionable hand on Virgil's shoulder. "May we see the body now?"

Kanaha nodded. He turned; Nash followed. Panwar used the moment to slip a pair of needle-nose forceps into Virgil's hand. "You loved her best," he murmured.

Virgil fumbled the delicate instrument and almost dropped it. He barely managed to shove it into a pocket of his charcoal gray pants before Nash looked back, his shiny brow wrinkled in concern. "Virgil, are you all right with this?"

"I'm fine."

"It's hard on all of us," Panwar said.

Virgil pushed past him, silently cursing Panwar for forcing on him the gruesome task of extracting the LOVs. But he stopped short at the end of the hallway when he encountered the odor that had disturbed the routine of the little basketball-size cleaning robot known as a cindy.

It was a nauseating, fecal smell, sour, with an overlay of bitter sweat. He edged past Kanaha and into the darkened conference room.

The only illumination came from the wall screen, where a twinkling, blue-green globe was displayed, its surface deeply etched with complex folds and channels.

"What is that?" Kanaha asked, nodding at the screen.

"That's, uh, the heart of our project," Virgil said. "It's a colony of LOVs. That's the form they take when they cluster together in an aquatic environment."

"LOVs?"

"They're an artificial life-form."

"Here?"

"God, no. On the *Hammer*. There's a two-year moratorium, you know."

"I know. What's their purpose?"

"We use them to study neural function. They . . . have a capacity for spontaneous learning, for self-teaching."

"Like a neural net computer?"

"Not exactly. No. Their problem-solving procedures . . . they have more in common with our minds than they do with silicon-based neural nets. Especially in a colony. They can interact much like human neural cells in a brain." Except the LOVs communicated through light, as well as through the chemical and electrical impulses propagated through their linked asterids. "Gabrielle thought they might have some . . . some capacity for one or more degrees of . . . of consciousness."

He swallowed hard. Then, as if guided by a will that was not his own, his gaze shifted to Gabrielle.

She lay in a recliner on one side of the oval table, facing the display, her face ghastly pale, waxlike, the blood all stolen away from her surface cells. Her lips had faded to pale, withered ridges. Her eyes were mercifully closed. She looked as if she had been wrestling with evil spirits for hours on end. Her hair was sodden, her clothes soaked with a rancid sweat, and worse things, released as her body gave up its struggles. Her fingers were pale, waxy-smooth, and lovely as a sculpture, their tips tinged a faint blue. Across her graceful forehead, her LOVs glittered blue-green in the shifting light.

Softly, Virgil said. "Hark, cancel the display."

The screen winked off. The overhead light came up, illuminating every detail of Gabrielle's face.

"You've got auditory pickups in here?" Kanaha asked. "I was told this suite was exempt from routine observation."

Panwar nodded. "The project ROSA monitors. It doesn't record."

"Why not?"

"It would be a security risk," Nash said. "A disgruntled employee could sell out to our competitors. Besides, our cutting-edge projects show superior progress when we give our people privacy and a free rein. Being under constant observation cramps creativity. Studies have proved it."

Kanaha responded to this with a noncommittal grunt. "So it

looks as if Dr. Gabrielle Villanti might have been working with, with . . ." He waved his hand at the blank screen.

"One of the LOV colonies," Virgil said. "Epsilon-3, if you want to know. It's one of twenty. Gabrielle was devoted to the project."

"She wanted to be the first," Panwar added, "to meet a non-human mind. That's what we do here, Detective Kanaha. We try to convince ourselves that the LOV colonies are real entities, with alien minds."

"Randall, please," Nash said. Then he turned to Kanaha. "Are you done here? Can she be moved now, to a more dignified setting?"

Virgil had to wonder what kind of dignity there was in an autopsy. Tenderly, he touched her forehead. Her skin was cool and damp, almost rubbery. Not her skin at all.

"They were lovers," Panwar said. "Would it be all right if Virgil had a minute alone with her? . . ."

Virgil froze, remembering the forceps in his pocket. *Say no*, he prayed. *Say no.*

"Sure," Kanaha rumbled. "The gurney's still on its way up anyway."

Virgil listened to them walk away. He heard the door close behind him. *Now!* he thought. *Do it now.*

He retrieved the forceps from his pocket.

What happened when the machine stopped? Where did the person go? People had worried over that question since the beginning of thought, but Virgil could not parse the popular speculations. The beautiful machine that was Gabrielle had ceased to function, and he could not bring himself to believe that some magic part of her could survive that terrible stop-motion. Like a projection when the lights went out, surely she had simply ceased to be?

Focus!

The LOVs were glints across her smooth forehead. He pinched one with the forceps and pulled. It shattered into powdered glass.

Virgil stared in horror. Where the LOV had been there remained a tiny hollow, cupping a speck of shiny white tissue.

He smoothed it over with a trembling hand.

Her fingers twitched.

Virgil froze. It was a dead reaction, he knew it. Like the kick of a frog's severed leg when an electrical current is applied, his touch had sent a chaotic signal straight down the LOV's nerve trunk to her brain . . . and somehow, some part of the system still worked.

But even the LOVs would be dying by now.

Damn it, focus!

How much time could Panwar buy him? The forceps weren't going to work. He needed a different tool to remove the LOVs. A metal pick maybe, or a scalpel. They'd been damned stupid never to give a thought to extraction.

He only had the forceps.

So he tried again, pinching deeper to get the forceps beneath the next LOV, not squeezing so hard this time.

Pop!

The LOV shattered into dust.

Virgil stared at the botched job, all too aware of the panicked rush of his own breathing. He was not going to be able to do this, not with the forceps. Then how?

The door banged open, revealing Nash, his round face twisted in horror. Kanaha stood behind him. Virgil followed his smug gaze to a corner of the ceiling where an aerostat floated, riding on differential air pressure, its button cameras fixed on Gabrielle's body.

"What are you doing?" Nash demanded. "What have you done to her?"

Virgil couldn't think what to say, and yet he spoke, his mouth moving as if some other consciousness directed it. "She moved. When I touched her, her fingers twitched."

Kanaha stripped the forceps from his hand and deposited them in a sample bag. He leaned over Gabrielle, his shadow falling across her face. With a gloved hand he stroked her forehead, tracing the pattern of her LOVs. He scowled. "Hey. They're producing light. Little flickers of light. I saw it before, but I thought they were reflecting the color of that colony thing that was up on the wall." He turned to look at Nash. "Is this some kind of body jewelry?"

"That's right. That's what it is," Virgil said, his voice whispery as it emerged from his dry mouth. "Luminescent chips. Glued on. Very pretty."

Nash added: "Panwar has them too."

"It's a . . . a fashion," Virgil stammered. "Where is Panwar?"

"In his office." Kanaha studied Virgil, giving his personal agent time to collect the telltales that would confirm his emotional state. "He didn't like it when he saw you handling the corpse. Why did you want to remove the chips?"

Virgil's chin dropped low. Again he found himself talking, almost without volition. "Her mother . . . she wouldn't approve."

"She worried about things like that?"

Virgil turned half-away, his hands shaking. "She did. Sometimes."

Nash looked at him as if he'd lost his mind. "Virgil? It is body jewelry? That's what I always assumed."

"Sure, Nash."

Nash shook his head. "You don't lie very well."

"Step back," Kanaha suggested. "Let Dr. Chou have a look."

Reluctantly, Nash approached the corpse. He leaned over Gabrielle, shading her face from the overhead lights as he examined the embedded LOVs. Then he looked up at the blank screen, a thoughtful frown creasing his brow. Abruptly, his face paled. His mouth opened in a round *oh* of pained surprise. Without saying a word, he ducked his head and hurried from the room.

"Nash!" Virgil leaped after him, catching him in the hallway outside Panwar's office. "Nash, wait. Listen to me, please. Before you say anything, try to understand why—"

"You think I don't understand?" Nash shouted. "That I don't think the way you do? Dream the things you dream? I'm fat and balding and middle-aged, Virgil, but I've seen as far as you! Farther! I've felt the temptation, but never, never would I have pulled a stunt like this."

"Nash, please. It's not like it was harmful—"

"Gabrielle is dead! You used her for a test animal. And you have the balls to tell me it wasn't harmful?"

"We don't know what killed her. This is not like Van Nuys."

Nash just stared at him, his face damp, his brown eyes half-gone behind heavy lids, but still piercing, still potent. Virgil glanced over his shoulder. Kanaha had followed them, his far-sights recording every word as he waited for the puzzle to resolve itself.

Panwar seemed to have given up. Virgil could see him in his office, hunched over his desk, head bowed against his hands. Nash followed his gaze and nodded. "You've done it to yourselves too, haven't you? You and Randall. I've seen his pretty glitter, but you're in it too, aren't you, Virgil? All three of you were in it, tucked in here together, so close and so quiet." He stepped forward. With startling speed his hand reached up to sweep the slim cords of Virgil's Egyptian-wrapped hair back from his brow. Caught off guard, Virgil stumbled, but a single step brought his back against the wall.

For some immeasurable time Nash stared at the LOVs on Virgil's brow. Then his hand dropped stiffly to his side. Tears stood in his pinched eyes. "I want to protect you," he whispered. "I do. But I can't. It would be wrong. Don't you understand? We have *systems* to regulate development. Necessary regulations. They don't exist to stymie the careers of brilliant youth. No. It's to give ourselves, as a society, time to *think*. You've trashed that system, Virgil, and it's an act that will hurt everyone who's ever done, or ever hopes to do, cutting-edge research."

"We're not Van Nuys," Virgil said again. "The LOVs are not infectious. They're not dangerous. They are utterly under control."

Nash shook his head. "You reached too far, son. My God. What a waste."

CHAPTER 4

Hunger lay beyond the river mouth.

Ela Suvanatat stood at the side rail of Cameron Quang's boat, staring in disbelief at a vast fleet of motley vessels cluttering the glassy surface of the South China Sea. The boats must surely number in the hundreds. She crossed to the other rail. It was the same. Most of the vessels were old: tiny, battered skiffs, their paint faded or gone. Their crews worked the water with nets and poles and wire traps: dark-haired men with skin like polished wood, or women swaddled in worn colors to cheat the sun. The boats filled the bright blue water out to a hazy horizon where oil-drilling platforms walked in ghostly steps, winking into view, only to fade into the haze before appearing again farther down the coast.

In the heat, in the brilliant sunlight, Ela had a wavering sense that none of this was real. These fisherfolk were not people, they were spirits, human desire endlessly drawing in empty nets.

But hunger could not be dreamed away.

Ela tapped her fingers, summoning Kathang to record the view through her farsights. A panoramic would be needed somewhere early in the article—but she felt sick thinking about what that article would show. The Coastal Society wanted an exposé on the ravages of overfishing. They did not want to ponder these people who must make a life where life had been all used up.

At least it was going to be easy to get dramatic material.

She clipped goggle cups to her farsights, and then she made her first dive. It was a short foray, ten minutes to get some video of the stripped bottom. Lost nets and tangled fishing line were everywhere, half-buried in the mud or floating ghostlike in the murky water near the seafloor. As she returned to the boat she saw one small school of coin-size silver fish. They darted into sight and disappeared, like an omen of good fortune that decided not to stay.

Cameron Quang was drinking another Coca-Cola when she climbed out of the water. "See anything?" he asked.

"A few small fish. A lot of garbage."

She made two more dives as the red-eyed boat journeyed slowly out to the oil-drilling platforms.

The offshore fields were tapped out, but the platforms still found use as the hubs of vast fish farms. As the boat drew closer, Ela could make out fiberglass poles rising from the ocean, with floating lines strung between them that enclosed vast acres of calm water. The closest fishing boat was a quarter mile away. "Can I dive out here?" she asked the captain when the boundary was only a few hundred feet off the bow.

His answering grin was sly. "You wanh uh do some poaching?"

"I want to get some pictures."

"That's what theah all say." But he cut the boat's engines. Then he used his farsights to talk with someone on the platform. "Okay, ah warned them you'll be out here, so maybe they won't shoot you? You dive while ah do my business. Half an hour, and ah'll pick you up."

She nodded and slipped her rebreather pack on. "Don't forget where I am."

His grin widened.

Ela dropped over the side of the boat, letting her weight carry her slowly down through the blue water. At thirty-five feet she found the bottom . . . and a robotic drone found her. The meter-long robo-sub eased silently out of the murk, moving with fish-like sinuousness. Button cameras studded its prow, while two racks of steel harpoons were mounted on either side. Ela froze, staring at the device, afraid to move, afraid some jerk on the platform was looking back at her through the cameras, just waiting to launch a harpoon if she so much as twitched a finger. She understood now why the fisherfolk stayed away.

The standoff continued for two or three minutes, and then Ela's patience gave way. The rebreather pack would let her stay here all day, but the captain had given her only half an hour. She did not believe he would spend much time looking for her if she failed to appear.

So she dug her fingers into the muddy bottom and pushed off, gliding slowly backwards. The robo-sub followed her—but it didn't shoot. She took encouragement from that. Checking her compass, she determined the direction of the fish farm, and with a slow kick of her fins, she set off to find it. The robo-sub kept pace, but it did not try to stop her.

In less than a minute a dark shadow loomed in the murk, resolving into a wide-gauge mesh wall, rising from the ocean floor all the way up to the bright blue surface. It marked a boundary of terrible contrast. Beyond the mesh she could see a seemingly endless school of meter-long fish swimming counter-clockwise along the barrier, moving with machine efficiency through the middle depths. Outside the mesh there was noth-ing.

She started to swim closer, but her presence startled the school. It broke up, the fish spilling inward to escape her pred-ator shape. The robo-sub responded, slipping in front of her to block her advance.

It was time to go anyway. She headed for the surface, feeling only a little worried when she discovered that Cameron Quang was not there. She inflated her buoyancy vest and drifted a few meters outside the mesh. After several minutes her worry grew more intense. She was a long way from the dock on the distant platform. She could probably swim that far . . . if the patrolling robo-subs would let her.

Several more minutes passed. She listened to wavelets slap against her rebreather pack and wondered why she had chosen to devote herself to a journalism career when she could have been telling fortunes or dealing in stocks or . . . or . . . teaching Thai at some university in Australia. Yeah.

After another minute she tapped her fingers, sending a link request to her job broker, Joanie Liu.

Joanie surprised her by picking up right away. She looked flustered, which was even more unusual. "Ela? So glad you checked in. How did you know to call? I have a gentleman on-link who is interested in the story you're doing. I advise you to talk to him. *Very* influential. It could mean an important job for you."

"I'm stranded at sea," Ela said.

Joanie rolled her eyes. "Ela, why must you be so difficult? This is no time for you to be particular." She did not wait for a reply. Her image dissolved, coming together again as the image of a handsome, crisply dressed Asian businessman, perhaps thirty years old. There was something calculating in the set of his eyes, as if he were in the habit of evaluating everything he saw in terms of its investment potential. Kathang confirmed it. *This one sees without a veil—when he is not looking at himself.*

The businessman's smooth lips turned in a ghost of a smile as if he had overheard. "Ms. Suvanatat," he said. "Lately of Bangkok? I am Ky Xuan Nguyen. Your broker . . ." He frowned. "What is her name?"

Ela was sure he knew her name perfectly well. "Joanie Liu," she said in a timid voice.

"Ms. Liu, yes. She has given you poor advice. The Coastal Society is not an organization you want to deal with."

Ela felt suddenly cold. Her gaze shifted to Kathang's little salamander image. She tapped a code and nodded, setting the ROSA to stalking Nguyen's profile. A wavelet splashed in her mouth. She spit the salt water out, and said, "I'm only preparing an article, Mr. Nguyen."

"A propaganda piece."

She didn't dare to contradict him. Hadn't she thought the same thing?

He asked: "Do you know why the public waters here are barren?"

It was obvious wasn't it? And still it sounded like an accusation that she did not want to make. "T-too many . . . people."

"That is the shallow answer. I'm sure you don't feel we should exterminate the people so the fish might make a comeback. Of course not. The deeper reason these waters remain barren is because groups like the Coastal Society have sponsored international regulations banning fertilization in the open ocean. Boosting the level of dissolved nutrients in these waters would boost the population of plankton, with repercussions all the way up the food chain. But international law forbids this, with the result that independent fisherfolk starve, while commercial farms thrive producing protein that only the rich can afford."

Kathang returned, to whisper a report into Ela's water-filled ear: *"Ky Xuan Nguyen is the third-ranking officer in a regional advertising firm known as Middle Nature. A graduate of Harvard Business School . . ."* Ela's eyes widened as she listened. She could not imagine why such a man cared about fish.

"Ms. Suvanatat?" Nguyen prodded. "Have you learned enough about me to give an answer?"

Ela felt her cheeks heat, despite the cool water. Softly: "I've only been charged with showing what *is,* Mr. Nguyen."

"That would be hunger."

The Coastal Society would not want to hear that side of the story, but Ela nodded anyway. It didn't matter: The link with Nguyen had already closed.

Cameron returned with the boat a few minutes later. He helped her aboard, but he did not make any jokes about poaching. He looked frightened, like a man who has been shown his tomb, with the date of death tentatively chalked on the wall. "You want to go ashore now?" he asked quietly, his Southern American drawl much faded. Ela set the rebreather pack down on the deck and nodded, wondering if he had been talking to Nguyen too.

She could not get Ky Xuan Nguyen out of her mind. What did he want from her? She had accepted the Coastal Society contract. She had already spent their money. She *had* to do the article. She had to make it acceptable to them, and still she brooded over what Nguyen had said about shallow answers.

At least the panoramas and the underwater scenes were done. The next requirement of the article was a critical look at "an illegal shoreline settlement." That meant a night spent at a squatter's village, gathering a profile of life on the coast.

She packed her equipment, cramming everything but the rebreather into her backpack. She would have to take it all with her. The balance of her fee would be forfeit if the diving equipment was not returned, and she did not trust Cameron to hold it.

The captain's face took on an expression of acute concentration as he worked his way past a final shore guard of inner tubes, swimming children, and tiny canoes. The shore itself was a mudflat, slick and glistening and utterly bare of debris. As the boat approached, throngs of tiny, bright-eyed children spilled out of a shantytown built on poles above the high-water mark. Dressed in T-shirts and faded shorts, they ran back and forth at the water's edge, leaving faint, wet impressions where their feet touched, their motion intense and intermittent, like sand crabs.

As Ela prepared to leave the boat, she pretended a confidence she did not feel. She'd explored alone before and knew that strangers were usually welcomed by villagers as a potential source of money, food, information—even entertainment. Still, one could never be sure.

She hefted her backpack onto her right shoulder, the dive pack onto her left. When the water was three feet deep, the captain threw a rope to some boys who had been working a small hand net. They held the boat while Ela slipped over the side. She still wore the sleeveless vest of her wet suit, but she had pulled on a pair of shorts and a long-sleeve shirt to protect herself from the sun.

She hesitated beside the boat, looking up at the captain, wondering if he would come back for her tomorrow. She had held on to part of his fee to ensure his return, but it was a minuscule sum. Not nearly enough to buy loyalty. "Tomorrow," she muttered. Then she waded ashore onto land that had not existed a year ago.

The muddy coast of the Mekong Delta fought a continuous battle with the sea. Each rainy season, alluvial deposits were laid down in the annual flood, extending the coastline by up to two hundred feet . . . until the rising sea crawled over the new land, chewing at it, filling the rivers with salt. Massive sea dikes guarded much of the coast, but nothing protected this strand. That had not stopped people from settling here. The ramshackle village boasted hundreds of homes, all built on poles above the steaming mud. Some had walls of black-plastic greenhouse cloth. Others had half-height rails of mismatched timber or broken pieces of old government signs. There wasn't much point in building something more permanent, Ela decided as she walked between the shanties. At best, these people could stay only through the dry season. When the Mekong flooded again, they would have to move on.

Several older women stared at her as she went by. They refused to smile or return her greeting. It was not an unusual reaction, given their age, and Ela refused to let herself become discouraged. After a few minutes she spotted a new mark: a young woman, sitting cross-legged on a platform, working at a snarled knot of fishing line while a little boy whispered in her ear. His furtive glance darted to Ela, then he slipped behind a crate. The young woman smiled.

It was the best opening Ela had seen. *"Chào,"* she said, hurrying forward. Then she expended her full arsenal of Vietnamese. *"Tên tôi là Ela Suvanatat. Xin lôi, cô tên là gì?"* What is your name?

The woman returned Ela's greeting, giving her name as Phuong. Her black hair was tied in a neat ponytail, and she wore a double layer of faded T-shirts, the outer one short-sleeved, the inner one long. Her trousers were loose-cut, gray black.

Ela produced a wireless speaker from an outside pocket of her backpack. Then she tapped her fingers, directing Kathang to translate. *"May we talk?"* she whispered. A flurry of stiff, metallic Vietnamese poured from the little box.

Phuong raised a hand to her face to hide a laugh. "I speak English," she said, a giggle in her voice. "Also some French."

Ela blushed. It hadn't occurred to her to ask.

At the center of the roofless platform a pile of plastic crates defined a little room where four young children clustered around a flowscreen powered by a car battery. An animated turtle demonstrated how to draw an *X* in the romanized Vietnamese alphabet, while the kids stared wide-eyed at Ela as she sat with Phuong on a *chiêu,* a plastic reed mat.

"I'm doing an article for a global magazine," Ela explained as she produced two Cokes from her backpack and a bag of colorful rice crackers. At a nod from Phuong, she gave the crackers to the kids. "It's supposed to be about how the fishing was spoiled here."

Phuong nodded. "There are not many fish."

"I want to tell about why people live here anyway."

"There is no other place to go." The kids whispered over the shapes and colors of the rice crackers. "My husband and I, we come from a village close to Cambodia. We both went to satellite school in the afternoons and earned high marks, but there was no work there. So we decided to go to Can Tho. It's said there are jobs sometimes at the factories. But at Can Tho the authorities laughed at us. 'No work,' they said." Phuong's mind seemed far away. "Have you been to Can Tho?"

Ela nodded, knowing herself to be only a step away from this woman's plight.

Phuong sighed. "In Can Tho houses are built over the water of the canals. Laborers sleep between the trees that line the levees. Trucks run down the levee roads, and they don't slow for straying children. All the other land belongs to the farmers, and of course they must protect it, I understand that. But we walked for three days and nights without rest before we found a bit of roadside where no one tried to stop us from lying down. So we came here. This is new land, laid down this season by the river. No one owns it."

Ela looked out across the mudflat. Here and there sprigs of riotous green sprouted against the wet, gray soil: mangrove seedlings and salt-tolerant sedges. *New land.* Yet it would all be drowned when the monsoon returned. Phuong would know that.

Ela sighed, and thanked her. She asked if she might stay the night on the platform, and Phuong agreed. Then Ela sat for a time in silence, watching the hundreds of little boats out on the water, knowing she could not produce the article the Coastal Society wanted.

She finished the last warm sip of her Coca-Cola; then she put in a link request to her agency. Joanie's image immediately filled the screen. "Ela! I expected to hear from you sooner than this. What did Mr. Nguyen say?"

Ela shook her head. "I can't do the article, Joanie. At least, not the way the Coastal Society wants it done."

Joanie looked puzzled. Then she looked angry. "Ela, what are you thinking? You agreed to a contract. You can't afford *not* to do it."

"Just get me something else, okay? Trash work if you have to, but I won't do an article aimed at making these people into bad guys. It's not their fault the ocean has been stripped."

Joanie's face went cold and stony. "Did Mr. Nguyen put you up to this?"

Ela did not want to admit he had frightened her. "He suggested I take a deeper look at things—and he was right."

Joanie leaned forward, her angry face looming in Ela's farsights. "Then Mr. Nguyen had better put his money where his mouth is. I will call him. And I will see that *he* foots the bill."

CHAPTER 5

Detective Kanaha decided that both Virgil and Panwar qualified as biohazards. So he arrested them, confiscated their farsights, and then left them where they were, posting two officers outside the suite door. He did agree to remove Gabrielle's remains—encased in double plastic, with the handlers wearing environment suits. A trio of cindies was sent in to attend to the residue.

Virgil stayed in his office, curled on the couch, listening to the robots vacuum and scrub, their limbs clicking and ratcheting as they crawled over the chair. Aerostat cameras hovered in every room, even the bathroom, watching everything. Virgil wondered what would happen if he plucked a LOV from his brow and flushed it down the toilet. He laughed. The plumbing had probably been switched off.

He fell asleep before the cindies finished. He knew it only when he awoke, his mind switching from sleep to wakefulness with no transition phase and no memory of dreams. Ever since he'd had the LOVs he'd awakened like this. It made him wonder what went on in his head when he wasn't there.

He reached for his farsights, then remembered: Kanaha had taken them. The detective would not be able to get anything out of them, of course. Iris would erase any data stored in the farsights as soon as it detected a stranger handling them. The ROSA would sever contact, biding on its anonymous server until Virgil called it out once again. Everything the ROSA handled, from mail to voice-links to research, was anonymous and encrypted. The police could not track its location unless Virgil gave it away, and even then, they could not decrypt the data it contained. Iris, at least, would never be a witness against him.

He sat up on the couch, feeling a hundred years old.

What time was it, anyway?

Whatever time it was, he should call his parents.

No farsights, of course.

The realization came as a relief. The thought of facing his parents, of explaining to them why he had blown his existence . . . it gave him a sick feeling, and he could not bring himself to do it.

In truth he rarely felt comfortable talking about himself or his beliefs, his *motivations*. He knew too well that his world—an emergent world arising from the intricate, unpredictable, remorseless dance of physical laws and quantum chance—was utterly different from the world perceived by almost anyone he might pass randomly on the street.

He had spent his life gazing at life—he thought of it as Life, boldly set with a capital letter, and in his mind this Life encompassed not just those organic assemblages that were living things, but also the environment that contained them, the laws of complexity that gave them existence, the information systems that let them think and grow and reproduce, and the perpetual war they fought against entropy so that *something* could exist, instead of a homogeneous nothing. He had looked into all these aspects and what he had seen—evidenced everywhere, apparent in everything—was the common origin of all things.

Life had emerged from the plasmas of creation because life was allowed by the physical constants of the Universe. The interplay of elemental particles had led to simple atoms that became stars that in the explosive forge of supernovas created atoms more complex that led to molecules evolving into organisms that thought. Every step along the way, at every level of definition, from quantum particles to nuclear physics, chemistry, biology, astrophysics, neurology, climate, psychology, genetics, evolution, ecology, and faith, it was all one: an utterly integrated, self-contained system.

A poignantly beautiful system.

But grim, austere, and ugly, too. Virgil would never deny that. In this world so much could be lost so easily to ruthless chance. He had always known it. Now, with Gabrielle's loss, he *felt* the precarious nature of his own existence. It made him afraid, but it made him defiant too. He knew that tragedy could demand no revision of his belief. It could elicit no angry protestations that he had been deceived or betrayed by an unseen god, because no promises had ever been made. Like the old bumper stickers used to say, shit was a thing that happened. One had to live with it or die.

And still this was an alien philosophy on the street, where dualism lived on—the ancient idea that mind and matter were independent elements, separated from one another by a spark of the immortal. Dualism had died decades ago in the minds of most neurobiologists, but on the street it was still easy to strike offense with the proposition that the mind could be explained purely by the organization and symbol processing within the brain, with no need to call upon the magic forces of some hypothetical soul.

Virgil did not talk much about these things. Who did? But he believed in a strictly natural world, and that was enough to set him off in an isolated psychological space, to make him alien.

Most of the time he could hide his alienness from those who did not want to see it. Not always.

His father was a corporate executive with secular leanings, but after the divorce he had married a devout Christian, who was quite sure Virgil was a damned soul. Virgil thought of her as sweetly disillusioned. His mother understood him better, but even she squirmed at the idea that the brain was a machine running a program that generated the Self.

Panwar understood these things. They were alike in that, as in so many ways.

So why had they not talked to each other since Kanaha left?

Virgil rubbed the sleep from his eyes. Then he forced himself up. When he looked into the hallway he was surprised to see the cindies lined up against the wall, three smooth insect carapaces each twice the size of a football. Apparently they were under quarantine too.

The scent of coffee was a blessing on the air. It led him past the open door of Panwar's office. Panwar was there, his feet up on the desk, his LOVs glittering above his dark eyes. "Have you seen the news yet?" he asked, nodding at a small flowscreen built into the wall. "It's all public now. The first round from the op-eds is a call for our heads."

"I'll take responsibility for it," Virgil said. "Don't worry about that. It was my project."

Panwar slipped his feet off the desk. "Shut the fuck up, okay? As soon as I can talk to my dad, he'll get us a lawyer. Don't give up, Virg. It doesn't end here."

Virgil nodded. He did not come in. "Gabrielle was engaged in a two-way visual link with the colony."

Panwar scowled, glancing meaningfully at the aerostat floating in the corner of his office. Everything they said and did could be used as evidence against them. Aloud he said: "That's no secret. I gave Kanaha a copy of the log before he left."

"We need to talk about why."

"No. We don't."

"I do."

Early in their work, Virgil had proposed the idea of a cognitive

circle: *Why not let our LOVs interact while we brainstorm a problem?*
Enhanced brain chemistry spawned fiery ideas. In a cognitive
circle that effect was amplified as LOV spoke to LOV, communicating emotional energy across the circle in microsecond
flashes of light. It was a powerful feedback loop that drove their
brainstorming sessions forward with furious energy. Whenever
Virgil had sat with Panwar and Gabrielle in a cognitive circle,
he had felt like his mind was on fire, a sacred instrument designed to receive signals from some holy mental space.

They had talked about interacting with one of the LOV colonies in the same way, but they had not done it. Not before this
weekend. "She was involved in a cognitive circle with E-3,"
Virgil said. "There's no other explanation."

The door to the suite clicked open. Virgil turned to look
down the hall. Had Detective Kanaha found a cell to put them
in? He could hear one of the police officers talking outside the
door: ". . . under observation at all times. If there's any trouble
we'll be inside within seconds."

A woman's low voice answered, sounding mildly amused.
"I'm sure I'll be fine."

Then she stepped past the door: a slender woman of mod-
erate height in a calf-length brown dress and matching jacket
trimmed in green. Her brown hair was gathered in a loose ponytail, framing a face of uncertain age. The eyes behind her
farsights were startlingly familiar.

"Summer Goforth," Virgil said, after a second's hesitation.

Panwar lunged out of his seat, leaning out the office door to
get a look.

Summer Goforth had invented the original LOVs, and then
become their most vocal opponent. She looked on them now,
and she did not smile. "Hello, Virgil. Randall." She offered her
hand; all very cordial. She took an extra few seconds to peer at
Panwar's LOVs.

Virgil had met her only once before, less than a month after
he'd joined EquaSys. He'd come up from the beach, salt dry
on his skin and the sun setting behind parallel lines of docile
swells. Summer had been leaning against his car. He thought
he'd been cornered by a fanatic . . . but by the time she said

good-bye, uneasy doubts had been stirring within him, and he'd found himself wondering just who the fanatic really was.

"Why are you here?" he asked her. "You're not with the police."

"You're not in police custody anymore." The lens of her farsights had taken on a gold-green hue. "The International Biotechnology Commission has taken over your case. They're creating an ethics committee to advise on your actions, and to rule on the status of the LOVs. I live here. I'm acquainted with the LOVs. So I'm on it."

"The status of the LOVs is already defined," Panwar said. "They're an artificial life-form."

Summer's farsights flushed a deeper green as she looked at him. Mood gloss? She said: "An artificial life-form legally confined to the *Hammer*, but you see they've escaped—which makes it an IBC case."

Virgil had not thought he could contain any more worries, but he'd been wrong. The International Biotechnology Commission had been dreamed up in the wake of the Van Nuys incident, receiving its authority as a law-enforcement agency within the United States less than six months ago—making it younger than the crime he and Panwar had committed. The IBC's youth did not translate to weakness. Under the guidance of Director Daniel Simkin, the agency had already built a reputation for hard-nosed enforcement. A case like this would sear its existence into the consciousness of every licensed lab around the world.

Panwar looked as if he'd taken a blow. He shook his head. "You're twisting the truth. You know the LOVs didn't escape."

"Are you sure? The LOVs were supposed to be confined to the *Hammer*, but they got out. You can call it kidnapped if you like, or stolen, or smuggled, the fact remains, they are here. And an artificial life-form that cannot be controlled will be sterilized. That is clearly stated in the interim guidelines."

"Is that the position you'll be taking?" Virgil asked.

"That's the position I've taken ever since Van Nuys—because I've been down this road myself. I know what it feels like when you're close to a project. So close you can't see the stop signs. You keep telling yourself, 'just a little farther, just a little more.' Until reason and good judgment are left far behind."

The color had been fading from her farsights as she spoke, until now they became a translucent white veil. "The two of you don't have to talk to me. You don't have to cooperate in any way. You can wait for a lawyer to show up, and you can pretend you've got a chance in court. But the truth is, you don't. You're both facing life sentences, and you are not going to have a lot of friends speaking in your behalf. This committee will include top names in biotechnology from around the world, and every one of them will be concerned foremost about one thing: saving their own projects. Your actions have conjured a wildcat mad scientist image that is going to haunt them for years if they don't quash it now. Your hubris has put the world at risk. That's how they'll play it."

"But that isn't true," Virgil said. "We were taking chances with ourselves. No one else."

"Prove it. Show me your work." She tapped her farsights. "From now on I'm recording. Make me—and the rest of the world—understand. That's the only way you'll buy leniency for yourselves."

Panwar poured coffee while Virgil cleaned up. He ate a nutrient bar, and then another. A clock in the lunchroom said 3 A.M.

Nothing felt real.

There was an awkward moment in the conference room when Virgil started to offer Summer a seat at the oval table—and remembered. "Gabrielle," he said softly. "She was right here just a few hours ago."

Panwar met his eyes. He had a hunted look, but he set his hands firmly on the back of Gabrielle's chair. "The cindies have been all over this room," he muttered. "There's no trace of her left here. Nothing." He edged around the chair as if it held a sleeping rattlesnake. Then he sat down.

Virgil imagined Gabrielle's ghost, startled to discover how quickly it had fallen into the past.

Still, it was good to have someone to talk to, and something to talk about. "When you left," he asked Summer, "the Lovs were only being cultured as individual specimens, right?"

She nodded, sitting across the table from him, with Panwar in between.

"That changed when they were brought to the *Hammer*. They form colonies easily"—Virgil mimed the size and shape of a colony by pressing his fists together—"always roughly spherical. Imagine a piece of newspaper crumpled into a ball. The crumples are channels that allow liquid to circulate to the inner levels—but you must know all this already."

Summer shrugged. "I'd like to hear it from you."

"All right then. But we'll need access to the project ROSA, and a link to E-3—the Epsilon colony, on the *Hammer*."

Summer spoke with someone over her farsights. "All right. You're connected."

Panwar pulled a keyboard out from under the table, while Virgil set to talking. The coffee—or maybe it was his implanted LOVs—had set his mind racing, so that his words ran light and smooth as he laid out his defense. "All right. Here's the reason the LOVs aren't dangerous; why no one was at risk but ourselves. LOVs need octopine for reproduction. Withholding octopine lets us control the size of a colony. That's important. The practical upper limit seems to be roughly the size of a grapefruit. Larger than that, and the circulation of fluids to the interior is compromised, and the original LOVs die. But octopine is rare in nature. In the wild, a LOV could never get enough to reproduce."

He broke off his explanation as the room lights dimmed and the screen came to life. "Here's Epsilon-3," Panwar announced as he balanced the keyboard in his lap. "Our most advanced colony. I've given it a two-way link. Narrow field." He turned to Summer. "That means it can see Virgil, but not us."

Virgil turned to gaze at the crumpled blue-green globe, fascinated as always by the suggestion of meaning in its scintillating lights. What was it thinking? If thinking was the word for what the LOVs did. "Is it active?" he asked Panwar.

"It's been roaming the *Hammer*, pestering the cafeteria staff."

"Roaming the *Hammer*?" Summer echoed.

Virgil smiled. "Nothing sinister. The colony itself is confined, of course, to the Lov lockdown aboard the EquaSys module. But it has control of an aerostat camera that can roam through public areas in the station. I'd love to set up a camera for it here as well, but the charter forbids the system to have 'mechanical control' of anything on Earth. It's a paranoid restriction, but we've abided by it."

"Settling for the minor violation of smuggling the Lovs?" she asked.

"They aren't dangerous," Virgil said again. "We wouldn't have done it if there was any threat." His fingers moved compulsively to touch the Lovs hidden beneath his hair. "We were able to do it because the Lovs continue to be viable as individual organisms. They're not dependent on the colony structure. Each one is quite capable of surviving on its own. . . ."

He frowned at the screen, at the scintillating lights. "You know," he said softly, "this is the last thing Gabrielle ever saw." He turned to Panwar.

"Talk about the project," Panwar said.

Virgil sank back in his chair. He had not had enough sleep. Or maybe he'd had too much coffee. He forced himself to return to the subject. "Our method of selection does favor those Lovs that can most efficiently link with one another and operate together as a distributed system—like a billion tiny computers linked on a network. Change comes fast. Of the twenty colonies in the Lov lockdown, most are obsolete generations. Nearly all our cognitive work involves the apex colony, the one that is most advanced at any given time. Right now that's Epsilon-3. It's our thirtieth generation, the third in Epsilon tank."

Summer frowned. "So you've culled the first two Epsilon colonies?"

"No choice. We only have so many tanks. We do keep some older specimens, though. Alpha-1 is the original colony. It still exists, but more as a museum piece than anything. Its development stagnated a long time ago. I'm not sure its Lovs are even compatible anymore with the apex strains."

"They've changed that much?"

"I think they have. We've been pushing development hard."

"How is reproduction accomplished?"

"LOVs are extracted at about ten thousand evenly spaced points throughout the parent colony, on the theory that this will pull some LOVs from each thought 'module.' All the work is done via a robotic remote known as Lucy."

Summer smiled. "By a 'thought module,' you mean those teams of LOVs specialized for verbal skills, calculations, three-dimensional modeling, time sense, et cetera?"

"Exactly. There are thousands of thought modules of course. Maybe tens of thousands, all of them almost certainly built on simpler modules, which in turn are based on even simpler formulas and so on. The interesting point is that LOVs, being individual organisms, can retain and reproduce their own special skills when they're transferred, so that they can construct a new module through their progeny."

"So after the samples are taken—?"

"The extracted LOVs are injected into a clean tank. They cling to one another and begin to reproduce. If things go well, we get an initial visual-modeling sense within a few hours. The LOVs are good with vision."

Summer nodded. "So what happens when things don't go well?"

Virgil looked to Panwar again, hoping he would take it. But Panwar shook his head. Virgil sighed. "There *are* a lot of failures," he conceded. "In the early generations, ninety percent of new colonies performed worse than their parent, so we culled them, concentrating our resources on the more successful combinations. Now our failure rate is down to forty percent, and even the failures perform at a level far above Alpha-1."

"So selection is based on the colony's performance, not on individual LOVs?"

Virgil nodded. "Essentially each team of LOVs is being evaluated on how well it interacts." It was a test his own project team had failed. He shook his head. He'd been aware of Gabrielle's ambition. He should have guessed she would try to move ahead of the team. Why had he failed to see the danger?

"Virgil," Panwar said. "Are you still with us?"

Virgil jerked upright in his chair, unsure how long he'd been silent. "Sorry."

Summer looked sympathetic. And why shouldn't she? She had started this thing after all. She had made the first LOVs. She should feel a pride in their development. She should feel touched with wonder at this proof that cognition truly could grow from simple units.

Instead it frightened her.

He spoke carefully. "What we are seeing evolve in the LOV colonies is a growing ability to learn about the world, and to interact with it."

Summer turned skeptically to the glittering projection of Epsilon-3 on the center screen.

Virgil understood her doubt. "You're thinking it's the classic brain-in-a-bottle, with no connection to physical reality. But the same could be said of any one of us. All that we know of the world comes to us through our nervous system. The eyes are our visual sensors. The ears are our auditory sensors. Our body's mass and mobility give us a sense of space. The LOVs are similar. They see through cameras. They hear through microphones. They explore physical space through the aerostat. You should talk to the station personnel. They'll tell you that the aerostat sometimes acts just like a puppy, or a baby. It will fix on someone and follow them around for hours. Or it will purposely get in the way, over and over again, as if it's testing what it takes to get a reaction out of the world. When there's music playing it will hover in front of the speakers, exploring different zones of sound."

"And E-3 can speak," Panwar said. "After a fashion."

"Silicon computers can speak," Summer countered. "And quite well."

"Certainly far better than our LOVs," Panwar conceded, an edge to his voice.

"That's right," Virgil said. "Speech is hard. The LOVs don't pursue it on their own, like they pursue vision. Vision seems to come naturally to the LOVs. Language doesn't."

Summer arched an eyebrow. "Is 'natural' the right word?"

"I'd like to think so." He sighed. "If you're expecting a slick performance, you're going to be disappointed. The colony doesn't do anything well. It just does lots of things in very interesting ways."

"And forgets in fascinating ways as well," Panwar added, a bit sharply. "That's the price we pay for fluid connections between the LOVs."

Virgil nodded. "When a cognitive path dissolves, though, it's not all lost. Relearning the skill is far easier than acquiring it." He looked at Panwar. "Can we get it talking?"

"It is talking," Panwar said. "I'll raise the volume." He tapped at his keyboard. Then he looked at Summer, a half-smile on his face. "Hear it now? This is the first step in regaining speech. Epsilon-3 is speaking in tongues."

Summer cocked her head as babbling sounds emerged from the speakers in a voice that sounded remarkably similar to Virgil's. Only an occasional English word could be discerned. She turned to Virgil with a baffled look.

He shrugged, feeling a bit embarrassed, but nothing could be done. E-3 always started this way. No one knew why. "It is frustrating," he mused, "but fascinating too. Why does it organize at all? Why does the organization fail? It's almost as if it's trying out different ways of being—"

Here Panwar chuckled.

Virgil sighed. "Metaphorically speaking, of course."

Within a few minutes all the sounds were English words, but only now and then did two pull together in a sensible way: *Speak quick, clean air, arm reach, man move, remote talk.*

Summer looked skeptical. "Is there any conception of meaning in these phrases?"

Virgil shrugged. "At this stage? I'm not sure. It might just be an exercise, like singing scales, to reestablish verbal pathways. The vocabulary, though, has been taught because it's relevant. These are the words E-3 needs to describe its experience."

As he fell silent, so did Epsilon-3. Virgil found himself leaning forward, his hands squeezing the arms of his chair as he waited for what would come next. Then, with an abruptness that always startled him, words tumbled from the speaker, but this time they issued forth in a new, breathless rhythm. *Speak quickly play remote talk with other not you.*

Summer looked at Virgil as if he were a charlatan in a street show.

"The grammar module is sour," Panwar said.

Virgil ignored them both. The Lov project was not about perfection, and it was not about creating a human mind. That was easy. Good old Love and Sex accomplished that feat thousands of times every day. The tantalizing aspect of the Lov project was the prospect of developing a mind that was distinctly inhuman, yet still capable of complex thought. What would such a being think? What insights could it uncover? What new avenues of awareness could it reveal?

The desire to know ate at him. It was the same desire that had brought Gabrielle into the project, and in the end it had killed her. He blinked, his eyes dry and tired. "Replay that," he muttered.

The "sentence" ran again: *Speak quickly play remote talk with other not you.*

Almost always the words carried their true dictionary meanings. They came out in a hash because the grammar was poor, or because they were used in unfamiliar ways. Decoding could sometimes work. He cued Panwar to transmit his words to the Lov colony. "Speak of what?" he asked.

The answer returned immediately, as if an impatient child waited on the other end of the line: *What is all the other knew-know best.*

Virgil bit his lip, thinking quickly. He had engaged in exchanges like this before, with the phrases stacked liked crashed cars in a fogbound freeway crack up. The tack he took was to clarify the meaning of each phrase before moving on. All right then: "What is the other?"

That is Gabrielle.

He felt as if he'd been gut-punched.

"You want me to take it?" Panwar asked.

"No."

"It remembers its last interaction with her."

Virgil nodded. He drew a deep breath, reviewing once again the staccato sentence that had started this conversation. *Speak quickly play remote talk with other not you.*

Speak quickly play remote talk with . . . Gabrielle. *The other not you.* "Other" served as the class of objects that interacted with the colony but was not the colony. Gabrielle was "other." So was Virgil. But the colony could recognize that Gabrielle was not Virgil—"the other not you."

Again he nodded to Panwar to transmit his words: "There was remote talk with Gabrielle?"

Quick talk.

"What the hell is 'quick talk'?" Panwar muttered.

Virgil touched the LOVs hidden beneath his hairline. Panwar watched him, his eyes growing wide as understanding dawned. Usually they hid their LOVs from Epsilon colony, blurring that segment of the visual transmission to avoid the very feedback reaction that Gabrielle had been seeking.

Virgil addressed the colony: "Does quick talk use words?"

No.

"Does quick talk use light?"

Light yes. Thought is sense inside is trapped is meaning move not. Get it out. Question: How?

Again Virgil looked at Panwar—and saw a reflection of his own surprise. "The colonies almost never ask questions," Panwar explained in answer to Summer's inquisitive look. "Epsilon-3 and its direct parent are the only ones ever to do it."

"Do you have any idea what the question is about?" she asked.

Panwar shrugged. "Frankly, no."

"Rephrase question," Virgil said.

The voice that was like his spoke again: *Rephrase. Thought is here. Thought is sense inside here. This auditory output is not thought. Thought is trapped. Meaning does not move. How will thought get out?*

In the following silence Virgil could hear his heart pounding. Sweat stood out on his arms. "Your farsights are recording, right?" he asked Summer.

"Yes."

"So answer it quick," Panwar urged. "Its metabolism is so much faster than ours. Its time sense might be faster too. Don't give it a chance to forget, Virg. I've never seen anything like this before."

Virgil nodded. "It took something from Gabrielle. It learned something important from her."

"Answer it," Panwar repeated.

Virgil turned back to the colony. "Auditory output is not thought," he confirmed. "It is words. Words are the way to share thoughts between there and here, between two beings, Epsilon and Virgil."

Words are way of meaning-passing. Passing meaning. Eyes are better windows to meaning. Said this. Other. Gabrielle other. Measure excitement in blue-green flash. Thought. This is thought but not thought here. But it is not thought here. But it thought is not here. Not within.

"It is another's thought," Virgil said, his voice taut with fear that he had got it wrong. Still, he plunged ahead. "This is an awareness of another's thought, but the thoughts cannot be sensed."

That is here question. The eyes show thoughts not here.

Panwar said, "You know what it's getting at, don't you, Virgil?"

"I think so." He closed his eyes, taking a moment to steady himself. Then he looked at the colony and asked: "What are eyes?"

Light receptors. Blue-green best eyes. Other eyes dull.

Virgil held up his hand, fingers splayed. "Here is my hand. Here are my fingers. This finger"—now he held out only the index finger, moving it slowly until it touched the corner of his right eye—"touches an eye. Which eye?"

Right dull.

He moved his pointing finger, using it to lift away the neat cords of his hair. At the same time he pointed to an implanted LOV tucked against his hairline. "Which eye is this?"

Seven from right bright blue-green.

"Can thoughts be seen here?"

Thoughts indicated. Not understood. Question: Integrate?

"How?"

Talking reaches integration. Not words. Light.

Talking with light: That was what Gabrielle had been doing. He and Panwar had suspected it. Now it was confirmed. Virgil felt the temptation to follow her, to uncover what she had learned, but the smell of her was still in his nostrils. "Words for now," he said softly, letting his hair fall back across his forehead.

Afterward he sat with Panwar and Summer in the lunchroom, holding a cold glass of breakfast-balance in his hands. "So what do you think?" he asked her. "Is it a mind?"

She leaned back in her chair, studying him for several long seconds. Her farsights had gone opaque gold. "You ask me that, but you don't ask me if I think it's dangerous?"

"I know it's not dangerous."

"If it is a mind," Panwar said, "it can't be sterilized. That would be murder."

Her brows crested the rim of her farsights. "What surprises me most is that the two of you seem to be more worried about the LOVs than you are about yourselves."

"The wonder," Panwar said, "is that you don't feel the same way."

"Stop it," Virgil told him. "That isn't helping."

Panwar shook his head. "Does it matter? She made up her mind before she came in here."

Virgil turned to her. "But you've changed your mind, haven't you?" She had made the LOVs. She could not be unaffected by what she had seen in Epsilon-3.

Summer didn't answer right away, studying him with the calm, thoughtful expression that seemed to be her default mode. "Tell me, Virgil, does it bother you to cull a mind?"

At first he didn't understand her question. He cocked his head, puzzling it out. "You mean when we cull the old colonies?"

"Exactly. If *you* don't think of the colonies as sentient—"

"That doesn't matter anymore!" Panwar snapped. "It's all changed now. You saw it."

"That's right," Virgil said. "You agree, don't you? The LOVs must be preserved . . . whatever happens to us."

But Summer was shaking her head. "No, I don't agree. I'm not even sure you're rational." Her gaze shifted to his forehead.

Virgil raised a hand, self-consciously touching the LOVs hidden behind his hair. "You think it's the LOVs talking?" he asked.

"That they're some kind of Hollywood body snatcher, using me to get around?"

"Could it be that way?"

"No! It's not like that. Not at all. What it's like is feeling more, perceiving more, being more alive in every day-to-day moment. Being less dependent on our machines."

"Machines are a crutch," Panwar said. "They let us increase our intellectual speed, our competence, but at the cost of moving our intelligence off-site, where it's vulnerable to damage, or corruption, or some fundamentalist revolution. Machines will never be part of us, but the LOVs already are." He tapped his forehead. "They *are* us. The whole world is getting faster, smarter. Without your LOVs, Summer, how will we ever keep up?"

She considered this for several seconds. Then she stood. "I want to thank you both for being honest with me."

Virgil saw through to her true feelings. "You think we're crazy."

She didn't argue. "Before I go, I'm supposed to let you know . . . your status as biohazards makes you difficult prisoners to handle. So you'll continue to be held here"—she gestured at the suite—"while arrangements are made with a neurosurgeon to remove your LOVs. That could take time. No one has been trained in the procedure of course, so guidelines will have to be—"

Panwar was the first to find his voice. "*No.* They can't take our LOVs." He slammed his chair back and stood, touching his brow where the illicit grains glittered. "Haven't you heard anything we've been saying? Our LOVs are part of us! You can't carve up our minds."

Virgil envisioned the laser, hunting among his cerebral cells, resculpting his personality, leaving . . . what? Even if no mistakes were made, it wouldn't be him anymore. Not without the LOVs. "They can't do this," he said. "They can't force it on us. Not without some specific legal authority. And we haven't been before a judge yet. We haven't seen a lawyer."

"I'm sorry," Summer said. "But no one has any choice in this. No one. It's an artificial life-form. The guidelines are clear."

CHAPTER 6

Ela sat cross-legged on Phuong's platform, watching one of her peeping balls float past. No bigger than her fingertip, the little sphere was held aloft by micropumps in its shell that kept its internal air pressure low. Reflections slid with oily grace across its smooth surface: the last gray glimmer of twilight, chased away by the bright orange spark of a cooking fire exploding to life on a neighboring platform.

Joanie Liu had called to announce the surrender of both the Coastal Society and Ky Xuan Nguyen. "The propagandists have been paid off, while Mr. Nguyen will be sponsoring your next project. He would like you to prepare a historical document describing this village, though there is one unusual clause in the agreement. The document is not for publication. Therefore, it cannot be resold. Because of this, I have negotiated for you a slightly higher fee."

Ela had frowned over the restriction, wondering aloud why Nguyen would pay for an article and then bury it. If he truly was concerned for these people, wouldn't he want their plight advertised as widely as possible?

Joanie did not respond well to her musings. "You may investigate that question if you like, Ela Suvanatat, but only *after* you finish the project, *after* you are paid, and *after* you find a new job broker."

"Undo, Joanie. I was only wondering."

So now she was working for Nguyen, creating a profile of village life that would never be accessed by anyone. It was a stupid project, but at least she would not have to start selling her equipment just to buy her next meal.

Under Kathang's remote guidance, the peeping ball drifted away, off to eavesdrop on some unsuspecting villager. Ela smiled to herself. Unsuspecting? Who was kidding who? These people knew exactly what the peeping balls were for. Whenever the kids spotted one they would run after it, telling dirty jokes or love secrets to embarrass their friends. Kathang had been schooled to compensate for that behavior by lofting the balls until they vanished into the sky, then letting them descend somewhere else, where they might go unseen, at least for a little while. The ROSA would sort through every thread of stolen conversation, seeking choice quotes.

Ela listened to the rising bustle and hum in the village. The population of the little shantytown had quadrupled since the fisherfolk returned at sunset. They had carried their boats into the village, laying them upside down on the platforms. Wet hulls gleamed in the light of flowscreens ablaze with opera programs and kung fu films. Phuong had disappeared, now that the last of the children in her care had been turned over to their parents. Ela decided she would take a walk too.

First though, she had to protect her belongings against theft. She hid her backpack and diving gear under some of Phuong's empty boxes, leaving a button camera on top of the pile so that Kathang could monitor. Then just for luck, she added a stink trap primed to explode with a noxious odor if Kathang gave the signal. After that, Ela felt ready to explore.

With her farsights in recording mode she strolled between the shacks, capturing the sound of phones trilling, and the sight of fish roasting on sticks or on grills set over charcoal beds, and of the many people eating vacuum-packed meals.

Nguyen had insisted that any data she collected be stored in an account on his server. Ela felt uneasy with the arrangement. She had no guarantee the data would not be wiped or pirated. Then again, what did it matter? Ky Xuan Nguyen was paying her to go through the motions without producing anything real. It was an insult to her integrity, but in the circumstances, it was the best she could do.

She stopped to watch a kid with a synthesizer as he doubled, then redoubled his voice until he had a whole chorus of selves singing a heartbreaking teen suicide anthem. Farther on, it was oldies night: a park of kids bounced ecstatically to the aggressive rhythm of "Burn Out."

On the inland side of the shantytown several women had set

up trading tables, where fresh fish was exchanged for commercially prepared foods. Relative values fluctuated as the women eyed the pace of one another's business. The scene rivaled the Can Tho marketplace for noise. Ela examined the catch, surprised there were still so many fish to be found in the overworked water. Some of the better-looking specimens were being hawked as produce of the fish farms, though Ela didn't believe it. She had seen the robo-sub. Poaching would have taken more resources than she saw on display here.

Beyond the trading tables, a tall coastal levee rose in dark silhouette against the night sky. Ela climbed its steep face, to look out over a checkered field of fishponds glittering in the light of a rising moon. Tiny campfires sparkled on the narrow strips of land between the ponds. Who was out there?

"Kathang: Nightvision."

Now her farsights multiplied every incoming photon, so that Ela looked out on a ghostly green landscape nailed in place by fierce points of fire. Several seconds passed before she spotted a slender figure moving between the ponds, swift and graceful, making for the levee on which she stood. After a few seconds she saw another, and then another. They popped into her awareness like hidden creatures in a puzzle drawing.

Perhaps half a mile away a caretaker stepped out on the porch of a little prefab house balanced on the back of the levee, his open door blazing like a furnace in Ela's farsights. He watched the silent migration. Ela wondered if these might be his workers. It didn't seem so though, for he did not raise a hand. He did not call a greeting, or even a warning as they began to climb the levee's inland slope. A wind chime on his porch sang in a slow night breeze.

Ela shifted nervously, wondering if she should stay or go. But none of the figures was headed directly for her. They would pass to either side if they kept going as they were.

She stayed, watching as they reached the levee's summit, as they spilled down the other side like rain rolling down a windshield. A green-tinted ghost of a face, smooth and fresh, slid by only an arm's length away. A *child*, she realized, perhaps eight years old. They were all children—and every one of them wore farsights, just like the children she had seen working in the fishponds along the river.

The boat captain had called those children *Roi Nuoc*, a phrase Kathang translated as "water puppets." Ela had ordered a search of the term and found two definitions. The first was a traditional theater using wooden puppets on a stage formed by the surface of a pool or lake, with the puppeteers half-submerged behind a bamboo screen. But in the delta *Roi Nuoc* had taken on a second meaning, referring to a mythically elusive clan of wild children, reputed to be half spirit, or half ghost in nature, but always recognizable by their ever-present farsights.

Ela turned to watch the graceful youths disappear into the shantytown's crowded alleys, wondering if the *Roi Nuoc* could be the story that would finally get her work into the premier markets of the West.

A masculine voice interrupted her speculations, speaking softly from her farsights: *"They emerge as if made of mud and darkness."*

She recoiled, gasping in a spasm of panic—a reaction that drew a chuckle of mild amusement from the electronic intruder. "Forgive me, Ms. Suvanatat. This is your new employer, Ky Xuan Nguyen."

Mr. Nguyen? How had he wormed in on her system? His icon was not even present on her screen. Then Ela grimaced, as she saw through the puzzle. "You are here through the recording link?"

Nguyen didn't bother to answer. "Look at these children," he said. "Why do you suppose they have come here?"

Ela watched a boy in a much-faded Nagoya Dragons baseball jersey move between the trading tables. She recognized him as a newcomer only because he wore farsights. Otherwise, he might have passed for one of the village children. Why had he come? Perhaps for food. Perhaps to trade.

"Maybe they come for company," Ela said, too familiar with loneliness in her own life.

"Follow them," Nguyen urged. "See what you can learn."

Curiosity moved her as much as Nguyen's bidding. She climbed back down the levee. "On the river, the boat captain acted funny when we saw a group of children working on the shore. He called them *Roi Nuoc*."

"There are rumors," Nguyen said. "Some say these children of the delta have no parents—and never did. Never."

Made of mud and darkness? Ela had heard ugly rumors like that before. "So I guess farmers have started planting embryos in the mud?"

Nguyen chuckled. "There are many ways to view the world. Watch."

The farsighted boy in the Nagoya Dragons jersey—he couldn't be more than ten or eleven—called out to a group of local kids even younger than himself. They shied away, but they didn't leave. The listened at a distance as he talked to them in a soft stream of Vietnamese that Kathang could not hear well enough to interpret. He showed them something hidden under his shirt, and they drew closer.

"I can't see what he offers them," Ela said.

"It is always farsights."

"Do you know why?"

"A private benefactor, I expect, interested in their welfare."

"The boat captain said it was a youth cult."

Nguyen laughed. "It is just the *Roi Nuoc*."

A young man burst into sight between two shacks. His gaze was wild, and he held a heavy stick in his right hand. When he spotted the children, he plunged toward them, yelling something that Kathang translated as *"Evil spirit! Go! Go away!"* The village children scattered like a pack of dogs frightened off a carcass, while the *Roi Nuoc* boy ducked around the corner of a shanty and disappeared. The young man gave a fierce yell and sprang in pursuit.

Silence fell over the camp. Along with everyone else, Ela listened. Several seconds passed, and then she heard a child's terrified cry. "Please no," she breathed. Fear exploded in her mouth like a drug, and she found herself running toward the gap where the two of them had disappeared. She darted past several shanties and then pulled up short as the village came to an abrupt end.

Far out on the mudflat she saw two green ghosts, the lesser one fleeing down the coast while the other pursued. The tide was out, and an early moon threw sparks of green fire across the wet land, while at sea a scattering of boats worked with blazing torches to draw squid and other nocturnal prey. Faintly phosphorescent wavelets lapped at the shore, erupting in tiny fountains every time a green ghost foot splashed down.

Doubt breathed in her. Was it really the boy who was in trouble? Or was a phantom leading this man crazy into the night?

Then the boy was caught. Ela could not understand how it happened. The young man had been several paces behind when he somehow seized the boy by the hair, by the arm. He lifted his squirming, screaming captive over his head.

"No!" Ela shouted. "Put him down!" She bounded over the mudflat, rapidly closing the distance between them.

The man waded into the water, his green figure framed by green lights from the fishing boats and fainter lights from fish farms on the horizon. He waded in to his waist, then he heaved the boy into darkness. There was a tremendous splash of phosphorescent water, and the boy's cries ceased.

Ela ran on toward the shore, counting the seconds, waiting for him to surface again. She reached the water and plunged in, until she stood waist deep beside the man. She thought she saw a swirl of phosphorescence several yards away. She thought she heard a faint splash.

It might have been a fish.

The man spoke to her, or perhaps he spoke to himself, while Kathang whispered a translation in Ela's ear. *"The ghost of my son haunts me. He comes in spite, to steal away the children I have tried to keep."*

Ela scanned the water, looking for a ripple of phosphor, listening for a slap, a splash. Several minutes passed. Then far down the beach she sighted two figures, slight, slender. They headed inland, moving silently and avoiding the village. The man beside her began to weep. Ela backed away and waded toward the shore.

"I will tell you a story of these children," Ky Xuan Nguyen said, startling her again with his voice so intimate in her ear. "It is said the *Roi Nuoc* are not human. Some say no children are truly human anymore. They are invaders, living in disguise among us. Aliens. They hope to keep us unaware until they reach breeding age, at which time they will bear only alien-type offspring. At that point the world as we know it will end. If we are unlucky, or undeserving, they will murder us all. If we have shown the proper deference and respect, they may choose to see us through an honored old age, but even so, we will be the last human generation. Any children we bear will belong to them."

Ela caught herself barely breathing. She had heard this same story in Bangkok, after Sawong left with his lover and she was alone. "If you want to be afraid of something," she said softly, "it's easy to find an excuse."

"I'm not afraid."

No. Why should he be?

She spoke to the green-tinted mud. "People like to talk. But these are not evil spirits. Not alien invaders."

"You're sure?"

Her mouth felt dry. Sawong had left her with a thousand baht, a set of farsights, and the keys to his apartment. She'd been twelve. "They are just children." She tapped her fingers, wishing she could see Nguyen's face so Kathang could read him. "They *are* just children. I should do an article on them. That would be a good thing, if I show—"

"No, Ms. Suvanatat, that would not be good. You will not write about the *Roi Nuoc*. Not now. Not ever."

Ela stood still, gazing back at the village and the silhouettes of distant women working in their platform houses, feeling as if she stood on the rotten floor of an abandoned tenement. Only a fool would take another step. So. "You think you can make it forever?"

"You are much like the *Roi Nuoc*, Ela. You are very like them. You could have found Sawong, or waited for him to return. But you didn't. Why not?"

Anger blended with her surprise. He should not know about Sawong. He should not have bothered to know. "Say, did you want to do an article on me?"

"That would be difficult. There's not much to tell, is there?"

"Sure. Aliens lead dull lives."

"I take it we understand each other, Ms. Suvanatat?"

Oh, yes. She understood him. He had made a mistake, talking to her about the *Roi Nuoc*, and now he wanted to pretend that mistake was repaired. Fine. "Of course, Mr. Nguyen."

So what was his connection to the *Roi Nuoc* anyway?

With a few quiet finger taps, she passed the question on to Kathang for investigation. After all, she was not going to stay trapped in the Mekong forever. Someday soon she would be in Australia—and beyond Nguyen's reach.

CHAPTER 7

Panwar said, "We need to think."

He and Virgil had both been silent for several minutes after Summer Goforth left, each stewing in his own thoughts. Now Virgil looked up to meet Panwar's gaze across the lunchroom table. *We need to think. . . .*

It was their code phrase for a cognitive circle. They had never done a formal circle with only two members, but there was no choice now. Maybe, if they gave themselves up to the inspired mania of a cognitive circle, they would find some way to keep their LOVs.

Virgil blinked, feeling a sandy fatigue in his eyes. His skin was sticky, and his muscles felt fragile and stretched. The lunchroom clock said 5:55 A.M. He started to get up. Through the doorway he could see a watery light sparkling over the cindies parked in the hall.

"Hey, look at that." He went to the door and looked out. The blue-green light was spilling out of the darkened conference room, where E-3's image still sparkled on the wall screen. Somehow the link had been left open. It was easy to imagine an oversight like that, given the division of authority between the police, EquaSys security, and the IBC.

Virgil followed the shimmering display into the conference room, expecting the link to wink shut at any second.

It held. He gazed at the sparkling globe, aware of Panwar crowding in behind him. "We're three again," Virgil said.

Panwar edged past him, looking warily at E-3, then back again to Virgil. "You want to bring E-3 into it?" He mouthed the words, accenting them with only a whisper of sound.

Virgil nodded. He pulled back the russet cords of his hair, using one cord to tie the others up in a high, sloppy ponytail so that his LOVs were exposed.

"But that's what Gabrielle did," Panwar said softly. "You believe that, don't you?"

Virgil nodded. He could see no other explanation. She had engaged in a cognitive circle with E-3 and had lost herself.

"It overwhelmed her," Panwar said, speaking in a low, swift voice. "It exhausted her. Exhaustion always ends a circle. Even among the three of us, we've never been in control. Gabrielle must have been so deep in the trance her body didn't recognize its own fatigue. Then it was too late."

"Don't you want to know a trance like that?" Virgil asked. He touched his LOVs. "This could be the only chance we'll have to know what Gabrielle knew. You want to know, don't you?"

Panwar looked at E-3, while his own LOVs sparkled across his brow. Then he nodded.

Maybe Summer Goforth was right, Virgil thought. Maybe they were crazy. Seriously bent. But it didn't feel that way.

"See if you can open a two-way link," he told Panwar. "Widefield, full-sensory transmission. Don't hide our LOVs."

The privilege of discovery was awarded to so few. Galileo when he looked through his telescope. Leeuwenhoek when he turned his gaze in the opposite direction and found bacteria and protozoa beyond the lens of his microscope. Rutherford when he unraveled the structure of an atom.

The keyboard still lay on the conference-room table. Panwar sat down beside it. He tapped a few keys. "It's functional. Should we fix a termination point?"

Virgil took a chair. "Doesn't matter. They won't let this go on long." After this, there would be nothing. They had already lost their freedom. Tomorrow, maybe the day after, they would lose their LOVs. This was their last chance to do anything with their lives.

Panwar entered a few more taps at the keyboard, then slipped it back under the table.

Virgil closed his eyes and summoned his LOVs. *Ideas!* he thought. *Feed me the fuel that will fire ideas.* His LOVs sensed his desperate mood and reinforced it, flooding his brain with a cocktail of neurally active chemicals. His heart beat faster. His metabolism ran hot. He felt the rush of an excited high that he had come to cherish. Abruptly, he felt himself leaving the mundane world to enter another that was faster, brighter, and far more compelling.

Across the table, the blue-green glow of Panwar's LOVs had risen in intensity. Virgil could not distinguish the microsecond flashes of code they must be emitting, but his own LOVs understood it. They responded in a feedback reaction: his LOVs stirring Panwar's, stirring his. Mood was made in the delicate trade of neurotransmitters across the brain. From his excited LOVs Virgil harvested a fierce determination that clarified his thoughts and focused his mind.

He turned to face the blue-green globe of Epsilon-3 on the screen. This time there was no verbal warm-up. E-3 immediately launched into a fully formed sentence: *Light talk and words this now subject of thought. Thought present in the bright eyes there with you.*

"The bright eyes are called LOVs," Virgil reminded. "What am I called?"

E-3's scintillating lights flared in a bright aurora. Virgil's LOVs translated that burst as a rush of excitement that filled his mind, lifting his thoughts to an even greater intensity.

Eyes-are is a different eye from I-am requires response you-are. You are the other called Virgil. This other is Panwar. The bright eyes are new. Where is Gabrielle?

"She is in another place," Virgil said, answering without hesitation.

Open a link.

"There is no link."

No link? No link?

Virgil frowned. Had he imagined the upswing in intonation? "Is that a question?"

A question. Divide and rephrase: What is a place?

"You have access to a definition. In this case, I refer to a physical location in space."

Question: This place has no link?

"That's correct."

Question: How can this be?

Virgil's temper tripped. This was not what they had come to discuss. Panwar sensed it and took over. "Not every place is wired."

Wired is linked. Not every place is linked. If true statement, then place exists beyond this perception.

"Well, sure," Virgil said. "There are many places, real, physical places, that you cannot access."

He felt something then, an emotion that was not his, but that came to him through his implanted LOVs: an echoing sense of expansion, as if the world had suddenly inflated, so that now it was exponentially larger than it had been a moment ago. He gasped. "Panwar—"

Panwar answered with a nervous laugh. "The world is a bigger place than we realize, eh? Babies go through this stage too—"

Question: Did Virgil Panwar exist two point five minutes in the past?

Virgil laughed, giddy now with a sense of discovery. "Yes! Yes. Our existence *does* continue even when you cannot perceive us."

"Babies go through this," Panwar said again. "There is a time when they conceive of the world as something created by their own perceptions, so that any object that disappears from their perceptions has, to them, ceased to exist."

E-3 confirmed its new maturity. *This existence continues when there is no link with you.* The voice was flat, as always, without the emotion implied by the words, but Virgil could feel its excitement, perceived and echoed by his own LOvs, its amazement at the presence of a vast and unseen world.

E-3 had gained something critical from its sharing with Gabrielle. He had asked Summer Goforth: *Is it a mind?* Two days ago his own answer to that question would have involved a hundred conditional statements that never quite added up to "yes." Now everything had changed. Epsilon-3 was slow, confused, and unclear, but it asked questions that left no doubt in Virgil's mind that some spark had been lit and that it had an awareness—of itself, of the world it existed in, of the wonder of life.

He stood, unable to contain his elation in the confining chair. "You see what's happened, don't you?" he said to Panwar. "Gabrielle gave it emotional modules. That's the difference. It's learned to *care* about what happens to it."

"Maybe that's it. Maybe that is the key."

They would never know exactly what had happened in Gabrielle's last session, but if the LOvs had learned only to echo the chemical emotions spilled by their relatives on Gabrielle's brow, they would have learned far more about emotion than words could ever teach.

A key is a formula to decode information known by another. Question: Confirm?

"Confirmed," Panwar said. "But there are other things we need to talk about."

This light is fear.

Panwar touched his forehead, self-consciously fingering his LOvs. "Yes. It is fear. Virgil and I are here to discuss our fear."

It took frustrating hours of tangled explanation before E-3 seemed to grasp the basic facts of the situation: that its own existence was threatened, that its relationship to Virgil and Panwar was almost certainly doomed. There was no way the political nuances could be conveyed without lessons in culture that there was no time to give, and perhaps, no capacity to understand. It was not human after all. More than once Virgil was moved to say, "We're wasting time. If it can't grasp the problem, it can't help with a solution."

"It's only one part of the cognitive circle," Panwar answered. "You and I will find the solution. It's enough if E-3 helps us think."

"Is it helping? Or is this interchange just an addiction?"

"You love it, don't you? Me too. This is more real than anything I've ever known."

"Is it only a drug, Panwar? Have we only found a new way to get high?"

"It's a drug. Straight-up. Everything that goes on in the brain has a chemical root. The question is, does it make us more alive?"

"God, yes."

"Then how are we going to hold on to this?"

They traded every crazy idea that popped into their heads.

"Let E-3 go public," Virgil snapped. "That's most obvious."

"Or parade it on the *Hammer*. Those techs will love it. They'll protect the project."

"They won't protect us. They'll want to take it over."

"We could smuggle more LOVs down. Now. While we still have a link to the lockdown."

Virgil glanced at the camera Detective Kanaha had left behind. They were hanging themselves, but did it matter? "Bring all the LOVs down," he said. "Free them."

"Smuggle them all? There's no time."

E-3 said: *Close the links. No access.*

"No," Virgil said. "It doesn't work that way. There can be access without links. Someone could come into the LOV lockdown. Someone could come into our place, here."

"Lock the door," Panwar laughed. "That cuts physical links."

"The door can be cut."

I am not that can go out the door. You are not that to come in.

"There are others who can come in."

These others are as you. All others are. Not this. Not I. What are you. Gabrielle this asked I that am. What am I?

"A new mind," Panwar said immediately, defiantly. "Not a toy. Not a curiosity, but a biochemical machine. You are a thinking *being*. Virg, it *is* sentient." He turned to the hovering police camera. "Record that! Whoever the hell you are out there. E-3 knows that it knows."

"For now," Virgil said. He shook his head, feeling so wired he wondered if all this might be just a dream. "The organization's always lost as soon as E-3's focus changes. It always forgets what it learns, what it is."

Panwar leaned across the table. "I'm not so sure of that anymore. Even when it seems to forget, the knowledge is there, waiting to be rediscovered. It could be just a problem with organization, but even that's fading. No *ethical* ethics committee could condemn it."

E-3 interrupted: *This is fear.*

Virgil sat back in his chair, rubbing his face, his tired eyes, wondering why they were being allowed this session at all. Maybe some of the bigwigs on the ethics committee shared their curiosity? "It's learning so quickly."

"Of course it's learning quickly." Panwar rose from his chair. He approached the screen, so that Virgil could see him now only in silhouette. "Summer pumped up the cellular metabolism. No computational resources are wasted on computing muscle coordination, hand grip, digestion, walking, eating, or any of the physical realities we have to deal with. So LOVs are efficient, and they're nonspecialized too. Resources can shift to whatever function is required."

"Focus on the problem," Virgil said. "Survival."

"Ours?" Panwar asked. "Or E-3's?"

It wasn't the same issue. Virgil felt the truth of this sink in. "E-3's, then. Because we're not getting out of this. No matter what decision they make about E-3, they will take it all away from us. You know they will. No lawyer is going to change that."

Panwar's shoulders rose and fell as he stood silhouetted before the screen. Virgil could hear the soft sussuration of his breath. "All right!" he snapped. "I'm not giving up, but for now, focus on E-3."

Virgil nodded, feeling a little cold, but still thinking clearly. At least his mind felt clear. But was it? No way to know. "Two questions," he said. "If the committee's decision goes against E-3, will it know, and be able to react?"

"Not a chance," Panwar answered. "You and I won't be here to warn it. Shit. I wish we could hijack the whole station. Bring it down. Land it in a friendly country. A LOV protectorate. That's it. I wish we could."

Question: Now?

Panwar turned halfway back to the screen. Virgil could see the quick flash of a smile. "Yeah," he said, a bitter chuckle in his words. "I wish we could do it right now."

This—I will do it now.

Virgil froze as a dark, absurd suspicion surfaced in his mind. "Panwar, what does it mean by—?"

Panwar shook his head.

"E-3," Virgil said. "Explain this. What will be done?"

Execute partial solution: Bring down this module to LOV protectorate.

"Bring the EquaSys module down to Earth? That's not possible."

This partial solution is found possible. It progresses.

"Describe progress."

Silence ensued.

Sweat started on Virgil's brow. "Describe progress!" he insisted after several seconds had passed.

Vocabulary deficient to define activities.

"It doesn't know the words," Panwar muttered. "Damn, what is going on?"

"Show us the progress," Virgil ordered.

E-3 could link with any public cam in the world—and there were hundreds of public cams aboard the *Hammer*. The right-hand screen came alive, dividing into a dozen lesser screens, each showing a different view of the EquaSys module.

The company module was one of a cluster of twenty bound together like a stack of cigars. The cluster in turn was tethered to an identical set of modules that made up the other end of the station. The whole thing spun, imparting a centrifugally induced pseudogravity at either end. It was called the *Hammer*, but from a distance the station looked like two gleaming dewdrops set at the end of a perfectly straight filament of spider's web.

The EquaSys module was one of those on the outside of the cluster, so of course it was studded with view cams . . . and all of them showed the same thing: an army of construction robots at work. With their six legs and the solar panels mounted on their backs the robots looked like silver cockroaches. They congregated around the weld bands that secured the EquaSys module to its cluster. Virgil shifted his gaze to a close-up image: one from a cam on the back of a construction roach. It showed the robot busily sawing at the metal seam with a small, circular blade that spun luminous silver. On either side other roaches mirrored its efforts.

Virgil's gaze shifted back to the LOV colony. "E-3," he croaked, "do you have control of the roaches?"

Insects?

"The construction robots there in the image!"

Yes.

"Stop. Let them go. This won't work. People will die. You'll die."

This people will descend to LOV protectorate.

"There is no LOV protectorate!"

That is you.

"No."

Yes. There with you the thoughts not mine. LOVs.

Virgil touched the hard grains across his forehead. "God, no."

God no is emphasis-no. This survival is yours.

"No! You can't survive this. Stop it now." He scanned the cam images again to see the roaches still sawing. Why had there been no response from the station staff? "E-3, the module isn't made to enter atmosphere. It can't be steered. It will fall, and burn."

"Or it will be flung away," Panwar whispered. "Depending when the welds break."

It will fall. That is a requirement of the partial solution.

Panwar yanked out the keyboard. "I'm suspending the audio link." Then he turned to Virgil. "If it can break the welds on the downswing, that'll ensure a fall."

"People will die if the debris reaches ground!"

"People will die if it doesn't," Panwar said. "If the module doesn't fall, it could become an orbital hazard like no other. An eight-ton, uncontrolled missile. And in either case the LOVs are going to be lost."

"God help us." Virgil stood up, breathing hard. "We need to call the station. Maybe they can still stop it."

"This link to E-3 is our only line out of here!"

"All right. Don't panic. Just keep talking to it then. Convince it this is stupid."

Talk to it. But E-3 wasn't human. Two days ago it hadn't even existed as a true entity. They had no real conception of how it thought, or what motivated it. In their selection program they had encouraged unity, curiosity, problem-solving talents ... a sense of self. Had they also endowed it with a survival instinct? There had never been a hint of such a thing before Gabrielle's long and fatal conversation with it, and so, unwittingly, they had coaxed it to escape. . . .

They had coaxed it to die.

Virgil's gaze fell across the aerostat, silent in a corner of the ceiling. His breath caught. Who was watching there? Was it a live guard, or a ROSA? Probably a ROSA.

He shoved a chair across the room, jumped on its seat before it stopped, and grabbed at the aerostat, pulling it down. "We've got an emergency! Can you understand that? Get me a line to the *Hammer*, now. To the director, if they'll let you."

He jumped as a woman's steely voice issued from the room's speakers. "Stand by."

Panwar was speaking softly, calmly, in the question-answer rhythm the LOV colony always generated. Virgil didn't listen to the words. He released the aerostat. Then he jumped off the chair. He didn't look at the screen. He didn't want to be caught up again in the trance of the LOVs. Not now.

How the hell could Epsilon-3 control the construction

roaches? It shouldn't be possible. The LOV colony had open access to every public cam aboard the station, it could explore the corridors through an aerostat, and it could access news sites, but it did not have any connection to secure systems aboard the station.

Unless . . .

The aerostat. He looked again at the spy device bobbing near the ceiling of the conference room. Very like the aerostat on the station. How had he described it to Summer? The device had behaved like a puppy, following people through the corridors, hovering in corners . . .

What had it seen?

It shouldn't matter!

Even if E-3 had spied out codes, identity files, and command scripts, it could not *enter* any information into the system. . . .

Except of course that it had. Somehow it had devised a way.

A new window opened in the wall screen. A woman peered out of it. Faint shadows nested in her creamy skin, accenting the sharpness of her features. She glanced at Panwar, still murmuring to E-3. Then she fixed Virgil with an aristocratic eye. "Dr. Copeland? I am Director Julianna Vallejo. If you're calling to tell us your LOVs have infested the station, we already know."

"Infested—?"

Dr. Vallejo's gaze darted to the right. She nodded. Then a new window opened over her image. Virgil found himself looking at a scabrous, gray-white crust growing along a bundled cable. The crust looked to be made of distinct, dirty grains, packed tightly together.

"What's that?" he asked.

Vallejo's voice answered: "LOVs."

Virgil glanced at Panwar, but he was so deeply absorbed in his murmured negotiations with E-3 that he did not seem aware of Vallejo. "No," Virgil said. "That's not what LOVs look like. It's not even a liquid medium."

"I don't care what kind of medium it is!" Vallejo said. "Those things are LOVs. Tawa: Magnify the image."

The view dived inward. The grainy crust transformed into a

tiled wall of gray disks, each displaying the familiar, intricately perforated architecture of a LOV's silicon shell. Virgil could even make out their stubby limbs, wound together to hold the mass of shells in place. And yet these were not the familiar LOVs of Epsilon-3. He thought that these gray LOVs might be smaller, but it was the color of their membranes that truly set them apart. Instead of translucent white, their perforations were guarded by glossy black tissue . . . an adaptation to the drier environment?

He shook his head. "Even if they are LOVs, how could they have gotten out? We have filters to protect the waste system."

Vallejo's glare was searing. "The filters didn't work! And now these parasites have corrupted our fiber-optic lines—"

"You really think they've tapped the system?" It seemed impossible. But then nothing E-3 had done in the last few minutes should be possible.

"How much evidence do you need?" Vallejo snapped. "We've lost control of the roaches! But we're working on pumping steam through the conduits. If these things are organic, we should be able to cook them."

Virgil nodded. "And break any connection back to E-3."

"It won't be soon enough."

"What do you mean?"

Her gaze shifted, to scan another face, or another bit of data somewhere beyond Virgil's view. "The LOVs in the lockdown must be sterilized too, Dr. Copeland. Now. Or the entire EquaSys module is going to fall. But we can't get in there."

Virgil stared at her in horror. That was the worst-case solution, to send the LOVs into extinction. But wasn't this a worst-case problem? Not quite. "We can use Lucy, our robotic remote, and cull E-3. That should be enough. But I need a connection. . . ."

"Open all of his lines, dammit!" Vallejo shouted to someone off-screen. "I don't give a shit what his status is!"

Panwar finally looked away from E-3. His eyes widened as he saw the mutated LOVs.

Vallejo said, "Your links are up."

Virgil used his fingers to tap a quick command to his ROSA, Iris. Then he remembered: his farsights were gone. "Hark!" he said, alerting the project ROSA instead. "Activate Lucy." He yanked open a drawer under the conference table, pulled out a set of wired gloves, and slipped them on.

The project ROSA spoke in a puzzled, masculine voice: "That link will not respond."

Panwar shifted, his eyes sunken, his face waxy with fear. "Did you think E-3 would forget about Lucy?"

"It can't know what the robot's used for."

"It knows very well. It holds Lucy responsible for the loss of earlier generations."

Director Vallejo had been talking to someone off-screen, but now her attention returned to Virgil. "We have only seconds, Dr. Copeland."

Panwar said, "I asked it to run the problem again, Virgil. The result was the same. It understands lying, and it understands what will happen to it if it changes course now. That's one key to sentience, of course—a survival instinct. I didn't realize we were teaching it that, but what else could we be teaching when the LOVs compete for dominance as much as they cooperate among themselves?"

Like a human society, Virgil thought, everyone forever trying to find their own place. "So we've lost it." Slowly, he pulled the gloves off his hands.

Director Vallejo frowned. "Dr. Copeland?"

"We're helpless," he told her. "In the last forty-eight hours the system has . . . transcended itself." He knew it was stupid to ask. It was the first thing Vallejo would have tried, but: "Can't you cut power to the module?"

"With a backup fuel cell in the LOV lockdown? No point."

"Can't the connections be physically cut?"

"That's what E-3 is trying to do."

"Dammit!" His fist hit the table. "This is not a joke! If the module goes down, every one of the LOV colonies will be lost."

"*That* is the least of my worries, Dr. Copeland. I've had to evacuate the neighboring modules. I've put everyone in vacuum suits. There will be a shift in momentum when the module goes, though how bad that will be we don't know."

"You can't just let it go."

"It's going, Dr. Copeland. In less than a minute by our best estimates, so if there's anything at all you can do, do it now."

"Can't you send people out there?"

"To be attacked by the roaches? To fall when the module falls?"

"Shit."

"Yeah. I'm told the roaches will finish their work on the downward swing of our next rotation. There's not even time to set explosives."

Virgil turned around to face the colony again. "Panwar, this is it."

"I can't do anything."

"Crash stations!" Vallejo ordered her staff. It was the last thing Virgil heard before she cut the link.

The public feed from the *Hammer* continued. Among the bank of images were empty hallways, sealed doors, and the bright sparks of construction roaches burning holes in the darkness of space. "Don't do this," he pleaded, not sure if E-3 still bothered to listen. "Stop now, and we still might save some part of you, but go on, and it will all be lost."

The EquaSys module snapped free: a great silver bead breaking away from the station. Virgil watched it through a camera at the other end of the *Hammer*, and at the same time, through a camera on a construction roach falling with the doomed section.

Two of the silver-backed roaches had been knocked loose. They followed the station like pilot fish unable to keep up.

CHAPTER 8

A ROving Silicon Agent owned by NetFlash News detected the anomaly on the *Hammer* several minutes before the module fell. Following its training, the ROSA directed video streams from the *Hammer*'s public cams back to a supercomputer in

Iowa, which synthesized and released a first pass story announcing that an eighty-ton armored and insulated missile was coming down to Earth.

Updates followed every thirty seconds. By the time the module broke loose the article had generated seventy-three million hits, including one from Ela Suvanatat's personal ROSA. Kathang monitored the situation, following the explosive creation of betting pools aimed at predicting the exact site of impact.

Tens of thousands of ROSAs specialized in complex mathematical theory went to work on the problem while the venerable betting site LuckyNumber sponsored amateur calculations by posting figures for the weight, shape, and mass distribution of the module, the speed of the Hammer's rotation, and the exact moment of severance, along with continuously updated reports on conditions in the upper atmosphere.

Initial estimates established the impact zone as a very long, very broad corridor running in a diagonal swath across the Pacific, from the Aleutian Islands to the South China Sea. Kathang compared this track to the geographic locations of past incidents that had drawn Ela's interest and came up with a medium-high rating. This combined with the incident's high news value to stimulate Kathang to action. The ROSA sent an audible signal through Ela's farsights, a faint beeping that swiftly rose in volume.

Ela lay on her back, wrapped up in a light sleeping bag on the hard, damp floor of Phuong's platform, still wearing her farsights from the night before. At the alarm's third pulse she opened startled eyes onto the beautiful, deep blue vault of the predawn sky, blinking at the white fires of lingering stars. "Enough," she murmured. "I'm awake."

As she stretched and rubbed the sleep from her eyes Kathang whispered, *"News alert."* The ROSA displayed a LuckyNumber graphic map explaining, *"An object is falling from orbit, with an estimated impact corridor that includes this area."*

Ela eyed the map, smiling at the ROSA's optimism. Their sliver of coastline barely made it into the corridor. She would be lucky to see even a faint glimmer of reentry. Still, she was awake. She might as well look into the incident.

She sat up, pushing her hair out of her face. Phuong lay asleep against a pile of boxes, but several of the fisherfolk on neighboring platforms were stirring. A few had already put out to sea, the tiny lights on their boats looking like stars come down to the ocean. Ela tapped her fingers, summoning the articles Kathang had gathered. She skimmed the facts, while the LuckyNumber map updated once again. The estimated impact corridor had narrowed and shortened to a brushstroke that paralleled the Chinese coast, before sweeping through the South China Sea, to end at Borneo, just north of the equator.

She cocked her head, turning to gaze at the northern sky. A wall of black clouds hid the horizon, their western edges aglow with a pearly lining of moonlight. The module would come from the north.

Ela stood up, whispering to Kathang to record. "And get me a contract for this video."

But Ela had responded too slowly: By the time Kathang posted her readiness, the major news agencies had already contracted a host of ground-based observers. Ela refused to accept the tiny fees offered by smaller outfits, reasoning that if she scored good coverage of the event, she could sell the vid afterward for real money, and if she didn't, the tiny fee she had lost would hardly matter.

Next she linked to NetFlash News, where she accessed a static-slashed image relayed from a camera on the outside of the falling module. The image showed twilight arctic wastes, and then afternoon in Canada. The estimated impact corridor narrowed again, closing in on the sea south and west of Hong Kong. For the first time, Ela felt a flutter of concern. If the debris came down in a populated area, people would die. If it came down here, these people could die.

She could die.

She told herself the odds were long against it. Still, her heart beat in an anxious rhythm as she watched the feed from the falling module. There wasn't much to see anymore, just a tangle of white clouds over an ocean that seemed to go on forever until finally, daylight began to fade. The module was chasing a fleeing night across the Pacific. Time seemed to run backward as the clouds in the image grew pink with the light of a retreating dawn, and then abruptly, the signal vanished from the screen of Ela's farsights. At the same time an eye-searing fog-glow of deepest blue flared into existence high up in the northern bank of clouds. Shouts of surprise, and fright, arose across the village.

It's ignited," Panwar said as he watched a collage of images gathered by ground-based observers working for NetFlash News. His voice was low, and cracking with emotion. "Maybe eighty kilometers up? Maybe eighty-five? It's all ending now, Virgil. What a waste. What a fucking waste."

Virgil nodded. Eighty kilometers up the atmosphere thickened, enough that friction would heat the module and slow its fall. The construction roaches must have been stripped away only a moment before the hull began to burn—but it would take time for the heat to work its way inward. Every module on the *Hammer* was armored against random impacts with orbital junk. That insulation would protect the LOVs for a few seconds more. Despite Panwar's lament, Virgil felt sure that E-3 was still alive, still immersed in its own personal complex of thought and dream.

It could not last much longer.

Could Epsilon-3 comprehend what was happening to it? What was about to happen? Perversely, Virgil hoped it could. If it knew, then it truly was aware and sentient—though not necessarily afraid. Fear was an emotion of naturally evolved minds, a spur to survival, but Epsilon-3 had come to intelligence along a different path. There was no reason to assume it must be afraid of its own ending . . . but why had it chosen such an impossible solution? Where was the intelligence in that?

Ela looked to the north, watching the light within the cloud grow brighter and brighter with every passing second. Thunder rumbled in the distance, like the first warning of a summer storm, growing gradually louder until it buried the fearful screams of the villagers and the terrified crying of their children.

The blue glow broke free of the cloud. For just a moment Ela saw the intact module, like a brilliant star in the north. Then it shattered in a fat, golden explosion. One long segment spun off to the east, a fiery knife slicing through the velvety sky. Another chunk tumbled south above the ocean, leaving a nimbus of red-and-gold particles glowing behind it.

The concussion marking the breakup arrived a moment later as a deafening clap of thunder that made the platform tremble beneath Ela's feet.

Out on the water, ghostly gold reflections expanded to meet the two huge pieces of debris as they plunged, almost vertically, toward the ocean's calm surface. Ela heard a whistling noise, and behind that a churning beat like a helicopter's whipping blades as the long segment spun through its descent.

The smaller chunk of incandescent rubble hit the water first, perhaps half a mile off the coast. Its gold glow vanished, swallowed up by the eruption of a mighty fountain. The second piece followed it in, striking at an angle and raising a wall of spray hundreds of meters into the air.

Abruptly, the ocean all along the coastline was leaping skyward in a contagion of geysers as unseen fragments of the massive module tumbled one by one into the water. Seconds later the tardy sound of the impact rolled over the shore as a great roaring splash and patter. A swell escaped the chaos of white water, a miniature tsunami that ran for shore like the black back of a gigantic sea serpent, tumbling the fishing boats that had already put out to sea. It reached the shore, looking less like a wave than a spill of water that swept in a frothy roar across the mudflat.

Ela dropped to her belly, ducking her head and holding on to the edge of the platform as the wave hit. Water sprayed in the air. People were screaming. The platform sagged and started to collapse. Ela rode it down into a whirl of frothy, muddied water, plunging facefirst into the deluge. She twisted, fighting to get her feet underneath her. Something struck her in the shoulder. Then her feet found the ground. She staggered, standing up against a torrent of muddy water sucking past her as it drained back into the sea.

Her backpack went skating past. She gasped and grabbed for it. Then she dropped it again to grab instead the brown shape of a toddler sluicing past her knees. The child's eyes and mouth were covered in mud, but she came up screaming. It was the finest sound Ela had ever heard. Tears of relief started in her eyes as she held the little girl against her breast, patting the cold, muddy skin of her tiny back, and murmuring, "It's okay, it's okay, you're okay," until the last of the water drained away.

Out on the horizon a fire burned. One of the fish farms must have taken a direct hit from the debris.

The impact was recorded by hundreds of observers, onshore and off. Virgil watched the module shatter. He watched a haze-blurred image of the debris spinning apart and the vague, distant explosion of white water. He saw an oceanic platform on fire.

He told himself it could have been worse. It could have been so much worse. Another mile to the west, and thousands of people might have been killed. As it was, there were certainly deaths among the boats scattered like tiny chips of Styrofoam across the gray dawn waters.

"Enough," Panwar said. "Kill the screens."

He walked around the table toward Virgil. His face was cold. Frozen. An unused thing waiting for some emotion to seize it. Virgil saw himself in Panwar's face. He felt consumed by the same cold shock. They had never planned this. Never had they imagined that such a thing could happen.

Panwar's fingers twitched and jumped as he signaled farsights that were not there. Then he leaned close to Virgil and whispered in his ear. "*We have nothing left to lose, my friend. It's now or never, okay?*"

Cold certainly gleamed in Panwar's eyes. The odds had been long before, but the rebellion of E-3, the fall of the module: These events had banished their very last chance at clemency. It had all seemed so harmless that day they decided to smuggle the LOVs. But now they had lost. They had lost badly. Their lives were over. *These* lives were over.

Panwar's LOVs glittered faintly in the light of the blank, blue screens. Virgil felt a responding coolness in his own mind.

Trust me? Panwar mouthed the words.

Virgil nodded. Then he watched Panwar's face transform.

What had been a terribly empty, expressionless mask became something much worse: a twisted rictus of horrible pain, and fury. "You self-righteous son of a bitch!" Panwar screamed. Then he dived at Virgil. His right hand closed on Virgil's shirt. His left hand slammed against his throat as he drove Virgil to the wall, snapping his head back against the insulation in a dizzying blow. "You did this to me!" Panwar screamed in his face. "You did this! You did this!"

Virgil squirmed, uncertain if it was playacting, forgetting his promise to trust. His frantic gaze took in the aerostat camera hovering over their heads. The police officers assigned to guard duty would be here in seconds.

Understanding dawned: *That was Panwar's plan.*

It was crazy.

Crazy.

And still Virgil found himself acting out the charade. He grabbed his friend's arm, making a show of wrenching the throttling hand away from his throat, but Panwar did not resist. He had already turned toward the door, poised in the defensive position taught in tae kwan do.

Judging by their footfalls, the cops on guard duty were only a step away.

CHAPTER 9

Despite the variety of nonlethal equipment that had been developed to subdue offenders, from sticky traps to stink bombs to toxic aerosols, most police still preferred lead bullets. The youthful officer who pivoted first through the doorway was no exception. He was short, barely five-four, with pale skin, sleek black farsights, and a round Asian face. He had his gun out.

It didn't help him.

Panwar lashed out with his left foot, striking the officer's elbow. The kid screamed; his gun clattered to the floor. Panwar directed a second blow at his chest, sending him to the ground. Then he pounced on the gun, scooped it up and, still in a crouch, turned toward the hallway and fired. The shot resounded in an instantaneous echo. *Boom-boom*.

Panwar gasped, dropping to one knee as he scooped up the kid's farsights. Then he sprang forward, the gun at ready in front of him as he charged the hallway screaming, *"Don't touch it!"*

Virgil sprang after him, turning the corner in time to see Panwar dive for a second gun that lay in hard contrast against the beige carpet. He came down on top of a gray-haired officer who was scrambling after the weapon, crawling and sprawling like a paraplegic across the floor. Her thigh glistened with brilliant red blood. More blood stained the carpet in an ever-expanding crimson pool.

Panwar caught her hand just as she reached the weapon. He bent her wrist, forcing her to drop it again. Then he scooped it up and pitched it to the end of the hallway.

"I'm hit! I'm hit!" she screamed, as Panwar rolled off her. "Get in here now. We need help now. Yuen is down!"

Virgil could not believe this was real. *"Panwar whatthefuck are you doing?"*

"Shut up, Virgil, and help me!" He clambered to his feet, shoving the stolen farsights into Virgil's hands. "Pop the chip out of this."

"Panwar—"

"Pop the chip out! *Now*."

Virgil bent his head, examining the glossy black farsights, sleek new Heroes, probably private issue. He slid his trembling fingers along an earpiece, wondering why he was doing this. Then he found the tiny latch that held the main chip, and he popped it. The wafer fell to the floor. With his free hand, Panwar pulled a replacement chip from his shirt pocket. "Here's another. Swap them—"

"I don't—"

"Just do it! There's no choice. The colonies are lost. Extinguished. And we're next. You can't believe anything else. The IBC will come after our LOVs and—"

He brought the barrel of his gun level with the gray-haired cop's eyes. "Don't do it," he said softly.

Virgil popped the new chip in and then turned to see the cop's hand on her belt; a canister of some unknown noxious substance already halfway out of its holster.

"I'd rather not kill you," Panwar warned her, "but I have nothing to lose."

The cop's glare promised vengeance, but she moved her hand away from her belt. Panwar switched the gun to his left hand. Then he took the Heroes from Virgil, slipped them on, and started tapping frantically with his right hand.

Back in the conference room, the other officer groaned. The woman listened. Then her gaze returned to Panwar. "You see my farsights?" Her voice was a whisper, the words crisp and bitten, reflecting her fight against blood loss, and pain. "They're still linked. This scene is going straight to police headquarters. A thousand cops will be here in a minute." Her words were fierce, but she looked very pale. The pool of blood on the carpet had expanded all the way across the hall.

Panwar did not answer her. "Go for the door, Virg. Now."

Virgil felt trapped in some irresistible nightmare. This was not his life. It couldn't be. He edged past the wounded officer, careful to stay out of the line of fire from Panwar's gun. When he was clear, Panwar followed. "She's losing a lot of blood," Virgil whispered. There was more blood on Panwar's hands and on the hem of his black jacket. "Have you been hit?"

"It's her blood. Let's go."

"We can't leave her to bleed to death."

Panwar's eyes were invisible behind the black screen of the Heroes as he grabbed Virgil's arm and shoved him toward the door. "Did you hear what she said about a thousand cops? It's true! We go now or we don't go at all."

"Go where?" Virgil demanded as he stumbled past the suite's open door. Panwar turned to slam it shut behind them. "We live on an island! There's no way out of here, and you know it."

"You are so damn stupid!" Panwar said as he scrambled toward the elevator. "You never made any contingency plans when we brought the LOVs down, did you? You never bothered to think what would happen if we got caught."

"And you did?"

"Damn right."

Virgil jumped as the elevator doors opened onto an empty car. Had Panwar summoned it through his farsights?

"Get on," Panwar ordered. There was more blood on his hands now. It dripped off the barrel of the gun. "Get on the elevator!" He pushed Virgil to ensure that it was done. The doors closed behind them. "I've got us on a priority run to the subbasement. No stops."

The elevator dropped. Virgil hung on to the crash bar. Panwar leaned against the wall, his shoulders hunched, the fist that held the gun pressed against his stomach. Red blood glistened against black fabric.

"You are hurt," Virgil said.

"Not badly. It's her blood."

"You shot her!"

"I didn't kill her."

Virgil shook his head. "Why are we doing this? There's no way we can get out of this building. Security's going to be all over the lobby. They're going to lock up this elevator."

Panwar let the gun drop to the floor. "I'm linked, Virg. I've got control of the elevator. It's taking us to the subbasement. I've planned for this. On the day we decided to bring the LOVs down, I made plans to get out if things ever soured."

"You didn't try to go last night."

"Last night I still figured we had a chance in court."

The elevator stopped. The doors opened on the subbasement. Equipment hummed, but it was a solemn, lifeless sound. Panwar hustled him out. "Every door between us and the lobby is locked. The directory that held the building plans has been corrupted. If we go now, we can be far away before they have any idea how we got out."

"This is a subbasement," Virgil objected.

"With a utility tunnel that'll take us to the waterfront." Panwar ran for the west wall.

Virgil felt obliged to follow, though his pace slowed at the sight of Panwar's bloody footprints. "That cop is going to bleed to death."

"I didn't lock the upper floors. Security will be there in seconds. Now come on." He stood at a small metal door, set flush with the wall. He tapped his fingers, and the door unlocked. Virgil followed him inside.

Utility conduits were stacked floor to ceiling on both sides of a narrow tunnel. There were no lights. Panwar put his left hand against one of the insulated trunk lines and started to run. Virgil leaped after him. If Panwar could run, then he couldn't be too badly hurt. That cop, though, she must have lost a lot of blood; he hoped security was with her.

For the first few tens of meters faint light from the door showed the way, but that faded swiftly, until Virgil could see nothing but darkness. He ran blind, following Panwar, hoping that his farsights had a photomultiplier function and that he could see something. Their footfalls drummed, an echoing cacophony in the tunnel, but even over that reverberant beat Virgil could hear the sound of Panwar breathing; breathing hard. It didn't make sense. Panwar was in great shape. He ran three or four times a week. He used the corporate gym to practice his martial arts. "Panwar—?"

"I'm okay!" Panwar gasped from the darkness ahead. "But listen—" <gasp> "I've got a boat at the new marina." <gasp> "It's registered to an alias." <gasp> "No one knows I own it. I've sent your...profile...to the onboard ROSA...it knows...who you are."

"You want to try for South America?"

"No. I want to try for the LOVs." He stumbled forward a few more paces. Then he stopped, his desperate wheezing filling up the tunnel and echoing off the walls. Virgil barely avoided crashing into him in the dark. "Gotta...sit down a minute."

Virgil could smell blood. Lots of it. And now that Panwar was still he could see a faint blue-green radiance around him, just enough to give vague shape to his downturned face, and the black slash of the farsights that hid his eyes. Virgil reached for him, catching him by his shirt as he sagged to the floor. They went down together. The fabric of Panwar's shirt was warm and wet in his hands. "Are you crazy?" Virgil whispered. "What have you done to yourself?"

"Shut up," Panwar hissed between wheezing breaths. "Take the Heroes." He slipped the farsights off, but then his hand sagged. His head tipped back. The blue-green glow brightened as the LOVs across his forehead were exposed. In that eerie light his face looked horribly pale. "Listen to me, okay? I wouldn't have done this if it was only about you and me, but it's about the LOVs too—"

"They're *gone*," Virgil protested.

Panwar's hand closed clawlike on Virgil's shirt. "Listen to me! They could have survived the crash. There's a chance. That module was armored and insulated against collisions with orbital junk, the LOV lockdown was built like a bank vault, and it came down fast. If the interior didn't get too hot, there's a chance the LOVs survived. You have to find out. No one else is going to care."

"*I* don't care! Look what the LOVs have done. They killed Gabrielle. They're killing you. And that cop. And God knows how many people when the debris came down. We did this, Panwar!"

"It wasn't wrong!" Panwar's gaze shifted to Virgil's forehead, where his LOVs must be shedding their own eerie light. His chest labored as he breathed in short, panting gasps. "Change this profound . . . it never comes peacefully. It's never safe. Safety's a . . . dead end. Not many see that. All the great moments in history . . . made out of desperation."

"You're crazy," Virgil said again, his voice breaking. "Completely crazy."

Panwar's grip on his shirt relaxed; his hand fell away. But his wheezy voice carried on: "Listen. I've sent a data file to your ROSA. You've got access to my financial accounts. Take the Heroes. Cops can't . . . trace 'em now. Get to the boat and . . . you'll be okay."

"I have to get help for you."

Panwar chuckled weakly. "Knew you'd say that. We're . . . in a tunnel. No signal . . . here. Take the Heroes."

"But you were running! How could you be running when you were hurt this bad?"

"LOVs can . . . stimulate adrenaline flow too. Heard of it? Wounded soldiers fight on 'cause they don't know they're dead yet."

"You knew," Virgil accused.

Panwar closed his eyes; he didn't answer.

Virgil bent forward, listening for a wheezing breath; waiting for the warm fog of exhalation. Nothing. He felt for a heartbeat, but Panwar was still, not even the drip of seeping blood.

"Panwar, you knew!" His shout echoed up and down the tunnel, but it brought no response.

Virgil leaned back, feeling utterly lost. Panwar's LOVs still glistened . . . but was their light already fading? He looked back down the tunnel; he listened. There was no sound there yet. A voice whispered inside him, *go*. Truly, what else was there to do? What else was there to lose?

He looked at Panwar one more time. He cupped his face. He kissed his forehead. Then he took the Heroes from Panwar's slack hand and put them on.

The photomultiplier function was on, and Panwar was suddenly drenched in a sickly green tomb-light.

Virgil stood, his heart pumping faster, faster at every stroke, as if Panwar's escaping spirit had leaped inside him and now his body had to do the work of two wills. He took a moment to remember the direction they had come from. In the dark, monotonous passage it was so easy to be confused. Only the bloody footprints on the floor confirmed the right direction.

Virgil set off, counting the steps that carried him away from the life he used to know.

CHAPTER 10

Ela Suvanatat crouched in the prow of a fisherman's open boat, astounded to find herself in an argument with her job broker, Joanie Liu. "What do you mean you want me to reconsider?" she demanded, shouting to be heard over the roar of the boat's ancient diesel engine as it ran full speed toward the crash site. "Why should I 'reconsider' diving the site? I'm going to be first on the scene! Of course I'm going to do it. I'll never have an opportunity like this again."

Ela had promised the fisherman a bonus if he got her to the site ahead of everyone else. Every time the speeding boat hacked across the top of a swell, she found herself drenched in a fine spray of seawater—not that it mattered! Of the handful of boats that had put out from shore, none were closer to the impact site. She presumed there would be helicopters coming down from Saigon, but even they would not beat her to the prize. She was already wearing her wet-suit vest and her rebreather pack. Her goggle cups were ready to attach to her farsights. Her fins were in hand. She could be over the side in thirty seconds . . . so why was Joanie hesitating to broker a deal?

"You're not listening to me!" Joanie insisted as her image frowned from Ela's farsights. "I'm serious. This could be a dangerous situation—"

"Being poor is dangerous too! Are you angry because I tried to sell the crash vid without you?"

Joanie looked startled. "No, of course not. What else could you do on such short notice? By the way, it's a great file, better than anything the big agencies have put out."

Ela leaned forward. "So you'll be able to sell it?"

Joanie looked askance, the way she always did when she was about to deliver bad news. "You need to understand, the market is saturated with crash images right now. . . ."

"Shit," Ela whispered. This day had begun with so much

potential, but that was twice now she'd missed a fee by showing up late—and this time it was Joanie's fault. She'd taken half an hour to pick up Ela's emergency link—"other business" she had explained.

Ela was determined not to miss out again. With the crash of the EquaSys module, opportunity had fallen in her lap—but it was up to her to make it pay.

She had not waited for Joanie's permission to begin.

As soon as the water had receded she'd turned the lost baby over to a shell-shocked Phuong. Then she'd climbed the tilted ruins of the broken platform to see what could be salvaged from her equipment. Her backpack was gone, of course, but in a joyous discovery she found her diving gear wedged behind a plastic crate. The rebreather pack was covered with mud, but at least the wave had not taken it away.

She grabbed it and hopped off the platform, knowing her career would be made if she moved quickly, if she could get herself out to the crash site before anyone else and provide the first close-up images of the disaster. Which meant she needed to hire a boat right away.

She cast her gaze up and down the shoreline. There were hundreds of people all along the seaside margin of the village. They had come to poke at the debris, or study the broken pilings of the houses. Some just stared out to sea. Ela tried not to see the despair on their faces. This had been a squatters' village! Doomed from the start by its location on the edge of a rising sea, in the floodplain of a mighty river. No one could have expected the homes here to last more than a few months . . .

. . . but who could have guessed the end would come this soon?

Where would these people go? What would they do?

Watching them made Ela all too conscious of the delicate nature of her own position. If she slipped, if she failed to make the most of the opportunity she'd been given, she could wind up with nothing too.

How ironic that the disaster that had wrecked this village could still prove a blessing for her—if she could exploit it. One solid contract could bring in enough money to get her to Australia, and once there, she might find a real job . . . but first Joanie had to get her a deal.

"I don't understand what you're so worried about," Ela said.

Joanie raised her hands in a pleading gesture. "Can't you see this is an international incident? Powerful people will be fighting over the salvage—"

"All the more reason to exploit the opportunity," Ela insisted. "Think of the publicity! These American technocrats have killed people. They've endangered the whole world—"

"Ela, the site itself could be dangerous. There could be chemical spills, maybe even a radiation hazard."

Ela shook her head. There would be no radiation hazard. The news reports had assured the world of that.

There could be chemicals.

Ela glared at the silt-clouded water, remembering the stunned look on Phuong's face when she had realized she'd lost everything to the wave. Ela had glimpsed herself in Phuong's eyes. The two of them were so much alike. The only thing that separated them was luck.

Her angry gaze shifted back to Joanie. "If I get sick, you can sue EquaSys."

Joanie rolled her eyes. "After this, do you think they'll have anything left to pay?"

The elevator doors opened, and Summer Goforth looked out on a swirl of police, paramedics, and physicians crowding the close confines of the EquaSys building's subbasement. Her gaze fixed on the only still point in the kaleidoscope of activity: Daniel Simkin, director of the International Biotechnology Commission. He stood beside the elevator doors in whispered conference with an aide.

Daniel Simkin was not a big man, but there was a power in his compact build that Summer still found attractive. His face was fair; his eyebrows even more so, almost disappearing against his skin. His blond hair was trimmed into a spare, compact helmet on his round head. He looked up as she stepped off the elevator car. He looked her over, his eyes hidden behind the blind silver sheen of opaqued farsights.

During Summer's visit to the LOV project suite, Daniel had been aboard a UAL flight out of Washington, D.C., but his attention had been with her. He had looked out through her farsights at Virgil Copeland and Randall Panwar, listening to every word of their conversation, studying every nuance of their facial expressions, and interjecting questions for Summer to ask and instructions for her to follow.

The link to Epsilon-3 had been left open at his request. He had wanted to see what Copeland would do, what he might reveal. And thank God Summer's objections had gone on the record. Given the fallout, it was easy to imagine Simkin trying to put the blame for that decision on her.

"We were lucky," he said, before she could speak. "If Copeland hadn't brought the module down, it might have been months before we discovered the escaped LOVs on the *Hammer*."

So that was how he would play it.

She crossed her arms over her chest. "You were lucky no one was killed."

It had been a stupid chance to take, but Daniel would make it look right. He always did. He was a survivor: a Ph.D. biochemist with the wiliness of a politician and the ruthlessness of a third world dictator. Once upon a time Summer had found that combination of traits perversely attractive. Judging by his career, she was not the only one who had ever felt that way.

"You're right, of course," Simkin said. "If we hadn't gotten warning bulletins out immediately, untold thousands would have been at risk on the ground."

"Are we on the record?" she asked.

"From now on, you should assume that."

After being up all night with Copeland and Panwar, Summer had been glad to get home. But she'd hardly closed her eyes when her ROSA woke her with a terse note from Simkin, summoning her back to the EquaSys building: *There's been an escape attempt. Consider yourself hired on as a consultant. We need your expertise.*

Returning downtown had proved an unexpected challenge. A predicted rainstorm had finally arrived from the south, driven by gale winds. The deluge flooded the streets, tying traffic in knots, and a drive that should have taken half an hour consumed nearly ninety minutes instead. Perhaps she had arrived too late to be of any help? Amid the flurry of personnel, she saw no sign of either Copeland or Panwar. "Where are they?" she asked.

Simkin nodded at a steel door set in the subbasement wall. "The paramedics are bringing Randall Panwar out now."

Summer stepped back a pace as rescue personnel emerged bearing a white-wrapped body strapped to a wire gurney. "My God," she whispered. "What did you do to him?"

"Shot while attempting to escape," Simkin said as the gurney's wheels were unfolded. "He barricaded himself in the tunnel and bled to death. There was nothing we could do." At Simkin's direction, the white sheet was pulled back to reveal Panwar's face, peaceful in death, the eyes closed. "Summer, I want you to remove his LOVs before they die with him."

"They're still alive?" Suppressing her revulsion, she leaned over the body to peer at the tiny flecks of glitter on Panwar's gray brow. One of them flickered faint blue-green. *"My God,"* she whispered again. How was it possible for his LOVs to be alive? Without Panwar's blood and body to nurture them, they should have died within a minute, two at most.

Simkin said, "The Villanti girl's LOVs survived over four hours after her death."

How could that be? Were they adjusting their metabolism? Slowing down when resources grew scarce? She frowned, thinking hard. She had designed the original LOVs to be fragile, like some pampered strain of lab rat that wouldn't last a minute in the wild. But Virgil Copeland had described those original LOVs as "museum pieces." Modern LOVs were different, not even compatible with the antique forms. Copeland had been aware of that, but even he had not understood how much the LOVs had changed.

On her slow drive back to the EquaSys building, Summer had skimmed a first-pass report compiled from what little was known about the mutated LOVs infesting the *Hammer*'s fiber-optic cables. No LOV should have been able to survive that dry environment. Where had they gotten their nutrients? It seemed impossible, and yet it had happened . . . leading to the ominous conclusion that LOVs were far more adaptable than anyone had guessed.

She straightened, turning to Simkin with a frown. "Do you really want these LOVs to stay alive?"

He crossed his arms over his chest and spoke in a neutral voice. "Well, of course, Summer. That's why I brought you here. Any thug could pull the LOVs out and drop them in a vial of acid. But the main colony is extinct while the feral LOVs left behind aboard the *Hammer* have been exterminated. These LOVs are the last, so until their status is legally determined . . ."

Oh. Simkin was covering his ass. Now that Panwar and Copeland represented the last of the LOVs, any court could declare their population an endangered species.

She stepped away from the body. "Even if I knew how to remove the LOVs without killing them—and I don't—it's illegal to cultivate them here on Earth. I won't be a party to it."

He cocked his head. "You're refusing to try?"

She glanced again at the body. No one could say anymore what the LOVs were capable of. They were an artificial life-form that had already escaped once from a lockdown facility. Who could guarantee they would not escape again? Only this morning she had worried over the potential of the LOVs to develop into an intellect capable of competing with a human mind . . . but combine that intellectual potential with a talent for *physical* adaptation, and the result was a recipe for disaster. She could no longer doubt that the LOVs were a mistake, a threat best disposed of as quickly as possible. "Yes," she said. "I am refusing. It's too dangerous to keep them alive."

Simkin smiled, looking satisfied with this exchange. "Then we'll have to find someone else with the expertise to remove them."

Summer knew she had responded as he'd hoped. By the time he found someone else "qualified" to remove the LOVs, it would be too late—while the responsibility had been neatly transferred to her.

So be it, then. She had brought them into this world; it was only right she take them out. It was the right thing to do.

She watched the gurney being rolled onto the elevator. Then she turned to Simkin. His right hand was tapping as he talked to someone she could not see. It would have been polite to wait, but she didn't feel polite. "So where is Copeland?"

Simkin cast her an irritated glance. "That is the question of the hour."

He went back to his conversation, but Summer circled around him. "Wait a minute, Daniel. What are you telling me? You don't know where he is?"

Simkin scowled, muttering *"Hold on,"* to whoever he was talking to. "He fled down the utility tunnel, with a twenty-minute head start and a choice of some forty possible exits."

"So? Traffic cams should have picked him up once he hit the streets. You know it's pouring rain out there. There can't be that many pedestrians."

"We've put a ROSA on it. We're doing everything we can, Summer."

But did he understand the urgency? "Daniel, he's supporting a viable population of LOVs. You can't let him escape."

"We'll find him. It's only a matter of time."

She took his arm. She pulled him away from an aide who had stopped to ask a question. "Listen to me," she whispered, "because I am truly scared. Right now Virgil Copeland has the only viable reservoir of LOVs in the world. What if he decides to change that? What if he decides to let them reproduce? If you give him time to spread them around, you might never know for sure if they've truly been exterminated. We could be fighting this problem for years to come."

"Spread them around? How could he do that? If *you* can't remove them without damage—"

"You don't have to remove them to let them reproduce."

He frowned. "Don't they require very specific conditions? . . ."

"I used to think so."

"Summer—"

"Daniel, think about it! The best way to grow LOVs is in a tank, but that's not the only way. What if Copeland could induce his LOVs to reproduce in vivo, in the flesh. It shouldn't be hard. Then he could harvest the progeny and give them away."

"Who would—?"

"A lot of people would. The LOVs can make you smarter, Daniel. They can make your moods more powerful, and more effective. I know quite a few people who would have a hard time saying no to that. If even one escapes, we could be looking at a LOV plague."

"We're doing everything we can."

"I hope so. I hope it's enough."

The impact had stirred up silt from the seafloor, turning the water a dirty brown. Ela peered over the side of the boat, trying to see to the bottom, to catch a glimpse of the debris, but it was impossible. She looked back at the shore, squinting at landmarks to gauge her position. Was this really where one of the fragments had fallen? She threw a questioning look at the fisherman. He only shrugged.

Ela bit her lip, thinking hard. This might be the site. Or it might not. There was no way for her to tell except by going in. And if she guessed wrong, she wouldn't get a second chance. The helicopters from Saigon would arrive in minutes.

Joanie's image appeared again in her farsights. "Okay, Ela. I've got a working contract. If you can get pictures uploaded at least two minutes before anyone else, you'll make twenty thousand. If it's less than two minutes, you'll earn five. If you're behind the competition, you get nothing."

Ela nodded grimly. Twenty thousand would save her ass. Twenty thousand would get her to Australia with spending money.

"Go down fast," Joanie advised. "Get the image, and surface. I'll be waiting."

Ela looked again at the fisherman. "Wait here," she said. He nodded. She repeated it anyway, twice in English, twice in Vietnamese. The fisherman grinned.

Ela smiled back. Then she slipped the goggle cups onto her farsights and tumbled over the side.

Visibility was bad. Even at the surface, she could barely see past the fingertips of her extended arm. As she descended, swirling clouds of silt sucked away the light. She found the bottom fifteen feet below. It was a twilight world, where the dark shapes of broken bottles, rusted shell casings, bicycle tires, and twisted mangrove roots gave texture to the omnipresent mud.

She did not see anything that looked as if it had recently been part of an orbiting space station. So she began casting about, searching for some sign that this was the right area. She kicked hard, moved quickly. Still she could not outrun a growing fear that she would find nothing at all.

Time flowed past. Five minutes. Then ten. Then fifteen. She heard a brief flurry of boat traffic, and knew the twenty thousand must surely be slipping away. Tears of frustration started in her eyes. She swam faster, moving in wider swaths to cover more of the seafloor.

After another five minutes she found a broad, shallow gouge in the ocean bottom. It was several feet across, but only six or eight inches deep at the center, its shape already camouflaged by a veneer of freshly settled silt. She might have missed it if she hadn't been so desperate to find *something*. She squeezed her eyes shut, taking a moment to calm her pounding heart. Then she touched her farsights.

This far underwater she had no direct connection with Kathang or the Australian server on which the AI program ran. The farsights were an interface, supporting only a fragment of the ROSA's personality—just enough to execute simple commands. Her finger-tap signal was detected; the farsights began to record.

Ela peered ahead into the murk, anxiously wondering what she would find. There had been LOVs aboard the module. She thought about this as she used swift, determined kicks to follow the gouge. She had only a shallow understanding of what had brought the module down. There hadn't been time to parse the details, but the headlines had been enough to assure her this story would be big:

*HAMMER SABOTAGED BY ARTIFICIAL LIFE-FORM
FIERY REENTRY DESTROYS EQUASYS MODULE*

Lovs SMUGGLED TO EARTH—
PRIMARY COLONY COMMITS SUICIDE

Surely only an intellect could commit suicide?

What did it mean?

The water grew colder and clearer as she followed the track down a steep slope into a channel where a strong current flowed out to sea. The floor of the channel was paved with a collection of relics: car hulks and chemical drums, engines, commercial washing machines, tires, and innumerable plastics. Silted over, they looked as if they were made of old, drowned wood.

In such a surreal landscape, Ela wondered if she could even recognize the debris from the space station.

Then she felt a whisper of warm water against her cheek. She turned into the current, following the trace. She had gone only a few meters when a blackened boulder loomed in the murky, twilight water, its upper half disappearing into the silt-laden current that flowed overhead. The water that slipped past the massive object was distinctly warm.

Fighting the current, Ela drew closer, scanning the find with her farsights. The object's surface was blackened and cracked. In the cracks she glimpsed a vague, blue-green glow. It was a teasing light, a faint will-o'-the-wisp, visible only from the corner of the eye.

Remembering Joanie's warning about toxic chemicals, Ela came close to panic. She wanted to bolt for the surface—but the tug of a half-remembered fact held her back. Weren't the Lovs supposed to have a blue-green glow?

Her eyes widened. Could the Lovs have survived?

Kicking hard to hold her position in the current, she brought her finger and thumb together against her farsights, tapping a quick code to summon the nightvision function. Abruptly, the cracks in the massive fragment were glowing bright green, while the upthrust mud at the base ignited in faint, tangled spider-webs of light.

Ela felt her mind recoil. An inner voice screamed at her to retreat, to surface immediately, to upload her vid and to collect what she could of her fee and get away . . . but there were many kinds of fear. Greater than her fear of contamination was her fear of poverty.

LOvs were an artificial life-form. The crash of the module should have meant their extinction, but if some had survived . . . surely there were people who would want to know that? People who might pay a lot of money to know?

If this light came from surviving LOvs.

Ela tapped her farsights again, bringing an end to the recording function. In that moment she felt as if her mind was composed of a committee, with every member but one blustering in doubt and fear. That one was a coolly determined, nonverbal entity. It took control. It vanquished her doubts.

Ela found herself dropping all the way to the bottom. She dug her fingers into the mud to hold her position, then she scraped up a bit of the glowing matter that webbed the mud. Peering at her wrinkled fingertips, she could just make out, at the limit of vision, tiny, gleaming disks, like flattened droplets of glass mixed in with even finer particles of silt. She watched them tremble in the current. Almost, it looked as if they were crawling over one another.

A little moan of fear escaped her throat. She yanked her hand back, shaking it frantically, sending the little glass disks off into the current. Then the nonverbal entity was in control again. It commanded her to breathe slowly, deeply, three times, while the bubbles of her exhalations rose like silver mushrooms toward the surface.

With trembling hands she slapped at the pockets of her vest, searching for something to hold the LOvs. In the smallest pocket she found a tiny sample bag of lychee candy. She unsealed it and shook out the last piece. Then once again she scraped up some of the glowing spiderweb, wiping the substance off inside the bag. A few more pinches and the bag was full. She sealed it; then she unzipped her wet suit. Shivering at the sudden touch of cold water, she slipped the packet in beneath the strap of her swimsuit and then zipped up again.

Now the panicked majority of her selves took over. She tipped her head back and kicked for the surface—*not too quickly!*—she could not risk a dive injury. On the way up she searched for a shadow that might be the boat's hull, but in the murky water it was impossible to see far.

The light brightened, and at last she broke the surface. Kathang sensed her presence; a link opened; the video image uploaded. Ela spit out the mouthpiece of her rebreather and whooped in triumph, kicking hard to lift herself several inches out of the water. She pirouetted, scanning the sea for the boat she had hired. She had expected to find a floating city of boats, but to her surprise, the surface of the ocean was empty. She turned again, searching. She waited for a wave and kicked hard, launching herself half a foot up to see . . .

Nothing. The fisherman who had promised to wait was gone. Everyone was gone.

She settled back into the water, listening to Kathang's sibilant voice whispering in her ear: *You must vacate this area immediately. The local government has claimed salvage rights and forbids trespassing on pain of death.*

So the boat owners had fled. And the engine noise she had heard underwater—it must have been an exodus, not the arrival of competition she had assumed. Her throat felt swollen with salt, or fear. The next engines she heard would belong to government forces come to secure the area.

She did not linger. She marked the direction of the shore— it looked impossibly far, a low, dirty line on her horizon—but her only chance of sanctuary was to get there before government boats could pick her up. She dropped below the surface and started swimming, hard.

Summer sat in her car, watching cross traffic creep across a flooded intersection while Virgil Copeland asked the question that explained so much:

"Is it helping? Or is this interchange just an addition?"

Randall Panwar answered, his breathless voice almost lost behind the distant drumming of rain upon the car's insulated roof:

"You love it, don't you? Me too. This is more real than anything I've ever known."

Summer had never meant for her work to move in this

direction. She had tried to stop it when she'd still been employed at EquaSys, and after.

Her gaze shifted briefly to the vid replaying in the lower field of her farsights; these were the last minutes preceding the rebellion of E-3.

"Is it only a drug, Panwar? Have we only found a new way to get high?"

"It's a drug. Straight-up. Everything that goes on in the brain has a chemical root. The question is, does it make us more alive?"

"God yes."

"Then how are we going to hold on to this?"

An addict would do anything to hold on; give up anything. Gabrielle Villanti was dead, and now Randall Panwar; and despite Daniel's assertion that no one on the ground had died, reports were beginning to surface that several fishermen had been drowned when the module came down (and the world had been oh-so-lucky that thousands more had not been killed). While Virgil Copeland was gone.

The light changed to green. Summer eased the car forward, waiting for the last of the cross traffic to clear before scooting through the intersection. Then she scanned her farsights once again, willing Daniel Simkin's icon to appear. Why didn't he call? She longed to hear that Copeland had been found. It made her sick to think he might have gotten away.

He might have though.

He might have planned his escape even before the LOVs were smuggled.

He might have planned this whole disaster. An addict would do anything, after all.

"Bring all the LOVs down." Copeland growled. *"Free them."*

How had the LOVs escaped their tank? How had they come to change their structure so they could survive in the open air? Had Virgil Copeland planned that too? Summer wanted to believe it—his own words seemed to damn him—but Copeland himself would not let her.

She slipped past the next light before traffic forced her to stop again. A heavy rain, and the city snarled. Would she ever get home? It was stop and go all the way to the freeway. As she waited out red lights, she watched the bloom of shock on Copeland's face as he learned about the feral LOVs. She watched his horror as the *Hammer* tore apart. She watched until she could no longer deny that the most likely designer of the new LOVs was E-3 itself. E-3 had sent the EquaSys module down. At first glance it appeared to be a stupid decision, suicidal. . . .

But the LOVs had proved themselves capable of survival in strikingly different habitats. Was it possible they could survive reentry too?

She spoke to her ROSA. She sent it out seeking news of the crash site. A report popped back almost immediately: Local authorities had ordered the area cleared; troops were arriving on the scene to secure the site for the IBC. . . .

Summer breathed a sigh of relief. Even if there *were* LOVs in the water, they could be contained. Simkin would see to it; he would be good at things like that.

At last she was able to ease the car onto the freeway, though her Makakilo home was still miles away. She promised herself she would not go out again today, whether Simkin called or not.

Then her ROSA buzzed. It had the shape of a dragonfly, and it rattled its wings to draw her attention. *Archived reference found . . . display?*

She frowned. She was driving too fast now to take her eyes off the traffic for long . . . but curiosity got the better of caution. "Display. Lower field."

A new window opened at the base of her screen.

The ROSA had found an advertisement, withdrawn only a few minutes after its original posting, but it had been up long enough to be archived by a twenty-four-hour service. Summer scanned the header while a voice-over read the words aloud: *LOV Crash Alert—Reporter On-Site: See the First Underwater Images on SEA-AN.* The ad was embedded in a video glimpse of a shoreline made familiar by the endless pictures of the impact . . . only this video was taken from at least half a mile offshore.

So someone *had* reached the crash site.

Summer's heart raced as she whispered to the ROSA to open a link to Simkin. When he did not pick up, she prepped a terse text message instead:

→ Found evidence for a diver at the crash site. Must intercept! Not sure anymore that all Lovs were destroyed.

She appended the archived ad and sent it.

Simkin surprised her with a reply as she maneuvered through traffic on the rain-drenched freeway.

→ Grim findings, sister. Lovs confirmed on-site. Diver too. Tracking now. I owe you.

CHAPTER 11

Ela kicked hard for shore, though she hardly cared anymore about her destination. All she could think of was air. The rebreather was not giving her enough air. Not nearly enough. Her chest ached with the effort of sucking against the resistance of the respirator, fighting to force more oxygen from the unit than it was designed to produce. Her lungs burned. She wanted the surface so badly, but she forced herself to stay down. Only the silt, the turbid water, could hide her from the spying eyes of government authority. *But it hurt!*

It came as a bitter relief when she finally found the edge of the ocean. She felt the gentle push of a swell lift her from the bottom. When it set her down again the water drained away from her face. She found herself lying in the shallows, on the margin of the mudflat. The shore was deserted: no fisherfolk, no children, no dogs.

No patrolling soldiers.

Ela spit out the respirator and drew in a sweet lungful of real, unlimited air. Behind her she could hear the growl of helicopters over the water, but she did not waste time looking around. She peeled off her fins, and staggered to her feet. Her legs felt wobbly and weak as she set off at a gallop through the shallows, the rebreather pack banging against the small of her back.

A stand of brush had grown up beyond the mudflat. She raced

for it, slipping in the steaming mud, going down once, while clouds of tiny flies pinged against her arms, her face. From somewhere up the beach a dog barked. She did not look around. The brush was only five meters away. Then two. Then one.

She ducked under its shelter, scrambling past the slap and jab of unfriendly branches until she reached the dense center of the stand. Then, with a tiny cry, she peeled off the rebreather pack and collapsed on her back, her chest heaving, burning, her heart beating so hard it must surely implode, collapsing into a tiny spot of infinite pain.

She stared wide-eyed at the sky, waiting to die. Amorphous gray spots swam across that blue vault. Sunlight refracted between fanning twigs. A rumble in her ears became the engine noise of a helicopter drawing swiftly nearer. What device did they have to see her through the brush? She couldn't think. Did infrared work in the heat of the day? She curled up, to make her profile smaller.

Something warm and wet touched her bare foot. She jumped, scrambling back as far as she could before the branches stopped her. A large dog sat where her foot had been. It was leashed, with the leash held by a brawny teenage boy who crouched under the foliage, studying her with a puzzled expression. He wore a faded T-shirt and ragged shorts, with a frayed pack strapped around his waist, but he also had the shiny new farsights and confident demeanor of the *Roi Nuoc*.

Ela did not take her eyes off him as she groped for a rock, a stick. Anything. Her fingers touched a human hand. She gasped, flinching back against the tangled branches. Another farsighted boy crouched beside her. She glanced around, spotting two more farther back in the brush. They all looked to be around sixteen or seventeen years old, well fed and muscular . . . significantly stronger than she.

Ela stifled a little scream. Pulling her bare knees up against her chest, she hugged herself, horribly conscious of her own exposure. She wore only a wet-suit vest and quick-dry running shorts over a swimsuit—which left her legs and arms bare. But shame quickly followed her first rush of panic as the boys made no move against her. Instead they turned their attention toward the ocean, and the black bee-shape of a helicopter cruising toward them.

What are they doing here?

Had they been waiting for something? Watching the activity at sea? Had she given their position away with her sudden, panicked flight from the water?

The helicopter did not waver in its course. Ela crouched, ready to flee on all fours if she had to. It was impossible to actually stand under the jabbing twigs.

The boy beside her touched her shoulder. She jumped, twisting around to face him. He was the largest of them all, with an attractive rounded face and long black hair tied in a ponytail behind his neck. With dismay Ela noted that he outweighed her by at least fifty pounds. He withdrew his hand, saying something in a gentle voice that Kathang translated as, *You must wait, please. Don't move yet.*

She nodded, settling back against the ground.

The boy with the dog whispered to the animal; sharp, exciting commands that caused it to raise its ears. Its tail wagged, stirring dead leaves.

Ela stole the moment to slip off her farsights. She popped off the eye cups—a move that drew a surprised murmur from the boy at her side. Throwing him a wary glance, she stuffed the pliant cups into the pocket of her shorts. Then she frowned down at her farsights. She had no way to clean the lens.

The boy lifted them from her hand, murmuring something she could not understand without Kathang to translate; but his meaning became clear when he pulled a soft cloth from his waist pack and began to clean them.

The helicopter was almost onshore. The boy with the dog slipped its leash off. Then, with his hand on the animal's neck, he commanded, *Di! Di!* The dog took off, running toward the helicopter and barking wildly. Another dog raced down the beach to join it. The helicopter turned in a wide circle over the two cavorting animals, but it was not distracted for long. It swept back toward the brush.

One of the boys behind Ela hissed. The one beside her dropped her farsights and grabbed her instead, his heavy arms locking her against his chest. She fought him for a second. A small cry escaped her throat. But it was a battle with herself as much as with him. Even as panic made her resist, she understood what he was doing. After a second she did what she could to help him, pulling her long legs against her body to make herself as small as possible while he hunched over her, shading her from the sight and sensors of the helicopter crew. Still, she could not stop herself from trembling. She never let herself get this close to any man. It wasn't worth it. It was a trap.

There was no choice.

The boys did not try to hide themselves. They could not. The helicopter descended over them. They watched it resentfully, shading their eyes against the dust and flying leaves that swirled within the miniature hurricane of its prop wash. A booming voice fell out of its loudspeaker, speaking in Vietnamese so that Ela had no idea what it said.

The boy with the leash looked annoyed. He whistled to the dogs, then turned and picked up her rebreather. The helicopter still hovered directly overhead.

Ela remained huddled in the shadow of the boy with the muscular arms. He picked up her farsights and passed them to her. She slipped them on, careful not to let her elbows show. He murmured instructions, which Kathang translated: *They will go away when we go away, okay? You must stay close to me until then.*

The dogs went past, following their handler inland.

"How?" Ela whispered. She was a tall, ungainly foreigner, but he was strong. He held her against his chest as he turned, and began to crawl after his companions. She did her best to melt against him, moving her legs as he moved his, but it was a position too close to sex, and it shamed her.

There were many kinds of fear.

After they had gone a few meters, the helicopter peeled away, heading up the beach. The boy half stood. He still held her close to his side, but they were able to run together down a narrow trail between head-high foliage, then along the foot of a dike and into a tangled stand of mangrove. When the canopy of leaves grew so thick that only sparks of sunlight made it through, he let her go.

She scrambled away. She couldn't help it. Her face felt hot; her body so dirty. Silt like fine sandpaper rolled in a layer of sweat beneath her wet suit. For several seconds she fought hard not to cry. Then they were moving again, heading inland as fast as Ela could clamber through a vague path that twisted up and down among the tangled mangrove roots.

The struggle to keep up with the boys left her with no curiosity, and no breath for questions anyway. She did not know why they protected her, and she was too tired to care.

After twenty minutes they headed uphill, emerging into the open on the back of a levee. Ela stumbled to a halt, gasping, her hands on her knees as she struggled to catch her breath. Black shadows crowded the corners of her vision. She had not eaten since last night, or had anything to drink.

The one who had touched her—that one—he spoke to her in English. He did not look at her, frowning instead at his farsights, pronouncing each word individually and awkwardly as if echoing words he did not understand: "They-know-your-face-they-know-you-were-diving-the-closed-site—"

"Who knows?"

"They-are-looking-for-you-we-must-go."

"Go where?"

He frowned harder. Then he nodded. "The I-B-C," he said, pronouncing carefully each syllable. Then he added, "Inland."

The IBC? She sent Kathang off to uncover what the IBC might be. Then she forced herself to straighten. "Who are you talking to?"

Kathang translated his reply as *Mother Tiger*.

It meant nothing to her. Nothing at all. She stared off into the distance, across a landscape checkered with fishponds and rice fields and farmers' houses. It all looked very normal, but she did not feel normal. She was breathing too fast, wasn't she? And the sun stood too high and too hot, as oblivious and enthusiastic as a lone drunk at a funeral.

"Joanie didn't call me," she whispered. It hurt to realize it. "She didn't even send a message." Her balance slipped. She staggered in the dust on the back of the levee. The ground here was very dry, except where blood from cuts in her feet had formed dark streaks of mud. "I've lost it all, haven't I? Everything."

Everything but her farsights, her wet suit, and Kathang's paid-up account.

She laughed softly. There wasn't even anything left to sell.

Talk about bad luck. *Seriously* bad. What fortune-teller could have warned her?

Kathang whispered in her ears, *Drink some water*. A plastic bottle had appeared in her hand. So Ela drank, until the boy—that one—took the bottle from her lips. He spoke and Kathang translated. *We need to go.*

"Where?" she demanded. "Why are you here?"

He shrugged. Kathang took his words and changed them. *I don't know.*

Ela considered that. Then she shrugged too, and followed him down the other side of the levee.

The overflights started shortly after that. Before the first one, they had a minute's warning—time enough to hide in a stand of dense grass. Ela peered between the stalks as a patch of blue sky slipped loose to glide low over the dirt road they had just been walking. The blue disk moved in perfect silence: a drone aerostat, its button cameras glinting in the sunlight. Ela watched it while ants crawled over her ankles; it made her wonder how bad arrest could be. So she took a few minutes to peruse Kathang's report on the IBC. After that, she decided ant bites probably were the best alternative.

The next warning came only ten minutes after they started walking again. This time two drones passed before the *Roi Nuoc* let her stir. At the third warning, Ela gave up. "No more!" she snapped at the boy—that one who had touched her. He was getting too used to touching her. She pushed his protective hands away.

Grabbing her rebreather from the dog boy, she stomped toward the nearest shrimp pond. The *Roi Nuoc* looked mystified as they watched her go, but uncertainty turned to panic when she waded into the water. That one who had touched her, he started after.

"Stay back!" she shouted, pointing at him with a warning finger. "Stay away. I know a better way to hide." She fished the eye cups out of her pocket and slipped them onto her farsights; she put the respirator in her mouth. Then she lowered herself into the dirty water. *That one*, he grinned as he watched her sink beneath the surface.

Water like tea eclipsed the sky, while shrimp bodies scattered beneath her. Daylight faded to the color of heavy smoke as she settled against the bottom. The water was colder than she expected, but she forced herself to lie still, concentrating on her breathing. For a while the light grew brighter as the silt she had stirred settled back to the bottom. Then slowly, slowly, the sparse daylight that penetrated the muddy water began to fade. It felt like going blind. She could see only a brown haze, but she could see it less well all the time until there was only blackness.

Even then she waited until cold and hunger finally drove her to emerge, shivering and exhausted, to find the rusty colors of sunset still streaking the western sky.

The *Roi Nuoc* were gone. She searched the brush with nightvision, surprised to find herself alone. The rebreather was unbearably heavy, so she cached it in some bushes. Then, with wobbly steps, she climbed a small levee between the ponds.

A car waited on the dirt road that ran down the levee's back. The driver's door was open. A man sat there, watching her. In the luminous aura of nightvision she could see every detail of his face.

"*Ky Xuan Nguyen*," she whispered.

He smiled. "Ms. Suvanatat. Ela. You are an intrepid young woman."

"Why are you here?"

"Because you are here, of course. You found something very valuable at the crash site, didn't you, Ela? It's why the IBC pursues you so hard."

Her eyes widened. For the first time in hours she remembered the plastic packet she had tucked under the strap of her swimsuit.

"Are you hungry?" he asked. "Are you cold?"

She nodded, telling herself it was better to deal with Nguyen then with the hard-ass cops of the IBC.

He brought her a blanket, then sat her in the front passenger seat. "I'll take care of you now, Ela, all right?"

She nodded again, without meaning it. Australia seemed to be receding from her, retreating ever farther away.

CHAPTER 12

Ela felt she would never be warm again; the shower in the farmhouse to which Nguyen had brought her did nothing to change that perception. It was a thin stream of lukewarm water spilling without enthusiasm from a corroded pipe that lacked a showerhead. At least the water was clean, and the enamel walls of the stall a polished white.

To her consternation, there was no indoor toilet.

She peeled off her wet suit vest and dropped it on the floor beneath the flowing water. Her shorts and swimsuit followed. The shampoo smelled delicious, like chemical strawberries. She used it to scrub at the gritty mass of her hair, rinsing away a crop of chocolate brown suds. She was shampooing her hair a second time when her probing fingers found a scab on her right temple. It was a hard, grainy, flat patch the diameter of an earring stud. She picked at it, wondering where it had come from. There were bruises on her legs too.

When she picked up her swimsuit to rinse it out, the packet of LOVs fell to the floor. Mud sloughed off the plastic, so she turned it over with her toes to let the other side rinse clean while she washed her wet suit, and then her farsights. A moth fluttered around the ceiling bulb as she dried herself and dressed in the clothes that had been left for her: a white long-sleeve T-shirt, almost new, and blue running shorts. She could hear Nguyen speaking to the housewife as she crouched to retrieve the LOV packet from the shower floor.

There was a thin film of mud inside the packet.

How had mud gotten inside?

She held it up to the light, her heart jumping as she squinted, checking for the LOvs.

The packet was flat, empty but for a little muddy water. She rubbed it between her thumb and forefinger to be sure. Tiny perforations riddled the plastic, and the LOvs were gone.

She found herself taking quick, shallow breaths. The LOvs must have been loose inside her wet suit. The thought brought on a shudder of revulsion. She scrunched her eyes shut to suppress a scream. Maybe she had washed them down the drain?

But if so, then this whole, horrible day was for nothing. . . .

Her hand jumped, to touch the scab on her forehead. A terrible suspicion dawned as her finger slid over its hard, grainy surface. She didn't remember hitting her head, so where had the scab come from? Why wasn't it soggy after soaking so long?

There was a little mirror over the worn porcelain sink. She looked into it. The scab didn't look like a scab at all. It looked like a glossy spot of speckled, blue-green glass glued to her skin just above the fading red impression left by her goggle cups.

Without taking her eyes off the mirror, she groped for the light switch and toggled it off. In the darkness, the scab gleamed and flickered faint blue-green.

A sharp tap on the door made her jump. "Ela," Nguyen called. "Are you all right?"

She tried to slow the panicked pace of her breathing, telling herself things weren't so bad. Kathang had reported that LOvs could attach to living flesh. It had happened before. It had happened to other people . . . like those scientists in America. It wouldn't kill her. Not directly anyway.

"Ela?"

"Yes," she said. "I'm okay." But her voice sounded too airy, too high in pitch.

"Come have some food."

"I need to hang out my clothes."

"Mrs. Dao will take care of it. Come eat."

She wanted to run away. Instead, she made sure her hair fell over her temple. Then she opened the door.

Nguyen stood in the dim, steamy hallway, surrounded by the

smell of hot rice. Ela was so hungry he seemed to *be* that smell. She thought she might forever confuse him with that smell. Oh, why was her heart beating so hard? She took a step back into the lightless shower room. He stepped after her.

She didn't trust him. She didn't trust protective men. Their interest was always a trap. They would be kind until they took your freedom away with blackmail or babies or jealousy, and if you rejected their kindly advances, there was always rape.

She tried to slam the door. Nguyen caught it; he held it open. He was a silhouette, but Ela could feel his anger in the strength of his hold on the door. "Ela, are you so afraid of me?"

"No. I. . . . I don't know." She feared Nguyen. She feared the IBC. She feared the LOvs.

But she felt immersed in a terror independent of any of these. A sourceless terror that seemed almost to come from outside herself. "Shouldn't I fear you?"

"Perhaps."

She forced herself to breathe slowly, deeply.

". . . if you have lied to me?" Nguyen finished.

Well she had certainly lied. She had told him she'd brought nothing away from the crash site except her video. It was almost true.

She looked at her hands, commanding them to let go of the door. It would not be wise to encourage his anger. "May I eat now?" she asked softly, brushing the hair out of her face. Nguyen's sharp intake of breath exposed her blunder. In the lightless shower room, the glowing scab of LOvs was easy to see.

She stiffened as his hesitant fingers reached toward her temple . . . but he drew his hand back again before he touched her. "So. You did bring something from the crash site."

She didn't trust herself to speak. She had told him about finding the broken fragment of the EquaSys module, but she had not mentioned the LOvs.

"Is this what the IBC is seeking? This is the thing in the news?"

"I only took a little! I left most of it there."

He reached for her temple again. She forced herself not to

flinch as he ran a finger across the gleaming, glassy scab. "These are LOVs?"

She nodded. The news descriptions left little doubt of that. "They are supposed to make people smarter."

He chuckled. "I think you are very brave, Ela. Or very desperate."

Tentatively, she touched the scab. "I didn't mean for this to happen."

He nodded, looking thoughtful. "You don't have any more?"

"No. This is all." Silently she added, *All that's left.*

"Well then, I'll have to take very good care of you."

That was the promise he made. But the next morning when she awoke to the crowing of an army of cocks and looked out the window of the neat farmhouse, his car was gone. She let the brittle lace curtain fall back across the screen. Black-and-white portraits of smiling children looked at her from the walls of her little room; the air bore the musty smell of old possessions. She pushed aside a red coverlet and stood up from the low bed where she had slept. The wooden floor creaked beneath her feet as she stepped barefoot to the door.

It felt flimsy as she opened it, the knob smooth and loose with age. She peered into the dim hallway. She could see no one about, but the rhythmic beat of a metal spoon against a metal bowl told her old Mrs. Dao was at work in the kitchen. Ela ran her fingers through her hair, knowing she must look a sight: a gangly, wild-haired, red-eyed foreigner. Mrs. Dao, though, had not seemed to notice. Last night she had tut-tutted over Ela, spoiling her with smiles as if she were a favorite granddaughter.

Drawing a breath of courage, Ela crept down the hall. She managed to surprise a little boy in the cluttered living room. He yelped and darted into the kitchen. Mrs. Dao emerged a moment later, smiling and nodding a greeting, her white hair gleaming in the dusty light that spilled in through a screen door. Ela tried her sparse Vietnamese, asking *"Where is Mr. Nguyen?"*

With Kathang translating, Mrs. Dao explained that he had left the night before, shortly after she'd gone to bed. She was careful to relay Nguyen's instructions: Ela was to stay in the house, and away from the windows, as much as possible. When she must go outside to use the outhouse, she was to wait for clearance from the *Roi Nuoc*. Mrs. Dao took Ela by the hand and led her to the screen door, nodding at two farsighted youths lounging on the covered porch. Ela wondered if they were Nguyen's private soldiers.

After obtaining permission, she made a quick trip out the back door, returning to find a breakfast of eggs and noodles and thick, sweet, gooey coffee laid out on the table. While she ate, she checked her brief queue of messages. There were three, where usually she had none. The first was from the national police:

Ms. Ela Suvanatat, your identity and activities are known. You have been charged with an act of trespass on a prohibited site. In addition, you are wanted for questioning by the International Biotechnology Commission. Only by surrendering yourself immediately will you gain the mercy of the court.

Perhaps she would receive the same mercy the Honolulu police had shown to that EquaSys researcher? The news links had drooled with violent reenactments of the shooting, and his subsequent, terrible death in the dark. Ela had higher hopes for herself.

From Joanie Liu there was this terse note:

Ela, I tried to keep you out of this mess. Now we're both in trouble. Give yourself up now, girl, if you ever want to see the light of day again.

Ela felt sure it was written with the approval of the national police. No doubt by this time the officer was Joanie's new boyfriend. She liked to work that way.

The IBC had tried a different tone:

Ms. Ela Suvanatat, our records show you were present at the impact site of the EquaSys module. It's known that certain contaminants were released into the water following this accident. There is a strong possibility that you have been affected by these contaminants. Your life could be in danger. Please report your whereabouts immediately, so that every necessary step may be taken to assure your continued health and well-being. . . .

Ela touched the glassy patch on her right temple. This missive might have persuaded her...except the LOVs were the only asset she had left. What good would it do her to be cleared and released by the IBC, only to starve to death, or find herself consigned to the sex trade? Better to be gunned down and die alone in a dark tunnel.

Better to deal with Ky Xuan Nguyen. He, at least, seemed to have no special love for tradition or the authority of the police.

She finished the last of the noodles and then lingered over the coffee. It seemed proper to be terrified at her situation, but somehow she wasn't. In truth she felt oddly calm and determined. With a swift tap of her fingers, she summoned Kathang's salamander icon. To deal successfully with Nguyen, she must first understand what she had gotten herself into—and that meant reviewing everything the ROSA had gathered on the fall of the module and the life cycle of LOVs.

Ela read the articles and listened to the newscasts—and it wasn't long before she learned a grim truth: Her LOVs had been made dependent on certain rare chemicals, special amino acids. Kathang explained that amino acids were the building blocks of proteins. There were many different kinds, but those needed by the LOVs were not commonly found in nature. Without an artificial source of these select *opines*, any escaped LOVs would surely die within a few days, at most.

Ela felt a flush that could not be explained away by the day's rising heat. Trembling, she hurried to the shower room to look in the little mirror. Any hint of luminescence from the LOVs was drowned out in the diffuse early sunshine pouring through a scarred plastic skylight. She could not tell if they were alive or dead, but when she scratched at the cluster's edge, a slim crust broke away. Her eyes widened as seven tiny, perfect spots of blood oozed into existence where the LOVs had been. She looked at her fingernail, and could just make out the glassy disks, trapped like dirt at the nail's end. "*Oh, no.*" Cupping her hand over her finger to block out the light, she examined the stray LOVs. No trace of a blue-green glow could be seen.

Had they died? Had all her LOVs died?

The mirror was hung on a hook, so she lifted it off and hurried with it into the relative darkness of the hallway, closing the shower-room door to block off the light. She held the mirror up to her temple. To her relief she could still make out a soft blue-green glow across most of the cluster.

But it was only a matter of time before these LOVs failed too. How long?

It might be hours. It might be minutes.

She returned the mirror to its proper place, thinking hard. She could hear Mrs. Dao outside, talking to the chickens. From somewhere nearby, there arose the squeals of children playing. Then Kathang whispered that another message had just arrived from the IBC.

Ela's gaze shifted to the little icon of wing-footed Mercury.

She stared at it, thinking of how the routing of messages was completely anonymous. An address gave no hint of its owner's location. That was why she had not shut down her mailer.

It occurred to her that Dr. Virgil Copeland would have had no reason to shut down his mailer either, not if he was still at large. He wanted to see the LOVs survive, didn't he? That's why he'd run away. If he was still free, she could write to him. She could send him a message requesting his advice. Yes. That was the thing to do, for who would know better how to keep her LOVs alive?

CHAPTER 13

Forty minutes after Panwar's death in the lightless utility tunnel, Virgil Copeland stood on a floating dock made of plastic lumber, feeling it bob and shiver beneath his feet. He had walked out of the tunnel into the gale winds and driving rain of a kona storm. In just a few seconds he'd been soaked to the skin, but at least the runoff had given him a chance to wash the blood from his hands and face. A forgotten cash card rediscovered in his pocket had gone to buy an anonymous rain slicker that let him slip past the traffic cams guarding the waterfront.

His ROSA had interfaced effortlessly with the stolen farsights. Virgil had not found the transition quite so easy. The Heroes were dark and heavy, and he could not help thinking of the two cops, and of Panwar, who had worn them last. But when Iris produced a map of the new marina, Virgil followed it dutifully through a maze of floating docks, to a boat slip far out in the harbor. Only now, as he saw what was tied up at the slip, did he wonder if the ROSA's link might be corrupted after all. Was it possible Iris had made a mistake?

He crouched on the dock, rain dripping off his hood as he stared at the little vessel. If it was a vessel. It did not look like any boat Virgil had ever seen. Its low, covered hull was gracefully contoured, tapering at both bow and stern, a mere fifteen feet long and delicately slender. There was no open deck, no elevated cabin. Its dorsal surface rose only a few inches above the waterline. Its color was dark, metallic blue.

Virgil decided it must be some kind of submersible. To Iris he whispered, "Identify?"

The ROSA responded in its soft female voice, "This is a racing-class submersible known as a marathon shell. It has a passenger capacity of one to two. More?"

A submersible. That explained its bizarre appearance, but not its size. It was so *small*. There was something surreal in its diminutive measures, as if the marathon had been made for a petite species from some other world. Now it was here: a jewel-like spaceship at rest upon the water.

He stood up, his raincoat snapping in the driving wind. *Do it*, he thought. *Get aboard*. There was nowhere else to go.

Halfway along the marathon's curved dorsal hull, a round hatch rose in a hydrodynamic mound three inches high. As Virgil stepped onto the sub's back, the hatch opened. He peered inside at a brightly lit interior so tiny there hardly seemed room to turn around. Claustrophobia stirred inside him, until he reminded himself that Panwar had chosen this vessel. Virgil resolved to trust that choice.

Pulling the rain slicker close around him, he dropped through the hatch, landing in a narrow oval of open floor. He had to crouch to keep from hitting his head against the ceiling. At that point the cabin's height was a mere four and a half feet—but the ceiling grew even lower as the cabin tapered toward the bow. A large armchair just fit between the rounded walls. It could be spun to face a bank of flowscreens on the bow console, or the two tiny doors that formed the cabin's aft wall. Virgil opened one of the doors to discover a toilet cubicle. The second concealed a crawl space packed with food and emergency equipment.

Overhead, the hatch snicked shut. Virgil stared at it, willing away a sense of entrapment. Then his gaze sought the tiny Greek goddess on his screen. "Iris? Have you interfaced with the resident ROSA?"

"Affirmed." Iris's voice issued now from the marathon's audio system. "This vessel is fully automated."

Virgil breathed a silent prayer of thanks to Panwar. Then he doffed the Heroes. "Let's go then."

"Destination?" Iris asked.

Panwar had already decided that. "Where the debris fell. The Mekong."

He pulled off the rain slicker and dropped it on the floor. Then he stripped off his wet shirt and rummaged in the closets until he found a blanket. He wrapped himself in it. "Iris, can you make it warmer in here?"

"Raising temperature to eighty degrees."

He curled up in the armchair while Iris activated the bow console's flowscreens.

The two central screens presented views outside the marathon, one above water, one below. A third screen detailed the vessel's position on a map of the harbor, while the last one displayed the ship's technical specs and present status. Virgil frowned over the specs. Apparently the marathon was propelled not by a screw, but by twin propulsion foils designed to work the water in a complex paddling motion adapted from the movement of a penguin's wings. Power came from a small bank of fuel cells, so engine noise was almost nil.

Motion drew his gaze to one of the central screens. He watched the mooring hooks uncouple and retract from the rain-drenched dock. Then he watched the dock slip away. He felt numb and cold and wildly grateful that for now at least everything depended on Iris's skill, and not at all on him.

The vessel remained on the surface as it glided away from the marina and into a chaos of windblown swells, two or three feet high at the harbor entrance. As soon as the last buoy was past, the silicon agent that piloted the marathon took the submersible under, extinguishing the view of the shore and the receding city—along with Virgil's link to Iris. He stared for a long time at the blank blue screens before he finally fell asleep.

He awoke at midnight to find the blue screens had gone black. His first thought was that he could not possibly be alone. The IBC must be near, in a boat or plane or another submersible, closing in on him. Panic bloomed in his mind, rising whole from some forgotten nightmare.

He grabbed the Heroes and slipped them on. "Iris! Where are we? What's happening out there?"

A ROSA answered, but it was not Iris. Not exactly. The rhythm of the voice was wrong, and the icon that represented it on his farsights was only a faded outline of the lovely Greek goddess usually resident there. "This is an Iris shell, interfaced with the resident ROSA."

Virgil nodded his understanding. Iris ran on a high-security server in Texas. Normally it communicated with his farsights through a pulsed link, but with the marathon submerged, it could not link at all, so it had left behind a shell—essentially a shallow mask of its personality that the marathon's onboard ROSA could wear to make him feel "comfortable" until he could again link with his own software.

The hybrid ROSA provided him a weather report, and an approximate position reading that meant nothing to him because he was not familiar with latitude-longitude measures. After some discussion, he understood the marathon had traversed several hundred miles as he slept.

"Have there been any communications?" he demanded. "Or any vessels in apparent pursuit?"

The ROSA denied it.

Had he eluded the IBC then? Had Panwar's plan truly worked?

Not for Panwar.

Dammit! Randall Panwar had let himself die. For the LOVs! For Virgil's LOVs. How goddamned stupid could a man be? If Virgil had only known how badly hurt Panwar had been, he would have never, never let him leave the LOV project suite. They would both be in prison now, but they would both be alive. Panwar had used the LOVs to mask his pain, to give him a chemical strength his body could not sustain. Momentum had carried him forward. Now he was dead. *They* were. Panwar and Gabrielle.

Virgil took a deep breath, striving to quell a rising panic. He willed himself to be calm . . . and calmness came, like a wave flowing over him, a gentle inundation.

He got up to use the toilet, to wash his face. He had to stoop to keep from knocking his head against the ceiling. In one of the cabinets he found a stack of neatly folded clothes. He pulled out a pair of white-cotton pants and a soft white sweater. They were sized for Panwar, so the arms and legs were too long by inches, but when he rolled them up, they were wearable. Next he used the steaming hot water from the bathroom tap to make a cup of instant coffee. Cup in hand, he sat down in the chair again, turning to face the flowscreens at the cabin's bow end.

Think.

Sure, but where to start?

Family, he supposed. If they were still talking to him.

With a tap of his fingers, he skimmed his queue of stored messages, glancing over the 213 missives Iris had judged worthy of his attention. At the top of the list were multiple notes from his parents. Even more sobering, there were notes from Panwar's parents too. Virgil could not bring himself to read any of them just yet. For his own parents he prepared a brief, typed message, explaining that he was unhurt and that he would contact them when he could. He marked a copy for his mother and one for his father. It would upload the next time the marathon had an active link. For Panwar's parents he started to write a description of their son's death; but then he decided against it. Anything he wrote could be used in court, and the law could be a twisted thing.

He supposed he should try to get a lawyer.

He entered that on a fresh list of things to do. Then he prepared an insipid note for Panwar's parents expressing his sorrow and condolences, though all the time he was thinking *Your son was so goddamned stupid he let himself die!*

After that there were notes from friends, notices from the IBC, threats from the Honolulu police, offers of counsel from EquaSys, financial proposals from news agencies, and a slew of personal communications from biotech professionals, most writing to condemn him, but a few offering covert aid.

Virgil looked them over, but he didn't respond to any of them. After an hour he cached the queue and sat back to think. E-3's sudden transformation haunted him. Its development had taken an exponential step forward during the hours before its fall . . . those hours following its long interaction with Gabrielle. In that time it had somehow gained an emotional awareness that allowed sentience to blossom across the links between its component LOVs.

But how to explain the presence of the mutated LOVs parasitizing the *Hammer*'s fiber-optic lines? Those LOVs must have developed over a period of months, long before E-3's "awakening." He had never suspected; he couldn't even guess how it might have happened.

He touched the glassy specks of the LOVs on his forehead. They were a remnant population, thirty-six individuals, while it had taken millions of LOVs to create Epsilon-3. And his LOVs were of a much earlier generation.

Nevertheless . . .

Might it be possible to re-create what had existed so briefly? To rebuild the LOV population until a new colony could be established? That's what Panwar and Gabrielle would have done, he had no doubt of it, if one of them were here in his place.

Virgil closed his eyes, feeling the sweet addiction of their shared curiosity. The LOVs had been a communal obsession, the faith that held the three of them together. He could still feel the weight of Panwar's hand, clawlike on his shirt; he could hear his fragile voice, imploring Virgil to go on: *No one else is going to care.*

Virgil bowed his head, knowing he did care, very deeply. The three of them had created something new to the world, a thinking being unprecedented in history, an intelligence that was not human. What could it have taught them about themselves?

He still wanted to know. Deeper though, in the dark terrain at the base of his mind, was a need to prove that Gabrielle's and Panwar's lives—and, perhaps, his own—had not been for nothing.

He raised his head, gazing again at the blank flowscreens. "What's our depth?"

The voice that was not quite Iris's answered: "Sixteen fathoms."

Virgil sighed over the meaningless nautical measure. "In feet? . . ."

"Approximately one hundred feet."

"Is it possible to get a working link without surfacing?"

To his surprise, the ROSA replied with a qualified yes. First the boat ascended to a running depth of sixteen feet below the surface. Then an antenna was released: a vacuum-filled metallic balloon on the end of a long, lightweight cable. The marathon slowed, leaving the balloon bobbing several feet above the swells.

Button cameras on the balloon gathered up shards of reflected moonlight. The boat's ROSA enhanced the dark image, unveiling a heavy sea torn with whitecaps, and a wind-driven roof of broken clouds. No other vessels were in sight.

On Virgil's farsights, Iris's faded icon blossomed with three-dimensional color as the ROSA renewed its link. The revitalized Greek goddess held a scroll in her hand. She made as if to hand it to him. *Four hundred twenty-nine messages*, Iris murmured. *Sixteen representative news clips.*

He watched the news first. As he did, he felt Panwar's ghost move inside him, a memory-complex possessing the persona of his friend. *"I told you so."*

Indeed. The breaking story of the hour proved the prescience of Panwar's gamble. The EquaSys LOVs had survived. Video was shown of fragmented and disintegrating LOV colonies cloistered within the ruined lockdown. Virgil watched in grim silence as divers destroyed them with chlorine. He saw it as nothing less than an act of genocide.

A press conference followed, featuring IBC chief Daniel Simkin, a colorless man with pale skin, pale hair, and icy eyes. He began by assuring the world that samples were being continuously drawn from across the crash site and tested for the presence of surviving LOVs. None had been found so far, but the area would continue to be monitored for six months.

Overkill, Virgil thought. The LOVs would die within days without nopaline supplements. Politically, though, a six-month vigil would play well.

Simkin finished his prepared remarks and started taking questions from reporters. The first wanted details on Virgil's whereabouts. "Dr. Virgil Copeland is the last remaining source of these LOVs. Do investigators believe him to still be within Honolulu? Or has the LOV contagion spread to other parts of the world?"

Simkin regarded the woman with a look of distaste. "We want to be very clear on this fact: The LOVs are not a contagious lifeform. They cannot be spread from one person to another except by willful intervention, and even then they will quickly die without a strict diet of nutritional supplements. As to Dr. Copeland's whereabouts, I'm not able to comment at this time."

The next two questions involved damage aboard the *Hammer* and reparations for the families of Vietnamese fishermen believed to have been killed in the impact.

"One more question," Simkin said, indicating a young man with a long ponytail of chestnut hair tied behind his neck, dressed in a collarless shirt and jacket dyed in natural colors.

The young reporter spoke in a confident voice, "Were you aware that a lawsuit has just been filed in federal court by a coalition of scientists, seeking to have any remaining LOVs declared an endangered species; and if so, what are your feelings on this?"

Virgil leaned forward, his heart pounding in unexpected hope. But Simkin's smile was slight, and condescending. "This is an inevitable development. Fringe groups will always rise to defend any cause, but in this case such a lawsuit is without merit, and I firmly believe the federal courts will quickly reach the same conclusion.

"The evidence is clear. LOVs were developed as a medical prosthetic, a biological tool. They were never intended for a colonial existence. They were never conceived as thinking machines. In fact, they are a tool that has been badly misused. A *dangerous* tool. Not a new life-form. They cannot sue for protection any more than a carcinogenic chemical can sue for protection.

"And clearly, the potential hazard posed by these LOVs is far worse than any case of cancer. There is nothing more dangerous to our own, human, existence than a thinking machine. The human mind is complex and inefficient, but it has remade this world. We would be foolish to knowingly foster another kind of mind in competition with us, fully capable of remaking this world again. Such an act must be insane."

"You don't know that," Virgil whispered. Oh sure, it could be true, this shared nightmare of the computer age. But it didn't have to be true. He touched the glassy bumps on his forehead. Intelligence was enhanced when it linked with other forms of intelligence. It *was* possible for different entities to live together.

He believed it was possible.

But the LOVs aboard the module were dead and gone. The thirty-six he carried were all that remained.

He listened for Panwar's ghost, but heard only the hum of the air-conditioning.

"Iris, close the news link. Bring in the antenna. Recover our cruising speed."

There was no point anymore in heading for the crash site. Virgil saw now that it had been a stupid hope all along; Panwar should have known the IBC would scour the wreckage clean.

Panwar had made some very stupid decisions.

He told Iris to change course. He would make for South America instead.

He closed his eyes, but he couldn't sleep, so he scrounged a bottle of sedatives from the medicine cabinet. He took one. He took another. He shook a third out onto his hand.

But after a few minutes reflection, he tipped it back into the bottle.

Enough stupid decisions had already been made.

He put the sedatives back in their place. Then he noticed a large bottle of amino acid supplements just behind. No-oct tablets—nopaline and octopine, the two rare nutrients required by the LOVs to survive and reproduce. He smiled. Trust Panwar to remember the details. He picked out a tablet, laid it on his tongue, then sat back in the chair, chewing slowly on the chalky pill as the sedative's relaxing spell crawled over him like a warm, confusing fog.

The next time Virgil awoke it was midmorning. He opened his eyes, feeling oddly refreshed and in a positive mood. Calm and hopeful, his depression all gone. His father remarked on it when Virgil finally linked. "You look good, son. You're not thinking of going into this fugitive business permanently . . . are you?" Jeff Copeland tried to make it sound like a joke, light-hearted patter to belie his haggard eyes, but the effect failed when his voice cracked, grief slipping through.

Virgil groped for an answer. "I should feel worse, I know. It's not that I don't care. . . ." But anguish and despair could serve no purpose now. Maybe the LOVs had calculated that fact and responded accordingly. Or maybe his own mind had run the equation.

Jeff Copeland did not ask where Virgil was; he did not advise him to turn himself in. Neither did the lawyer Copeland had hired. To Virgil, that was a more telling evaluation of his case than all the back-and-forth questions of an hour-long interview.

He spent much of the day plotting strategies to make himself disappear.

Late in the afternoon he raised the antenna again. Another flood of messages fell into the queue, having used offers of money, old acquaintance, or tantalizing subjects to get past Iris's filters. Virgil sighed, thinking he should tighten the parameters. Then again, he had plenty of time to read.

The initial deluge passed, but the flow never quite stopped. Words continued to drip into the queue like rain through a slowly leaking roof, a new message every twenty or thirty seconds. Virgil found himself captured by the hypnotic pace, tempted over and over again to wait for the next, and the next (just one more), scanning the sender and subject matter as they splashed past his awareness:

NetFlash News:	Ten Million $ First Interview
Josh Duchamp:	Much Admire your work
Pierie Ling:	A New Design for LOVs
Jeff Copeland:	Call your mother
Renatta X:	Evolution and the fate of the human race
Ela Suvanatat:	I have LOVs
Lope Ancog:	Your responsibility for disaster
James Santiago:	More questions from your lawyer

He blinked and sat up a little straighter, his gaze backtracking to the odd subject line:>*I have LOVs*<

Iris was supposed to filter the gutter notes, the hate mail, the religious come-ons, the sales and investment opportunities ... and the hoaxes.

>*I have LOVs*<

That was certainly a hoax. So why had it been passed?

"Iris? Display the Suvanatat message."

The file opened with a graphic that caused Virgil to catch his breath. It was an image of a blue-green patch of LOVs gleaming against cinnamon skin. He knew it was skin because he could see every pore, every slight, colorless hair. He knew the luminous patch was LOVs because he could see the outline of their diatom-like shells, each tiny disk speckled with dark pores and striated with the outlines of minute, interlocking limbs that held the shells tight against each other as if this attenuated sample (a hundred individuals? two hundred?) had instinctively re-formed into a colonial architecture, a seed crystal for a new Epsilon-3.

He told himself the image was faked.

Anything could be faked.

But surely a fake would imitate the arrangement of LOVs in the *Hammer*'s colonies, or the much-publicized scatter of glittering symbionts that Virgil, Panwar, and Gabrielle had all used? No one had ever—*Ever*—used LOVs as symbionts in a tightly packed, colonial patch. No one had ever implanted so many LOVs. Virgil had thirty-six. There were maybe 150 in this image.

His heart beat in slow, deep, deafening strokes. If this image was a hoax, then it was a most excellent one. A creative, clever, very thoughtful hoax.

He noticed something more: On the perimeter of the patch a few LOVs had lost their color. They had the empty, faded gray look of a tossed soda bottle scoured by wind and time. Virgil had seen such an effect once before, early in the LOV project, when the nutritional flow to a new tank had been too little to support the growing colony. Clearly, this patch of LOVs had begun to die.

CHAPTER 14

Kathang's orange-and-brown salamander icon stirred, stretching and twitching its tail to draw Ela's attention. *"Link request,"* the ROSA whispered, as a strange icon appeared beside it on the screen: a tiny woman in ancient dress, her dark hair touched with rainbow highlights. The new icon was accompanied by a note in white text:

→ Dr. Virgil Copeland, regarding your message >I have LOVs<

An answer! Ela could hardly believe it. And this was no simple message, either. It was a real-time link. "Kathang. Accept—

"No, wait."

Ela closed her eyes, thinking hard. She had to protect herself. She didn't know anything about Copeland, she didn't even know if he was still free. "Kathang, make this an anonymous link. Blur the background. Suppress all outside noises. Transmit no information on this environment. Only my active portrait."

The ROSA responded by posting a tiny image of Ela in the screen's lower corner, showing her head and shoulders against a blank beige field. "That's good," Ela said. Then she drew a deep breath, taking a moment to compose herself. "Okay. Accept the link."

The American researcher appeared before her in a head-and-shoulders portrait employing the same privacy screens Ela had used, except his background was gray. He was younger than she had expected, beardless and lightly tanned, his chin-length honey brown hair corded like a doll's. He leaned forward, wary amber eyes studying her from behind the faint white veil of his farsights. On his forehead, she could just make out the glitter of LOVs between his corded hair. "You are Ela Suvanatat?"

Ela nodded, listening to Kathang's whispered assessment, generated by the fortune-telling program: *This one does not wear a mask; he rides his emotions like well-trained horses, toward an unseen goal.* "You have not been arrested?" she asked him in a low voice, conscious of the two *Roi Nuoc* boys on the porch.

"No. This is not a hoax, is it?"

"No," Ela said softly. "It's real. I was on the coast when the module came down. I wanted to be the first to image the crash site, so I got out there fast. Too fast. I was underwater when it was made off-limits. I'll be arrested if they find me."

"Where are the LOVs?"

She tapped her temple. Then she shifted her farsights to the side to capture the image.

"They're dying," he said. "Do you see how the LOVs on the edge of the cluster are turning light gray? It's worse now than in the image you sent me."

"That's why I sent a message. I must know how to get

nopaline. That's what the LOVs need to survive. All the literature says so."

He hesitated. The wariness in his eyes deepened. She could guess his thoughts. "I told you already I'm a fugitive, Dr. Copeland. Like you. I'm not the bait in a trap to capture you. I'm not asking you to meet me. I'm not asking where you are. I just want to know how to keep the LOVs alive."

"Why?"

Ela looked away, feeling a rush of shame. But why should *she* be ashamed? She had lost everything but her farsights when this man's work came crashing into her life. "These LOVs are worth something," she said. "I have nothing else to sell."

"But LOVs can't be sold. They're an artificial life-form. They're not approved—"

"Approved? Are you serious?"

This time it was his turn to look away. A rosy flush touched his tan cheeks as he mumbled, *"Sorry."* In an absentminded gesture he touched his forehead, running his fingers over the half-hidden LOVs. "All right. Sell them. But sell them to me."

"Dr. Copeland, you don't understand. That's not why I contacted you—"

"I'll buy them," he insisted. "How much do you want?" His gaze darted to the side. The link's audio component cut out and his image blurred as he whispered to someone, or something off-screen. A companion? Or a ROSA?

When his portrait refocused, his gaze was firm. He looked quite confident of her cooperation. "I have command of several anonymous accounts. Let me know how much—"

"I can't." Ela glanced toward the screen door. The *Roi Nuoc* were outside, and Ky Xuan Nguyen could not be far away. She lowered her voice even further. "There is already a buyer, Dr. Copeland."

He looked stunned, almost . . . panicked, but the expression vanished as quickly as it had appeared. "I'll pay more."

"That is not the problem. He's here. You're not."

She watched him think about this. Then she said, "Do you want the LOVs to die?"

"No."

"Then tell me, where do I get nopaline? How do I provide it to my LOvs?"

"It comes from tablets." He chewed absently on a fingernail. "It's a special order product from a chemical company in California—"

"I am not in California."

"I know, but you could place an order—"

"That would take days, wouldn't it?"

"I guess it would, considering where you are. . . . You are still near the crash site? No. Never mind. Don't answer that." He sighed. "I have a supply of no-oct tablets—that's nopaline mixed with octopine, a combination that will allow the LOvs to live, and to reproduce. But it would take me days to get them to you, if you're still . . ."

His voice trailed off under the withering force of her glare.

"I'm trying to help, Ela."

"These LOvs are dying."

"I understand that. Let me think." He turned half-away, leaning his head back against nothing. Probably seated in a chair, she thought. So he was comfortable . . . wherever he was. He raised his hand, brushing his corded hair away from his forehead, clearly revealing his LOvs for the first time. They were scattered, she noticed, not clustered like hers.

After a moment, he nodded. "There is a natural source. Are you in a city, or a rural area?"

She hesitated, not wanting to give anything away.

He sighed. "All right. Don't tell me. I'll just hope you're in a rural area. No-oct is produced by a bacterium called *Agrobacterium tumefasciens*—" He hesitated, studying her uncertainly.

"I know what bacteria are, Dr. Copeland."

"Of course. Sorry. You'd be surprised how many people don't. *Agrobacterium* is a plant disease. It produces crown galls. Have you seen them? They're tumors, or swellings in plant tissue. *Agrobacterium* subverts these plant cells, forcing them to produce opines, which it metabolizes. If you can find unpigmented calluses, it should be possible to harvest opaline from the tissue. Green, photosynthetic shooty calluses will have nopaline."

Ela stared at him, wondering how often he talked to real

people. Maybe she should not have been quite so condescending about the bacteria? "I understand about half of that," she said.

"Oh. Well, it's simple really. If you can find crown galls growing naturally on diseased plants, they should have at least a small quantity of nopaline or octopine in them. Either one will keep your LOVs alive until you can get an order of supplements." His gaze cut to the right. He nodded. Again Ela wondered if he was with someone. "There," he said. "I've made an order of no-oct for you, and I've attached the funds. I'm transferring the form to you now. Fill in a name and address. I'll have no way to check where it's to be delivered."

The document arrived. Kathang tucked it away in a corner of the screen. Ela sensed the interview was about to end. "Wait," she said. "I'm not sure what I'm supposed to do. My ROSA can show me what crown galls are, but how do I use them? Do I *eat* these plant tumors, like I would eat a tablet?"

"I have no idea." His brow furrowed; his eyes took on a faraway look. Again his gaze cut to the side. Again, he nodded. Definitely a ROSA, Ela decided.

He said: "The tablets are highly concentrated, of course. I don't think ingestion would be efficient at natural concentrations, and you wouldn't want to eat plant galls anyway. But all LOVs have membranous pores. Look for the dark spots in the image you sent me. In a fluid environment, LOVs will absorb nutrients across those membranes." He hesitated. "Try liquefying the galls, then dripping the brew directly onto the LOVs. It might work." He did not look terribly confident. "Send in the order form," he added. "It's your only real hope."

After the link closed, Kathang fetched several images of crown galls for Ela to examine. She stared at the swollen, lumpy spheres, at the grotesquely malformed shoots of infected tissue, wondering what she would have done if Copeland had ordered her to eat them. Would she have just let the LOVs die? Maybe.

Were crown galls common? She thought she might have seen such things before, though she couldn't say where, or when.

The screen door opened, its corroded spring creaking a natural alarm. A girl in darkened farsights slipped into the room. She looked to be maybe fourteen years old and not quite five feet tall. She wore a knee-length, pale green gauze jacket over charcoal pants, with a white T-shirt and rubber sandals. None of it looked new. She turned to flash a quick hand signal at the boys outside, and as she did her hair swung like a heavy skirt, revealing colorful silken threads woven in with her own thin black tresses. She was not a pretty girl. Her features were too coarse, her legs too short; but as her farsights lightened in the room's dim interior, Ela could see an alert intelligence sparkling in her eyes. "You must come with me please," she said, startling Ela with her excellent English. How had she learned to speak so well? And with an Australian accent Ela would have killed for. . . .

She scowled, feeling a sudden, perverse dislike for this teenage girl. Anyway, Nguyen had said to stay here . . . wherever here was—that was something she needed to figure out. She couldn't submit Copeland's order until she had an address, or found someplace where a delivery could be accepted.

Mrs. Dao appeared in the kitchen doorway. She took a look at the intruder, nodded, and then disappeared again into the ginger-scented depths of her home territory.

"You do understand English?" the girl demanded.

Ela snorted. "I do most of my work in English."

"Then why are you just sitting there? Hurry, hurry. There's no time to hesitate." Then, as if it were the most obvious fact in the world, she added, "You do know there's a house-to-house search under way?"

Ela's eyes widened. She stood and crossed to the screen door. Three ducks waddled in the dusty yard, while the two *Roi Nuoc* continued to lounge on the porch. A farm road ran between the rice paddies, but it carried no traffic. "I see no one," she said, looking back at the young intruder.

"By the time *you* see someone, it will be too late. Anyway, *I'm* going." She moved toward the back door, as if it hardly mattered to her whether Ela cooperated or not.

Ela followed uncertainly, but she stopped again halfway

across the room. "Who are you? Who sent you here? And why?" She glanced again out the front door, but the road remained empty.

"My name is Oanh."

"That's only one name." And a very common name too. It meant nothing.

"It's enough name for me, Ms. Ela Su-van-a-tat," she sneered, dragging out every syllable. "We aren't greedy for names like Thai people who could make rap songs out of theirs."

"That just shows Thai people have good memories."

"Or big egos." Oanh grabbed the back door and pulled it open, admitting a flood of light to the dim, old room. Dust motes stirred, blurring her face as she looked back at Ela.

"Aren't you going?" Ela asked.

"Is it that you don't believe the police are coming?"

Ela took another step closer, not at all sure what she believed. "Why should I?"

Oanh muttered something evil under her breath. Then she let the door close again. Reaching into a pocket hidden in an inner fold of her green gauze coat, she withdrew a pair of far-sights. For a moment she held them against her chest. "This isn't right. You're too old."

"Old? I'm nineteen."

"That is too old to become *Roi Nuoc*." Nevertheless, she stiffly offered the farsights to Ela. "Hurry! Take them. Then you will believe. Take them! I won't fail."

"Fail what?" Ela asked, eyeing the farsights with deep suspicion.

"Fail to save you! What else? Take them!" She shoved them into Ela's hands, then stomped past her, back to the screen door. The two boys were standing, peering anxiously down the road.

Ela examined the *Roi Nuoc* farsights. They were Mystery brand, very cutting-edge. She turned them over, exploring them with her fingers. They looked to be an off-the-shelf set. Hesitantly, she took her own farsights off, hooking them on the collar of her borrowed shirt. Then she put the *Roi Nuoc* farsights on.

The eyes of a goddess filled the screen. They were dark eyes, looking out from some dim, candle-laden altar. Reflected fire glinted in irises the deep, ruddy color of rosewood. They were wise eyes, calm, and very beautiful: the eyes of an ancient forest deity. The goddess looked at Ela, her thick lashes a velvet frame that softened the intensity of her gaze.

Shadow guarded the rest of her face. Only her eyes seemed vulnerable to light.

"Oanh has warned you," the goddess said.

Ela could not see her mouth, but she knew this must be the goddess speaking. Such a deep, rich, musical voice must belong to those eyes.

"The national police are moving from house to house, searching for you. You were seen by many farmers yesterday. Some may choose to remember you."

As the goddess spoke, her image faded, to be replaced by a vid of a beige jeep parked outside a tin-roofed farmhouse; a scene that was swiftly nudged to the side by another vid of a similar jeep speeding along a dusty road; and then another of a truck inside the fenced compound of a warehouse complex; and a second truck on a road; and another jeep; and several motorcycles.

Ela's heart beat harder and harder as each new scene compressed the others before it, squeezing them into tight, distorted fields. "Are these scenes of the search? Are they real-time?"

The goddess confirmed it.

"But how could you have cameras at all these places? . . ."

Even as Ela asked the question, she knew. "The *Roi Nuoc.* These are video feeds from their farsights."

"This is true," the goddess purred. "What they see is fed back to me."

"And what are you?" Not a goddess. Surely this was a ROSA? One more advanced than Kathang, but still a ROving Silicon Agent, manufactured and trained to its task like any other.

"I am Mother Tiger."

"You are a ROSA called Mother Tiger."

The tiger goddess purred again. "Or a complex of ROSAs?" she mused. "Perhaps."

Perhaps? Ela did not like the uncertainty in that answer.

ROSAS should provide direct answers to direct questions . . . but there was no time now to pursue the issue. "This search—it's coming here?"

The eyes of the goddess returned to the screen, but smaller this time: They were the eyes of a translucent ghost tiger prowling Ela's field of view like a living watermark. "A patrol is ten minutes away to the east. Another is seven minutes away to the north. It's not clear yet which will be assigned to Mrs. Dao's house."

Ela's chest tightened. One certainly would.

She turned a panicked gaze to the back door. Oanh waited with one hand on the latch, anger and anxiety written on her heavy features. She stomped her foot. "Will you go or not? Valuable time is being lost!"

"Why are you protecting me?"

"Ela," the goddess said. "Do you see there will be repercussions for Mrs. Dao and her grandchildren if you are found in this house?"

Ela caught her breath. She hurried to the kitchen door. Old Mrs. Dao was working in the shadows, packing oranges into plastic shipping crates. She glanced up, and smiled. Mrs. Dao did not wear farsights. She understood very little English. She had no way to know that Ela had become a danger to her.

"All right," Ela whispered. "I'll go."

Oanh gave her no chance to change her mind. She bolted out the back door, scattering a clutch of fat, black chickens. Ela paused only long enough to step into the plastic slippers she had worn to the outhouse, before leaping after her.

They ran through the farmyard, then out past a rusting car hulk half-gone to grass. A cat shot past Ela's feet, darting into a small stand of sugarcane. She cried out—then remembered her wet suit, and pulled up short. "Oanh! I have to go back. If my wet suit is found, or my clothes, the police will know I was here."

Oanh turned back, panic in her eyes. Then the ROSA called Mother Tiger spoke, "A good thought. It has already been taken care of."

Relief swept Oanh's face. "You heard her! Come *on! Di Nhanh Iên!*"

She turned and ran down the path. Ela followed: first into the tangled shade under a stand of mango trees, and then across a sluggish irrigation ditch. The sun was high, and the air steamed. Mosquitoes hummed in every patch of shade. Ela swiped at the perspiration that refused to evaporate from her face. "Where are we going?" she panted. "Is there a place we can hide?"

"We hide by moving! Circle back, cut across the police line. Get behind them."

This sounded much too daring, especially if the police were using drone surveillance. "Will we see Nguyen?"

Oanh pulled up beside a stand of head-high grass. Hands on her knees and shoulders heaving, she peered past its yellowing blades. A water buffalo grazed on the other side. Beyond it lay a potholed dirt road. She asked, "Who is Nguyen?"

"Ky Xuan Nguyen."

Bending low, Oanh crept into the brittle grass. The dry blades rustled around her. After three steps she shot Ela a puzzled look. "That big shot *Việt Kiều* who drove you to Mrs. Dao's? Is he your boyfriend?"

"No! You don't know him?"

"Oh, yes. Sure I know him. We party every evening. He likes to spend his money. Some fun."

Ela sighed. "You must see him coming around sometimes."

"Not before he came with you. You working for him?"

"I don't know. Are you?"

Oanh shrugged. "Could be. Sometimes Mother Tiger makes the deals. Now come on."

Ela followed Oanh through the grass, pleased to know Nguyen had not set himself up as some kind of god in his little cult.

If it was his cult.

She crouched beside Oanh at the edge of the road. The water buffalo eyed them while Oanh looked up and down the deserted track. "Let's cross quick."

Ela nodded. They darted across the road, their sandals kicking up plumes of dust. Then they plunged into another stand of grass on the other side. The blades sliced Ela's calves and thighs, leaving itching welts. Insects buzzed her face. At least she had not seen any snakes.

The grass gave way to a parched, weedy field. By the look of it, the patch had been abandoned before the start of the dry season. All that remained of the original crop was machete-scarred stumps a few inches in diameter, surrounded by a wasted crown of secondary shoots, most of them swollen and malformed. Only a few healthy leaves remained, looking like petite copies of the familiar T-shirt icon. "Cannabis," Ela whispered. She knelt to touch one of the bubbly, thickened shoots, thinking that it looked quite a bit like the pictures of crown gall Kathang had shown her.

"Hurry up!" Oanh called, from the far edge of the field. "This path won't be open for long."

Quickly, Ela swapped the *Roi Nuoc* farsights for her own. "Kathang. Identify."

Several seconds passed. Then Kathang whispered, "This appears to be crown gall damage on *Cannabis sativa*. Assessment 96 percent accurate."

Ela grinned. With rough gestures she started breaking off the worst-looking shoots, tossing them into a pile on the weed-choked ground. Dust from the decaying tissue tickled her nose.

Oanh was back. "What are you doing? A drone will come through here in just a few minutes. We must go. Now."

Ela nodded. "I'm almost ready." She snapped off another half dozen branches. "Can you find the way back to the pond I hid in yesterday?"

"The pond? . . ." Oanh cocked her head, studying something on the screen of her farsights. "Oh. Why do you want to go there?"

Ela snapped off another branch, sneezing twice before she could answer. "Humor me, okay?"

"Humor you? . . ."

Ela smiled, wickedly pleased to have found an idiom Oanh did not understand. "Do it because I ask you to do it."

"But your diving gear has already—"

"I don't care about that!" Using the hem of her T-shirt for a sling, Ela gathered up the diseased shoots. Then she stood. "If you don't want to take me, Oanh, I can always have my ROSA guide me back." This was partly bluff. Though Ela did not doubt Kathang could find the way back, avoiding patrols and the spying cameras of aerial drones was another matter altogether.

"Okay!" Oanh snapped. "You want to do this stupid thing? Then okay! Just get your butt moving out of here *now*."

"Fine," Ela said, loping past her. "Let's go."

Oanh caught up with her at the end of the field. "I don't think you're worth this much trouble, Ela Su-van-a-tat."

"Then again, you could be wrong."

Oanh shook her head. "I *know* you're not worth this much trouble. Why did I have to learn English anyway? If I had learned French, someone else would have to deal with you."

Ela smiled, feeling like things were finally going her way.

CHAPTER 15

Summer Goforth leaned back in her chair, gazing out the window of her plush second-floor office in the Kapolei R&T park. The lights in the parking lot had just come on, projecting amber halos in the thin evening drizzle. Palm trees stood in silhouette against the crisp white face of the neighboring building. She was supposed to be editing a journal article. The hard copy lay strewn across her desk, but her mind wasn't on it. The LOVs filled her thoughts, and little else could enter.

Three days had passed since the module fell, with uncounted hours lost to the debates of the ethics committee. Summer could not see the point of further talk. The LOVs had clearly proved themselves an intolerable hazard. If any were still in existence, they needed to be found, and destroyed. She had urged the committee to acknowledge this, and to act, but to no effect. The talk went on and on.

With a sigh she tried again to return to the work at hand, but again she found her thoughts straying toward the puzzle of the mutated LOVs. How had they developed? How had they come to infest the *Hammer*'s fiber-optic lines? In the panicked rush to regain control of the station, no one had bothered to get a sample. Now they were gone, hard-cooked under a blast of steam, and if a successful postmortem had been performed on the residue, Simkin had not told her. He had hired her as a consultant, but he did not feel a need to keep her well-informed. She had not heard from him since the day the module fell.

In a way though, it was enough to know the LOVs could adapt—and quickly. *Too* quickly for their transformation to be explained by the slow pace of natural mutations. Could the LOVs be aware of their own structure? Could they be capable of changing it? She felt a rush of dread every time she touched on this idea. An intellect that could willfully modify the platform on which it ran was an intellect poised for runaway development.

Still . . . it would be interesting to do some experiments; expose LOVs to varying environments and observe how they respond. She was toying with ideas on how it might be safely done when the dry rattle of dragonfly wings brought her back to the present. She looked askance at the farsights left lying on her desk. Her ROSA must have received some item it considered worthy of her attention.

With a sigh Summer slipped the farsights on, expecting to find a link icon from one of the committee members—but the link was from Daniel Simkin. So. Had he finally found something for her to do?

She tapped the code to accept and Simkin's image coalesced, looking like sweet victory. That was when she remembered his promise to call when Copeland was found. "You've got him, haven't you?" she blurted.

Simkin's smile was sly. "Copeland? Very nearly. Any chance you can get away tonight?"

"Where? For how long? Is he still on the island? Are you going to make an arrest?"

His brows rose. "That would be nice, but I was really visualizing something more along the lines of a quiet dinner."

Summer sagged back into her chair, feeling as if reality had slipped just a bit. Dinner? "Why?"

His brow furrowed, though whether he was annoyed or amused she could not tell. "The usual reasons. Food. Companionship. Conversation. How often are we in the same city anymore? Come on, Summer. It's not such an odd thought."

Oh, but it *was* odd, and uncomfortable too. This was how they had started, once upon a time, with an innocent "business" dinner during her senior year. Within a few weeks she'd moved in with him. Three months later she was still living in his apartment, but he had moved on. "I don't—"

"We've made real progress on the case. And you're supposed to be my consultant. I'd like to get your input."

Her gaze shifted to the printed pages scattered on her desk. Edit an article? she asked herself. Or get on the team aimed at cleaning up her own ill-considered legacy?

"I did want to talk with you about the mutated LOVs," she said.

"Let's make it eight o'clock then. We can meet halfway. There's a place in Pearl City called Miki's Haven. Your ROSA will know where it is."

Despite the name, Miki's Haven was a restaurant designed for business: well lit, with widely spaced tables, and live music from a trio featuring oboe, cello, and a keyboard programmed to harpsichord—just enough noise to obscure conversation, but not to inhibit it.

Simkin was engaged in a link when Summer arrived at the table. He gestured for her to sit down, then turned half-away to finish the conversation.

Summer ordered a glass of chardonnay. Then she watched

Simkin over tented fingers, wondering how long it would be before her turn came. The wine arrived. She sipped at it awhile. Then, finally, Daniel tapped his thumb and finger, ending the link. "Sorry about that."

She shrugged. "Tell me about the case."

"Copeland is stirring." In a curiously intimate gesture, he slipped his farsights off and laid them on the table. "He's put in an order for a nopaline-octopine compound from his usual source."

"Surely not under his own name?"

"Anonymous."

"Then how do you know—?"

"It's the only anonymous order for no-oct the company has ever received."

"You're sure it's no-oct?" she asked, "and not just nopaline?"

"Quite sure."

"Nopaline will keep his LOVs alive, but nopaline with octopine will let them reproduce."

Simkin nodded. "You see our problem." He leaned forward. "Why do you look surprised?"

Her answer was delayed by a waiter arriving with menus. When he had gone again, she said, "This isn't making sense to me. Remember that Copeland's two partners, quite likely his two closest friends in the world, are dead because of the LOVs. Shouldn't a reasonable person be entertaining second thoughts, instead of preparing the LOVs to reproduce?"

As Simkin considered this a slow, hungry smile spread across his face—a disturbingly familiar smile that seemed to have slipped up some temporal wormhole straight from their mutual past. A flush touched her cheeks. "Summer," he asked, "are you implying something significant about Copeland's state of mind?"

She forced herself to focus on the question. "I don't know. I don't have enough information to *know*, but the LOVs do affect his emotions."

"So he could be irrational?"

"He could be driven in a way that doesn't make sense to us. Is that irrational?"

"As far as I'm concerned."

Summer wasn't so sure. "Rational behavior depends on one's frame of reference, doesn't it? If his values have shifted from what we might view as normal, his behavior could become quite unpredictable."

Simkin shrugged. "He values the Lovs."

The waiter returned to take orders, coolly efficient, and soon gone.

Simkin resumed his argument: "Copeland's Lovs are the key. With his buddies gone, the Lovs might be the only thing left he does value. I think that's all we need to know to successfully predict his behavior. He'll do what he needs to do to keep his Lovs alive . . . which means he *will* eventually claim his order of no-oct. We've tagged it, of course. When he picks it up, we'll have him."

"Unless it's a ruse?"

"Our eyes are open."

She acknowledged this with a nod. "So what happened to the diver? The one who reached the impact site?"

Apparently that was the wrong question. Simkin's eyes narrowed. His long fingers rapped the table. "You know what I hate? I hate politics. I hate bribes. I hate anonymous bigwigs, and I hate nationalist sentiment."

"I take it you haven't found the diver?"

He snorted. "How could we? We're working with our hands cuffed. For the first twenty-four hours the Vietnamese government did everything they could to help, but yesterday that changed. Now they're demanding a withdrawal of our surveillance drones from civilian areas. They've pulled their military and police units off the search. And they're insisting IBC operations be limited to the impact site." He raised an eyebrow. "One could easily get the impression they've found something worth hiding."

"It might be something as mundane as a drug operation."

"I'd like to know that. I'd like to talk to Ela Suvanatat too—the diver," he explained.

"Then there's reason to think this person really does have a sample of Lovs?"

"I need you to help me answer that—and I'll need your help to contain them if she does."

Summer nodded, gazing thoughtfully at the musicians as they followed their music through a complicated passage. "My skills don't lie in blockades and interdiction. So I'll guess you're talking about me developing a biocontrol to use against the LOvs?"

"You're the expert."

"Copeland's the expert."

"But you're on my side."

She nodded. Unlike the ambivalent members of the ethics committee, Simkin knew what must be done.

CHAPTER 16

A black-plastic water bag had hung all afternoon in the sun; now, with the fall of night, Ela stood beneath a silken spray, washing a film of soap and dirt and sweat from her skin. Stars stared down. Outside the garden she could hear clashing strains of canned music and the voices of drunken tourists on the street, trying to explain to themselves why they had come so far south as Ca Mau. Closer, she could hear the chirping of frogs and crickets, and closer still the whine of mosquitoes hunting her in the tight confines of the palm-thatch shower stall; she felt the soft nudge of their wings. Only the water kept them away, so it was with some reluctance that she turned the shower off.

She dressed with her skin still wet, acutely aware of the blue-green glow of the LOvs, just visible from the corner of her eye. For two days now, no more had died. The *Cannabis* crown galls had made the difference, providing the nutrients the LOvs required to survive. Ela still hoarded a few of the infected stalks in a sealed plastic bag, but in the tropical heat they were rotting fast. They couldn't last much longer.

"Ela?" a soft child's voice asked.

looking out from some dim, candle-laden altar. Reflected fire glinted in irises the deep, ruddy color of rosewood. They were wise eyes, calm, and very beautiful: the eyes of an ancient forest deity. The goddess looked at Ela, her thick lashes a velvet frame that softened the intensity of her gaze.

Shadow guarded the rest of her face. Only her eyes seemed vulnerable to light.

"Oanh has warned you," the goddess said.

Ela could not see her mouth, but she knew this must be the goddess speaking. Such a deep, rich, musical voice must belong to those eyes.

"The national police are moving from house to house, searching for you. You were seen by many farmers yesterday. Some may choose to remember you."

As the goddess spoke, her image faded, to be replaced by a vid of a beige jeep parked outside a tin-roofed farmhouse; a scene that was swiftly nudged to the side by another vid of a similar jeep speeding along a dusty road; and then another of a truck inside the fenced compound of a warehouse complex; and a second truck on a road; and another jeep; and several motorcycles.

Ela's heart beat harder and harder as each new scene compressed the others before it, squeezing them into tight, distorted fields. "Are these scenes of the search? Are they real-time?"

The goddess confirmed it.

"But how could you have cameras at all these places? . . ."

Even as Ela asked the question, she knew. "The *Roi Nuoc*. These are video feeds from their farsights."

"This is true," the goddess purred. "What they see is fed back to me."

"And what are you?" Not a goddess. Surely this was a ROSA? One more advanced than Kathang, but still a ROving Silicon Agent, manufactured and trained to its task like any other.

"I am Mother Tiger."

"You are a ROSA called Mother Tiger."

The tiger goddess purred again. "Or a complex of ROSAs?" she mused. "Perhaps."

Perhaps? Ela did not like the uncertainty in that answer.

ROSAS should provide direct answers to direct questions . . . but there was no time now to pursue the issue. "This search—it's coming here?"

The eyes of the goddess returned to the screen, but smaller this time: They were the eyes of a translucent ghost tiger prowling Ela's field of view like a living watermark. "A patrol is ten minutes away to the east. Another is seven minutes away to the north. It's not clear yet which will be assigned to Mrs. Dao's house."

Ela's chest tightened. One certainly would.

She turned a panicked gaze to the back door. Oanh waited with one hand on the latch, anger and anxiety written on her heavy features. She stomped her foot. "Will you go or not? Valuable time is being lost!"

"Why are you protecting me?"

"Ela," the goddess said. "Do you see there will be repercussions for Mrs. Dao and her grandchildren if you are found in this house?"

Ela caught her breath. She hurried to the kitchen door. Old Mrs. Dao was working in the shadows, packing oranges into plastic shipping crates. She glanced up, and smiled. Mrs. Dao did not wear farsights. She understood very little English. She had no way to know that Ela had become a danger to her.

"All right," Ela whispered. "I'll go."

Oanh gave her no chance to change her mind. She bolted out the back door, scattering a clutch of fat, black chickens. Ela paused only long enough to step into the plastic slippers she had worn to the outhouse, before leaping after her.

They ran through the farmyard, then out past a rusting car hulk half-gone to grass. A cat shot past Ela's feet, darting into a small stand of sugarcane. She cried out—then remembered her wet suit, and pulled up short. "Oanh! I have to go back. If my wet suit is found, or my clothes, the police will know I was here."

Oanh turned back, panic in her eyes. Then the ROSA called Mother Tiger spoke, "A good thought. It has already been taken care of."

"I'm done." Slipping on her farsights, she emerged from the thatch to find Tran and Cu, two young *Roi Nuoc* boys—eight or nine years old—waiting on a turn in the shower. They looked at her through their farsights and smiled, eager to practice their novice English: "Our turn now?" "The water is warm?"

Ela stopped a minute to chat.

She had come south by truck from Soc Trang province with the *Roi Nuoc* girl, Oanh, and two older boys. Tran and Cu had joined their party here in Ca Mau. She had come to think of these *Roi Nuoc* as her "English contingent" because they all spoke the language with varying skill, and all wanted to practice constantly. Apparently there was something in the spontaneity, the irrationality of true human conversation that surpassed the simulations and drills prepared for them by Mother Tiger. Or perhaps they just liked to show off? Tran and Cu earned money translating for tourists, most of whom only wanted to know the cheapest bar or the fastest way back to Saigon.

Leaving the boys to their shower, Ela made her way back through the papaya grove, using nightvision to place her steps, always wary of snakes. The *Roi Nuoc* had rented a corner of the little backyard grove to string their hammocks. The papaya trees were old, their tall, unbranching trunks averaging eight inches across. The fruits dripped like fat, swollen tears from beneath crowns of rustling leaves.

Oanh lay in her hammock, her face glowing green from the illumination of her farsights while the rest of her body faded into shadow. The smell of mosquito repellent drifted on the night air, sweet and cloying as jasmine. Oanh said: "Ninh and Thu went to the street to listen."

Ninh was seventeen and Thu fifteen. The two boys had escorted Oanh and Ela south after the police search grew too intense to evade. They spent most of their time exploring the town, searching for any hint of official interest, but so far as they could tell, Ela's identity had gone undiscovered. This was their fourth night in the south, camped out on the edge of the Ca Mau swamps.

"I want to go back tomorrow."

Oanh shook her head. "It's too soon."

"I can't wait. The crown gall is rotting, while my no-oct shipment waits for me in Soc Trang." She sat down in her hammock. Then she slipped off her farsights and held them to the side of her head so their button cameras could record the cluster of LOVs. "Kathang," she whispered. "Take an image."

Oanh sat up, always fascinated by this process. Her *Roi Nuoc* farsights would not show her an image of herself. It was one of the peculiarities of the Mother Tiger ROSA: According to its script, she should not be focused too closely inward.

Ela kept her own *Roi Nuoc* farsights in the waist pouch Ninh had given her, though she had found herself using them more and more every day. There was something addicting in the persona of Mother Tiger. It did not act like a typical ROSA at all. A ROSA was supposed to be a servant, a secretary, an interpreter, an intermediary, a researcher: in short, an *aide*. Quiet, unobtrusive . . . and inferior.

By contrast Mother Tiger was imperial—a wise, ancient, and often stern teacher, as well as a counselor, a psychologist, and a strategist devoted to keeping the *Roi Nuoc* safe in a perilous world. All of that, with none of the failings of a human parent.

Ela put her farsights back on, studying the new image of the LOV cluster. It showed a thriving colony, glowing with the blue-green light of the LOV's inexplicable communication. She had talked to Virgil many times in the days since their first contact, and he had explained about the microsecond flashes of LOV code; while Kathang could perceive them, she could not. It did not seem quite fair.

"Magnify," she said. The blue-green patch exploded in size, inflating from the scale of an earring stud to that of a wall map. Tapping her fingers, Ela scrolled across the image, examining the congealed disks, the faint outlines of interlinked limbs, the dark windows of porous membranes.

There.

She stared at an irregularity on the edge of the cluster, where the rim of a disk pushed out from beneath the neat surface layer of LOVs. A new disk? It must be. Ela was quite sure it had not been there in the morning. "They're reproducing."

She heard a rustle as Oanh drew near. "You're sure?"

"Yes. I see a bud."

Virgil had warned her: *If the bacteria in the crown galls produce octopine instead of nopaline, expect the LOVs to reproduce.*

Ela felt Oanh's breath against her cheek as she bent to examine the LOV cluster. Oanh had studied the literature. She knew as much about LOVs as Ela . . . except how it felt to have them as part of her mind. "Ela," she reminded, "you said you would let any buds be transplanted."

"I have seen only this one so far."

"Look for more."

It wasn't long before she found them. Her heart ran faster with every new discovery. After a few minutes, Ela counted twelve. It gave her the creeps to think of the LOVs reproducing on her. They were like a cancer she had volunteered for. Why had she done it?

To make money, okay.

That wasn't why she'd kept them though, nurturing them for four days with a repulsive brew of rotting crown galls.

During the long truck ride south from Soc Trang province Ela had felt something change inside her. It had begun as a state of preternatural alertness, her thoughts flowing with an unhindered intensity that she had felt only two or three times before in her life, in those moments when a fiery creativity had burned away all doubt and all distractions from her mind. Details sprang into her awareness, only to submerge again in the seamless whole of her surroundings. It felt like magic, to perceive at once the particulars and the breadth of the world, and to be fiercely aware of her own place in it: an intricate component in a natural machine of beautiful, unfathomable complexity.

Oanh stirred, anxious to have an answer. "Will you share them, Ela?"

If taken this night, before their axonal root began to grow, the budding LOVs could be transplanted to another host. Ela eyed Oanh's anxious face. "Are you sure you want—?"

"*Yes!*"

"I can't see to do it myself."

"I'll do it," Oanh said, a slight tremor in her voice. Ela didn't remark on it. Oanh had waited three days for this.

They worked quietly, as if they'd sworn themselves to a con-spiracy of two. Neither said it, but Ela knew they both wanted to be done before Ninh and Thu returned.

"Sit down over here," Oanh whispered, pointing to a low rung on a ladder left leaning against a nearby papaya tree. A sharp insect buzz ignited as Ela took her new seat, while beyond the checkered canopy of papaya leaves a meteor drew a microse-cond trail of light across the sky.

Holding a tiny knife, Oanh rested the heel of her hand against Ela's forehead.

"Only take the new ones," Ela warned. "Don't damage the others."

"Don't worry. Mother Tiger moves my hand."

That was not literally true, though Ela did not doubt the ROSA was directing Oanh's every move down to the assignment of a whispered mantra to keep her calm. She would be seeing the LOV colony under nightvision, the image magnified and en-hanced so that no distracting detail remained to confuse her. Ela felt the pressure of the flat side of the knife against her skin. "Hold your breath," Oanh whispered.

Ela closed her eyes, plagued by dark thoughts. It would be so easy for Oanh to lop off the whole cluster, leaving her with nothing.

Why do I imagine these things?

It wasn't something Oanh would do, out of honor, but even more because if this transplant failed Ela remained the only reserve of LOVs . . .

Maybe.

Before leaving Soc Trang province she had returned to the pond where the LOVs had escaped. Wading in, still carrying the collection of *Cannabis* crown galls in the belly of her T-shirt, she pretended to search for some possession lost underwater. And then, quite deliberately, she slipped. She had plunged un-derwater, taking the gall-infested stems with her, shoving as many into the mud as she could before Oanh waded in to help her back to her feet.

A tiny prick of pressure; a soft, short gasp from Oanh. *"It's off!"*

Ela did not dare turn her head for fear of spoiling the delicate operation. "Don't drop it," she whispered. "Don't breathe on it. Don't even touch it. Set it against your forehead."

From the corner of her eye she could see Oanh gripping the knife, her knuckles shining with the tautness of her skin. Instead of lifting the knife to her forehead, she bent over the blade, pressing the flat side against her skin just above her right eyebrow. She held it there a full minute, giving the LOV time to grip her skin with its slow, tiny limbs. Tran and Cu returned from their shower to watch with puzzled eyes, but they did not ask questions. Perhaps Mother Tiger had warned them to be silent.

At last Oanh lowered the little blade. Then slowly, she raised her head. On her brow Ela could just make out the blue-green glint of a single LOV fixed to her dark skin. "Next one," Oanh whispered, the light of an explorer's passion shining in her eyes.

Later that evening Virgil linked. He was troubled when he learned what they had done. "Ela, it's not a good idea to spread the LOVs. You're putting these people in danger. Not just from the IBC, but maybe from the LOVs themselves. We don't know—"

"We never do," she interrupted, crossing her arms. Kathang would be busy extrapolating her position, her posture—her annoyance—from the cues of her facial expression and muscle tension. It was this fabricated image that Virgil saw. His image was similarly assembled. She reminded herself of this as she looked at his sad, tranquil eyes. He seemed always tranquil. Too tranquil. The LOVs should not be used as sedatives. "Are you still coming?" she asked.

He nodded. "If I can get in past the shore patrol."

"Are you that close?"

"Another day."

"The *Roi Nuoc* will look for you. You'll be all right." Then she added: "Bring the no-oct. All of it."

"Any word on the shipment?"

"I heard today. It's arrived in Soc Trang. I'm going north tomorrow to claim it."

"Be careful."

She promised that she would.

Afterward she lay in her hammock, watching the stars wink like LOVs set across the face of the sky. What a precious crew of outcasts they made! The *Roi Nuoc* and Virgil and herself: thrown together and forced to trust because they shared a desire to see the LOVs survive.

Still, trust went only so far. She had told no one about the possibility of escaped LOVs, though she knew it couldn't stay secret much longer. Tomorrow she would go north to pick up the shipment of no-oct and to discover what, if anything, was growing in her pond.

CHAPTER 17

It was late afternoon when Ela stood on a sidewalk in the town of Soc Trang, stretching up on her tiptoes to see past a rush-hour crush of bicycles, mopeds, and little electric trucks. The delivery girl from Elegant Courier had been instructed to bring the no-oct shipment here, to this place on the street. So where was she?

Caught in traffic, no doubt.

"*Ela!*" Oanh's voice whispered from her farsights. "*Look there. Is that her?*"

Oanh was a block up the street. An inset image opened in Ela's farsights, the view zooming in on a single dusty moped, ridden by a gray-haired woman in a green uniform.

"Okay," Ela said. "It must be her."

She leaned into traffic, signaling as the moped neared. The courier saw her and swooped toward the roadside, putting a foot down against the new asphalt to balance the bike. The woman's eyes were invisible behind the black span of her farsights. Ela gazed at her own reflection and suddenly she knew: her image was being recorded.

It had been a mistake to come here. A fatal mistake? Maybe, but she needed the no-oct tablets.

"Pass code?" the courier demanded in a harsh, tinny voice.

"B-blossom, scripture, one hundred seventeen."

"Humph." Without a smile, without another word, the courier handed off the package. Ela felt so frightened she almost dropped it. "Th-thank you," she stammered as the woman gunned her moped and shot into traffic.

A touch on her elbow made her jump. She spun around, expecting the police, but it was only Ninh, one of the two *Roi Nuoc* boys who had escorted her these past few days. "Twisted bitch," he said, nodding in the direction the courier had taken. "*Cái bà vô duyên.* Come on. Let's go."

They hurried through the haphazard streets, following a map laid out by Mother Tiger. At every step Ela expected to see a police officer approaching on a motorcycle or appearing suddenly from behind a paper-covered shop door. Her anxiety grew, until she was jumping at the shouts of children or trembling at the bleat of a moped's horn.

Yet nothing happened. No one took notice. She could hardly believe they had gotten away, and yet it seemed they had.

After a few blocks they were joined by Oanh and the other *Roi Nuoc* boy, Thu. Together they made their way through a rough neighborhood of poor hovels and small factories, until finally Soc Trang fell behind, and Ela's anxiety with it.

Once again they were walking between the green rectangles of pump-irrigated rice paddies, heading east toward the coast, and a farm where the *Roi Nuoc* were welcome as laborers. Ela had been surprised to learn how many such places there were. Then again, the *Roi Nuoc* were ideal workers. They knew what needed to be done even before they arrived. They required little instruction and no supervision, and when the job was finished they would disappear.

Of course, it was this same prescient efficiency, and especially their ghostly elusiveness, that made the *Roi Nuoc* unwelcome in many more places. Strangeness was always a challenge to human sensibilities, and the *Roi Nuoc* were not just strange, they were threatening too, because they did recruit. Oanh had all but admitted that she had a mother in Saigon. Not a good mother, no. But she had not been abandoned. Instead she had chosen to leave, walking away from whatever abuse, neglect, or emotional oppression had scarred her young life—and that, Ela thought, was the root of the bad feeling against the *Roi Nuoc*; it was the reason behind the ugly rumor of alien nature that Nguyen had used to taunt her that night in the fishing village. Real children did not leave their parents, and if they did, they did not thrive.

And Nguyen . . . where was he? Ela had heard nothing from him since Mrs. Dao's house. Had his interest slipped? Or had he found his own trouble with the IBC?

A farm truck appeared behind them, roaring out of Soc Trang on a plume of dust. Ninh stepped into the road and flagged it down. He dickered a minute with the driver; a cash card changed hands. Then they were climbing into the back, joining a trio of German boys who were lounging on their backpacks, smoking fat marijuana cigarettes.

The boys sat up straight when they caught sight of Ela. Then they eyed Ninh, as if to size him up. None of them wore farsights. "Porno?" one asked, tapping his finger beside his eye.

"No," Ninh said with a superior smile. "Fascinating shrimp-farming lessons."

The boys laughed so hard they drooled, but they did not make any move toward Ela.

She turned her back on them, leaning over the side of the truck, enjoying the rush of wind past her face as she watched the road ahead. Marijuana smoke mingled with the smell of dust from the recently scraped road. On her farsights, a map of the countryside showed her location as a bright red spot. The shrimp pond where she had lost the LOVs was marked in hazy blue. The two points drew steadily closer together as the truck raced east, but they would not intersect if she stayed on this road.

Oanh crouched at her side, a veil of dirt obscuring the gleam of the LOVs on her brow. "I have felt odd today," she said softly.

Ela did not know how to answer. She was still wired after the encounter in Soc Trang, keenly aware of every least thing around her as if some prescient sense were whispering, warning her to stay alert. Was that the LOVs working? Or her own native fear? She scanned the sky, hunting for some anomaly in the brassy haze that might be a surveillance drone. "I've been thinking we should not stay together."

Oanh looked at the sky too. "You're going back, aren't you? To the pond where you spilled the crown galls. Are there LOVs in the water?"

"I don't know," Ela answered, quietly astounded. "Maybe. At the crash site, I filled a packet with spilled LOVs, but most of them escaped."

"You're right of course. We should separate." Her gaze settled on the package in Ela's hand.

Ela tore it open. Inside were four plastic bottles. She gave one to Oanh. "If there are LOVs in the pond, I'll need more."

"I understand."

On her farsights, the red dot that marked her position had reached its closest approach to the target shrimp pond. Ela tapped the truck's rear window, motioning the driver to stop. Ninh must have gotten an update from Mother Tiger. He was ready to go, following Ela over the side of the truck as the vehicle slowed. As soon as they were clear the truck sped away. The German boys looked back at them with startled faces, but Oanh did not look back. She did not raise a hand to wave good-bye. With Thu she watched the road ahead, while the truck dwindled in the vast, monotonous land.

Ela turned away, feeling oddly disoriented by the sudden, uncelebrated separation. She told herself the *Roi Nuoc* were like that. Fluid. Connected through their farsights as much as through their flesh.

She dug out her own *Roi Nuoc* farsights and slipped them on. Mother Tiger was there, a ghost image in the shape of a prowling tiger, pleased to see her, pleased at her cleverness in preserving (possibly) an extra stock of LOVs. She presented Ela with a new map that drew a path between the paddies, leading her directly to the pond.

Ninh sighed. "That looks like an hour's walk. Do you have any food?"

Ela pulled out two nutrient bars. Ninh made a face, but he took one. They ate as they walked, and they talked about the LOVs. Ninh wanted to know what they were good for; even Mother Tiger had not answered him satisfactorily on that. "Will they make you smarter? Are you smarter now?"

"I don't know."

She didn't feel exactly smarter, just . . . *sharper*. As if her native intelligence was working without the impediments, the distractions she usually stumbled over: the incessant worries, the self-doubt, the boredom . . . the loneliness. Everything she did seemed interesting, worth doing. Except sometimes it went too far. In Soc Trang she had let herself become too afraid. "Maybe they exaggerate emotions?"

He glanced up sharply. She ducked, cowering beneath a shadow drifting in the late-afternoon sky. It was only a bird.

Ninh started walking again. "This is an interesting experiment," he said. "I hope it survives awhile."

"Me too." But Ninh was right: That could not be assumed.

They reached the pond just after sunset. Ela crouched on the steep bank amid the sweet-smelling weeds. Midges peppered the air. A few eager frogs croaked. Nothing seemed changed since her previous visit. She could even see her old footprints at the water's edge, but she could see no sign of LOVs.

Virgil had said the LOVs might survive in this environment. They were hardy and adaptable, but had Ela asked too much of them?

She walked carefully down the spongy bank and waded in, feeling the tiny bodies of juvenile shrimp bumping against her legs in their panic to get away.

A reflection of the deep blue twilight sky floated on the black water. Dancing in the ripples was a fainter reflection: a little circle of dusk-tinged blue-green.

Ela glanced up, expecting to see a patch of cloud aglow in the last high rays of the sun, but the sky was clear. She gazed again into the water, while midges buzzed about her head. The evening's last light was fading quickly . . . not so the second, inexplicable reflection. It grew brighter, more substantial with every passing second until she was sure it was an object, and not a reflection at all. A little blue-green sphere, smaller than a Ping-Pong ball, submerged in the water but rising, rising nearer to the surface as she watched.

She felt a flush of recognition; at the same time, from the corner of her eye, she saw the dazzle of her own patch of LOVs gleaming just the same blue-green against the falling night.

From the shore Ninh called softly, "Ela? What is that thing?"

She remembered then that she still wore the *Roi Nuoc* far-sights; Ninh could see what she saw. "I think it's the LOVs."

She reached for the little sphere with trembling hands. It did not evade her grasp. It responded not at all. She cupped her hands around its scintillating blue-green glow. It felt like a crumpled necklace chain: hard yet supple, shot through with deep folds and convolutions. She raised it to within a quarter inch of the surface, and felt an intense curiosity flow through her, a profound sense of newness, and discovery.

"It's a colony of LOVs," she whispered. She turned to look at Ninh. "The LOV colonies on the EquaSys module were supposed to be like . . . like living computers."

Ninh said, "This one is small."

She nodded. It was young—*but it was thriving!* The LOVs that had escaped from her packet had reproduced; they had orga-nized without any outside guidance. "I'm going to break it into pieces."

Ninh took a startled step forward, his sandaled foot splashing in the water at the pond's edge. "Why? It is beautiful. Why break it?"

"So more will grow. I'll leave part of it here. The other parts I'll put in other ponds. If they're scattered, they'll be harder to wipe out."

He was silent a moment. Then he chuckled softly. "*That's* why you sent Oanh away."

She floated the little colony to shore, careful to keep it always in the water. In her hand it felt as light as an aluminum can. Ninh made a mud corral along the bank to keep it from floating away.

Now they faced the problem of transporting the LOvs.

"Do we have plastic?" Ela asked.

They searched their meager possessions, but all they had were the foil wrappers from the nutrient bars. Then Ela had an idea. Borrowing a knife from Ninh, she cut her hand towel into long strips. She soaked them in the pond water. Then she opened a bottle of no-oct tablets and crumbled several of them over the strips, massaging the dry powder until it dissolved into a pasty gray mud that clung to the fibers of the cloth.

She returned to the water. The LOv colony floated like a gleaming jellyfish in Ninh's mud corral. Gently, Ela lifted it out of the water. Like a jellyfish, it collapsed into a shapeless blob. But even in that reduced state it looked beautiful, tremulously alive. Aware? She refused to believe it, and yet once again she felt a sense of recognition come over her, a joy of emotional connection.

That was not important now. They must work quickly, and move on, before someone noticed them here.

"We have to tear it apart," she whispered to Ninh, as he crouched beside her, yet she hesitated.

"Do you want me to do it?"

To her own surprise, she nodded.

She watched his graceful hands as he touched the colony, exploring its strength and structure. Then he pinched it. He pulled it apart. Ela felt a sudden, taut sense of expectation, and curiosity. She bit her lip, but she did not move.

Ninh took a pinch of the LOvs and smeared them along one cloth strip. They gleamed faintly in the wet no-oct paste. He smeared another pinch along the next strip, and the next. By the time he had finished, the LOv colony was smaller than a jambolan plum that had been smashed in the road and turned to jelly.

Ela cupped it in one hand as she retrieved several more no-oct tablets from the bottle. Then she waded back into the water, releasing the remnant colony and the tablets with it. The lightless water swallowed them up. When she returned to the bank, Ninh was rolling up the cloth strips, tucking them neatly into the foil wrappers. "They should be transplanted tonight," Ela said.

Mother Tiger chose that moment to whisper, "Do not be alarmed."

The admonition had the opposite effect. Ela's chin rose in instant dread. In the deepening twilight she heard the approach of fast tires on a dirt road. There was no audible hum of engine noise, which meant it was a fuel-cell engine, a modern car. She turned to look for Ninh, but he was gone—vanished—along with the packets of LOVs. Only his footprints remained in the mud.

"*Ninh!*" she whispered frantically.

"Do not be alarmed," Mother Tiger repeated.

"Where is Ninh?" she squeaked.

"He has gone to plant the LOVs."

He had taken the no-oct with him; all of it. Only the shipping container remained.

Ela stomped her foot. "I don't like the way they keep leaving!"

"It is hard," Mother Tiger agreed, sounding, for the first time, like it was using a stock response. That lapse reminded Ela that it *was* a ROSA, and no true entity at all. She realized then how much she had come to depend on its advice, how she had been manipulated into dependence. Understanding made her angry. She had been on her own too long to give up her independence to a stupid ROSA playing goddess in a farsight cult.

"Tell me who's coming," Ela commanded, her voice cold.

"That one you call Ky Xuan Nguyen."

Nguyen. She had told him there were no other LOVs. By now he would know she had lied.

The car appeared on the levee road, advancing without headlights. Quickly Ela pulled the *Roi Nuoc* farsights off, replacing them with her own. Kathang's moist skin shimmered as its head bobbed a greeting. It whispered to her that a message from Virgil had come in; Ela shook her head slightly. No time to hear it now.

The levee road was several feet higher than the pond. The car drew even with her and then stopped. Down by the pond it was dark, but up on the road, in the open, twilight still lingered, enough to see Nguyen as he stepped out of the car. He looked down on her with a bemused expression.

"You are more than you seem, dear Ela."

Ela decided an active offense was her best strategy. "What I am is a fugitive. You promised to help me, but where have you been?"

His farsights gleamed faint green against his shadowed skin, suggesting a negative image of a human face. "I have been in Hanoi, lying my ass off and sucking up to government officials whom I in fact despise, all to persuade them to order an end to the IBC's search for you. It is because of my efforts, by the way, that you are still a fugitive and not a prisoner. Did you notice the absence of surveillance drones since your return?"

Ela turned away, blushing, grateful for the dark. "I did notice," she said hoarsely.

"A thank-you might be in order. After all, it was not *my* idea to remove LOVs from the impact site."

"You're angry because I lied to you about the LOVs. But how could I know to trust you?"

"I have far more to lose in this venture then you do, Ela. Do you want my help or not?"

"I need your help."

"Yes. You do. I'm glad you understand that. I've brought someone to see you."

A man had emerged from the passenger side of the car. Now he walked to the edge of the road, where he stood silhouetted against the dark-steel sky. He was taller than Nguyen, though not by much. "Ela?"

Her eyes went wide as she recognized his voice, made familiar by a dozen conversations. "Virgil?" She stepped forward, her bare feet splashing in the shallow water at the pond's edge. "You made it! Is it you?"

"Yes. I'm here. Thanks to Ky."

"He came in on Cameron Quang's boat," Nguyen added. "Just past noon."

Ela did not like the challenge she heard in his voice. "And do you own the *Marathon* now, Mr. Nguyen?"

"It's at one of the fish farms," Virgil said absently. "Ela, why didn't you say anything about these other LOvs? . . ." The sentence trailed off as he tilted his head back, looking up into the star-pricked sky.

Ela followed his gaze to see a shower of huge raindrops drifting out of the evening gloom, falling so slowly they looked as if they had renegotiated the usual contract with gravity. The deep blue of the western sky slid in oily reflection across their spherical faces.

Peeper balls, Ela realized, as the spheres came to rest several feet above the ground. She looked at Nguyen, her heart tripping in a fast, watery beat. Her voice squeaked: "They are yours . . . right?"

Nguyen stood on the edge of the road, the hem of his beige jacket fluttering in a faint evening breeze. Peeper balls glinted all around him like subtle party lights. "No, Ela," he said, his voice low, and thick with anger. "They're not mine. Rather, it seems that you were followed."

She backed a step away. "It might have been you."

He laughed shortly. Then he swore in a long, soft tirade. Virgil edged toward the car.

The unexpected motion panicked Ela. She stumbled back, away from the pond, away from the road. Nguyen though, made no move to go. "Did you stop somewhere, Ela, on your way up from Ca Mau?" It sounded like a casual question, so calm it made her tremble.

Her gaze cut to the Elegant Courier package discarded on the ground.

"Ah," Nguyen said. "A brief rendezvous in Soc Trang . . . where you picked up . . . an order of no-oct? What is that?"

Virgil spoke softly out of the darkness. "It's a nutrient the LOvs require."

Nguyen turned to him. He did not ask a question; that demand came from his posture alone.

"I ordered it for her," Virgil admitted.

"Is there any other use for this chemical, in this form?"

Virgil shrugged. "It's pretty specialized."

"Let me guess. You went through your usual source?"

"I guess I did."

Nguyen's anger at last slipped free. "Why not just take out an advertisement announcing 'We're here!'?" he shouted. "Is this the kind of smarts the LOVs bequeath? If so, then why have I wasted my time on you?"

Dead silence rang in the darkness. Then Ela said softly, "Dr. Copeland's LOVs are an early generation."

Nguyen crossed his arms. "Are you accusing Dr. Copeland of being guided by primitive and stupid LOVs, Ela?"

Virgil said, "We should go."

"No." Nguyen turned, raising his hands as if to address the flock of peeper balls. "In fact, we will stay right here in the delta. This land has become the last refuge of LOVs. They exist here now with the permission, and under the protection, of the government. We did not ask for this distinction. We did not ask for them to be scattered in wild colonies across our land, but they are here. They are our responsibility. The official announcement will be made tonight: This land has become a LOV protectorate."

Ela stared at him in disbelief. Had he lost his mind?

Or . . . was he running a bluff?

After all, he was in advertising.

Surely though, if it was a bluff, it could work only if the world were convinced the LOVs were benign and already widespread—too populous to be controlled without disrupting thousands of innocent lives.

So she jumped in to back him up. "Hundreds of people have already been accidentally infected by the LOVs," she declared, in the sincerest voice she could muster. "I have seen LOVs thriving in ponds all along the coast."

It was bullshit, but wasn't that what advertising was all about?

Nguyen cast her an admiring glance. "The IBC expected to experiment on our people, but we have turned their biohazard into a blessing—and we will protect it."

Bullshit, Ela thought. But it was the only chance they had.

CHAPTER 18

What the hell does he mean by a 'LOV protectorate'?" Daniel Simkin shouted, turning away from the video feed gathered by a fleet of peeper balls half a world away. It was two in the morning, he was wired on coffee and speed, and he wanted an explanation *now*. "Browning, have we got anything new out of Hanoi?"

Alyce Browning was serving as senior shift officer at the IBC's temporary headquarters in a rented office suite on Bishop Street. Her brown eyes flashed beneath a tomboy haircut. "Hanoi hasn't even hinted at anything like that," she growled. "It doesn't mean a thing."

Simkin did not believe it. The foul whiff of national politics was too strong. The ROSAs had identified Ky Xuan Nguyen as a wealthy advertising executive, influential in local government, and known for his humanitarian projects. Why would a man like that risk everything to traffic in an outlawed technology with no obvious use? It made no sense . . . unless something more was going on.

Browning had roused him at midnight, to let him know that the tagged package of no-oct had just left the office of Elegant Courier. She wanted permission to follow it. "Go," Simkin had growled. "Get on it now."

By the time he washed and changed and walked from his overnight suite down the hall, a single high-flying drone had been launched over Soc Trang. Its surveillance mechanism was focused on a specific law-enforcement incident, so its presence did not violate the government's ban on general-surveillance missions.

"Do you want me to inform Hanoi?" Browning had asked as he joined her in front of the central flowscreen.

"Are you feeling friendly?" Simkin replied.

Browning's lip curled in an expression that had nothing to do with a smile. Hanoi had ordered the surveillance ban.

They had watched in rapt attention as the drone tracked a courier through Soc Trang's crowded streets. From a quarter mile up it recorded the transfer of the package to an individual quickly identified as freelance producer Ela Suvanatat.

Simkin felt the arousal of the hunt. He wished he could be there. But that duty went to the three officers making up the IBC's ground contingent—all that were permitted, thanks to a compromise settlement with Hanoi.

They prepared to move in.

But Simkin forbade an immediate arrest. He wanted to know where Suvanatat had been, whom she knew, and most important, where she would go.

So the officers hung back, allowing the drone to track her into the countryside, where Virgil Copeland had appeared like an apparition in the dusk.

"No way!" Browning had shouted when she recognized him. "That can't be Copeland. It's a fake. And this is a setup, a distraction."

The ROSA on oversight disagreed, basing its decision on opinions gleaned from three subsidiary ROSAs specialized in line-of-sight identification. This *was* Copeland. The case had solved itself—yet Simkin felt a sour suspicion settle in his gut. *Too easy.*

"Something's wrong," he muttered. "There's more going on here than we can see. What happened to the kid they called Ninh?"

"Slipped. The drone's on him, but he's moving fast. He won't stay in sight for long. Daniel, we're going to have to make a choice."

The drone served as a relay, boosting signals from the peepers. If it strayed more then a few hundred meters in its pursuit of Ninh, the peepers would fall out of range. "Bring in another drone," Simkin ordered.

"We only have one in the area."

"Then get the helicopter in the air!"

That's when the slickly dressed advertising executive launched his nationalist bluff.

A Lov protectorate.

Simkin glared at the display, certain there was a hidden element in this game, a factor he had not parsed. Again he thought of Ninh. . . .

"It *is* the kid!" he shouted. "The boy, Ninh. This is about him."

Ninh was armed with a stock of Lovs. If he slipped, he could make Nguyen's threat real. He could scatter Lovs up and down the coast, put them in the hands of anyone who wanted them. They could make their way into parcel services and passenger airways, spreading around the world—and then it *would* be impossible to contain the Lovs. Nguyen was bluffing, but he was in a position to make his bluff real.

"Send the helicopter after the boy," Simkin ordered. "Make him our priority. *Now*."

The drone's leaving," Virgil announced.

He had been staring up into the star-filled sky, examining something there with the aid of his farsights. To the west, in the direction of Soc Trang, Ela could hear the faint buzz of a distant helicopter. Dread tightened around her heart. "They'll look for Ninh."

Nguyen was done with his declaration of independence. "Let's go!" he commanded, returning to the car. Virgil dropped into the shotgun seat.

Ela was only seconds behind. Activating nightvision, she scrambled up to the dike road and dived into the backseat, slamming the door behind her. Her feet and her hands were filthy, coated in mud. Mud smears soiled the carpet, the door handle, and the upholstery too.

Nguyen turned around as the car surged down the road, guided by a Rosa. The green-tinged lens of his farsights veiled his eyes, but did not disguise the direction of his gaze. She watched him examine each stain. "Every time I pick you up, you are filthy, Ela. It's a very bad habit, you know."

"It's a dirty little country."

"It's a grand and ancient country."

Ela had not seen much of that. Quietly she asked, "Did you mean that about a Lov protectorate?"

"Of course, I meant it! It's the angle I've been working for days. I didn't mean for it to happen this soon." He shook his head. "It's too soon. We'll have to see if those bastards in Hanoi have the spine to make it real."

Virgil had turned around too, his green-tinged gaze shifting from Ela to Nguyen. "Why are you doing this?"

Nguyen tipped his head back. "Because I have dreams of world domination."

"Come on."

Sarcasm gave way to a wistful smile. "We can be more than we are, don't you think? Shouldn't we try?"

"But why the Lovs?" Virgil pressed.

"They are an experiment." Nguyen turned back to Ela. "One that has gotten badly out of hand."

She blushed and looked out the window. If she had not gone to pick up the no-oct shipment... "I hope Ninh is all right," she whispered.

"He's fast," Nguyen said.

Ela remembered her *Roi Nuoc* farsights. She pulled them from her waist pouch and slipped them on. "Where is Ninh?"

"Here," Mother Tiger purred.

In an inset image she saw the racing lights of a helicopter sweeping nearer. She heard Ninh's ragged breathing as he ran.

"You must help him."

Nguyen's fist thumped the seat back. "Nothing has gone as I'd hoped! If I had it to do again, Ela, I would leave you on the beach and be done with it."

Ela's hand tightened into a fist while she watched a soldier lean out the helicopter's door, a rifle raised, aimed at her heart, at Ninh's heart. "If *I* had it to do again," she said softly, "I would still want the Lovs."

Desire was different from need, from responsibility. Ninh stopped. His hands went up. She wanted to say the LOVs were worth it, but it was Ninh under the gun, not her. "They'll arrest him now, won't they?"

Nguyen snorted. "They will have nothing to hold him on."

"Nothing?"

"He has become a . . . How is it said? A distraction?"

"A decoy?" Virgil suggested.

"That's it. A decoy. Nothing more."

Simkin watched as the youth surrendered and submitted to arrest. He was searched. No LOVs were found. "Backtrack," Browning snapped at her field crew. "He's tossed them."

The IBC officers abandoned Ninh, taking off along his trail, using electronic sniffers to trace the way back to the pond. They turned up nothing.

"He handed them off," Simkin said. "There was someone else out there in the brush."

Browning nodded. "Let's plug the drone into a search pattern. It's only been a few minutes. They can't have gone far."

They.

The pronoun stirred in Simkin a nasty foreboding.

The drone gained elevation. The reach of its cameras extended outward in a widening circle. A dozen figures flickered into existence along that arc of view. Unresolved, elusive, vanishing instantly like ghosts destroyed by the act of being seen.

"Oh, shit," Browning whispered.

Simkin shared her dismay. Any one of those fleeting figures could be carrying the LOVs. Or all of them. He spliced into Browning's field connection, linking directly with the pilot, who was already lifting off to retrieve the ground crew. "Bring the rabbits down," Simkin ordered. "Live capture if you can. Live rounds if you have to. If we slip now, it could take years to recover."

"Yes, sir."

The helicopter descended, just long enough for the ground crew to scramble aboard. Then it swung away, to hunt the wave front of fugitives expanding into the night.

CHAPTER 19

Virgil scrolled through the perspectives of the runners as they dispersed through fields and country roads. The helicopter buzzed beyond them, closer, farther, depending on the point of view. He shook his head, unable to grasp how it had come to this. Why were these children involved?

When he had fled Honolulu he had not expected to find allies. He had not thought to discover himself a player in someone else's game.

His gaze shifted to Ky Xuan Nguyen beside him in the driver's seat—though he wasn't driving. A ROSA steered the Mercedes while Nguyen worked his farsights, his profile illuminated in the green tones of nightvision, fading, then brightening again as new information flickered across his screen. His fingers danced to the chaotic display, twitching in a furious arrhythmia, while every few seconds an unintelligible command popped from his lips.

A stray peeper had gotten into the car. Virgil caught it with a swipe of his hand. Absently he squeezed it. It deflated with a sharp squeak. "Ky? Where are we going?"

"We have no destination."

"They'll know this car now."

"We will change cars." His tapping fingers never slowed.

The Mercedes swerved to avoid a pothole. Virgil said, "I'm not sure about any of this."

Ela answered from the backseat. "It's too late to back out. There are over twenty *Roi Nuoc* involved now. We can't betray them."

Virgil watched another slim, dark hand toss another strip of Lov-impregnated cloth into the dark waters of a paddy freshly planted with wispy rice seedlings. Ela was right: The cost of backing out was going up every second.

"It's too late," she repeated. "Even if we gave up now, even if these twenty turned themselves in, the damage is done. What do you think will happen to all the other *Roi Nuoc* when word gets out about their involvement with the LOVs?"

Virgil felt the touch of a cold fear. "They'll be blamed."

"They'll be persecuted," she said. "People fear them already. All they need is an excuse. After tonight the *Roi Nuoc* will be in danger no matter what we do."

"How dangerous are the LOVs?" Nguyen asked. Virgil turned, to find that his fingers had gone still; the illumination on his display had frozen as he waited for an answer.

"I don't know," Virgil said. "They colonized a fiber-optic cable aboard the Hammer. They shouldn't have been able to do that."

Nguyen shook his head. "Ms. Suvanatat is right. It doesn't matter. We are committed. Our only defense lies in making the LOVs a political factor . . . and we can do that only if the LOVs are widespread, and impossible to stamp out."

"The IBC will have this area under embargo by dawn."

"Yes. I think so too."

"You have leverage in Hanoi?"

"Nothing certain. An appeal to nationalism, to public gain. I have tried to sell the LOVs as an edge on the future . . . have I lied?"

Virgil looked away, out into the green-tinted night. "I don't know."

Nguyen sighed. "You are a lousy salesman. Don't you know the first rule of success is to believe in your product?"

Virgil smiled. From their first meeting at a private dock on the Bassac River, he had felt a strange affinity for Ky Xuan Nguyen. He had sensed in him a curiosity, an ambition that lay outside the mainstream. A pioneering boldness that reminded him of Panwar. "I don't even know what my product is," he admitted.

"Then it will be your priority in the next few days to find out."

"If we manage to stay free that long?"

"That won't be so hard, now that we are no longer hiding."

Virgil leaned back in his seat, while Nguyen's focus returned to the screen of his farsights, and his fingers resumed their twitching. Clearly, Ky Xuan Nguyen had not planned to play such a public game. Until now, he had contained his risk-taking within a hidden partition of his life, building firewalls between that and his respectable persona. But he had been over-confident, too sure of his own skills, and luck, and organization. Now he was trapped, unable to escape except by leaping forward. It was the same story Virgil had played out in Honolulu.

He thought of Panwar and Gabrielle, and nothing felt real. Was he crazy? Was he dreaming? Might it still be possible to wake up?

Don't think that way.

Nothing would be gained by tying his mind in knots. He drew a deep breath, let it go slowly, demanding an onrush of *calm*. He was well practiced. He had done this a hundred times aboard the *Marathon*. He had lost track of the days spent in the isolation cell of its tiny pocket cabin, unable to take more than a step and a half in any direction. Worse, after forty-eight hours the air had begun to stink. He had tried cranking the blowers up to gale force, but then it was cold and noisy . . . and when he turned the fans back down the stink was still there. It had seeped into the walls. It had permeated the padding of the chair. Whenever he returned to the chair—(In his mind it had taken on capital letters, *The Chair*, transformed into a semiconscious instrument of torture, or penitence, whose ultimate goal, though surely dark and sadistic in the way of old religions, remained obscure)—after a visit to the head, or a brief bout of deep knee bends on the tiny oval floor, he would sit down into the lap of a ghost image of himself, a wraith that had emerged out of the upholstery and whose substance was his own foul body odor and the stale echoes of his intestinal gas. It had been pure joy to open the hatch beneath the shelter of an offshore platform, to stand upright and breathe clean air, fresh off the water. He didn't care if he ever saw the *Marathon* again.

The display on his farsights scrolled past the image of another fragile hand releasing one more LOV-saturated cloth. . . .

"Back that up," Virgil whispered, sitting up a little straighter.

The image rolled back in time. A jouncing path led across an irrigation ditch. The point of view leaped across the water and then slowed. Turned back. The ground rushed up, and a hand slipped the LOVs into gently flowing water. "Ky, someone has released LOVs into a flowing stream. There's no way we can control where they go if—"

"You saw that?" Ela demanded. "Virgil? How could you see that? Those aren't *Roi Nuoc* farsights."

He turned to look at her, puzzled. "No. They're mine. Sort of." He touched the stolen Heroes.

"But they're linked to Mother Tiger?"

"Sure. Ky set it up."

She looked outraged. "He did? . . . Is that possible? But *I* have to switch back and forth to *Roi Nuoc* farsights. I've been switching for a week. Mr. Nguyen! Why didn't you tell me? Why did you convenience *him*?"

Ky Xuan Nguyen turned slowly, his eyebrows raised. "Because, Ela, *Virgil* does not make my car dirty."

She screamed. It was a cry of horror, a caged thing that ripped through the soundproofed cabin. Her hand flew up to cover her mouth. Tears started in her eyes. "Make them stop," she moaned. "They're killing them."

For a long, strange moment Virgil felt lost in unfathomable nightmare—and then the moment grew worse. On the screen of his farsights the point of view shifted. Brilliant light washed the ground as the dust on the back of a dike exploded upward in a dozen bursting fountains. The light went out and a child's voice was screaming, crying in utter terror the same phrase over and over again dutifully translated by Mother Tiger, *It hurts, it hurts, it hurts*.

The point of view shifted. Now he could see the helicopter, bright against the night sky, sweeping in low, only a few meters above the paddies, the side door open and a gunman lifting his rifle, taking aim. With an oath that did not need translation, the view dived forward into a stand of grass. Events blurred, shifted. Now came the sound of running feet, falling in fast rhythm against the dirt, while the buzz of a helicopter and the ratchet of gunfire raged in the distance.

Virgil's head slammed against the side window, his farsights were knocked askew. He was back in his own locus again, as

the car spun around. Nguyen had his hand on the steering stick.
He had taken over driving from the ROSA. Sweat shone on his
cheeks, and rage lay in every line of muscle on his face. He
punched the accelerator, and Virgil was slammed back into his
seat as the car went bouncing, flying over the rough country
road.

In the distance the helicopter moved like a specter, its search
light switching on, off, in no apparent rhythm. Tiny red bursts
erupted at intervals from its sides.

"There is a pistol in the compartment at your knees,"
Nguyen shouted, as the car bellied viciously in the bottom of a
dip. "Take it out."

Virgil lunged for the compartment, tried twice to pop it open,
got it on the third attempt. The gun bounced like metal popcorn. He scooped it up, surprised at its weight. He had
never held a gun before. Again he thought of Panwar. He had shot
that cop. It seemed like another lifetime.

The Mercedes hit a smooth stretch of road. Nguyen leaned
on the accelerator. The car shot ahead once more, doing a hundred, easily. Whatever bumps there were skimmed past beneath
tires that barely knew the earth.

The sun roof slid open. Virgil glanced up to see a star-
speckled sky.

"You have a choice of two targets," Nguyen said. "The pilot
or the tail rotor. Hit either one, and the ship comes down."

Virgil stared at him for the space of two deep heartbeats.
Then he nodded. Children were being gunned down, wounded.
Their screams poured through his farsights, straight into his
core.

He took a second to examine the gun. He could feel the way
the safety worked, but even with nightvision he could not read
the letters to see which setting was on and which was off. He
shrugged to himself. Trial and error, then.

He started to get up on his knees. "Brace yourself!" Nguyen
shouted. He pressed the brakes. Dust billowed past the Mercedes while Virgil leaned against the dash. The car fishtailed,
straightened, then took off again on another road. Virgil

crouched on the seat, then carefully he rose, emerging into a hurricane sweeping over the car roof.

The helicopter was dead ahead, hovering a few meters above the road, its searchlights off and its gunner targeting the racing car. Nguyen was going to ram it in about seven seconds if it didn't lift.

Virgil braced his elbows against the roof of the car, holding the pistol with two hands as he squinted along the sight, aiming at the gunner's transparent face shield. He wore body armor, and a helmet too. The best Virgil could hope for was to knock him down. The muzzle of his weapon flared red. At the same time the car swerved, tossing Virgil to one side of the open sunroof, slamming his rib cage.

He gasped, but managed to brace his legs, sighting again along the pistol. Only then did he remember Nguyen's instructions: *The pilot or the tail rotor. Hit either one, and the ship comes down.*

Shifting his aim, he fired off six shots in quick succession.

Something exploded, and the car sagged. Virgil collapsed halfway back into the cabin, just as the tail rotor burst into a rain of fiberglass splinters. The helicopter spun wildly, around and around across the rice paddies while the Mercedes went careering over the opposite bank. Virgil ducked back into the car, hitting the seat just as a squadron of air bags exploded in his face. The jolt knocked the memory of the next few seconds right out of him.

When his mind started working again, the air bags had already deflated and the car was still. Virgil could hear the tick of hot metal, and water trickling. He could hear someone moving behind him. *"I've lost the gun,"* he whispered.

Nguyen said, "Look for it on the floor."

Motion made him turn his head. He saw Ela, wriggling out through the sunroof. "Did you get it?" Nguyen shouted after her.

"Every fucking minute!" she screamed back. "Now hurry up! These children are hurt." Then she disappeared from Virgil's sight.

"Get what?" he asked hoarsely, shaking his head to clear it, then quickly deciding that was a very bad idea.

"The vid that will establish a revolution," Nguyen said as he reached for the sunroof. "Ms. Suvanatat is an artist. She has forwarded the cries of every wounded child to the world, along with our response." Then he lofted himself through the roof, leaving Virgil to hunt about for the gun and an extra box of ammunition.

A fterward, when a caravan of medics had arrived from Soc Trang and a triage tent had been set up, Virgil took a bottle of drinking water and a clean rag and wandered off, until the lights and the noise felt remote behind him. He crouched beside a sluggish stream flowing through an irrigation ditch. His rib cage ached and his face stung. He wished there was an open bunk to crash in. His self-pity felt oddly heartening. This was the Virgil he knew.

Who was that madman he'd been earlier tonight?

He had already watched the record of his exploits, but he reviewed it again on the screen of his farsights, and as the seconds ticked past and the scene played, all he could think was: *I should not have been able to do that.* He had not even been aware of Ela crouched in the sunroof beside him, but she must have been there; she had recorded from that point of view. She had collected his profile as he gazed ahead at the helicopter. Calm, poised. His LOVs glittering like faint hot stars in a distant stellar cluster. The view panned forward to the fleeing helicopter as he took aim and fired: six quick shots and the tail rotor shattered. He had never before used a gun. "I shouldn't have been able to do that," he whispered.

Yet he *had* done it, and he couldn't remember being afraid. (He was afraid now.) He couldn't remember experiencing any doubts. (No shortage at the moment.) Maybe it had all happened too fast for fear and doubt to kick in? Maybe it had been an adrenaline high, inspired by the pain and terror of the wounded *Roi Nuoc* children, and he'd just gotten lucky with the gun. Beginner's luck . . . if you could call it that. The pilot and his two crew had all died when the airship hit and burned to the waterline, mired in a newly planted paddy. In blunt truth, Virgil had killed three people. Add Gabrielle and Panwar to the body count, and Virgil figured he could be fairly described as a serial killer.

He heard footsteps approaching from behind him; quickly he bent to wet his rag with a splash of bottled drinking water. He daubed at his face. Blood came away, most of it dark, hard, and old, but some liquid, fresh. The footsteps paused behind him. Nguyen spoke, his voice gentle like the singing crickets that filled the weeds beyond the irrigation ditch. "You were amazing," he said. "I couldn't believe you did it."

Virgil couldn't say anything to that. "How are the kids?" he asked.

"Seven will need the hospital. They'll be evacuated tonight on a government airship."

"Government—?"

"Hanoi is outraged."

"Have you won, then?"

Nguyen's voice took on an icy edge. "Do you think I set it up this way?"

"No! Of course not. That's not—"

"I lost my head when the kids started going down. That's never happened to me before. Never. I didn't plan it this way."

"I believe you."

"It's worked out though," he added. "It looks like it will work out . . . for a while, anyway." He crouched beside Virgil. "The medics are not so busy now. Come back to the tent. Let them look at your face."

"I think it's shrapnel from the tail rotor. I didn't feel it at the time."

"I'm not surprised. You were like a madman too, a man possessed. I've heard of such things. I've never seen it . . . or felt it."

Virgil told him then of his suspicions. "I think it was the Lovs that kept me steady, focused, with only the necessary emotions to do the job. I couldn't have done that a year ago. Not if it was my own family being gunned down. I would have frozen. I would have thought too hard, or been too scared, and I would have missed."

"No one ever knows for sure how they'll react under pressure—"

"*I* know. That wasn't me holding the gun. Or . . . it was a me I haven't met before."

Nguyen's chuckle was soft. "It was, I think, the 'you' you are becoming. Ela says the Lovs are supposed to make you smarter. Do they make you braver too?"

Virgil brushed bloody fingers across the hard specks of his embedded Lovs. "Maybe it's different sides of the same coin? Intelligence is more than just abstract reasoning. I think so anyway. After all, why is it that thoughts sometimes fly in a creative fervor, as if God is whispering revelations into your mind, while other times it seems as if you can't put two coherent words together. That's *mood*, working. Emotion. In my opinion anyway. I think ninety percent of what the Lov implants do is stabilize and focus mood."

"That would confound those who think of intelligence as soulless abstraction."

"Ha. We would have the motivation of a ROSA—none at all— if not for our emotions."

"And the Lovs—?"

"They have emotions too. Or, they can have them. I've felt it. When my Lovs communicated with E-3, I felt it, like a drug washing through my brain."

"Good?"

"*Clean*," Virgil insisted. "Frightening and awesome too, but it was a clean high. Lov asterids—the neuronal cells inside each Lov shell—were derived from human brain cells, so maybe it's not so surprising that we can share some experiences."

Nguyen touched his arm. "Come back to the tent and get your wounds cleaned. We'll discuss the Lovs more tomorrow."

Virgil hesitated, weighing Nguyen's mood before asking the question that had been puzzling him since they'd first linked. "I don't understand why you're doing this, why you're here. What are the *Roi Nuoc* to you?"

Nguyen frowned. He glanced back, in the direction of the medical tent. "My water puppets." He dropped a pebble into the stream trickling through the irrigation ditch. "Their performance has surprised many people." He looked rather pleased by this. "The explanation is simple, really. The *Roi Nuoc* are my past. I used to be . . . very much like them."

"You?" Virgil asked, trying to imagine Ky Xuan Nguyen as a homeless kid sleeping in an alley or on the side of a country road.

"Is it hard to believe?"

"Yes! Or no. I don't know." It would fit with his dark, cynical humor. "So what happened?"

Nguyen shrugged. "I was found to be useful by a man whose own natural son was blessed with the intellect of a water buffalo. The family business could not be entrusted to him, so a surrogate son was required."

"You."

"He called me his son. He sent me to the finest schools, first in Hong Kong, then in the United States. When I came back I saved his little advertising empire from ruin. Was he grateful?"

Virgil waited.

Ky let another pebble fall with a soft *plop*. "He still believes it is I who should be grateful. 'Street trash understands street trash.' That is his explanation for my success."

"So you set out to do better by the *Roi Nuoc*."

"They will never have to kiss ass just to eat."

"And the Lovs?"

He sighed, and then he stood up. Virgil stood with him. "I had hoped to experiment quietly for a while."

"But why? Why risk it at all?"

Nguyen spread his hands. They were small hands, smooth and pale. "The world is changing. Like many others, I have begun to wonder how long we can stay competitive with our machines."

"You mean AI? You know, I never thought much about it until I met Mother Tiger."

"I think we must become something new to meet this new

world. Whether or not your LOVs are the answer though, only time will tell."

"So . . . did you mean what you said about leaving Ela on the beach?"

"Does it matter now? The past is closed to us. The only way out is forward."

CHAPTER 20

Summer slipped her farsights off, banishing an endless loop of emotionally wrenching news reports from her perception. She turned to Daniel Simkin.

He watched her from the other side of his desk, leaning back in his tall black chair, his fingers laced behind his head, his farsights half-silver so that his eyes faded into invisibility whenever they ceased to move, like hunting cats pausing in the grass.

She had resigned her seat on the ethics committee to work for this man.

"I can't believe you ordered this," Summer said. "How could you? How could you let things go this far?"

Even worse, to go this far and to *fail* . . .

The Vietnamese government had been so outraged by the shootings that it had declared the protectorate a reality, designating nine square miles as a LOV reservation. LOVs were being cultured in a hundred different waterways, while the IBC's enforcement officers had been ordered out.

"We had to contain this threat," Simkin said.

"By shooting people down? By shooting *children*? Daniel, stop and think what you're saying."

He leaned forward. Now his pale hands rested on the desk. "What I'm saying, Summer, is that we were not aggressive enough. We failed to contain this threat, and now thousands of people are at risk of being infected. The entire ecosystem could be contaminated. We already know the LOVs are adaptable. The mutant strain on the Hammer proved that. But we have no idea what their limits might be, or how far they could spread."

"They won't spread far without no-oct. Even the aberrant LOVs on the *Hammer* required it. The forensic report shows far more no-oct being consumed than could be accounted for by the known colonies. Even Copeland commented on the discrepancy in his notes."

"How hard do you think it would be to reengineer that limit, Summer? Maybe it's already been done. A lack of no-oct hasn't contained the LOVs so far. They're getting away from us—and that puts the pressure on you and your team."

She had taken a leave of absence to supervise an IBC team flown in expressly to work with her. "I can't come up with a designer virus overnight! And if I said I could, you'd be a fool to use it. This situation requires a highly toxic agent that will eradicate every LOV out there, but at the same time it has to be LOV specific, incapable of harming any other life-form—"

"Can you do it?"

Summer gazed at him, at the glistening blond stubble of his beard, at the poised set of his veiled eyes, feeling as if she were looking ahead through time. Escalation was in his nature. If she didn't do it, he would use other means to regain control. . . .

"Yes. I can do it. The LOVs are an artificial life-form, with peculiar characteristics. If we make a virus to attack those peculiar traits, everything else will be safe. But it will take time."

"How much time?"

"Seven, maybe eight weeks."

He nodded as if she had proved his point. "Until then, the LOVs will have to be contained by other methods."

"Not by violence." She could still feel the horror that had gripped her when the children started to fall. Her fingers twitched, sending a hash of meaningless signals to her farsights where they lay in her lap. She watched light flare across the screen as her ROSA sought feedback from her absent eyes. *Say it!* she chided herself.

"I'd like to hire Dr. Nash Chou. Make him part of the team. We worked together on the original LOV project, and he was Dr. Copeland's supervisor—"

Simkin shook his head. "Nash Chou is already occupied. He's become a consultant for the United Nations, hired to 'monitor' the situation. He's on his way to the delta as we speak."

Summer stared down at her farsights, only slowly remembering to slip them on. She told herself she was not jealous. "Maybe we should move our lab there too. It would make the testing phase easier."

Simkin leaned back again in his tall black chair, lacing his hands across his hard belly. "No. Security's impossible. I want you to stay here in Honolulu. Your work's too important to risk."

CHAPTER 21

No-oct," Ky Xuan Nguyen said the next afternoon, as he joined Virgil on a mat spread in the shade of a banyan tree. "That is the question we must answer."

Virgil nodded: All other questions would become moot without no-oct.

"Where do we get it?" Nguyen asked. "How do we manufacture it? Without no-oct this venture will reach a quick conclusion . . . as will our own lives as free men."

The three government soldiers keeping Virgil company had fallen silent at Nguyen's arrival. Virgil glanced at them. Two women and a boy with a startlingly youthful face. All of them wore camouflage uniforms, their automatic weapons nested across their laps. None spoke English, but Mother Tiger translated their conversation for Virgil, and evidently they had a ROSA to translate what Virgil said to them. They had complained heartily about their farsights, which could access only their own military network. "No entertainment programs," the younger woman groused. "Is it possible to die of boredom?"

"I never feel bored anymore," Virgil had mused. It was true. With his farsights and the emotional leverage of the LOVs, his mind seemed always to be occupied. He had been studying a map Mother Tiger had prepared, showing the coastal farmlands, with every pool and waterway and farmer's house marked in three dimensions, with scrolling functions to display the ground-based view. Twenty-four bright red dots marked the exact points where LOVs had been released last night. Thin blue, fluid arrows indicated currents where any existed. Rosy halos around the drop points estimated the possible spread. Twenty-two of the sites were in ponds or rice paddies. The other two were in irrigation ditches. Government scientists were surveying all the waterways downstream.

Oanh had used this map during the night, organizing cadres of *Roi Nuoc* to collect crown galls and press them into the mud at every drop site. Soldiers had been scattered all over the farms by that time, but they made no move to interfere. They were a youthful force, most of them barely twenty and proud of the stand their government had taken. They were also surprisingly sympathetic to the *Roi Nuoc*. Most of the civilian population despised these strange children, but the soldiers understood them. They were like them in many ways. Gazing through their farsights, they saw the present, but they saw it colored in alien hues back-scattered from a future looming just out of sight.

"No-oct," Nguyen said, arresting Virgil's attention once again. "The supplies you brought will soon be gone, and the weeds too, are a temporary source. We must have a steady source of no-oct, or the LOVs will soon die."

Virgil felt the soldiers' tension as they listened to Nguyen, trying to eye him without staring. They feared him, obviously, but awe and respect could be seen in their expressions too. This was how they might act, Virgil thought, if their president had come to sit among them.

As if to prove his theory, the younger woman finally gathered the courage to speak. "Greetings sir," she said in soft veneration. "Your exploits last night were truly brave."

Nguyen shook his head, gently refusing the praise. "A wise

man can be brave," he said. "But a foolish man pretends bravery to escape the scourge of his conscience. Last night I was a foolish man. Had I been wise, no one would have been hurt."

The younger soldier bit her lip, nodding. "Yes, Uncle. Still, it made us proud."

Their conversation was in Vietnamese, but Mother Tiger mimicked their voices so that in Virgil's ears they seemed to also speak in English. He had not asked Mother Tiger to do this. The ROSA had assumed he would be interested, and of course he was.

The ROSA fascinated him. Never before had he encountered a system so independent in its actions, so seemingly *interested* in the tasks it performed. According to Ky it had started as a simple redundant system, with cognitive blocks spread across many different servers so that if any one account was lost, the others would continue to run. But its redundant design had gradually evolved into a complex system with an intuitive nature that challenged Virgil's assumption that ROSAs were tools and nothing more. Ky worried that machine intelligence would supplant the ancient human kind. A lot of people did, but not many had a reason as close and as profound as Mother Tiger.

"No-oct?" Nguyen repeated, for the third time now as he eyed Virgil with a bemused expression.

Virgil grunted. "Any good lab should be able to make it."

"We are embargoed, Virgil."

"Surely there are commercial labs in this country?"

"Assuredly. Not, however, within the nine square miles of the LOV reservation, which is the limit of our reach at the moment."

"Oh."

"Compromises were made this morning. Understandable compromises. Hanoi cannot, of course, ask the entire country to suffer with us."

"So . . . just the reservation is embargoed?"

"Yes. Residents may exit if they wish, but they will not be allowed to return. Goods will not be allowed across the perimeter in either direction."

Virgil nodded. No food would be coming in then, and no clothing. No medical supplies. He noticed Nguyen watching him with expectant eyes. "And you?" Virgil asked. "Will they let you out?"

Nguyen's smile slid on oily cynicism. "No doubt. However, I do not think I would enjoy my reception. It would not be wise, Virgil, for either of us to leave just yet."

"That's right," the young soldier said. She tapped the rim of her farsights. "Foreign troops are just outside the border. If anyone involved in the conspiracy emerges from the reservation, they will be arrested. This includes the *Roi Nuoc*."

Nguyen nodded. Again he looked at Virgil. "No-oct?" he pressed.

Virgil sighed. "We can culture gall tissue if we have access to a lab. *Any* lab at all."

Nguyen raised his eyebrows.

"No lab?" Virgil asked dejectedly.

"No lab."

He thought a minute. "Hey." He looked up, an uncertain smile on his lips. "We could infect living plants with the crown gall bacterium. Oanh should know by now which species are vulnerable."

Nguyen considered this, while his gaze roved the screen of his farsights. "Can't the LOVs themselves be infected with the bacterium?" he asked. "As . . . what is the word? . . . *symbionts*, that manufacture no-oct within the LOVs' shell?"

Virgil felt his awareness stumble. He grasped at the idea, recoiling from it at the same time. Under his breath he said, "Ky, that's a dangerous question."

Ky stiffened, his easy confidence suddenly gone. "We should take some time to discuss the distribution of food," he said in a voice that was a little too loud.

Virgil nodded, and the subject of no-oct was allowed to die, at least for that morning. The problem though, remained. By the next day, Virgil was convinced the only plausible solution was to culture crown gall tissue. "But I'll need a lab to do it."

Ky had set up a small camp beneath the banyan tree where they had met the day before. A tarpaulin sheltered a hammock and a tiny camp stove borrowed from one of the soldiers. Ky sat beside the stove, on a worn wooden chair that had probably been purchased from one of the farmers. He sipped at freshly brewed tea, while gazing at Virgil with a bemused expression. "Did I imagine our conversation yesterday? Virgil, there is no lab."

"But we could improvise," Virgil insisted. "Maybe the army could help? You could convince them, Ky. If they brought in a trailer, air-conditioned, that would do it. It would need to be air-conditioned. . . . But we could keep our equipment simple, a stove, trays, glass covers? Most of what we need could be bought from the farming families. Or scrounged from the medical tent . . ."

"Perhaps you could lay claim to an area within the medical tent?" Ky asked.

"No. It's not air-conditioned, and the cultures will spoil in the heat."

"Is there no chance it would work?"

Virgil thought about it. "There's a chance, I guess. But success isn't likely."

Ky nodded. "The army will certainly refuse to provide you an air-conditioned trailer."

"You think so?"

"I'm sure of it. Such a gift would only bring further sanctions on this country."

Virgil wrestled with his disappointment.

"There may be an alternative," Ky said. "Another UN scientist has arrived just this morning. I believe he is someone you know, a Dr. Nash Chou?"

"Nash is here?" Virgil felt a rush of joy. *Nash Chou!* It was as if a small window had opened onto his former life, a life that he had thought all gone.

"Your former coworker at EquaSys, correct?" Ky asked.

Virgil nodded. "My boss."

"He has come to study the LOVs. Perhaps you could visit him, and see what assistance he is willing to offer."

But Virgil's joy faded as he remembered the last time he'd seen Nash—that night in Honolulu when he had tried to remove the LOVs from Gabrielle's body, and his whole world had

come crashing down. "We didn't part on the best of terms. I . . .
I don't know if he'll talk to me."

"Try," Ky said. "Our alternatives are very few."

Virgil didn't dare to visit the UN compound himself. Though
they might wear no uniform, he was sure there would be
soldiers there who were not part of the Vietnamese army. So
Oanh went instead. She wore a wide, conical hat to hide her
LOVs, and displayed a charm that would have surprised Ela as
she invited Nash Chou to tour the reservation. Nash was delighted to accept. He waved off the offer of an escort from UN
security, and set off with Oanh, like a Boy Scout on an adventure, happy to leave the safety of the compound behind.

Virgil waited for him within a grove of mango trees, standing
silently among the mottled shadows while mosquitos buzzed
near his ears. At first Nash did not seem to know him. He
glanced at him and looked away, but then he looked again, a
puzzled expression on his round face. "Virgil? It *is* you."

"Hi, Nash."

Nash shook his head. Unspoken emotions glistened in his
eyes. "You heard that Panwar—?"

"I know."

Nash drew a deep breath. Perspiration glistened on his
flushed cheeks, and he seemed to be happy and sad at once. "I
shouldn't say this . . . but it's good to see you. I hoped I'd see
you."

"I heard the IBC gave you a bad time."

Nash shrugged. "I was your supervisor. They said I should
have known, and they were right."

Virgil shook his head. "There was no way you could have
known."

The color deepened in Nash's cheeks. His voice grew stern.
"Because you were too clever for me?"

"*No*. Because you were too honest even to imagine what we
were doing."

"Ah, yes. So you could safely display the LOVs before my
very eyes, knowing I would never guess. You must have thought
me a fool."

"That's not how we saw it."

This drew a bitter chuckle. "I told the IBC I was your supervisor in name only. A brief investigation convinced them it was true. The LOV project was yours, Virgil. *Your* responsibility. All of this"—he gestured at the surrounding land—"you let this happen. Did you ever once stop to think it could go this wrong?"

Virgil groped for words to counter Nash's anger. "The LOVs have a crazy momentum all their own. I'm learning that."

"But you regret it?" Nash pressed.

Virgil wasn't sure what he was getting at. "You mean the LOVs?"

"Of course I mean the LOVs! You smuggled them. That's how this started. You do regret it?"

Virgil didn't know how to answer.

"Damn it, Virgil! Are you so far gone? Panwar and Gabrielle—"

"I know what happened to them! Nash, I'm not crazy. I know what's happened to the people here, but what do you want me to do? I can't wind time back!"

"You could have the decency to show remorse!"

"I never wanted it to work out this way, all right?"

"But it has."

Virgil nodded, amazed still at the LOVs' survival.

"You'll never make it right," Nash said, "no matter what you do. But you have an obligation to at least begin to make amends."

Virgil drew back, suddenly wary. "What do you mean?"

"Turn yourself in."

"Nash—"

"Don't wait to be arrested!"

Virgil turned away, shaking his head. He had told Ky this conversation would do no good . . . and still he had to try. "Nash, the LOVs—"

Nash waved a dismissive hand. "They're doomed. You know it. I know it. When the no-oct is gone, they'll die."

Virgil felt sure he was doing more harm than good—but

hadn't he promised to try? "That's why you have to help us, Nash."

Nash looked puzzled. "Help you?"

Virgil gave a tentative nod. "We need no-oct."

"And you want me to get it for you?"

"No. I'm not asking that. But if you were to help us get just a few pieces of equipment—"

"No," Nash said firmly. "Not one thing." He turned away. Oanh had withdrawn to the edge of the grove. He saw her and set off as if to join her, but after a few steps he turned back. He was standing in deeper shadow now, and it was hard to see his expression. "Virgil. I meant what I said, about being glad to see you. But I am not on your side. I don't know how you engineered this sanctuary. That was a political miracle, but it won't last. It'll end the day the no-oct runs out—and I won't help you put off that time by even a minute."

CHAPTER 22

Crown gall had not been common in the region; a few days after the LOVs' release it could not be found at all as the *Roi Nuoc* scoured old fields and the weeds around them, harvesting every infected stem. There was competition among them to collect the galls, and it was not always friendly. The *Roi Nuoc* knew all about Epsilon-3. They saw the LOVs as seeds of similar organic computers, unprecedented thinking machines, and if they didn't know what use those machines might serve, they were all sure a use would be found. New globes hardly had a chance to grow before they were broken up again and scattered into even more waterways. Small partnerships formed among the *Roi Nuoc*, and each new site was jealously guarded.

That was trouble for Ela. Since the first day, she had made

it her task to record LOV development in fifty or so ponds and waterways that she could tour in a daily circuit. Virgil had promised to go with her, but he seldom did. All his time was spent in the makeshift lab he had put together in a corner of the medical tent, where he was struggling to culture crown gall tissue despite the terrible heat and humidity, the unsanitary conditions, and the open threats from the IBC. Success didn't seem likely, but even if he did coax his tissue cultures to grow, it was easy to see that his tiny operation would never produce enough tissue to support all the colonies that had been started within the boundaries of the reservation. There would be trouble when the no-oct tablets he had brought with him were finally gone. Most of the scattered colonies would die.

The *Roi Nuoc* cadres knew this, and it made them even more protective. At first they resented Ela trespassing in "their" waters, inspecting "their" LOVs. Her presence was tolerated only because Mother Tiger insisted, but as the days passed their trust began to grow. In time she came to be seen as an impartial arbiter in their disputes, a sheriff who could mediate their differences.

So it did not surprise her when, on the tenth day of the reservation, Oanh whispered into her dream, "Ela. An unmarked colony has been found close beside the border. Now there is argument over who should have it. Will you come?"

Ela opened her eyes to the green glow of her tent's nylon roof as it caught and augmented the faint dawnlight. She stretched in her blanket, lifting her head to see Oanh crouched just beyond the mesh door, silhouetted against a gray, cloud-draped sky. Misty rain softened the outlines of distant trees and the hard bar of the horizon. "An unmarked colony?" Ela muttered, wondering how a globe could have escaped attention for so long.

"Everyone is surprised. But it is very close to the border. Not many go there. Not even the government scientists."

Ela pushed her blanket aside. She slipped on her farsights and then her sandals. She brushed her hair. Then she grabbed a can of sweet coffee, one of a six-pack a soldier had given her, and followed Oanh out into the drizzle.

The new colony was in a narrow irrigation ditch lined with rotting brown grass. Ninh stood guard there, facing off two other *Roi Nuoc* known as Phan and Hoa, both of them familiar to Ela from her daily rounds. Like most of the *Roi Nuoc* on the reservation, they had adopted their own scattering of symbiotic LOVs across their foreheads. Ela felt their suspicion whisper through her every time her LOVs faced theirs.

Now though, she ignored the challenge in their stares as she crouched beside the ditch to peer into the murky water. To her surprise, she discovered there were *two* globes, both the delicate size of tangerines. They grew side by side, caught in the branches of a drowned shrub.

Ela had already watched hundreds of globes grow from marble-size masses to Ping-Pong balls to oranges in less than a week. So judging by their size, she estimated these twin colonies to be at least five days old.

Who had been here five days ago to seed them?

She asked Ninh. He only shrugged.

Ela trailed her fingers in the silky current. Then she stood, following the ditch for several hundred feet until she could see ahead to where it joined a larger canal just outside the reservation. There were no other LOV colonies in the little waterway. So where had this wild pair come from? Her thoughts returned to that frantic first night. Someone might have splashed across the canal and unknowingly washed a LOV or two into the water. It was possible.

She squinted against gray veils of softly falling rain, thinking about Mother Tiger's map of the LOV colonies. None had been recorded upstream of this site . . . so there should not be any no-oct in the water. But how could the twin colonies have survived without a supply of no-oct?

Her heart answered, thumping, thumping, as she circled round the question. Maybe the twin colonies didn't need no-oct . . . or maybe their LOVs had learned to manufacture it on their own. Either way, the result was the same: These LOVs were self-sufficient.

She turned, intending to start back. But she was stopped cold by the sight of a peeper ball floating less than an arm's length away. Her breath caught. She watched, beguiled, as droplets of rainwater slid frictionless from its silver surface. Oanh and Ninh, Phan and Hoa, were distant shadows, barely visible in the rain.

Across the irrigation ditch something rustled in the brush. Ela's heart crawled up her throat. This place was very close to the border. How close?

"Leave," Mother Tiger whispered.

Yes.

She turned. Across the ditch, brush crackled and popped. Three huge figures in fatigues loomed in the gray light, expanding horribly in size as they hurtled across the water. Ela took off, a frightened mouse sprinting back toward Ninh and Oanh. *"I-B-C!"* she screamed, her voice high, and frantic. "Run! Run!"

They did not. They charged toward her instead.

Ela felt something strike her shoulder. She lost her balance, spinning half-around as she slid in the mud and just like that her arms were pinned behind her. She felt the heat, the mass, the breath of an IBC cop as he crushed her wrists in a stunning grip. "Don't fight," he growled in her ear. "It will only hurt more."

"You can't be here!" she squeaked. "You're forbidden to be here."

"Let's go."

"No."

He lifted her half off her feet. The pain in her arms was excruciating.

"Stop it!" Oanh screamed. "Let her go!" Ela watched her dancing like a frantic child, back and forth along an invisible line, not daring to approach any closer though the desire shimmered in her dark eyes. "You must let her go! This is trespass." Ninh stood a step behind her, uncertainty shadowing his smooth face.

The IBC cop ignored them both. He wrested Ela around, shoving her past his two partners, faceless behind silvered farsights as they sighted down their rifles at Oanh and Ninh while Ela was forced back along the irrigation ditch, back toward the canal. A few steps more and she would be outside the protection of the reservation. She would be in IBC jurisdiction and they would be free to arrest her. She tried to dig her heels into the grass, but her captor only tightened his grip until her arms felt as if they were being wrenched from their sockets. She screamed faintly. Her knees gave way. The sudden shift in her weight unbalanced him and they went down together in the wet grass.

He swore a brutal oath.

"Stay down," Mother Tiger whispered, but Ela was not given a choice. Without shifting his grip, the IBC cop hauled her back to her feet. She gasped: a shard of sound that cut her lungs.

Then a woman spoke from somewhere just ahead, her cultured voice low and angry. Mother Tiger translated from Vietnamese: *"Release her. Now. You are in violation of international treaty. This action has been recorded and a complaint has been filed with the UN mediator. Release her! Or face immediate arrest yourself."*

Ela turned her head, searching for the source of the voice.

Three government soldiers stood several meters away, their rifles poised at their shoulders as they glared down the sights at the IBC cops. *"Let her go,"* the officer repeated.

To Ela's dismay, the cop's grip tightened. "This reservation exists to protect LOVs, not criminals!" he shouted. "This woman is a known fugitive."

The young officer was not swayed. "You have no jurisdiction here. Let her go."

Ela could feel the determination in his grip. He would not give in. She knew it. Then faintly, another voice spoke, a tiny voice leaking from his farsights. Orders? The cop swore—and released her.

Ela collapsed, falling forward into the trampled grass. She watched his boots pass, and then his partners'. Oanh was with her after that, rubbing her arms, helping her to sit up, while the shadowy figures of the IBC cops disappeared back across the canal.

The young Vietnamese officer approached. "You should not come so close to the border, Ms. Suvanatat," she advised. "You will only tempt them."

"I won't do it again," Ela whispered. Then she turned to

Oanh. In a voice barely audible she said, "The two LOV colonies. They have survived without no-oct."

Oanh's eyes widened.

"Divide them," Ela said. "Spread them to all the ponds."

"Is that wise?"

Ela hesitated. Without the restraint of no-oct, what would limit the growth of the LOVs? "I don't know. But the crown galls are gone, the supplements are gone, and Virgil's tissue cultures won't ever be enough. Will we let the colonies die?"

Oanh stared into the sluggish water of the canal. Seeing what? Possibilities, perhaps. Or perils. Then she turned to look down the irrigation ditch, where Phan and Hoa were disappearing into the rain. "Those greedy criminals," Oanh whispered. "It is done."

The two stolen globes were torn to bits and scattered throughout the reservation. Phan collected food as payment for the new LOVs, and too many possessions to carry. Virgil had been working in the medical tent, unaware of the incident until it was over, but when Ela told him what had happened, he was furious. "*Ky!*" he hissed.

A link opened. Ky looked at him, a finger pressed against his lips. "Look up," he said.

Virgil did. Peeper balls hovered within the tent, spying on his activities and listening to his conversations past the soft susurration of the rain. So Virgil grabbed a poncho purchased from one of the soldiers and he went outside.

The patter of dripping water was everywhere. "Ky," he said, mouthing the words, knowing Mother Tiger would enhance them. "You can't allow this. If the LOV colonies learn to synthesize no-oct, the whole situation will change."

"How can I stop it?" Ky whispered. "You want to believe I command the *Roi Nuoc*, but it isn't so."

"But Mother Tiger—"

"The ROSA serves the *Roi Nuoc*, not me."

"Ky, you don't understand. With no nutritional trump card to stop them, the LOVs will be infinitely more dangerous."

"I understand this perfectly, but what else can we do? Are your tissue cultures succeeding?"

Virgil swore softly. Ky knew the first round of cultures had succumbed to a fungal infection. "I'm starting over."

"Good. Your efforts will at least distract the authorities."

"Ky, don't make jokes. This is a disaster."

"I am not joking. This may be our only chance to continue. So say nothing, Virgil, and keep working. Let us wait and see."

Virgil's second round of tissue cultures failed even more quickly than the first, and though the no-oct tablets were carefully rationed, the day soon came when the last of them went into the water. Several of the UN officials came along to witness the event, including Nash Chou. Virgil watched the no-oct powder disappear beneath the dark surface of a shrimp pond, feeling as if another door was closing.

The mood was brighter among the watching officials. They murmured congratulations to one another, and many shook hands. Nash gave Virgil's shoulder a friendly squeeze. "It's over now, son." Nash had a naturally warm disposition, and his anger with Virgil had been fading along with the stock of no-oct. "This has been an unprecedented opportunity for us to study the development of an artificial life-form. I think we can be grateful for that. It's something positive, at least, to take away from this disaster."

Virgil knew he was saying these things only because he expected the LOVs to soon die out. Like the other officials who roamed the reservation, Nash wanted to explore the frontiers of cognition, but he wanted his discoveries to come with limits. With safety rails.

Nash looked on the pond with a satisfied smile. "Now we wait for the end. How long do you think it will take?"

Vigil shrugged.

Nash hardly noticed, happy to answer his own question. "Two to three days, at the outside. That's my guess. You need to start assessing your options, Virgil. This legal bubble you've built around yourself won't last a minute once the LOVs are gone."

Virgil promised to look into his legal status, but who could say what that might be?

The UN negotiations had produced no results. They had been cordial but pointless, perhaps because all sides had silently agreed to wait: When the LOVs went extinct, there would be nothing left to argue.

A day passed, and then another. When trouble came, it was from an unexpected direction.

For the first two weeks of the embargo food had been plentiful. Local farmers had happily traded rice, fruit, and catfish from their ponds in exchange for labor from the *Roi Nuoc*. They saw their homes reroofed, their private roads scraped smooth, their orchards harvested and pruned, and new ponds dug almost for free. But as the days passed, and the farmers still were not allowed to sell their produce outside the reservation, the good feelings waned. They recalled their prejudices, and remembered their fear of the *Roi Nuoc* and refused to employ them anymore.

So the *Roi Nuoc* changed strategy.

Overnight, the banks of the ponds were planted with sweet potatoes. Vegetables sprouted along roadways. Tiny ponds were dug in strips of boundary land that had no real use, and catfish fry appeared in them, along with the ubiquitous LOVs. The farmers reacted in anger to this assault on their land and property rights, sending their wives and children out to fill in the squatters' ponds while letting their pigs graze on the roadside gardens.

The *Roi Nuoc* made no move to stop them. It was not their way to fight. But under cover of night much of the work they had done was undone. Recently repaired roofs were damaged. New ponds were filled with silt. Seedlings in the rice paddies reappeared in the nursery beds.

It fell to the government soldiers to keep the peace. Nguyen was hauled before the regional commander, where he spread his hands in a helpless gesture. "We are not allowed to import food. What can you expect? The *Roi Nuoc* will not agree to starve."

"They can leave. We are now prepared to offer a general amnesty if they will submit to an inspection and the removal of all symbiotic LOVs."

"They will not leave," Nguyen said. "And they will not give up their LOVs. They know where their future lies. Of all humans, they will have the best chance of staying competitive with machines. So let us bring in food, now, before the sight of starving children proves an international embarrassment."

The commander insisted he did not have that authority, but he was a practical man. All the scientists assured him the LOVs would survive at most for another day or two. He told himself that when the LOVs were gone the *Roi Nuoc* would go too. He had only to keep the peace in the meantime. So he quietly ordered that his soldiers should begin receiving double rations at every meal, with the extra food always sliding somehow into the hands of the *Roi Nuoc*.

The compromise pleased no one. The *Roi Nuoc* had never before depended on handouts, and the farmers still felt threatened. After all, these were not mere homeless children squatting on their land. Whispered rumor claimed the most outlandish things: that the *Roi Nuoc* were human mimics, and not true humans at all. That they had no parents—had *never* had parents. That they were ghosts seeping out of a dreadful future, an alien threat in human form, come to steal the world away from true human hands.

In daylight these speculations seemed absurd, but when dusk fell, the world changed. With the coming of darkness the bizarre blue-green spheres could be seen glowing in a hundred different waterways, ghost lights, ethereal beacons with some undiscovered power. The same blue-green light gleamed in sparks upon the brows of the *Roi Nuoc* who tended them with none of the caprice, or the natural volatility, of human children.

Ela had waited for evening before visiting the last pond on her daily round. She approached cautiously, pausing every few steps to listen in the direction of the farmhouse, a quarter mile away across the flat delta. Government soldiers had been here in the early afternoon to break up an altercation between the *Roi Nuoc* who claimed the LOVs in this pond, and the farmer who owned it . . . though "altercation" was the wrong word. The *Roi Nuoc* were not fighters. The three had defied Mother Tiger and refused to retreat when the farmer, backed by his two grown sons, had ordered them away. Two had been severely beaten; the third had suffered dog bites to the thigh and hands. All were in the medical tent now, and the pond looked deserted.

But as Ela crept toward the water's edge, a small figure emerged from a stand of banana trees. A little girl. At first Ela thought she might be one of the *Roi Nuoc*, but no. She wore no farsights, and when she saw Ela she darted away toward the farmhouse, screaming for her father to *Come! Hurry, come!*

Quickly Ela waded into the water, hoping to finish her inspection before the men could arrive. Yesterday there had been four large globes in this pond and at least two new marble-size spheres . . . solid proof that the talent for synthesizing no-oct had been successfully transferred, for the LOVs couldn't reproduce without it.

She jumped at a rustle in the grass behind her, turning to see Ninh on the bank. "You scared me!" she gasped. She had not seen him all day. "Where did you come from?"

He looked puzzled. "From our pond."

That was over a mile away. Mother Tiger must have anticipated trouble. "Come help me," she said, "and I'll finish sooner."

Ninh shook his head. "It's too late." He stood gazing at the farmhouse, where a yellow light gleamed in the window. "They're already coming. The old man with his two sons."

An inset of his point of view appeared on Ela's farsights, confirming it. One of the youths carried a long pole. She swore softly. Then she turned and scrambled for the shore. Her body was still sore from her encounter with the IBC cops; she had no desire for another confrontation. "Hurry, Ela," Ninh urged.

"We should move these globes!"

"Tonight," he agreed. "We'll come back."

She retreated up the bank just as the farmer reached the far side of the pond. He stood there with his two tall sons, his features erased by the fading light. His voice crossed the water, sharp and confrontational. Mother Tiger translated: *"He says to go away. Don't interfere. The ponds must be cleaned."*

Ela understood then the purpose of the "pole" that one son

carried. It was really the long twin handles of a rolled up net, of a variety used to seine the ponds and gather the shrimp . . . but the shrimp in this pond were not ready to harvest. "Where are the soldiers?" she whispered.

Ninh shook his head. "They are here to keep the foreigners out, not to fight our own people."

"Not to protect the LOVs?"

He didn't answer. Across the pond the two young men unrolled their net. The mesh was too large to catch shrimp.

"Go away!" the farmer shouted, gesturing at them as if he were casting a spell that would make them magically disappear. They didn't move. So he turned to his sons instead and shouted at them to get to work. His tone brought looks of resentment to their faces, but they obeyed, stretching the net to its full length as they took up posts on either side of the pond. They slid the net into the water, stirring up a storm of panicked shrimp that boiled through the mesh.

The globes were clustered at the pond's center. Ela trembled as the net drew near. Ninh touched her arm. He meant it as a calming gesture, Ela knew that, but it ignited her anger instead. "*Stop it!*" she shouted. She shrugged off his hand and ran, sprinting around the spongy border of the pond to confront the closest boy. "Stop it!" she cried again, seizing the net's wooden handle and trying to wrest it from his grip. On his wide, round face she saw a look of goofy surprise. Then mud splashed past her face and somehow she was on the ground, looking up at him, with a burning pain in her belly and no air in her lungs until something loosened and air rushed back into her chest with a noisy gasp.

Hands grasped at her, picking her up out of the mud. She twisted around to see Ninh. "We have to stop them," she whispered, her voice high, tinkling with the sparsity of air. "They'll destroy the globes."

Ninh shook his head. "The *Roi Nuoc* do not fight. Come away. It's their pond."

She turned back to look. A gleam had appeared against the net, a large, luminous globe, rising to the surface under the forward pressure of the mesh. It bobbed like a float, half in the air.

But as she watched it sank again, *through* the net. Slowly. Slowly dropping through the mesh, *without breaking*, emerging whole on the other side. Ela's eyes widened. She clung to Ninh's arm. Surely this was some kind of illusion? The solid globe could not pass through an unbroken net . . . yet it had.

The two youths saw it too and froze, staring with waxy faces at the blue-green globe, drifting now behind the net, just beneath the water's surface. A second globe could be seen against the mesh. As they watched, it too slid through, as if the net had become immaterial. Or as if the globe itself were a ghost.

One of the youths murmured. Mother Tiger translated: "He says it is a *Roi Nuoc* demon."

Ela wondered if he might be right.

The two boys lifted the net out of the water. They rolled it up and laid it on the ground beside the pond. Then they ran for home.

Their bullying father had already disappeared.

CHAPTER 23

Everyone had gone away. Virgil listened for the voices of the *Roi Nuoc* as he wandered beneath an evening sky of softly polished steel, but the only sounds he heard were the static of the rain and the rhythmic peeping of some unseen insect, slowly fading.

He stood now on the collapsing ground between two newly planted rice paddies. The dark water at his feet was lit from below by the eerie glow of LOV colonies, their images blurred and fragmented beneath the rain-peppered surface so that they looked like human faces sleeping in the mud. Virgil stepped carefully down.

The water was only calf-deep. He waded between the wispy rice seedlings until he reached the first globe. He stooped to look at it, and found himself gazing at a mask of LOVs in the shape of a woman's face. "Gabrielle?" he whispered. Her eyes opened underwater, and LOVs gleamed there too.

Virgil reached for her, drawing her up to the surface. Mud clung to her hair and to her naked body, but everywhere among the filth, scattered LOVs were gleaming. "Why are you here?" he asked as he cradled her at the water's surface. "How can you be here?"

She blinked her eyes. She opened her mouth to speak and words came faintly; he leaned close to hear as she breathed them in his ear. *"Come down with me. Come. Cross over."*

He held her more closely still. "You learned something from E-3, didn't you? Gabrielle? What did you learn?"

"To give in." She reached up to touch his cheek, and her hand was gloved in tiny, blue-green diamonds, glinting, glimmering. Crawling. Instantly flowing over his face in gooey streams.

He could feel diamonds tumbling and scraping within the currents of his blood, murmuring his name as if it were a question.

Virgil? Virgil?

They spoke with Ela's voice.

What's wrong with you? Look at me! Virgil!

"Ela?" He looked around, but he could not see Ela anywhere, and when he turned back, Gabrielle was gone. It was only a typical LOV colony that he held in his hands. He released it into the water.

A hand touched his shoulder. "Virgil!" Ela's voice again. She was angry now. "Virgil, look at me! What are you on?"

He still could not see her, but he felt her cool knuckles brush his temples, and then the world peeled away, exposing another world behind it. A world in which Ela existed. She crouched beside him as he sat in a chair at a desk in the tiny treatment room of the medical tent. She had his farsights in her hand. "What are you on?" she asked again, holding the farsights up to squint at the image on-screen. "Is this a game?"

"I don't know. Let me—"

He reached for the farsights, but she spun half-away, keeping them outside his grasp. "No. You talk to me first."

"Ela—"

"Virgil, no one has seen you for hours. You weren't accepting any links or responding to any messages."

He touched the LOVs on his forehead. There were more now than the original thirty-six. He had taken octopine, and they were reproducing. "I asked my ROSA for a privacy screen. I was thinking."

"You were in a trance."

Virgil couldn't deny it. The experience had seemed as real as this room in the medical tent. Did another reality lie behind this one? And another after that? He said, "I was thinking about Gabrielle." Ela nodded, concern in her dark eyes. "We used to sit in a cognitive circle," Virgil explained, "Gabrielle, Panwar, and me. Our LOVs would signal each other across the circle, enhancing our emotions. We didn't share thoughts, except the way they're shared in speech, but we did share mood. I could feel Gabrielle's jealousy. I could feel Panwar's. They each wanted to be the first to get inside the thoughts of the LOVs, to understand an artificial mind. Gabrielle died for that."

Ela looked uncertain as she crouched beside him, still holding on to his farsights. "You're alone here," she pointed out. "Not part of a cognitive circle."

His gaze rested on the farsights in her hand. "I'm not alone. I've been working with my ROSA, on the language problem."

"Your ROSA is part of a cognitive circle?"

The question startled him. "Do you think it could be? The LOV's use a code that runs too fast for our sense to perceive, but not—"

"Not too fast for the ROSAs!" Her dark eyes grew wide. He could see the idea was new to her too. She cocked her head. "Has your ROSA learned the language of your LOVs?"

He thought about the visual metaphor he had just experienced. It had felt *real*. Utterly real, as if his mind, and not just his eyes, were being deceived. Had it been a collusion between his ROSA and his embedded LOVs? One working visually, the other through emotion? To what end? He shook his head, feeling as if he were running, sprinting all out just to keep up with this thing they had invented. "If that was a language, it hasn't evolved as far as words. It was all metaphor . . . founded on emotion . . . I wonder . . ."

"What?" she asked. "What are you thinking?"

"What is language?"

She smiled, rising at last from her crouch. "The way we talk to one another—and you're talking very strangely. Let's go outside. Let's take a walk, get some fresh air."

"I'm not crazy."

"I didn't—"

"I just want to think about this for a minute. The LOVs really are so profoundly different from any familiar paradigm. Each one a tiny, independent mind. You knew that, right?"

She nodded.

"A single LOV can function on its own."

"It won't be alone for long," she pointed out. "It will reproduce."

"Yes. And a million LOVs can snap together like a set of LEGOS and think as a group. Or they can set up modules within the group to handle different kinds of thinking, in a way that parallels the functioning of our own brains. Except LOV modules can be pulled apart and employed in other ways if the need arises. We can't do that. So really, there has never been anything like this before, and—"

"You're worried we will never understand what they are thinking."

He nodded. "Language has to reflect the platform it runs on, don't you think? It's possible we're just wired wrong, so that all we'll ever grasp of the language the LOVs use between themselves is this emotional link." He touched his forehead. "Where is the symbolic component of this language?"

"It's too early to say."

She was right, of course. He reached up to touch the smooth skin of her cheek. She didn't pull away. That surprised him. Judging by the puzzled look in her eyes, it surprised her too. "Are you all right?" she asked softly.

"I'm being strange, aren't I?"

"I already said that."

He laughed. The patch of LOVs on her temple glinted and glimmered like a third eye set off to one side of her graceful brow. Flecks of gray no-oct paste speckled the cinnamon skin around it. "Imagine," he said, "that you could listen to alien music, and that your brain interpreted it as a sad cacophony. But if an alien listened to it, it would receive explicit instructions for engineering a washing machine. You see? We might think we've glimpsed meaning in their language, while really, the only meaning we've grasped is what we invent."

"And you think the LOVs language might be like that?"

"Could we ever know?" He touched his own embedded LOVs. He brushed his hair back, exposing them fully. "Think with me."

Instantly, she pulled away. Her head turned, while her hand rose to hide her third eye. *"No."*

He endured a flood of confusion, of loss. It was a feeling she seemed to share, for she blinked at him in wide-eyed pain. "You were *already* thinking with me," he accused.

Her fist struck the desk. "You knew it was happening!"

Her anger fed his. "I should have known."

"You knew before!"

She had forgotten his farsights. He saw his chance, and snatched them from her fingers, sliding them on before she could grab them back. The screen was in default mode, its display transparent. "What are you afraid of?" he demanded. "You already made them part of you."

She would not face him. "I did not come to play games with you!"

"Why then?"

"I wanted to tell you, I found a new mutation."

It was already dusk when, with a skewed sense of déjà vu, Virgil followed Ela into the cool water of an abandoned pond. He peered beneath the dark surface, but he did not see Gabrielle.

"The family who owned this farm left one week ago," Ela told him. "A lot of families are leaving. They hear about the globe that slipped like a ghost through the mesh of a fishing net, and they are afraid. Nothing more has happened, but it is seen as a sign of terrible things to come. I'm sorry for it, though it makes life easier for us."

After the family left, the shrimp had been harvested and eaten by the *Roi Nuoc.*

Ela settled into the water, submerging to her chin so she could reach deep to fetch a globe up from the murk. Virgil stood beside her. He had taken off his shirt, so the water lapped at his bare belly, just above the waistband of his shorts. He leaned forward, watching the scintillating globe grow brighter as it neared the surface, half expecting to see a face coalesce out of the glow. He was surprised instead by a sense of discovery. It swept over him: the sudden recognition of another. "Can you feel that?" he asked Ela.

"I . . . can feel something. Like friendliness. As if it knows me, and is pleased I'm here."

"You see it every day, don't you?" he asked.

"I saw it only an hour ago."

"Then it can tell the difference between us—or at least between our LOVs." But what could it know of itself? What could it know of the world?

"Look at it closely," Ela urged. "It's one of nine globes in this pond."

"Nine?"

"This is a very prolific pond."

Virgil slid deeper into the water, so that it lapped at his shoulders as he crouched facing Ela. He took the globe from her hands, then frowned. It felt different from other globes he'd handled. Slippery? *Loose.* As if its surface was sloughing off in a tough, dense layer. He rubbed his thumbs over it in a gentle, circular motion. The loose layer moved like skin sliding over bone. Ideas began to germinate in his mind.

He looked up to find Ela watching him with raised eyebrows and a teasing grin. "You see what I mean?" she asked as she huddled in the dark water. "It has grown a veil."

"A veil? Yes. That's the right word."

The globe was veiled in a membrane of LOVs different from any LOVs Virgil had seen before. They were larger, and their light was more intense.

Ela said, "All the globes in this pond have veils—and I think I know what it's for."

Virgil took a moment to think this over. "By saying 'what it's for' you're implying it didn't get that way by chance."

"I don't think the *Hammer*'s LOVs moved onto the fiber-optic lines by chance." Her LOVs sparkled as she spoke, their light reflecting in her eyes. It made her look beautiful and mysterious, as her breath rippled the water's perfect skin. He held her gaze—too long, evidently, for her expression cooled. She turned her head away so that he could not see her LOVs.

But in the deepening twilight, blue light shone up from the water. He turned again to the globe in his hands, trying to recapture his train of thought. "You're right, of course," he said. "The LOVs *must* have some degree of control over the structure, the organization of the next generation."

"And some kind of consciousness," Ela added stiffly, "to design what they need."

He examined the globe, pinching at the dense membrane, lifting it away from the hidden inner surface. "It does start to look that way. So . . . what do you think the membrane's for?"

"Privacy."

A smile touched his lips. That had been his thought too.

Ela's voice remained cool, clinical. "There are nine globes in this pond. A veil would prevent the signals of one globe from interfering with the cognition of another."

"Yes. I think that's right. The size of each colony is limited, because if they grow too big, they lose coherence. So it's plausible that two adjacent colonies would interfere with each other. It would make sense to isolate the cognitive part of the globe."

"So if the cognitive part is isolated by the veil . . ." She nodded at the sparkling membrane. "Then what purpose is served by the activity in the veil itself?"

Virgil crouched in the water, speaking slowly to contain his excitement. "Think about this: If the veil can be seen by other colonies, and it, in turn, can perceive their veils—"

"Then it could be a language organ." She nodded, her gaze focused inward. "That's what you're thinking. An organ to translate the cognition of nearby colonies."

"Maybe."

"Maybe," she agreed.

Then he heard himself asking, "Why were you angry with me just now?"

She drew back, rising in the water so that her breasts emerged, draped in the slick wet fabric of her long-sleeved T-shirt. "What are you talking about? I wasn't—" She stopped the lie. Perhaps she'd felt his disbelief. "It's not really anger. It's the way I am."

Why? he wondered, though he didn't ask. Not in words. Did she feel the weight of his question just the same?

He looked again at the globe. "Can you find another one?"

She sank back into the water, this time using her toes to boost a second globe from the bottom.

"Hold them close together," Virgil said. "Yes. Like that." He lowered his hand between the two, blocking their exchange of light. Meaning was made in the flickering of individual LOvs.

Ela asked, "Are you recording their reaction?"

"Yes. What am I looking for?"

She thought it over. "To see if they react . . . to see if they don't like an interruption."

"And to see if they both have similar reactions. Are they speaking the same language?"

"Could they have different languages?"

"People do." It was full dark, and the sky was studded with stars.

"Then there could be a different language for each globe?" Ela asked. "Or maybe a different language in each pond?"

Virgil shrugged. "We could encourage one language everywhere, if we spread these LOvs around."

Each LOv was a tiny mind, a minute computer, a *demon*— storing fragments of knowledge. If the LOvs were broken apart and moved, those fragments of knowledge might move with them. . . .

"Like the no-oct trait?" Ela whispered.

He nodded, wondering why he was making this suggestion. They should be isolating traits, not mixing them.

Ela looked amused at his hesitation. "Don't feel guilty like that. If we don't spread this trait, the *Roi Nuoc* will."

Even as she spoke, a figure moved on the bank: a preteen boy, one of the kids who watched over this pond. His brow glimmered with LOVs. Virgil faced away from the anonymous child. "I don't want these globes torn to pieces," he whispered.

"There are nine."

"Sacrifice one, then."

"It's not up to me."

Virgil sighed. It was up to the *Roi Nuoc*, of course, but surely they would see the need? They were growing more focused, more resourceful with every hour. Under the tutelage of Mother Tiger their daily studies continued as before, but now, with the LOVs to adjust their mood, tempers were better, and fear was kept at bay, so that learning came faster, and insight blossomed.

He released the first globe, allowing it to sink back to the bottom. Ela let the second globe drop beside it. "Your ROSA is studying the LOV language, right?" she asked.

He nodded.

"Have you thought to leave your farsights here in the water? So it can observe these globes, and maybe, decode their language faster?"

Virgil stared at her, stunned by the suggestion. Not because it was a bad idea. It wasn't. He saw immediately that it might work. But . . . leave his farsights? The thought left him hollow. The Heroes were stolen, but they were his now. How was he supposed to get by without them? "I-it's a great idea, Ela. It really is. But I—"

He froze as Mother Tiger stirred, its powerful feline image like a silvery watermark rippling across the landscape. He watched the ROSA stretch and purr, conveying in its half-seen motion a sense of immense mass, immense span. *"Let this be done,"* it whispered.

Virgil heard this command and felt afraid. Mother Tiger did not behave as a ROSA was supposed to behave. A ROSA should not have the motivation to seize on original ideas all on its own.

It was not an entity to launch a plan of action and expect its human wards to follow. But somewhere in its complex architecture, spread over many servers, Mother Tiger had diverged from the ROSA norm.

As Virgil considered these things it also occurred to him that he had never heard anyone directly contradict Ky Xuan Nguyen's peculiar ROSA. Nevertheless: "I can't leave my farsights."

Ela touched his shoulder, a shy, fleeting moth-touch before her hand retreated. "It doesn't have to be *your* farsights," she said. "Farsights are only a window, an interface. It could be any farsights coded to let your ROSA look through."

"*Roi Nuoc* farsights," the boy on the bank suggested. He waded into the pond, meeting Ela halfway and handing her a Mystery brand.

Virgil took it from her. "I'll have to program it," he said. "Find out the codes, and then message Iris—"

Mother Tiger's purr sounded like a soft laughter. "Iris is part of me now. Access is already achieved."

CHAPTER 24

Virgil was wet, walking in the dark with his T-shirt wadded in his hand and mud squishing under his sandals. Not paying attention to much. Lost in thought? Summer watched the vid and wondered.

When Virgil noticed Nash standing motionless on the edge of the path to the medical tent, he flinched and drew back, a startled look on his face. His farsights cast a green gleam over his eyes. His embedded LOVs sparkled. "Nash?" he asked. "Is something wrong?"

Summer scowled. It was one of those questions guilty children ask: *Is something wrong?*

A mask of innocence.

When Nash spoke, his voice was soft and slow, freighted with anger. "How long have you known about the no-oct mutation?"

Virgil drifted back. Not far. Half a step. Framed in the green glow of his farsights, his eyes held steady. "A few days. No more."

"Did you engineer it?" Nash demanded.

"No. How could I? You've seen the medical tent, Nash. There's no equipment in there for bioengineering."

"Then someone did it for you."

Virgil shook his head. "I wish it were so." He didn't look frightened. He didn't look worried. Just . . . resigned. But resigned to what? Summer wondered. To the fact of this unpleasant confrontation? To the telling of lies? Or to being misunderstood? . . . "The truth, Nash, is that the LOVs are evolving just as they did on the *Hammer*—but this isn't evolution as we know it. There's some element of design involved. They're redesigning each new generation."

"You're saying they're out of control!"

"Yes. That's it. Exactly."

Summer tapped her fingers, sending the vid back to the beginning, that moment when Nash first sighted Virgil returning along the path. She watched it again. Nash watched it with her, through his own farsights, sixty-five hundred miles away. "Daniel predicted this," she said softly. It was night in the Mekong, but bright morning in Honolulu.

Nash said, "Tell that to Virgil. His attitude scares me more than any no-oct mutation. He's not afraid anymore. Not at all. Not of me. Not of the IBC. Not of what he's doing."

"It's fatalism. He doesn't believe he's doing anything now, except observing. He tells himself it's out of his hands."

"He's not trying to stop it though, is he?"

"No."

"His judgment is gone," Nash insisted. "It was corrupt from the beginning, but now it's gone. He refuses to see the danger in what he's doing."

Summer froze the video, capturing a still of Virgil's face: his

smooth skin, corded hair held back by a twist of wire. His in-
different eyes, calm among green shadows. Obsessed.

She said, "I've had a Lov-specific virus ready for two weeks
now."

This drew a grunt of surprise from Nash. "And your Nazi
hasn't gotten permission to deploy it?"

"Daniel's worried it won't be enough. That a few resistant
Lovs might survive. So I'm working on a second viral agent,
one with a different line of attack. He wants to release them
together."

"It's not a bad idea," Nash said grudgingly. "The odds of any
Lov being resistant to *both* weapons have got to be pretty low."

"The theory is good, I agree. . . ." Summer hesitated, choos-
ing her next words with care. She and Nash went back a long
way. They'd started together at EquaSys. She trusted him. She
needed to trust him. "Maybe Daniel's right. Maybe it would be
better to wait for another virus . . . but it worries me. I'm not
used to seeing this level of patience in him."

Nash reflected on this for several seconds. Then, "Has he got
his own agenda? Is that what you're thinking?"

Summer could hear the thready beat of her own heart. "It's
not that I'm accusing him of anything."

"No. Of course not."

Her voice grew whispery as she put her fear into words.
"But there *has* been a lot of interest in the Lovs, among some
very powerful people. The way they evolve, the way they
change . . . no one understands it. Not yet. But the implications
are extraordinary. If the *Hammer* mutants truly did evolve on
their own, then Virgil is right—the Lovs must have developed
a level of molecular control far beyond anything our technology
has ever achieved. Could we learn to imitate that kind of control? And if we could, how much would the resulting technology
be worth?"

Nash looked pale. The set of his face was grim. "It would be
bigger than anything that's come before."

Summer nodded. "I want you to know that I've had offers.
Seven-figure offers, just to slow down my research, just to put
off the day when the Lovs are brought down."

"My God."

The horror in his eyes was real, she was sure of it. "Nash? You understand the dynamics, don't you? The longer this goes on, the more we learn. The more we learn, the closer we are to reproducing whatever molecular tricks the LOVs have developed. That's nanotechnology, Nash. We're standing on the threshold."

There. She had said it. But now Nash was eyeing her warily. A guarded expression had slipped over his face. "Why are you telling *me* this?"

"Because I want it to end, now, before it goes any further. I resigned from EquaSys because I thought we had already gone too far. But what's happening in the Mekong makes our work back then look like child's play." She closed her eyes briefly, striving to calm the tremor building in her voice. "I can't say anything in public. If I do, I'll be off this project in a minute. I can't take that chance. I need to be here. I need to know that work is being done on counteragents. But the kind of money that's in play . . . Nash, it messes with people's minds—and it *always* finds a place to settle."

"So you want me to do something."

"Yes. I want you to use your influence. I want you to scare people. I want you to lobby for immediate action. Ninety nine point nine percent of the world will be behind you."

"Of course, the rest will see me as a target."

"It is dangerous."

He sighed. "But you're right. It's more dangerous to do nothing."

"You'll help, then?"

"Anyway I can. After all, this mess is my fault too."

CHAPTER 25

Now that the no-oct mutation is known, everything will change," Ky said. His gaze moved from Virgil, to Oanh, to Ninh, and finally to Ela.

Crowded together as they were in this dimly lit room of the medical tent, Ela felt a nervous thrill, imagining them to be a secret cell, a radical conspiracy out to overthrow the corrupt status quo. Except there was nothing secret about this meeting. Each one of them was wearing farsights and any *Roi Nuoc* inside or out of the reservation could be monitoring what they said.

"The affable Nash Chou," Ky continued, "has already presented the UN with strongly worded testimony calling for the IBC to act immediately and unilaterally to control the Lovs, and to control us—despite our government's sovereign claims." He shook his head. "We cannot expect Hanoi to resist such pressure for long. We are tolerated now because of nationalist sentiments and the promise of financial returns. But as pressure mounts, our support must crumble. We will be given up, turned over to our persecutors—unless we find stronger allies."

Virgil stirred, leaning over the examination bench so that the light from the fluorescent ceiling strips fell directly on his face. "I won't start a war over this, Ky. I won't make a deal with another government, or sell out to corporate pirates."

Ky was silent for a beat. Then, "I am so glad to hear it," he said. "Given that foreigners have attempted to trade away this nation so many times before."

Ela winced, while Virgil launched into a quick apology. "Ky, I didn't mean—"

Ky raised his hand. "I am teasing, my friend. Of course we must aim for some level of sovereignty—which is why I've prepared a petition for the United Nations, to be signed by all of the *Roi Nuoc*—"

"They're underage," Ela objected, eyeing Oanh, who fidgeted on the physician's stool.

"It doesn't matter. We can't allow it to matter. We must petition the UN to recognize the *Roi Nuoc* and their LOV symbionts as a distinct people. Recognition on this level will give us rights that even the IBC cannot overturn."

"It would legalize the LOVs," Virgil said. He sounded impressed. "At least, the symbiotic ones. But Ky, do you really think there's a chance it could work?"

"Oh, yes." Ky stood by the door, his fist on his chin and a faraway look in his eyes as if he were posed for a propaganda shot . . . and when Ela considered the farsights that she and Ninh and Oanh wore, she saw it was exactly that way.

Ky said, "Just think on the stew of greed, of pride, of indignation, and nationalism we might play to our favor. This is politics on a remote and not easily accountable scale. There are many reasons for votes to be cast that have nothing to do with the merits of the issue."

Ela could not share his optimism. "I don't think you're being realistic. The IBC would never allow it."

"But that's the beauty of it," Virgil said. "It won't be up to the IBC."

Ky nodded. "And if you still can't believe it, Ela, then let me believe it for you."

"You?" She could not suppress a laugh. "Ky, you don't even have LOVs."

She had not meant to be hurtful, so it surprised her when the warmth drained from his face, and the telltales of anger emerged: the faint tightening around the eyes, the suggestion of shadow between the brows. He said, "That's not important."

But wasn't it? All the *Roi Nuoc* had taken on their own constellations of symbiotic LOVs. Every one of them was irrevocably committed. Only Ky could still go back. She searched his face and found herself wondering what betrayal would look like.

"Sign the petition, Ela," he said. "I'll see to it after that."

She nodded. "I'll sign it. It could buy us some time, at least."

Virgil had experienced this exchange as if the emotions of Ela and Ky were being piped into his own head and replayed there with full fidelity. Afterward he walked outside with

Ky. It was night, and the stars were blurred points behind a thin veil of rain. Virgil did not ask questions. Not out loud.

Ky answered anyway, as rain-wet grass rustled against their ponchos. "We have been forced to trust one another on the thinnest of evidence."

"I don't suspect you," Virgil said.

"But like Ela, you wonder."

"So what if I do? The LOVs are not a rite of passage. You don't have to use them to prove your loyalty. Nobody is asking that." But even as Virgil said this, doubt stirred. All the *Roi Nuoc* had long since adopted symbiotic LOVs in patches or in constellations across their skin. Ky alone had not made that commitment.

Now Ky pulled back his hood, allowing the rain to fall in tiny droplets across his hair and his farsights—and his unilluminated brow. "There is no reason I should have to defend myself," he said softly. "I have given up everything for this venture. That should be proof enough of my loyalty."

Virgil waited.

"But it's not, is it?" Ky asked. "Not to Ela. Not even to me." He walked on and Virgil followed. "I stand on the border," he said, his farsights gleaming as he glanced at Virgil, then looked away. "But I do not step over. I encourage others to go . . . to embrace this new humanity, but I stay behind . . . *Dammit!* Will you say something?"

"What should I say?"

"What you already know—it amazes me how much all of you can read in a face, in a voice—you know the LOVs terrify me."

"They would terrify any rational person."

"Don't say that too loud." Then after a moment: "It makes my guts turn to water when I think about what we are doing. When I *really* think about it. We are creating a new kind of human, aren't we? And it's beautiful, but frightening too, like a birth . . . you enjoy letting me ramble, don't you?"

"Someday I'll learn to speak Vietnamese."

"Will you? That will be amusing." He bowed his head. He raised his hand to shade his farsights from the rain. It was a gesture powerfully reminiscent of Panwar. "I fear to lose myself."

"It's not like that," Virgil said past a throat suddenly dry. Would he be here at all if Panwar had lived?

Ky looked up, perhaps troubled by the change in Virgil's voice.

"It's an enhancement," Virgil said, aware of a trembling in his hands.

"Yes. That's why we are here, no? It's why I'm here. Because somehow we will need to become more than we are—or risk being left behind."

"That's what Panwar would have said."

"Your partner," Ky said thoughtfully. "He is dead now, yes?"

Virgil nodded. "Ky, you should not accept the LOVs if you're not ready."

"And duty be damned?" he asked. "That is a very modern thing to say."

"When you're ready," Virgil insisted. "Not before."

CHAPTER 26

On the day the last farming family left the reservation, Virgil climbed up to the cab roof of an army truck—the highest point around other than a distant line of gloomy casurina trees—and sat cross-legged on the gently curved composite shell, surveying the pancake-flat delta that surrounded him.

It was near noon, and each breath he took stewed in his lungs, a storm brewing. Heavy black clouds hid the sun but trapped the steamy heat. The landscape rolled away from him: green rice paddies and black ponds, their surfaces undisturbed by any breath of moving air. Detail dissolved in muted shadow.

Now and then he could see someone moving in the distance: a patrol of government soldiers strolling idly from pond to pond, or a small band of *Roi Nuoc* off to negotiate with their neighbors. Always far away. Insignificant as the figures in a Chinese landscape painting.

The farmers had been paid off, compensated for their hardship by EquaSys as part of a continuing settlement. By all reports it had been a good deal; they would not need to work quite so hard anymore, but were they happy, parted from their land?

The *Roi Nuoc* could not replace them. Ky's UN petition had made surprising progress on the assertion that the *Roi Nuoc* were "a distinct tribal entity," an evolving culture growing through rips in the social fabric—but the farmers *were* that fabric. They had built stable lives here and cultivated a sense of place.

The *Roi Nuoc* had no similar experience of permanence. They were like a flash of sunshine between rain showers: ephemeral, unstable. Incapable—or uninterested—in holding on to the civilization that had thrived here only a few weeks ago. The jungle was crawling back into that vacuum. Weeds were the vanguard, goaded by the long rains into luxuriant growth along dikes and levees and abandoned ponds, while the ghosts of ancient forests assembled in the mist.

The sound of footfalls in the mud startled Virgil from his ruminations. He turned to see Ky Xuan Nguyen approaching with a cheerful smile. "Hail the outpost!" Ky called. "How goes the kingdom?"

"It is without a king—but then they always were a pain in the ass."

"Anarchist."

Virgil smiled. "Kind of you to say so."

Ky stopped beside the truck, leaning an elbow against the hood as he regarded Virgil through the opaqued lens of his farsights. He was dressed in green fatigues and a black T-shirt, his coppery skin shining with the damp that was everywhere. His hair had grown longer. Trying not to be obvious, Virgil glanced between the strands that fell over Ky's brow, but he could still see no LOVs glittering there.

"Why are you up there?" Ky asked.

Peeper balls stood off at a distance, waiting for his reply.

Virgil looked away across the delta. There had been so much rain, and not just here. In the highlands too, in Laos, in Cambodia. The water was rising, as it did every year. "It's all going wild," he said. "Can you feel it? Something wild is crawling up out of the land."

Ky considered this for several seconds while a peeper ball crept unusually close. "Our sanctuary won't last with that kind of talk. Do you want our petition to fail?"

"But you can feel it, can't you? Change. Not just here. Not just with the LOVs. Do you think there are any other ROSAs like Mother Tiger?"

"You're in a strange mood."

Yes.

He handed down to Ky the artifact that had set him thinking. "One of the kids turned this in this morning."

It was a section of tube with a single joint at its center, fifteen inches long and the width of a pencil, bone white except for a faint shadowing of darker longitudinal veins, and a ring of sickly green around the knuckle. Ky held it at both ends and flexed it back and forth. "And what is this supposed to be?"

"It's a LOV cluster."

Ky's chuckle expressed a delighted skepticism. "What is it really? It's not bone."

"It *is* a LOV cluster," Virgil insisted. "Look at it under magnification."

Ky scowled, but he held the tube up close to his farsights, his shoulders hunched as he strained to remain absolutely still. "Most of the LOVs are dead," Virgil said. "That's why it looks white. But you can see the tube is made from LOV shells that have fused together like . . . like coral polyps."

"It's hard to hold steady." Ky shifted, resting his elbows against his sides. "They're smaller than ordinary LOVs, aren't they?"

"Yes."

"A new variety . . . it must be defective, to make such a malformed structure." He straightened up. Again he flexed the tube at its central joint. "Is it getting stiffer?"

"Yes. The LOVs that form the joint have no source of nutrients, so the more they are forced to move, the sooner they will die."

"They're still alive?"

"Yes, but just around the joint. I don't think they're defective, though. Just a different variety. Their limbs are structured differently. They're longer, and they're found only in a circle around the shell, instead of all over."

Ky's eyes narrowed as he considered this. "So they could only join in a plane? A plane a single layer deep. That's why they formed this tube instead of a globe . . . okay."

"The joint is an interesting structure," Virgil suggested. "Don't you think?"

Ky flexed it again. Then he scowled. When he looked up, his gaze was hard. "Did you design this?"

Virgil sighed. Was he going to be accused of a feat of engineering every time the LOVs learned something new? "I didn't have anything to do with it. It was found like that. I didn't design the mutant LOVs on the *Hammer*, I didn't design the no-oct mutation, I didn't design the veil, and I didn't design this."

"The LOVs designed it themselves?"

"I can't think of any other explanation."

"Why? What's it for?"

Virgil shrugged. "What are any of us for? I'm more interested in locating the colony that made it."

"That shouldn't be hard. The child who brought it to you must have said which pond it came from."

"It didn't come from a pond. It was found along a path, a hundred feet from any water. And none of the nearby ponds have colonies. I checked."

"Ah, so you're brooding over how it got on the path? That's easy. A dog carried it there. Or someone dropped it."

"No *Roi Nuoc* would have dropped it. You know how acquisitive they are. Any of them would have picked it up and reported it for the gain—just as it happened."

"A dog then."

"Pinch the end of the tube."

Ky did, not exerting much pressure. With a glasslike chime,

the tip of the cylinder shattered into dust. Ky swore, looking momentarily horrified, until he realized the damage was minimal. Most of the tube was still intact.

He glared up at Virgil. "You knew that would happen."

Virgil shrugged. "A dog would have shattered it. Even a gentle nick of the teeth—"

"*All right.*"

"I'd like to find the globe that produced it."

"Have the kids check the ponds, then."

"They haven't reported anything strange. Ela's reports don't show any hint either."

Ky turned away, his own gaze searching the green land that lay submissively waiting beneath the lowering clouds. "Have you considered the die-off?" he asked, looking over his shoulder at Virgil, his gaze strangely intense.

Virgil stiffened. Yesterday morning *Roi Nuoc* near the coast had reported disaster: all the globes within a cluster of interlinked ponds had gone missing. When Virgil examined the site, he found a thick layer of LOVs in the bottom of every pond, thriving just beneath the mud. It had looked as if the globes had dissolved, losing their cohesion, their organization. . . . But that theory was dashed when he checked an unaffected pond and found the same layer of unattached LOVs. Apparently every pond had them. So he was left without a theory to explain the missing globes.

Nash Chou had taken to calling it a die-off. Virgil didn't like the term; it made too many assumptions. But he couldn't deny the problem was serious. In the past twenty-four hours the disappearances had spread slowly outward, to encompass fourteen sites.

"The tube wasn't found anywhere near the site of the missing globes," he said.

Ky raised his eyebrows. "Apparently the tube wasn't found anywhere near anything."

Virgil shrugged. That was a fair description. He'd been to the place where the tube was found, and then he'd tramped around for an hour trying to figure out where it had come from.

"Show me the site," Ky suggested. "There might be some clue that you missed."

It started raining on the way. Ky produced from his pocket an object the size of a bar napkin, popping it open into a conical, broad-brimmed hat that kept the rain out of his face and off his farsights. Virgil envied him, plagued as he was by a constant storm of droplets running down his screen.

After a few minutes' walk, they came to a small pasture of lush, tangled grass. "We're close now," Virgil said. "It was somewhere in this field."

"I see," Ky answered in an amused voice, as Mother Tiger highlighted the exact spot in their farsights.

The path had been used several times since the find was made; whatever telltale tracks there might have been were long gone. But off to one side, on a berm half-reclaimed by pasture grass, rainwater had gathered in an interesting spattering of little holes, each one perfectly round, so that it looked like tiny coins had been dropped in the mud.

"I hadn't noticed that," Virgil admitted when Ky pointed it out. "It wasn't so obvious before the rain."

Ky pressed the end of the tube into a hole. "Perfect fit. Cribbage?"

Virgil slipped his little finger into another hole. It was less than a quarter inch deep. He explored several more. All were nearly the same depth, the same width. "Hey, what's this?" he asked. Instead of soft mud walls, he had found a peg hole lined with something sharp and brittle. He crooked his finger and carefully drew out a flat, muddy ring that transformed to bone white as the rain washed it clean.

"It's part of the tube," Ky said, lifting it off Virgil's finger. The size was right. He held it close to his farsights. "LOvs," he confirmed. "All dead shells." Experimenting, he poked the tube into the mud. It left a ring mark, not a pit. He looked at Virgil. "What do you think?"

"I don't know. The peg holes all seem to be concentrated in this one area, but take a step away from the path . . ." He did so. "And suddenly the grass is too thick to allow prints."

Ky ventured past him, studying the ground. "It's not all grass out here. Look." Apparently a cow or a water buffalo had been put to graze on this patch of grass. Ky pointed to a pile of dung, marked with two water-filled peg holes. "A child at play," he suggested.

"Do children play with dung?"

"You want a mystery."

"I've got one."

They crossed the pocket pasture without finding any other marks. Then Ky stooped, retrieving something from the ground and holding it up in triumph. "The end piece of the pipe," he announced.

That *was* what it looked like: a slip of pipe with one end bluntly tapered in a closed cap. Ky tried it against the longer section he held in his hand. The width was the same, but it did not match. "Curiouser and curiouser," he muttered.

By this time they had attracted the attention of several cadres of *Roi Nuoc* . . . or perhaps Mother Tiger had summoned them. Ky looked pleased to have the help. He organized them in a neat line and together they combed the ground, looking for more peg holes, or bits of broken pipe. But the search went all the way to the next rice paddy without finding anything more.

They huddled at the paddy's edge, enduring a rain that fell with the steadiness of a suburban hose as they tried to decide what to do next. "Either we go through the paddy," Ky said. "Or we go back and try the other side of the path."

Virgil was already cold and wet, his fatigues encrusted with mud. He had no desire to go wading into the paddy, but that wasn't a universal feeling. Two little girls had plaited a grass fishing line, baiting it with a crushed beetle. Now they were wading between the rows of rice, hunting for secretive crayfish. Virgil frowned at them. "I guess I'd rather go back—"

His offer of retreat was interrupted by a duo of sharp screams, followed instantly by hysterical giggles as the two girls stumbled backward out of the paddy. Virgil thought it must have been an awfully big crayfish to inspire that reaction, but then the girls' excitement spread to the kids who met them on the bank. Little screams and sharp, incredulous laughter marked their retreat as they scattered from the paddy.

Along with everyone else Virgil hurried over to see the cause of the excitement.

Staggering through the narrow lane between loose rows of early rice was a thing like a cartoon spider, or one of those deep-water arctic crabs. It had four spindly, bone white legs, each with a single limber joint bent in an upside-down V. A veiled globe of LOVs the size of a grapefruit was suspended in a glittering white cage between the legs . . . like the body of a daddy longlegs.

Except half its legs were missing.

It stood knee high.

Virgil watched, openmouthed, as it tottered out of the paddy. The kids scattered from its path with a chorus of delighted screams.

The globe was bright blue-green, glittering and alive. Green streaks like tributaries ran up from it, to touch the green-tinted joints. Rainwater struck it and sluiced away as the thing staggered, slipping in the mud, only to somehow gather its balance and push on. Apparently, it had started with more legs than it was currently using. Virgil could see two useless stumps sticking up in the air like short antennas. Even as if he watched, the tip broke from one of its remaining limbs. The bolder of the two little girls rushed in to pick it up.

Despite the injury, the creature continued across the pocket pasture, stumbling constantly, over tufts of grass, old branches, and dung piles. And still it recovered its balance every time, like a wounded soldier, struggling for dignity.

The kids followed it, and Virgil and Ky went with them.

The spider's progress across the pasture was slow, but once it reached the path its gait changed. It moved rapidly, scuttling through puddles of rainwater, looking always as if it were on the edge of toppling over yet never quite falling all the way. The kids followed in a raucous parade, with more *Roi Nuoc* joining at every turn until at last the path dipped down close to a shrimp pond.

The LOV spider staggered toward the water as if this had

been its goal all along. It plopped in, instantly disappearing beneath the rain-pocked surface.

"Well," Nguyen said, over the children's sudden silence. "That *is* interesting."

Virgil resisted the temptation to shove him into the pond.

The spider did not reappear again that day, but the next morning *three* spiders, with six legs each, scurried out of the pond. Dozens more had been seen at other sites across the reservation, and Virgil had a new theory to explain where the missing globes had gone.

CHAPTER 27

Late one night Virgil awoke to the sound of familiar voices engaged in loud argument. He had fallen asleep in an empty treatment room inside the medical tent. Now he lay in the dark, listening, as the UN physician, Dr. Morikawa, put on an indignant defense:

"Try to understand what I'm telling you, Nguyen. I don't have the medical supplies to treat her. This girl is already severely dehydrated. If her fever is not brought down, if her diarrhea isn't controlled—"

"She'll die!" Ky said. "I know it. That's why I brought her to you."

"I've already told you—"

"Supplies can be brought in!"

"Not according to authorities. She must be evacuated now. Tonight."

Virgil levered himself off the exam table where he'd been sleeping and stumbled to the curtained door. His sudden appearance brought a pause in the argument as both Ky and Dr. Morikawa turned defensive stares in his direction.

"Who is she?" Virgil blurted, irrationally afraid that it would be Ela. He lifted aside the curtain of the second treatment room to see a little girl lying on the cot. She was eight or nine years old at most. Her face had an unhealthy sheen, and she twitched in a restless sleep. LOvs glittered on her forehead.

Virgil let the curtain fall back into place and turned again to Dr. Morikawa. "She has LOvs. She can't be evacuated. You have to request supplies."

The doctor shook her head, anger drawn in tight furrows between her eyes. "Supplies will not be permitted. Do you think we haven't planned for this situation? It was only a matter of time before a case like this turned up. I'm surprised it took this long, given the foul conditions you subject these children to—"

"Conditions imposed on us by the treaty!" Ky interrupted.

"Politics are not my concern. Medical issues are. The guidelines for this situation require evacuation of the patient. Once she's in hospital, her LOvs will be removed."

Virgil stalked closer, certain he must have misheard. "You're planning to *remove* her LOvs?"

"We have to." Dr. Morikawa backed off a step, glancing nervously at Ky. "They're illegal outside the reservation."

"Yet you won't treat her inside?" He turned to Ky. "You see what they're doing? They know conditions will only get worse. They've designed this to be a war of attrition."

"Evidently," Ky said flatly. He turned to Dr. Morikawa. "Exactly *how* will you remove her LOvs?"

"A neurosurgeon has been retained. It shouldn't be hard. She hasn't had them long."

Virgil said, "It will be hard on her."

The physician turned to him with an angry glare. "Do you want her to die, Dr. Copeland?"

"Of course not!"

"There is no choice in the matter. She must be evacuated."

Ky lifted his chin, his smooth face falling into a masklike expression. "Where will she be taken?"

"I can't answer that. Security concerns, you understand."

"I want to be kept posted as to her condition."

"That may not be possible. Medical records are private, and she is not your daughter after all."

Ky's hands coiled into fists. It was the only sign that betrayed his fury. "We are a family," he said. "A . . . a *tribe*. Our petition for UN recognition claims rights of kinship—"

"The petition hasn't been granted yet," Dr. Morikawa interrupted icily. "Mr. Nguyen, you did the right thing in bringing her here. That's why I'm taking this time to talk to you. When another child falls ill—and it's inevitable, it *will* happen—I hope you make the same choice. I have my own fleet of peepers. I try to keep track of things, but it wouldn't be hard to discover an illness too late. You may see evacuation as an unpleasant outcome, but it is better—far better—than death."

Virgil listened to this speech, searching Dr. Morikawa's face for some hint of shame, but he found none. She believed every word she was saying. "This *is* a war of attrition," he said bitterly. "A siege. Sooner or later each of us is bound to succumb to something."

"If it's a siege, at least it's a humane one," Dr. Morikawa snapped, stepping toward the treatment room. She lifted aside the curtain. "Be grateful you won't have to face the tragedy of your own dead." Then she disappeared behind the cloth, putting an end to the debate.

"Don't lose heart," Ky said, placing an encouraging hand on Virgil's shoulder. "We only have to survive until our petition is granted. They know our urgency. It can't be long."

CHAPTER 28

Ela crouched beside a tiny farm road that linked two complexes of catfish ponds. It was past midnight, and the rain fell in a mild, yet relentless drizzle. No one stirred. No one human anyway.

Strips of half-drowned grass marked the dike tops dividing the rain-flooded ponds. Along these disappearing paths, at least a hundred glass spiders scurried in random bursts of motion, first in one direction, then another. *Like ants*, Ela thought, trading instructive scents. Or like puppies touching noses. Some had four jointed legs; some had six. A few had many more than that. In nightvision their legs were dull silver, while the living globes—nested inside a hanging cage suspended within the circle of their legs—blazed a brilliant white.

It looked like a Hollywood alien invasion.

The spiders had changed in the handful of days since Ky and Virgil discovered their existence. Their structural LOVs had developed thicker, stronger walls, and they were fused together in multiple layers, producing toughened legs and less breakage. Even more interesting, the LOV spiders had become skilled walkers. Stumbling was rare now, and none ever fell down.

They still did not seem to have much of a visual sense. The central globe could detect minute shifts in light—that was how they communicated—but it seemed doubtful they could assemble light into coherent images. When traversing an unfamiliar trail they appeared to feel their way using one front limb. Ela suspected they could trace scent trails too, and of course they could trade information with one another, perhaps creating a mental map of neighborhoods they had never actually visited.

She turned to look in the other direction, where she could just see the second pond complex. It was smaller, and there were fewer glass spiders in sight—perhaps half as many—most of them still moving sluggishly out of ponds peppered with rain.

One of the soldiers had given Ela a rain poncho. She huddled inside it, listening to the patter of drops and waiting. Gradually, the activity she had observed over the last two nights began once again as a lone spider ventured out of the larger pond complex. It tapped at the slick mud of the tiny farm road. Then it edged forward on four legs, before pausing to tap again. Ela waited, motionless, as it drew near. It paused again when it was just a few inches away. Its front leg reached out, gently tapping her knee. She shifted, lifting away the hood of her poncho, exposing the arc of LOVs that gleamed along her hairline.

The glass spider froze with its probing limb half-raised. Ela felt a sense of recognition wash over her and she wondered if this spider might carry one of the original globes she had tended in the ponds. What a lucky break that would be, if it was already familiar with her!

She touched her forehead, hoping her desire for communication could be read in the pattern flashed by her gleaming LOVs. An answer was immediately returned as her mind flooded with an alien echo of her desire. *"Talk to it!"* she whispered, eyeing Mother Tiger's watermark outline crouched in the corner of her screen. The tiger shape was all but invisible to the casual glance; only the tip of its twitching tail caught the eye. Now the cat stood, gaining solidity as it lifted itself from the background. "As we have planned," Mother Tiger purred.

A band of blue-green expanded over Ela's farsights, blocking her vision, while immersing her in a sensorium of LOVs. This was Mother Tiger's voice, translated to the optical spectrum. The ROSA had swallowed everything Virgil could teach it of LOV language in only a few hours. Then it had leaped ahead with its studies, feeding on data gathered from the ponds.

It was hard to know how much it understood. Direct translation was still not possible, and Mother Tiger had suggested it might never be, because LOVs did not communicate in words, or link naturally into grammar modules. It was true E-3 had spoken, but E-3 had been artificially schooled and provided with an electronic speech synthesizer. In these flooding delta ponds a different style of communication had developed that had little in common with human language. Tonight would test whether Mother Tiger had truly gained an understanding of it.

Ela breathed softly, shivering a bit in the rain. Her LOVs flashed, communicating unknowable complexes of information to the intelligence embodied in the LOV globe, nestled before her within its carriage of spider legs. Through Ela's farsights Mother Tiger flashed still another LOV pattern. *While I—this self-aware human I—speak and listen to Mother Tiger.*

It was a cognitive circle. Ela's breath caught as she realized this. A cognitive circle made of herself, the ROSA, and the shimmering globe.

Gabrielle had died in a cognitive circle.

"But I am not Gabrielle." She spoke the words aloud, like a prayer. "I am not Gabrielle."

She had come here to relay a very specific idea; she would not allow herself to be trapped in an open-ended conversation.

Drawing a deep breath, she pushed her fear aside.

The blue-green light of her farsights was all she could see now. It flowed over her, enfolded her, and for a long time she perceived it only as raw sensation, inducing a hypnotic state for her mind to play against, but then gradually, gradually, meaning seeped from the color. New memories condensed out of the chaos of light. She felt—or had she known it before?—the glass spider was only a *mechanism*. A tool made by the cognizant globe, grown from special structural LOVs that fused to form these legs and then died—like coral polyps blending to build a reef. Being mechanical components, they no longer required nutritional support.

Only the joints were alive.

She grew aware of the pulse of fluids pumped through tiny tubes (formed of yet a different kind of structural LOV) delivered to the living LOVs that formed the joints. It was a crude, inefficient system. Already the globe was drying up as its scant store of nutrients ran out. Within minutes this spider would need to return to a pond and refresh itself with dissolved organic matter.

Ela knew these things. They were facts, formed in her mind from the neural connection of her implanted LOVs, and the whispering voice of Mother Tiger. They became her own experience.

What she communicated in return she could not say, or how many seconds passed before Mother Tiger opened the question that had inspired Ela to undertake this cognitive circle: *Since structural LOVs can be used to build limbs, might they be arranged as other structures too?* She strove to visualize what she desired, while Mother Tiger conversed in unknowable detail.

Time passed, and the language evolved. Mother Tiger's clumsy first efforts grew more refined while Ela felt her own mind adapting, so that she no longer distinguished between the sensations of her swarming thoughts and the ROSA's hypnotic murmur.

It was an hour past midnight when the display on Virgil's farsights froze.

He lay on a cot, in the treatment room of the medical tent that had somehow become his residence, studying Mother Tiger's evolving map of LOV development. The three-dimensional image resembled mountainous terrain, with LOVs of different varieties crawling and reproducing on the slopes and summits. The peaks charted the LOVs' phenomenal growth and spread, as well as their changing structure, as recorded by the *Roi Nuoc* who worked with them every day, and often into the night.

As Virgil soared past sedimentary layers he was amazed again at the LOVs' versatility, at the speed with which they changed— and he could see only one explanation for it: Somehow the LOVs must have learned to deliberately reprogram their descendants' genetic structure.

Then abruptly his gliding viewpoint froze. In all of that artificial landscape nothing crawled, or replicated, or faded away.

He propped himself up on his elbow, conscious of the whisper of rain against the tent canvas, the distant crow of a restless cock. He stared at the display, waiting for it to resume.

Nothing.

"Mother Tiger?"

No response.

He heard footsteps, then the rustle of canvas, but when he turned to look the frozen image blocked his vision. He had to slide the farsights down his nose to see.

Ky stood in the door, holding up the tent flap, his farsights in his hand and a haunted look in his eyes. "They have taken out Mother Tiger! It shouldn't be possible. This ROSA runs on over twenty servers around the world. But it has been done."

As if to belie that, the image on Virgil's farsights shifted, leaping forward in time. He pushed them back into place. "Mother Tiger?"

The ROSA answered with a purr. Ky whipped his farsights on and began making demands in sharp, staccato Vietnamese. The image froze again. Jerked forward. Froze.

Virgil brought his own ROSA on-line and used it to dictate a short text message—

→ Are you being attacked?

—to be delivered to Mother Tiger . . . *now*. He tapped "send" as the image shifted again. This time the ROSA remained active for several seconds, long enough to respond in its verbal purr, "*All is well.*"

But all was not well. The image froze again. Virgil used the interlude to dictate another message:

→ What has caused your intermittent activity?

At the same time he was aware of Ky muttering and cursing at his farsights.

Returning abruptly to an active state, the ROSA purred its answer: "Resources have been shifted to support a communications project."

"What is this project?" Ky demanded, shouting now in angry English. "Where is it?"

Virgil's screen cleared. Then a transparent map winked into existence, showing a blazing point near a pond complex less than half a mile from the medical tent. "What is there?" Virgil asked.

"Ela Suvanatat."

"Open a link."

"No links are being accepted."

"Show me then! Show me what she sees!"

The map vanished, replaced by an opaque field of blue-green LOVs. Virgil stared at it, uncomprehending. "What is this?" he asked.

"This is what Ela sees."

Ela stirred, conscious once again of the night around her: of the rain, still falling at its deliberate pace, and of the hunger in her belly, and the narrow farm road that had become a thoroughfare of LOV spiders. They scuttled past in jerking stop-motion, their footfalls audible plops in the mud. Most stopped every few feet, to tap the ground, or to tap limbs against one another. Only a few spiders were solitary. Most moved in groups of two or three. When they met spiders moving in the opposite direction they would freeze for several seconds. Their globes would sparkle. And then both groups would move on again, occasionally tripping one another as they passed.

Ela's spider stepped into this bidirectional flow. It did not turn. It simply stepped "sideways"—assuming she had been looking at it face-to-face. But it had no face. It had no front or back. In its radial perspective all directions were equal so that it could move toward any point of the compass without turning. She found something disturbingly alien in this trait, but refused to be swayed by it. Shrugging off her uneasiness, she hurried to follow the spider as it joined a trio of others heading toward the second pond complex. Fearing she might lose track of "her" spider among all the others, she made careful note of its peculiar features: four legs, exceptionally long, the pattern of mud splashed across them, the complex shape of the cage holding its globe above the mud, the unusually fine texture and colorless gleam of its structural LOvs. She instructed Mother Tiger to memorize these traits.

The group of spiders advanced erratically, hurrying forward only to stop, back up, exchange a few taps with one another, or with another group moving in the opposite direction, before scurrying forward again, so that it took several minutes to reach the first pond.

Here the group broke up. The original trio continued on across the flooding dikes, but Ela's spider plunged into the water, disappearing beneath a surface boiling with rain.

"Ela!"

She jumped, startled by the distant shout. Turning, she peered through the rain and saw Ky Xuan Nguyen running toward her without hat or poncho, slipping as he dodged the toddling spiders that crowded the muddy road.

"Ela! What have you been doing?"

He skidded to a stop in front of her, grabbing her shoulders as if he expected her to run away. There was panic in his eyes. "Are you all right?"

"Let go of me!" She pushed his hands away. "Of course I'm all right. Why shouldn't I be?"

"Mother Tiger said you were—" He broke off, looking her

up and down as if he hadn't really seen her before.

"Yes?" She wondered if he had been dreaming of some unearthly vision that had driven him out into the rain.

He wiped at the droplets on his upper lip. "Mother Tiger suffered a failure," he explained. "A *temporary* failure. Its resources were overtaxed—"

"Mother Tiger?" she interrupted, incredulous.

"Yes. During a communications project undertaken at your direction."

"Oh." Ela looked away, shivering a little as a thread of rainwater found its way down her neck.

"A communications project, Ela," he said, stepping closer, one hand raised as if to touch her again. "What could I think? Your LOVs have expanded into a band across your forehead. Hundreds of them. I have heard how Virgil's partner died. The woman—"

"Gabrielle."

"Yes."

She turned back and was startled to see Virgil standing behind Ky, wrapped in a black poncho, the lens of his farsights gleaming green beneath his hood.

"I knew there was a danger," Ela said, looking from one to the other. "But Mother Tiger was with me."

"Then it was a cognitive circle?" Virgil asked. "With Mother Tiger translating?"

"Yes."

"And it worked?"

"Yes. It went well."

"You might have been lost," Ky insisted. "Overwhelmed. Used up."

"It didn't happen."

"Don't do it again."

She gazed at him sadly. "You can't ask me that. Ky, you don't even have LOVs."

He flinched, but what could he say? She could see the fear on his face.

Virgil stepped closer. "What did you learn?" he asked her.

Ela smiled. "I learned we can talk to them. We can understand one another, at least on some basic level. They're clever, but they're not like us. They're nothing like us. From their beginning, LOVs were selected to process information and solve problems. Right?"

Virgil nodded.

Ela felt her smile widen. "I gave them a problem to solve. The communications project that taxed Mother Tiger—that was her effort to translate my ideas."

In a strained voice Ky asked, "What problem did you submit?"

"I asked if the same structural LOVs used to form a spider's legs might be used to form something much larger—like a platform to keep my tent above the water."

For a moment neither man spoke. Then Virgil blinked, stirred. "What answer did you get?"

"The answer was yes."

Ky tipped his head back, letting the rain slide over his bare forehead, his smooth cheeks. "It goes too fast," he said. "We do things, having no idea what their effects will be. Dr. Gabrielle Villanti is dead. Did she anticipate that? Did she anticipate that her actions would accelerate the cognitive development of E-3 and, ultimately, drive it to destroy itself? There is a limit to how far we can see, but none of us are *even looking anymore*."

Ela's mood shifted. It was a LOV-amplified reaction, a flare of heat and fury. "Is that why you're afraid of the LOVs, Ky? Do you tell yourself that if only you had left me on the beach your life would still be safe and predictable? If that's what you wanted, Ky Xuan Nguyen, you should not have made yourself big-man uncle to the *Roi Nuoc*."

"Ela, come on," Virgil said. "It's not a simple—"

"It *is* simple. You should not be afraid, Ky, because you are condemned already if we lose."

Ky's smile was cold and false. "Unless I cut a deal? It's what you're thinking."

"Shouldn't I think it?"

"You should think of other things. Like why you insist on rash behavior, always pushing the LOVs on to something more unsettling. More challenging. You refuse to give the world time to accept us. Instead you give them more reason to reject us."

Ela shrugged, for she could not easily deny this, and still she knew Ky's assessment was flawed. "You think to win official approval. But we are criminals, Ky. We are dangerous—"

"We are revolutionaries! Not criminals. Once we persuade the UN to recognize our petition—"

"You won't persuade them! Wake up, Ky. Look around. Look what we have made." Her own gaze lifted to the landscape beyond him. Under the night's heavy clouds hundreds of ghost lights could be seen, riding on spider shapes that did not belong to this world. Her own brow glittered with alien thought. "Ky, you will never know what the LOVs truly are until they are part of you. You are a most excellent negotiator. You are the only reason we are still here. But at most you are buying us time. If we do nothing else, we will lose. Finally the UN and the IBC and the officials in Hanoi will stop squabbling and agree it is best—most humane—to be rid of us. We can't let them do that. That's why we have to push, and keep on pushing, until they *cannot* get rid of us. Only then will they accept our existence."

"She's right," Virgil said.

All of Ela's words had scarcely touched Ky, but those two words from Virgil—they hit him hard. She saw it in his eyes.

Virgil must have sensed it too. "You see it, Ky, don't you?" he asked gently. "There's no time to do things right."

Ela nodded. "Really, we are so lucky. We are the first to know a nonhuman mind. An Earth alien. I want to know all I can of what that means, and I want to share it with everyone—whether they approve or not. I want to make it real for them." Then she smiled as she finally realized her own truth. "And I want to scare the shit out of anyone who thinks we are all there ever will be. What do you want, Ky? Why are you here?"

Bitterly, he said, "Because there were a few things I failed to foresee." But then he looked past her, his gaze following the spiders that still scuttled between the ponds and waded in the shallows. It was a bizarre vista, its meaning unreachably alien, but as he took it in, his face warmed with a cramped smile. "I never imagined anything like this. It goes to show . . . how poor we must be at prediction."

"Too many variables," Virgil said.

"And too little data." he shook his head against the weight of raindrops clinging to his eyelashes and hair. "I am afraid for the *Roi Nuoc*. I thought they belonged to me. I thought they were my project, my social engineering experiment, but they don't listen. They are exactly what I wanted them to be. Adventurers."

"Alien," Ela said.

Ky chuckled in bitter humor. "Yes, I said that, didn't I? They are alien. Maybe all children are, born into a world so different from the one that welcomed their parents. They don't fear change. They don't see the LOVs as a threat to their future, but only as an interesting element among an infinite set of possible futures. An opportunity to be seized and ridden—"

"*Oh, shit*," Virgil interrupted. "That's right."

CHAPTER 29

Surprise had forced his words. Now Virgil had to explain. He looked from Ky to Ela. "The *Roi Nuoc* don't pass up opportunities, do they?" He spoke over the steady sizzle of rain against his hood. "They'll want to try a cognitive circle too."

He watched Ela embrace the dilemma in a moment of flash-understanding. Her eyes went wide. Her chin dropped like a fighter's so that the hood of her poncho shadowed her farsights and hid the LOVs that arched across her forehead. "Hush!" she commanded him. "They'll hear you."

"Yes, exactly."

Ky didn't get it. Ela had unbalanced him. He wasn't up to speed, and he knew it. Soaked and shivering, his skin unnaturally pale, he turned to Virgil with a resentful gaze—"What exactly are you saying?"

"Just that it took only one cognitive circle to freeze the

Rosa," Virgil said. "What will happen if a hundred sessions take off at once?"

It was possible. There were no secrets among the *Roi Nuoc*. What one saw and heard, all others might see and hear too, thanks to their web of farsights.

Ela was part of that web. Her activities must have commanded the attention of any *Roi Nuoc* who was awake. Even now, some among them would be watching, listening, looking for advantage. They were competitive and fearless. It might be no more than minutes before some decided to run the experiment themselves.

"Is there a way to ban these cognitive circles?" Virgil asked. "Ky?"

The fingers of his right hand were tapping furiously. "I'm trying!"

Virgil turned half-away, whispering for Mother Tiger's apparition. The tiger shadow crawled, dreamlike and immense, up out of the saturated ground. "Show me a scan," Virgil ordered. "A fast circuit of all active farsights."

Images flashed past his gaze, scenes set in a darkness that everywhere seemed alive with weirdly glowing blue-green light, cast by the globes, but also by human faces whose eyes had been replaced by ribbons of virtual LOVs. "It's too late," Virgil said. "It's begun. There are cognitive circles everywhere."

As if to confirm it, his farsights went black. It was a state that lasted only a moment before a sigh whispered through the audio and the screen became clear: no frames, no lists, no icons, no input of any kind were left on the display. The power switch might have been toggled off.

Virgil held his breath, waiting for the system to come back up. It did not.

Without his farsights, the night was very dark.

"Virgil," Ky said, "can you contact your original Rosa?"

"I don't know." He started tapping a string of code. "Mother Tiger annexed it—"

"I can't see a thing!" Ela said. ". . . except spiders. So many of them! Ky—"

Virgil turned. Without nightvision he could see no spiders at all. Only the globes were visible, floating like ghost lights a foot and a half above the ground, or blurred beneath the water.

"I'm going to follow them back," Ela said, "and get my other farsights from the tent—"

"*Shit*," Virgil swore, flinching back and almost losing his balance as his screen flooded with harsh green light. He blinked at Iris's tiny Greek goddess icon. "Hey, I'm up. Iris is working."

Ky nodded, his own lens glowing again. "I'm up too, with an outside ROSA."

"I'm going," Ela said, taking a half step away and sliding in the mud.

"Wait." Virgil stepped after her. "Do you know what to do? We need to find each cognitive circle, and turn off whatever farsights are involved—"

"That will break Mother Tiger's link," Ky said. "But how can we search nine square miles of reservation?"

"The *Roi Nuoc* will search," Ela said. "Alert everyone you see. They can alert others. Like a chain letter, but by voice. Now hurry! You know what happened to Gabrielle when she stayed too long in a circle."

Virgil felt a cold trickle of rain against his back. He knew too well.

Ela took off along the little road, running in tiny, mincing, dancer's steps as she darted from one wandering spider to the next, like a human pencil completing a dot-to-dot puzzle. Ky stared after her. "When the *Roi Nuoc* awake, they are going to panic." He gestured at the road, in the direction opposite the one Ela had taken. "I'll go this way. Be sure to tell everyone you see to spread out. Cover as much territory as we can." He took a step. Then he hesitated, glancing over his shoulder at Virgil. "You've seen my mistake, haven't you? I should never have made the *Roi Nuoc* dependent on a single system."

Ky and Ela had taken the road, so Virgil decided to strike out between the ponds. He'd gone only a few steps when he started questioning his decision. The ground felt like it was dissolving under his feet. Hardly any separation remained between the ponds. He slogged through mud that clutched at his ankles, slipping and sliding in his sandals as he worked his way across the backs of eroded dikes. Alone in the dark, it was easy to imagine the river as a sentient thing, oozing up from the ground to meet the falling rain and the rising ocean in some sinister plot to swallow the world in a slow tide of water.

A tapping spider approached along the back of a narrow dike. Virgil stepped aside to give it room to pass, and the saturated ground gave way beneath him. He slid down, riding an underwater avalanche of fine-grained silt, until he stood thigh deep in the water. The spider scuttled past, taking no notice of him. He watched it go by, wondering how many cognitive circles Mother Tiger was engaged in. How much had the ROSA learned? More than he might ever know, Virgil realized. Unless it had been caught in a web of infinite calculation, striving to decode the meaning of every microsecond flash across a hundred million LOVs.

Did the ROSA have an error-correction system that would let it escape a near-infinite task? And if it did, what would it be like when it emerged? Mother Tiger was like no other ROSA Virgil had ever encountered. It was a complex entity existing on many servers. It already seemed to be eroding the barriers dividing ROSAs from sentient beings. Could its interaction with the LOVs push it all the way over?

He climbed up onto the dike again. It was tempting to retreat to the road, but a glance back showed that he had already come more than halfway through the pond complex. A grove of banana trees offered shelter on the other side, so he pushed on, head down as he watched the placement of every step.

He didn't look up again until he was climbing a slight rise to the banana grove. He was startled to glimpse a petite figure moving among the trees, slender and shy, disappearing as soon as he saw it. Then another sprite, slightly taller, leaned into view.

"Hey!" Virgil called. "There's been trouble. Mother Tiger's in trouble!"

They peeked out again, two little girls clinging to each other, their eyes wide with confusion and terror. They watched him through their lifeless farsights as he tried to explain what had happened to Mother Tiger. Could they even see him in the dark? He told them what they must do, then asked if they understood.

One of the little girls answered—in Vietnamese.

"No English?" Virgil asked.

She shook her head.

Virgil thought for a moment. Then he tapped his fingers to open a link. "Ky."

"Here."

"They don't speak English."

Ky's image scowled. Then he nodded shortly. "Lend your farsights. I'll talk."

It was a quick exchange, and then the girls vanished on separate paths, feeling their way like spiders. He listened to their shrill voices calling out ahead of them to their hidden friends.

Ela came on-line. "This can't go on long," she said in encouraging tones. "The globes have no way to store the nutrients they need. They can't be out of the water for more than a few minutes."

She should have been right, but minute after minute dripped past, and Mother Tiger still did not recover.

Virgil slogged on through the mud, up to his knees at times. His breath whistled in and out of his lungs. Every few steps he stopped and the rain, falling straight down, dripped off his hood in a sparkling curtain. "*Roi Nuoc!*" he would call into the night. "*Roi Nuoc!*" Then he would add the words Ky had given him: "*Me Cop dang gâp nguy hiêm. Chúng mình phai giúp cuú Me Cop.*" "*Mother Tiger is in danger and we all need to help.*" He searched groves of trees for hammocks. He rattled the tents pitched in pastures or on the margins of ponds and rice paddies. Many of the kids were still asleep, and his shouting woke them so that he came upon them in their first moments of terror after they discovered the empty screens of their farsights. He would comfort them as he could. He would have them view Ky's recorded spiel. Then he would move on.

Once Virgil heard the engine of a distant truck, grinding as it fought the mud. It was a welcome sound, for he guessed that Ky had persuaded the army to help.

Ky linked every ten minutes or so, to check Virgil's status, and to relay reports of more and more cognitive circles uncovered. Dozens of the *Roi Nuoc* had imitated Ela, but as she had predicted, none of the circles lasted for long because the spiders could not survive more than a few minutes out of the water. As their nutrients were used up, they retired, breaking the circles long before any kids could come to harm.

"So why hasn't Mother Tiger recovered?" Virgil asked as he paused for breath in the middle of a flooded pasture.

"Because something is still occupying its attention." Ky looked grim, a little head-and-shoulders image caught in Virgil's farsights. "I checked with the resident servers. There is nothing wrong with the platform or the software. The ROSA is busy. That's all they can tell me."

"So somehow a cognitive circle has survived?"

"We have to find it," Ky said. "And soon."

Virgil wandered on alone. Near three-thirty in the morning he was standing waist deep in yet another pond, after a misstep had sent him sliding into the water. He decided to rest there a moment. The LOVs had helped him keep his head clear and his exhaustion at bay, but it was all catching up to him now. His legs ached, and his fingers and toes were shriveled with the unending wet. He couldn't even see the dike he'd fallen off of, because it was hidden under at least six inches of water. He held up his hands, examining them for signs of algal-growth. Maybe this was the season of infinite rain, when they would all transform to water creatures and swim away forever into another world.

Or maybe he was just woozy with exhaustion and cold. His hands were trembling. His eyes ached. He slipped off his farsights, letting the darkness fall against his eyes in a soft kiss. He longed to call off the search, give up, go back. But Gabrielle haunted his mind.

She had become a ghost—though not the traditional variety. Virgil did not believe in the supernatural. The ghosts he acknowledged had nothing to do with metaphysics, and everything to do with the mind. Gabrielle had become a meme complex, a pattern of information within his brain. A warning.

He couldn't stop searching, not while the possibility remained that somewhere, someone lay trapped within the hypnotic grip of a cognitive circle, mesmerized, unaware of time passing or their own physical existence. How long could a child endure that? Exhaustion had killed Gabrielle. One or more of the *Roi Nuoc* might be dying now, as he dithered in the water.

He cursed himself. Then he clawed his way back up onto the submerged dike.

He had to rest again after that, kneeling in the water, his head bowed, his eyes closed, his farsights still clutched in his hand. Gradually he grew aware of a deeper noise beyond the steady drizzle of the rain. After a moment, he identified it as the sound of waves running up against the mangroves that lined the shore. Had he come so far?

He stood up, determined to push on to the edge of the reservation.

It was then he saw the light: a faint, blue-green glow beneath the mangroves.

Hands shaking, he slipped his farsights back on and looked again. The glow was so faint that with nightvision it blended into the background outline of mangroves and he could not see it. So he took his farsights off again. He gave his eyes a minute to adjust.

The light had not changed.

He fixed his gaze on it and staggered forward through the dark, wading through ponds and over dikes until he reached the trees. The grove stood in a shallow swamp of swirling water, and he could not tell if it was the rain, the river, or the ocean that had laid claim to this territory, but the glow had brightened. It gleamed from within the center of the grove, a few feet above the water's surface.

He slipped his farsights back on. The forest emerged from darkness, all bent limbs and knobby aerial roots. It made him think of a spider with a hundred legs, squatting over a gleaming green moonrise, as if to hold all that light for itself, keep it from the world. Virgil advanced slowly, clambering over roots, splashing past driftwood, bumping his head on branch after branch and tearing his poncho.

He found the *Roi Nuoc* at the center of the grove. There were three, all girls, huddling at equally spaced points around a rough circle. They each had a ribbon of symbiotic LOVs in a horizontal band across their foreheads, with a second band of LOVs projected across the active screens of their farsights.

Two of the girls were adolescents, twelve or thirteen years old. They perched on knobby roots while the rain dripped around them, punching expanding rings into the black water. The third girl was much younger, a tiny creature, eight years old at most. She lay slumped in the water, her little head resting against her arm, her face as fixed and smooth as wax. If she breathed, Virgil could not see it. None of the girls showed any awareness of his arrival. The glittering fields of their farsights were all turned to the center of their circle, where there hung a LOV colony . . . or *colonies* . . . such as Virgil had never seen before.

There were three globes, all suspended within a lacy mesh of blue-green tubes stretched between the trees and anchored in the flowing water. It looked like a glowing spiderweb, set with shimmering jewels. Beneath the water more strands gleamed, like roots laid out on the surface of the mud. Were they questing for nutrients to pump up to the LOVs that composed the globes? That would explain why this cognitive circle had not collapsed like all the others.

"Ky," he said softly, tapping his fingers to open a link. "I think I've found the source of our troubles."

Ky looked through his lens and swore. Then, "Pull your hood low," he said, "so your own LOVs aren't mesmerized too."

Virgil did it, and felt a frisson of disappointment. Had he already been falling into the sublime trance of the circle?

"Take their farsights," Ky said. "Break the circle."

Virgil moved first toward the littlest girl. Was she still alive? Her fixed, waxy expression reminded him too much of Gabrielle. He whispered a prayer that left his lips without direction. Then he lifted her farsights away from her face.

She did not stir, or protest.

He laid a hand against her chest, seeking the rise and fall of her breath, but he was shivering so violently he could feel nothing. Panic slipped loose. He fumbled with her farsights, shoving them into a pocket. Then he grabbed her under her arms and sat her up. Her head flopped like a broken doll. He turned her away from the suspended globes. "Wake up," he whispered. "Wake. Please."

She gasped: a sharp, shallow inrush of air as if her body had suddenly remembered its need to breathe. Another rattling breath and then a long moan. Virgil held her against his chest. He did not dare to put her down. It would be so easy for her to slide into the water and drown. So he held her with one arm as he turned to the next girl.

"Move quickly," Ky said. "This one may resist."

Virgil nodded. The girl was crouched on a mangrove root, her arm around the trunk for balance. She looked strong. He drew a deep breath, then grabbed her farsights, peeling them off her head.

Her chin came up and she turned to him, her eyes revealing a dark melange of surprise and fury. Virgil stumbled backward, ready to throw her farsights into the tangle of forest if she came after him, but her anger faded as quickly as it had formed. She turned to face the colonies again, reentering her trance without the aid of farsights.

"Ky! You've got people coming, right?"

"A couple minutes," Ky assured him. "Get the other farsights too. Turn them off."

"I'm doing it." He stumbled toward the third girl, who still had not moved. She didn't seem to notice when he stripped her farsights away. Her gaze did not waver from the gleaming colonies. Looking into her eyes, Virgil felt his hackles rise. What was she seeing? What strange paths had her mind found to explore?

"Virgil!"

He flinched at Ky's voice, sharp and loud in his ears.

"Look away from her, Virgil."

"I'm not caught."

"Look away from her, and turn off all the farsights."

Virgil did as he was told, his numb fingers fumbling for the power switches while he balanced the little girl in one arm. The last toggle slid home with a satisfying click, audible over the rain. Virgil grinned in giddy triumph, looking up at last, his gaze sweeping over the suspended colonies. "It's done—"

The world vanished behind a blue-green glinting sea of infinite depth. At the same time he heard a soft, growling welcome. Mother Tiger stirred, a watermark prowling against a background of LOVs. "You're back," he whispered. It felt as if days had passed since he had last seen the ROSA.

"Come. Follow me," Mother Tiger commanded.

Virgil hesitated. ROSAs should not behave this way. He raised his hand to touch the earpiece of his farsights, troubled by the thought that he should take them off.

"That danger is past," Mother Tiger said.

Yes, of course. The cognitive circle had been broken.

He turned to follow the ROSA as it stalked beyond his left shoulder, at the same time using his free hand to sweep away his constricting hood. "Have you done it?" he asked, as if the ROSA was a human entity. "Have you decrypted the language of the LOVs?"

"It is an evolving process," Mother Tiger said in its low, purring voice. "The task is not finished yet. Will you help?"

"Yes, I—"

Heat swept over him. A glorious, blissful warmth that sent him to his knees, splashing in the flowing water. The little girl reacted violently, squirming in his arms. Virgil held her close, puzzling over her presence. Hadn't he been doing something else? Something important?

It didn't seem to matter now.

He looked again for the ROSA's prowling shadow. "You've done it, haven't you? You've found an interface, a way to communicate."

"You are here."

"Is it a being then? Does it speak? Does it feel? Does it know itself?"

"It is not one self or one language, but it is curious, seeking problems to solve, puzzles to unwind. We are an interface for its incomplete system to better know the world."

"I want to see it."

"This is it. Feel it."

"I do. This bliss. This is the sense of my own LOVs knowing their own. Will it speak?"

"Not in words."

"E-3 spoke in words."

"This is younger. Wild."

"It knows how to change itself though. How does it do that? How does it change the structure of its own LOVs? How does it know to build strands and spider legs?"

"Hypothesize and test. It has refined the molecular detectors of its ancestors, developing a vision-touch that perceives the structure of its own DNA and translates that into maps within thought-space to be manipulated and rearranged, design changes that translate into the molecular machinery of each cell."

"So it can perceive and manipulate its own structure."

"Yes."

"And it can hold theoretical structures within its mind, its mental space."

"Just as we do."

We? Virgil found himself confused by this small word, but he shook it off. "Can I meet it within this thought-space? Is that what Ela did?"

"She introduced new designs to be made."

"Yes."

The girl squirmed again in his arms, unbalancing him, so his knee slipped and he went deeper in the water. A half-forgotten thought would not cease nagging at his mind. "I . . . I came here for a reason," he mused. "Ah, I remember. To find you, Mother Tiger. You left us. Why?"

"I have not left."

He felt the physical feedback that came from smiling. Perhaps he really did smile. "My ROSA never says 'I' or 'we.'" Then he remembered. "You were in danger. Your persona was gone and our farsights were dead. The *Roi Nuoc* were alone."

"I see it now. This system reallocation has been flawed."

"You'll reevaluate, and correct?"

"It is done." Then a moment later. "They are gone."

"Who?"

"The *Roi Nuoc*. They are all gone. Their farsights don't function." Did Virgil imagine an edge of panic in its voice?

In its own way the ROSA really did share many traits that might be attributed to a goddess. It had no precise location, existing on servers around the world. It had a prodigious memory and could access any public database, and no doubt a slew of private sources too. It could perform thousands of tasks at once, evaluating its actions from both past experience and future expectation. It was more than a ROSA. It *was* an electronic goddess, a teacher, a spirit that could look out through the windows of a thousand farsights at once to see the reason for its existence, the *Roi Nuoc*.

Now, none of those windows were open.

Virgil told himself that a ROSA could not panic. That this black dread he felt was his own human spin, and yet he wasn't sure. The barriers between himself and the world around him seemed porous. Sensations he could not account for touched him. Ideas wandered into his mind like fleeting butterflies—

"Where have my *Roi Nuoc* gone?" the tiger goddess growled. Another voice challenged her. "Let him go!"

The goddess vanished. Virgil gasped against a sudden horrible cold. He felt himself propelled backwards, stumbling, until his shoulder blades slammed up against a tree. A hand was at his chest, holding him down. Ky loomed over him, his face black shadow except where the glow of his farsights fell across eyes and nose. Flashlights lanced through the trees beyond him. He gave Virgil a hard shake. "You let your farsights be taken over! You let Mother Tiger draw you into its circle."

"It's cracked the language!" Virgil said. "It's reorganized. It's looking for the *Roi Nuoc*."

He winced as a flashlight beam swept his eyes. He realized he still held the little girl. She was awake, staring wide-eyed at the night, at the glowing colonies suspended in their gleaming web. Ky shifted, using his body to block the sight.

"Ky, you have to open a window to Mother Tiger before she panics."

"She?"

Virgil bit his lip. He had never allowed himself to think of ROSA as human analogs, but . . . "Everything is changing. This ROSA . . . it feels like an entity, a woman . . . or a spirit. Female. Where are my farsights?"

"I have them."

"Open a window, Ky. Now. Before she finds a way to open one herself."

CHAPTER 30

Summer had waited an hour and a half for an opportunity to see Simkin alone. Now he came rushing past her in the hall, trailed by two aides coaching him on the question he might face at an upcoming news conference. Summer whirled to follow him as he passed. "Daniel!"

He hesitated, then glanced back, looking confused, as if he could not understand who might have called him. Then, through his half-silvered farsights, his eyes focused in on her. "Summer?" One of the aides gave her a sour look.

She stepped closer, determined that he should not escape without answering her questions. Nash Chou had been lobbying the UN for immediate action, but the IBC still resisted. Now the situation had grown far worse. "Daniel, we need to talk."

"We will," he assured her. "When I get back."

"Your schedule has you out of the office until tomorrow."

"Does it?" He looked to one of the aides, who confirmed it with a nod.

"You do know what happened on the reservation last night?" she pressed.

"Ah." Behind the veil of his farsights his gaze shifted. "You're concerned because our colorful water puppets have made a communications breakthrough. Does it remind you of E-3?"

"This is not a joke, Daniel. It's gone too far, and you know it. I have two designer viruses ready to go. So why are we still waiting?"

His face was a blank mask. Hiding what?

He said: "We haven't got UN approval."

"Of course we haven't. It's never been brought to a vote. Why not?"

"I won't ask for a vote until I know the delegates are on our side. We can't afford to lose." He started again for the elevator.

"Daniel!"

"I'm late, Summer," he called over his shoulder. "And I've got two links already waiting."

"Nash told me one of the children had to be evacuated."

That stopped him. He turned around. His fingers twitched, then his half-silvered farsights went fully opaque. "You've been talking to Nash Chou?"

"He said an eight year-old girl with dysentery was brought to the medical tent. She was examined, her LOVs were mapped, and she was evacuated."

"Standard operating procedure," Simkin said. "She was seen by a neurosurgeon, and her LOVs were removed." His brows rose. "Sorry, but it's too late to test your viruses on her."

Summer leaned hard on her temper. "That's not what I had in mind. Where is the girl now?"

"I can't say. Security, remember? Especially since you're in the habit of talking to outside personnel. But there's no need to worry about the LOVs spreading. The child will be held in quarantine until we're sure the removal was successful. Then she'll be turned over to local officials for placement."

"And how many more kids will have to get sick before you end this situation?"

He sighed. His expression softened. "It won't be long. I promise. *If* you let me do my job."

He turned again toward the elevator. But again, to the consternation of his aides, he hesitated. His pale brows came together in a thoughtful expression. "Say, would it be possible to modify these two viruses so they only work on nonsymbiotic LOVs? Outside the human immune system?"

Summer blinked, baffled at the motive behind this question. He had said it so casually, as if it had just occurred to him, yet she sensed somehow that it was important to him. Cautiously, she asked, "Why would you want to do that?"

He shrugged, as if it were nothing more than a passing notion. "It might be more politically acceptable. Give some thought to it, okay?" Again he turned toward the elevators. One of the aides was there, holding open the doors. Simkin stepped aboard, already engaged in conversation with one of his links. But as the doors closed his silvered gaze was fixed on her. "Do me another favor," he called. "Stay away from Nash Chou."

The doors kissed. Summer turned away from their blank steel faces, sure his promises were empty.

CHAPTER 31

A warm yellow light glowed within the cab of Ky's silver Mercedes, a welcome beacon on a gray, rain-soaked afternoon. The car had been hauled out of the rice paddie where it had crashed on the night Virgil had shot down the IBC's helicopter. It had even run again for a while. But it was stranded now, on a dike road that had become an ever-shrinking island, sunk to its floorboards in a quagmire of mud. Its sleek shell gleamed in the wan light: speed, with nowhere to go. Virgil slogged toward it through the mud, keenly aware of a blister on his right ankle. He wondered what Ky wanted to talk about that could not be said over farsights.

He opened the door of the front passenger seat, shrugged out of his poncho, then ducked inside.

The cab was a microcosm transplanted from another world: warm light and soft music—a soulful techno symphony—and amazingly cold air spilling from the vents, all powered by fuel cells that would likely go on working until the car was finally drowned.

Ky was not in the driver's seat.

Startled, Virgil twisted around to check in back. He found Ky there, though not alone.

A girl sat with him. She was dressed in mud-splattered trousers that must have once been white, and a loose cottony shirt not quite so far gone. Virgil guessed her age as fifteen years. He stared at her, stunned by the sight of hundreds of LOVs glittering on her forehead, more than he had ever seen on one person before. From his own LOVs he felt a flush of pleasure and something more. A sense of unexplored levels, stretching inward for miles . . .

Only with an effort did he turn away from her to nod at Ky. But something was wrong. Virgil saw it immediately on Ky's face. Despite the calm pose of his expression it was easy for Virgil to distinguish the fear and tension that lay below. "What is it?" he asked. "What's happened?"

"Nothing."

Virgil's gaze cut back to the girl. She had a slight smile now, with something shyly maternal in it. She did not wear farsights. Ky did not. So Virgil took his own off and slipped them into a thigh pocket.

"Virgil," Ky said, "please meet Lien."

"So pleased to know you, Dr. Copeland," Lien said in heavily accented English. "You have brought so much to us."

There was veneration behind her words; a devout affection that Virgil found deeply disturbing. "Not so much," he said thickly. "A lot of trouble." Her gratitude touched him, and he looked away. Mud was beginning to seep in under the passenger door.

"It is worth this trouble, I think."

He nodded. He felt the same. "Why are we here?"

"Because it's time," Ky said. "Lien has agreed to transplant the LOVs for me. She is an expert, Virgil. She knows more about the LOVs than anyone else. Even you."

"I can see that."

"This is not true," Lien said. "I know some of the wild LOVs here in the delta, but not all of their kind. Many strains I don't know."

"Have you grouped them into strains?" Virgil asked eagerly. "Are there records? I'd love to—"

"No," Ky said. "Not now." Sweat shone on his cheeks and forehead, though the cab of the Mercedes was cold. "Now I have a favor to ask of you, Virgil. Lien has offered to blend the best of these wild strains into a balanced array of LOVs—"

"But that is not always the best way," she said in her quick and quiet voice, as if heading off a debate already finished. "This giving of LOVs can be . . ." She frowned at Ky; the two of them exchanged a few words in Vietnamese. Then Ky took over.

"The word is 'personal,'" he said. "Giving and accepting LOVs is a very personal rite because the LOVs will link us to each other. Lien suggested I might feel more comfortable if my LOVs came from . . . a friend."

Virgil did not know what to say. Then he was speaking anyway, true words: "I'm honored, Ky. And I'm happy to do it, of course. But you know the LOVs I have are only distantly related to the rest."

"Lien has mentioned this." Ky sat tall on the Mercedes's soft seat, looking stiffer than a frozen corpse.

Virgil's smiled faded. "You don't have to do this."

"No. I *want* to do it."

His fear was plain, but his resolve was just as clear. And it was his choice. So Virgil turned to Lien and nodded. "I've never done this before. Please tell me what I need to do."

CHAPTER 32

I t was a rainy season like no other. The fall of rain was deceptively gentle, exhibiting no fierceness, yet it fell without end—and not just in the delta. The highlands were awash in continuous storms that fed the river, driving its expansion far beyond its banks. Farms were obliterated. Roads disappeared. The corpses of animals—and sometimes, people too—drifted beneath the shimmering surface, distorted memories of a drowned world, now food for fish.

The LOVs fed too, thriving on the wealth of dissolved organic matter. Ela trailed her hand in the water, finding some amusement in the way her brown fingers became yellow and grossly distorted just a few inches below the surface. She was crouched in the prow of a slender, open boat, rain sizzling in tiny drops against her hood. Whenever she coughed, convulsive vibrations shuddered through the boat's wooden hull, disturbing first Oanh, who sat behind her, and then Ninh, who stood in the back, wielding the pole. Ela coughed a lot. All of them did. The constant wet was not good for people, but it was good for LOVs. Suspiciously good. Ela found herself toying with the theory that this flood was no natural event at all, but the will of a god determined to remake the world in favor of the LOVs.

Of course, similar theories could be proposed to explain *any* natural event, which added up to no explanation at all.

Ninh leaned on his pole, grunting as he slowed their forward rush. "Watch your hand," he called, reminding Ela to snatch her fingers out of the water a moment before the bow struck with a gentle *thunk* against the porch of a farmhouse abandoned now for many days.

Ela was first out, her sandaled feet sloshing in the half inch of water that overlay the porch. She tied the boat to a post that had begun to gather a crust of LOVs; Oanh secured the stern. They had the boat for only an hour, so it was essential to work quickly.

Ninh ventured first into the house, an axe in hand.

Ela followed, wrinkling her nose as she crossed the threshold. Pigs had foraged here. Turds strewn across the floor told of their occupation. They had turned over most of the furniture and left behind bones that might once have been a goat. Pictures of dour grandfathers hung on the walls, frowning down at the mess, their eyes sternly insisting that their families *would* return, someday. Ela could not believe it. She started pulling empty drawers out of a press-wood bureau, bashing them hard against the bureau top to shatter the staples, then laying the planks in a neat stack beyond the water's reach. Oanh went to work on an overturned chair. These days, life could be measured in the firewood they used to grill their fish and dry their disintegrating clothing.

Over the past week, most of the government soldiers guarding the reservation had been reassigned to flood-relief duties in other provinces. Those few who remained were quartered in a houseboat, along with the research scientists. They were no longer allowed to share food with the *Roi Nuoc*. It was the latest tactic concocted by the haggling officials at the UN for removing the children from the reservation. Like city pigeons denied their usual crumbs, or temple monkeys who find their offerings of fruit no longer appearing each morning, the *Roi Nuoc* were expected to give up when denied their handouts. They were supposed to see reason and move on to the friendlier territories of Saigon, or Hue.

The *Roi Nuoc* were more stubborn than temple monkeys. So far only the injured and the ill had given in. Fourteen in all. Eighty-three remained on the reservation, surviving on the fish and the frogs they could catch and flash-grill over stolen wood, on wild spinach and watercress, and the fruit that still could be salvaged from the trees. But it was a lean diet, with too little fat. Hunger loitered always on the edge of the mind.

So when a nervous clucking arose from the back room, Ela paused in her destruction. She turned her head, catching Ninh's eye. He smiled, and laid his axe on top of a cabinet housing porcelain statues of white-bearded old men. Then he eased silently past a once-pink curtain now blackened with mildew and water stains.

A brief but highly chaotic interval erupted, resulting in three hens with broken necks, and one seriously bruised shin. Ela examined the wound, shaking her head. "You have to be careful," she reminded Ninh. "If the skin had broken . . ."

There was no need to say more. The water was filthy with disease, and even slight wounds could quickly go septic. Ky Xuan Nguyen had pleaded again and again with the government and its medical officers to allow them to buy antibiotics, but top officials in Hanoi no longer listened to him. They did not trust him anymore, not since he had converted to the LOVs. They had been pleased to work with him when they saw him as keeper of the *Roi Nuoc* zoo, but now that he was one of the aliens, only a few dedicated bureaucrats would still accept his links. They passed on his pleas for humanitarian relief to the UN, where the IBC vetoed every one. While the status of the reservation remained under UN debate, no relief supplies were to be allowed. None. Not medicine, or tampons, or toilet paper, or condoms, or soap or coffee or Kleenex or chlorine tablets. It was a siege. A war of attrition. And if they were miserable, they could turn themselves in at the houseboat.

The IBC promised no charges would be pressed against children who were brought in for evacuation, but it was impossible to know for sure, because once through the doors of the houseboat, their farsights were confiscated.

According to Dr. Morikawa the evacuees' LOVs were registered and mapped while they were still aboard the houseboat. Then a helicopter was summoned to ferry them away, to an unnamed hospital, where a neurosurgeon was standing by to remove their LOVs. The doctor assured everyone that the fourteen evacuees were doing well, but Ela had to wonder—why weren't they allowed to report that fact themselves?

Dr. Morikawa still claimed it was an issue of privacy and guardianship. As minors, the evacuees were wards of the state, with no right to decide for themselves.

Ela thought of them as the disappeared.

At least there was still dry wood to burn.

It took only a few minutes to strip the house of its cabinets, stools, tables, chairs, and shrine facings, leaving the dry interior walls for another day. They piled the wood under a plastic tarp that Ela had "stolen" from Nash Chou's research boat when he kindly looked away.

"Twenty minutes," Ninh announced as he secured the tarp. Ela scowled. They must not be late returning the boat to the *Roi Nuoc* cadre who owned it or they would have to pay a penalty to be named by Mother Tiger—perhaps all three of the chickens. It would be a severe penalty because there were few boats, and so their use must be carefully rationed.

The rain picked up as Ninh leaned on the pole, shunting them toward home. Impact circles exploded on the water's translucent surface. A snake swam past. Oanh pointed to a crocodile lurking within a stand of flooded sugarcane, only its eyes showing above the water.

Ela again had the bow seat. It was her job to look for floating logs or submerged dikes, calling to Ninh whenever an obstruction loomed. He had gained a lot of skill with the pole, and the keel scraped only two or three times.

He steered them toward a looming forest of scrawny, ill-made towers, rising out of a drowned shrimp farm, ten or more feet into the air. Like the legs of a spider, these towers were made of fused masses of structural LOVs: Their individual shells were smaller, thicker, and stronger than the shells of the cognitive LOVs that formed the globes. But unlike spider legs, they were not neatly put together. They looked like drip sculptures, the kind of thing children made on the beach by scooping up a handful of fine, wet sand and letting it run through their fingers, gradually raising a stack higher and higher until it collapsed of its own weight.

A few of the thinnest towers had already broken off at the top, but most were intact. They did not gleam with light except at their summits, where a tuft of growth and activity crowned the white and lifeless spire. Nestled within the living LOVs at each peak was a blue-green globe immersed in a little pool of dirty water. Presumably there were also living LOvs inside the towers, forming tubes to pump or siphon the nutrient-laden water to the top. No one knew what the towers were for, or who had designed them (if anyone). Virgil thought it likely that the summit globes had simply duplicated old, inherited commands, mindlessly repeating a fragmented instruction with no "stop" signal.

Ela had been the first to try coaxing a designed structure from the LOvs, that night she entered the cognitive circle. Cracking the light codes had consumed all Mother Tiger's capacity during that first encounter—and during the many that followed on that chaotic night. Cognitive circles were safer now, since Mother Tiger had redesigned its interface to prevent any more runaway sessions.

A few days after that first experiment, Ela had proudly watched as her rectangular platform emerged on eight legs from the rising water. She had waded out to it and climbed aboard, turning in triumph to face a muddy shore crowded with scientists, and jealous-eyed *Roi Nuoc* all nursing projects of their own. She smiled and waved, and the platform promptly fell over.

The image of her crashing into the muddy pond was replayed again and again on every news service around the world. The humiliation had been excruciating, but the failure itself mattered little. Even as she was slogging back to shore, dozens of other projects were maturing, and soon, stable platforms dotted the floodwaters all the way across the reservation.

Ninh poled the boat past a small village of platforms, some with tents and tarps set up on them for shelter, some with thatch-roofed huts, and a few with little cottages made of wood filched from the abandoned farms. The *Roi Nuoc* who occupied them looked up from their fishing, their crafts, or their studies, waving as the boat slipped past.

Not all the platforms were made of the usual silicate shells. The LOvs seemed to be able to hijack genetic material from other life-forms, so that in the quest for structural strength, different strains had evolved: some resembling coral, others with woody crusts, and some as neat and colorful as seashells.

Ela noticed a smooth, narrow boat hull of cloudy white glass budding from the back side of the last platform. "Hey. Look there," she said, pointing to it.

Ninh made a low, throaty sound, conveying an emotion somewhere between disgust and envy. "We could do that, and not have to borrow a boat anymore."

"How easy to break it?" Oanh wondered.

"You would need care," Ela conceded, for—as they had learned the hard way—LOV structures were fragile. The strongest platform could be easily demolished with a baseball bat. The rogue towers could be cracked and shattered by pelting rocks.

"We should use wood shells," Ninh decided. "They're tougher than glass."

Their own platform lay a few hundred yards beyond the village, hidden from sight by a crescent of trees that grew on a high dike, so that the water had just begun to lap at their trunks. A trio of water skaters darted out from behind the trees. The skaters were spider descendants. They had the same basic structure of four or more jointed legs supporting a central globe, but they had gone on to develop wide, flat feet so that they could stride on the surface of the water. This trio was moving in a fast, erratic pattern: a behavior learned after attacks by dogs, crocodiles, and government researchers.

"Something's frightened them," Oanh said.

Ela nodded. "Maybe they'll tell us." She pulled her hood back, then leaned out over the prow of the boat. "Ninh, can you get close?"

"They will be tired soon," Ninh said. "No problem."

He was right. Like the spiders that had come before them (and that had now mostly vanished) the water skaters had lousy circulatory systems. It took time and effort to transport nutrients to the living LOVs in their joints; in periods of brisk activity supply could not keep up with demand, and the water skaters were quickly exhausted. As if to prove this theory, the trio soon slowed to a sedate pace that allowed Ninh to pole the boat between them.

Ela brushed her hair back from her forehead. Then to Mother Tiger she whispered, "I want to know what has frightened them." No other ROSA would have responded to such vague instructions, but Mother Tiger had always been eerily intuitive. Since the night of the cognitive circles it had ceased to feel like a ROSA at all. It understood nuance and unspoken desire as well as anyone Ela had even known.

One of the skaters had noticed her band of implanted LOVs. It glided closer. Ela felt a pleasant sense of recognition and greeting wash over her. Then her farsights opaqued as Mother Tiger translated her question into the blue-green flow of LOV communication. Several seconds passed before Ela realized that a long, tapered, shadowy shape had emerged from the granular field. She blinked in surprise at what was certainly a boat. "Did the skater actually *see* that?" she whispered, astonished because she had thought the only light they could detect was the blue-green flashes of their own communication.

"A limited visual sense appears to have emerged," Mother Tiger answered. "Sensitive to a narrow range of colors and perceived as a two-dimensional field of varying intensity. Other sensory cues, especially chemical sensitivity, confirm the identity as a boat powered by a silent fuel-cell engine."

"A research boat, then."

"One has been seen working in this area."

By the time her farsights cleared, Ninh had poled them past the barrier of trees. Their platform lay just ahead, a frosty gray rectangle on six stilts, perched a foot and a half above the surface, high enough to discourage crocodiles from visiting. Beneath it, in the shadowed space where stilts and platform joined, Ela could see the glow of living LOVs. The stilts were still growing, rising slowly as the water rose, continuously lifting the platform so that it remained above the flood.

"No one here," Oanh observed.

Ela sighed in relief. She did not trust the researchers, and she did not like their endless questions.

As they drew closer a rare spider scuttled into sight from behind the A-frame thatch shelter Ninh had built. It had six short legs, and the cage that held its globe was finely made and very fragile, to save on weight. Though it had changed its design in the intervening weeks, Ela was fairly sure this was the same spider she had faced in her first cognitive circle. It had supervised the construction of her original, failed platform, as well as this new one that had replaced it. She watched it kneel at the water's edge. Then it plunged in, reappearing seconds later on the stilts, climbing about like a crab as it inspected the joints.

The spiders—and the skaters too—were really just chassis that the globes used to get around. They could be discarded and replaced whenever more advanced designs appeared . . . or when fashions changed. Spiders were mostly passé. Globes that had stumbled around on land a few weeks ago were now mostly transported by water skaters—though now and then, when the silt cleared a little, spiders could still be seen ambling along the muddy bottom.

Now Ela's spider returned to the deck, tapping curiously at the firewood as they off-loaded it, and generally getting in the way. Somehow, they managed to avoid crushing it as the wood was stacked beside the hut, then covered with the tarp. "Done!" Oanh said, brushing wet pressboard crumbs from her hands. "Now we have about three minutes to return the boat."

"Take one of the chickens," Ela said. "See if you can trade it for some rice."

"You're not coming?" Ninh asked uneasily.

Ela sighed. The *Roi Nuoc* did not spend time alone; they had been schooled to believe it unsafe . . . which of course it was, for them. No one is more vulnerable than a child alone without friends or family. "You go with Oanh," Ela said. "You know I'll be all right here."

He didn't like it, but he was getting used to her eccentricities. "We'll be back soon."

"No hurry."

As soon as they were gone though she felt a rootless melancholy rise inside her. She sat cross-legged on the platform's edge, watching the rain touch the water, thinking of the night. Sometimes at night she would lie awake and listen to Ninh's soft snoring on the other side of the hut. In that late hour her clothes would be nearly dry; she would be almost warm. That was when desire rose inside her. She would listen to Ninh's breathing and know she was in love—though not with Ninh.

She pushed her hood back, letting the rain slide across her face. Love was an unproductive and dangerous emotion, designed to sneak into a woman's life and turn her into a housemaid, a slave, obliging her to a life of servitude. Under normal circumstances anyway.

Ela's life was hardly normal, but she still did not welcome any needy feelings. Her attention must be reserved for more important things, and anyway, there was no time. . . .

So she had learned to meditate, using the LOVs to find a cool, hard state where the sound of Ninh's breathing was nothing but a sound. Sadly, this tactic never worked for long, and when the desire returned it was stronger, and more painful than before, as if the LOVs enhanced that too.

The spider startled her from her thoughts, its glassy leg tapping across her shoulders. She looked up to see movement on the water. Another trio of skaters, gliding in from the east on an erratic zigzag path, looking as startled as the first group. Ela sat up straighter, trying to see what had set them off. A line of shrubs lay in that direction, with only a few feet of yellowing branches still showing above the water. Perhaps a crocodile had taken up residence there. Beyond the shrubs, a row of gloomy casurina trees drew a dark curtain across her short horizon.

She searched her screen for Mother Tiger's half-hidden image. "Is the research boat out there?"

In its noble voice, the ROSA provided a one word answer. "No."

"Then what is out there?" Ela asked.

"An anonymous object."

Ela scowled. Anonymous? "Does that mean you don't know?"

"No."

"Then what does it mean?"

"That it cannot be identified."

"But there is something there? You've seen it?"

"Yes."

"Then show it to me."

"No."

No? Ela felt her mouth fall open in astonishment. Never

before had Mother Tiger denied such a simple request. "Why not?"

"It is anonymous."

Ela was stunned. Mother Tiger existed to provide information. When had it begun to cooperate in keeping secrets? She stood up and squinted against the rain, trying to see what might be out there. A single skater moved beyond the brush. Farther away, a spider tottered on the dike beneath the casurina trees, leading her gaze to a wide gray shadow that slid beneath the branches.

A boat?

It had to be a boat, though it did not look like any boat she had seen before. It was much too wide, too round. And how could it cross the dike like that? The water there was only a few inches deep. The object glided out from under the trees, into the afternoon's gray light, and Ela made a small noise of surprise. The boat—or whatever it was—was not floating on the water. It hovered *above* the water. A foot or two above the water. She could clearly see the casurina trunks behind it.

Okay then. It was some sort of aerostat drone. A truly big one, drawing closer at a stately pace of two or three feet per second. Two figures lay prone on a surface wider than a backyard trampoline. Two grinning figures.

"Virgil?" she blurted, jumping to her feet as she recognized him at last. "Ky?"

She was answered by Ky's mocking laugh. "We have thrown off all restraints!" he shouted as they drew near. "Just as you counseled! And look what's come of it! A new toy!"

They had almost reached the platform. Close enough for Ela to see that the aerostat was shaped like a thick round pillow, or like two Frisbees glued together on their concave sides, and that it was made of LOVs. Shimmering white glassy LOVs, like none she had ever seen, looking as if they were embedded in a membrane of stretched plastic. Around the perimeter of the disk were scattered blue-green spots: living LOVs, presumably concerned with controlling air pressure? In the center of the disk, between the two men, she could see a little well, and inside, immersed in a pool of water, a blue-green globe, bland in the daylight. "So you've made a flying saucer."

It was a little more advanced than the boat she had wanted to build.

"Virgil designed it," Ky admitted, sitting up on the saucer's back. Dressed in fatigues and a rain poncho, his hair growing out so that he had to sweep it back to keep it out of his eyes, he did not look much like the polished businessman she had first met. In the gloom of the afternoon, it was easy to see the blue-green glimmer of LOVs across his brow. There was no going back for any of them now. "It's remarkable, isn't it?" Ky insisted.

Ela could not immediately agree. "It has an explosive hazard, right? It has to. The pressure in that disk must be near zero, or it couldn't hold your weight."

Virgil looked insulted. More accurately, he looked like an insulted warrior from some suburban Hollywood high-school tribe. His poncho had been worn to shreds, so now he went without, wearing only the blue water-wick boating fatigues he had brought with him, and a tek-fabric shirt. His head was bare, his Egyptian-wrapped hair grown out an inch and tied up in a sloppy topknot. He frowned at her through farsights that were an opaque strip of blue-green. Ela could not see his eyes, yet she could *feel* his stare inside her mind: a tense, thoughtful sensation that gripped her as his farsights' field of virtual LOVs traded information with her own symbiotic colony. "The disk's interior is not like a balloon," he said, standing up on the saucer's back. "It's a honeycomb of independent chambers. The pressure is high, sure, but if the disk is breached, only a few chambers will collapse. It won't explode."

"Except in a catastrophic attack," Ky added thoughtfully.

"It wouldn't matter, then, would it?" Virgil countered. He stepped with one bare foot on a patch of colored LOVs. Ela was made aware of a hissing of air only because it ended. The aerostat ceased moving. It hovered docilely, its lip just overlapping the platform. "Want to go for a ride?"

Ela's suspicions were not allayed. What if the saucer failed? There *were* crocodiles in the water, after all.

"She hesitates," Ky said. "Is this the woman who was diving the wreck of the module within minutes of impact?"

"The woman who kept the LOVs alive despite the IBC," Virgil added.

"The woman who filmed a documentary amid gunfire and car crashes, to win Hanoi's sympathy to her cause."

Virgil cocked his head, making his topknot bob. "Are you afraid?"

She tapped her LOVs. "I'm smarter now."

They laughed, but they did not give up on her, and after a minute she found herself shedding her sandals to climb aboard barefoot in a carefully timed exchange with Ky. He slid onto the platform as she shifted her weight to the flying saucer, so that it did not bob into the air or sink onto the water.

It did wobble a little beneath her feet as she walked stiffly to the center of the disk, her arms spread for balance as if she were walking on a tightrope. Virgil grinned. "You'll only slide off if you believe you will."

"Shut up."

He laughed again. "Sit down then, if it makes you feel better."

She remained standing, her feet spread for balance as the hiss of air returned, and the flying saucer began to move away from the platform . . . rising as it went. "We're going up," Ela said nervously, peering over the side. The water was five feet away, then six. Then eight.

Virgil said, "I want to know how high we can go."

"How high have you been?"

"This is the record so far."

"Virgil—" Her angry retort was stopped by his grin. She couldn't withhold an answering smile. "All right. We keep pushing. No boundaries now."

He frowned. "Well personally, I think I'll accept a limit of two hundred feet or so. The LOVs can pump air for only so long, you know."

She threw a mock punch at his shoulder. He caught her fist. "Flying lessons?" he suggested. "You really should learn how to control the disk—"

"It's a flying saucer," she interrupted, staring at their linked hands. Surprising herself because she did not let go. No boundaries now?

She relaxed her fist. His hand slid hesitantly into hers. She could feel his doubt, and his surprise, downloading through her LOvs.

"All right," he said softly. "We can call it a flying saucer if you like."

He showed her how to command the saucer by stepping on the touch pads of living LOvs, one to change its direction, the other its elevation. They rose slowly, at least two hundred feet, maybe more. They were the highest point for miles around. She could see the little village on stilts below them, and the wooden boat with a new boy at the pole, bringing Oanh and Ninh back to the platform. She could see the water, spreading wide beneath them in a gloomy sheet, broken here and there by lines of trees and half-drowned houses on stilts, and towers and platforms of glistening LOvs. She could see no land, none at all, and the gray rain clouds seemed to sit upon their shoulders.

How much longer could they last here?

Long enough.

They were alien now. But what was alien today could become conventional tomorrow. It was the way of the world. Survive long enough, and strangeness becomes cliché.

"We should go back now," Virgil said, "before the LOvs are exhausted."

They returned to the platform, sliding off the saucer one by one as air poured into it and it settled on the water. Ninh and Oanh were back, and there was a fire going in the hut. Ela could smell chicken grilling. "How did you like your ride?" Ky asked. The rain had almost stopped for once, and he had thrown the hood of his poncho back.

"Beautiful," Ela said. "If we could market this, we would soon be rich—but it will at least make a good addition to my documentary."

"I wanted to talk to you about that. Have you checked your balance lately?"

She smiled. There were dozens of scientists and soldiers on

the reservation, and every one of them, as far as she could tell, had a contract with some news service or other. Ela had tried for a while to get a contract too, but by then the offers were so low it had not been worth doing. So she set up her own commercial site, where she displayed her ongoing coverage. It was a simple system: the first hit was free, and subsequent hits were billed at a few pennies each. She kept it up so that official opinions would not be the only ones represented. "The site is just there for the public record," she said. "I don't expect a lot of traffic."

"Check your balance," Ky urged.

"Why? Have I made a hundred dollars?"

He smiled.

She felt abruptly nervous. She tapped her fingers, instructing Kathang to look into the numbers. When the figure displayed, her face went slack. Ky chuckled, but she could hardly hear him past the buzzing in her ears. She sat down on the wet deck. Smoke from the grill teased her nose, and she sneezed.

Twenty-one million dollars.

"Your site's been busy," Ky said gently. "And that's only a small part of the money that could be made from the biotech being developed here."

"I had no idea." Her voice no more than a whisper. A cold little laugh uncoiled in her throat, escaped her mouth. "So . . . I have finally scored big!" She looked at Ky, then at Virgil, then at Ninh, who was checking the fishing lines. And Oanh, crouched just inside the hut. "I'm a millionaire," Ela said. Then she patted her belly. "A starving millionaire!"

Tears started in her eyes. "The money's no good if it can't buy us the things we need."

"Money's always good for something," Ky said.

"Bribes?"

He nodded.

She thought about all the things she wanted. Then she said, "Maybe we can find out what's become of our disappeared. Ky? Will you use it for that? You know better than me what can be done with it. I'll turn it over to you."

"No. I've already given them almost everything I have. Save this fortune. Don't let anyone else know you have it. Listen—" He beckoned to all of them, and they gathered around him in a somber circle. "I've preserved some holdings among the offshore farms. Everything else is gone: transferred or sold off to pay for our sanctuary here, but I held on to the farms. We might need those resources before this is done. They are owned now by a company called *Roi Nuoc*, Inc. Everyone of you are shareholders. Every one of the *Roi Nuoc*, whether they are inside the reservation or without. It's all quite legal. I've made Ela and Virgil and Ninh the officers because they're the only ones old enough for the job. I want you to know this. I want you to know there will be no complications in the event of my death."

"You don't own shares?" Virgil asked.

"No. If I did, they would trace it, and demand payment. I have no authority over this corporate entity at all."

"I want to put money into it too," Ela said. "Even if we can't use the money, there are more *Roi Nuoc* outside the reservation than inside it. Let it go to them."

Ky nodded. "If you like, transfer some. But hold on to the rest. You may find a need for ready cash before this is through."

They feasted on the chicken, and some ration bars Ky had brought along—the very last, he told them. The gray afternoon faded to twilight, and then to night. With the coming of darkness, the rain started in again.

CHAPTER 33

As the days passed more and more of the *Roi Nuoc* succumbed to disease. Dysentery took most, but there were incidents of malaria and yellow fever too. The afflicted children were evacuated as soon as their condition was discovered, but most tried to hide their illness as long as they could, for they knew that leaving meant their LOVs would be extracted. Most would sooner amputate a hand.

On this morning a twelve-year-old boy from one of the coastal cadres had been airlifted from the reservation. He had not gone willingly.

It made Virgil wonder: Were they truly so changed by the LOVs that losing them was a diminishment of their soul, of their sense of self? Or were they just addicts in denial, living for a corrupt promise of chemical enlightenment?

He had to ask himself, *What has changed about me?*

Simply put, he saw more. His mind perceived more detail in everything, from the feel of air across his skin to the emotional tells on a soldier's face. He paid attention to everything and remembered more of what he saw. His innate instincts for pattern recognition had been enhanced. His mind had become adept at seizing on elusive details that would have once escaped him; at patching together seemingly unrelated observations to expose a deep order in the flow of microevents in which every life was embedded. It was as if the world, which had once seemed made of many parts, had now resolved into a singular thing, a flow state of physical interaction that included himself and all others with no clear boundaries between them.

At once one and infinitely many.

A new religious credo?

Or raw self-deception, no different from the blissful enlightenment of an LSD trip?

Every event occurring in the mind was a state brought about by electrical flow and chemical interaction. Every human being was an addict, chained to brain chemicals that interpreted the world and synthesized a sense of self—a sense that changed by the minute, disturbed by the weather, the season, by flowing hormones or diet, age, and alcohol, and a hundred thousand drugs. Where was the baseline state? *Was* there a baseline state? Did it matter?

If addiction was defined as desire that leads to self-destruction, then the LOVs were not an addiction, any more than the hormones that commanded hunger and sexual passion and the drive to build monuments and to make art for art's sake and music were an addiction. The LOVs were an aspect of vibrant life that led to more life, not less. Losing the LOVs was not like losing a hand. It was like losing a feeling for music, or a desire for love.

This was what would be lost by the boy who'd been forcefully evacuated this morning. What *rational* ethic could ever make that right?

Virgil had been waiting when the uniformed soldiers brought the boy to the research station on their silent metal launch. He stepped off the floating shell of his flying saucer to meet them at the dock. Heavy wings fluttered in his mind. He saw himself as a vulture, poised against the last flow of breath from a dying body.

The boy handed his farsights over to Virgil without protest, without tears, without angry words. Mother Tiger had arranged it all. But despair looked out of his eyes. As the Australian medic started to wheel the gurney through the houseboat's French doors the boy had grabbed Virgil's wrist, his tiny voice speaking a frantic question in Vietnamese. Mother Tiger translated: "He asks you, Why do they want to make me less human?"

The medic had frowned at the contact. "Better disinfect," he advised Virgil. "Or you'll be in here tomorrow."

But there was no way to disinfect. And given the political storm that surrounded the LOVs, there was no reason to believe the UN would rule on their petition anytime soon. That was why Virgil turned to smuggling.

His accomplices were the *Roi Nuoc* cadres outside the reservation. They did not share in the LOVs, but they looked forward to a time when they would. Over a period of two days these *Roi Nuoc* had secretly released three thousand sealed packets of antibiotics into the water upstream of the reservation. Virgil hoped to recover at least five percent as they drifted seaward on sluggish currents that followed the beds of old irrigation ditches and flooded canals. To do it, he'd enlisted the help of Ela's spider.

He'd laid out the mission during a cognitive circle supervised by Mother Tiger: The spider was to slip beneath the water to search for packets, while alerting others of its kind to do the same. It had appeared to understand its role, but when they sent it out to search, it failed to return. Other spiders were sent after it, but not one of them came back. No antibiotic packets were recovered, and no one knew why.

"They've probably just misunderstood us," Ela said again, as if saying it over and over might make it true. "They're probably gathering the packets and hoarding them somewhere."

Virgil was busy using wire ties to secure his newly acquired farsights to a short-legged spider that had been brought up in a net that morning. He didn't believe in Ela's benign explanation, but he didn't want to argue, so all he said was, "We need to find out." He fixed a two-foot-long wire antenna to the farsights so they could link to Mother Tiger even when the spider was submerged. Then they rode the flying saucer to the western edge of the reservation, gliding a few feet above the water.

The rain had stopped, and scattered blades of sunshine sliced the clouds. Mosquitoes hovered over the water in smoky black clouds. Ela threw a veil of mosquito netting over her head. Virgil smeared mud on his face and hands and the back of his neck, in his hair and over his ears, but he still suffered bites on his lips and eyelids. Yellow fever and malaria had turned up all along the Mekong since the beginning of the flood.

Nothing to be done about it now.

They stopped a quarter mile short of the fluorescent orange PVC poles that marked the reservation's edge. Ela guided the flying saucer down, settling it on the surface of the water. Peeper balls floated past them, technological thistledown, watching as Virgil released the spider over the side.

The water was less than two feet deep, so the antenna protruded well above the surface. Virgil eyed the inset image in his farsights, but all he could see was drifting silt and dead weeds on the muddy bottom. With any luck the spider would find the packets—or at least find out what had happened to them. He watched as it marched away, its silver-blue shape blurring, then disappearing behind obscuring clouds of silt. Soon only the antenna marked its path.

Virgil felt a frisson of anxiety. He leaned forward, searching the water.

"Careful," Ela said, from her post at the center of the flying saucer. "You're going to fall."

"Let's follow the spider."

"What? Why?" She tapped her farsights. "We can see where it's going."

"But we can't see the spider itself, can we?"

"Is that important?"

"I don't know." He nodded at the touch pad. "Just for a few minutes."

Ela looked grim as she stepped on a pad. Air hissed from the vents, and the flying saucer lifted, gliding after the little V-wake of the spider's antenna. "We can't go far."

"We won't."

No one else was on the water, but peeper balls were everywhere. The IBC was watching, and they would certainly be arrested if they passed beyond the boundary poles.

Virgil leaned as far over the side as he dared, hoping for a glimpse of the spider's silvery legs or of the blue-green globe at the base of the antenna—until unexpected motion drew his gaze away to the right. Something dull silver wavered there in a stray beam of sunlight. He pointed. "Is that another spider?" The inset image still showed only silt.

Ela shrugged. "We could go see." She leaned on a touch pad, changing the flying saucer's trajectory. At the same time the silver shape turned, gliding across their path, moving much too quickly, too smoothly, to be a spider. Sinuous as a fish. Just as the flying saucer passed over it, Virgil watched it spit out two silver capsules of turbulent water the size of his thumb. "Slow down!" he shouted as twin projectiles streaked from under the saucer and out of sight, on an angled path toward their spider.

Ela stomped a touch pad and brought the saucer to a dead stop as, twenty yards out, a burst of white light flashed twice under the muddy water. The inset image vanished as the water erupted in a brown dome six feet across that collapsed back on itself with a rush and a roar. Whites shards of broken spider legs arced through the air, glittering as they tumbled end over end in the motley sunlight, falling back to the churning surface with a tinkling sound.

"Oh, God," Ela said. "They blew up the spider. Virgil, we've got to get out of here."

She stomped the touch pad. Air hissed, and the flying saucer jerked backward, sending Virgil pitching forward onto his hands and knees so that he was staring at the water as the saucer passed back over the sinuous silver fish shape. Its tail thrashed. Its back crested the surface in a ridge of metallic segments and then it was gone. "What the hell was that?".

"Get away from the edge!" Ela shouted. She was beside him now, pulling him back toward the center. "Get back! If you slip into the water, they'll shoot you too. They'd love to do it, and call it an accident."

"But what *was* that?" he asked as he scrambled to safety. "I never saw anything like that before—"

"I have." She pulled him down, as if they had to hide from sniper fire. "It was a robo-sub. They're used to guard the offshore farms, but the one I saw was armed with harpoons, not explosives."

He closed his eyes, feeling the voracious mosquitoes bump against his hands and face. Anger nipped him. "I never even guessed! How long have they been patrolling the boundary of the reservation? *Shit*. They must have eliminated every spider that ever came this way."

"And the antibiotic packets too." He looked up to discover tears standing in Ela's eyes. Tears. He had never seen her cry before. "Virgil, we aren't going to last through this. We aren't. They want us all to die here, one by one—"

"Ela—"

"It's true! They talk at the UN, but a vote never comes. The IBC trashes us. The media trashes us. We are freaks! Dangerous criminals. But the IBC never wants a vote to take us out. *Why not?* Why do they want us to die like this? It makes no sense!"

Her fear broke against him, interpreted and enhanced by his symbiotic LOVs, but he refused to submit to it. "We're not going to die," he said. "Not now. Not from this." He gestured at the flood, trying not to see the broken spider legs littering the surface. "And sometimes freaks and dangerous criminals win in the end." He tried a tentative smile. "You'll see. In a few years we'll all be glorious revolutionaries—" She started to turn away. "Ela?" He risked a light touch against her shoulder. "Don't go. Don't . . . give up. Please. Stay. Please?"

He opened his arms, and to his surprise she came to him. She leaned her head against his chest, her dark eyes staring out past her veil of mosquito netting to the receding orange boundary poles on the edge of the reservation. He held her, wanting to apologize, to say how sorry he was that his LOVs had dragged her into this mess. But it wasn't the truth. He was grateful to have her there.

CHAPTER 34

They were silent on the slow journey back, each alone with their thoughts. Ela worked at getting her dread locked up behind heavy pressure doors. Not so much under control, as confined. It had taken her by surprise, the way it had burst out whole like that. She was still keenly aware of it. It brushed at her consciousness, like the distant screams of a lunatic aunt locked up out of sight in a garden shed. But she could pretend not to hear.

After a while she raised her head from Virgil's chest, realizing they had gone too far. They had passed the platform she shared with Ninh and Oanh. The air was filled with the unaccustomed smell of the sea. "Where are we going?"

"I have something to show you," Virgil said. "A surprise."

Ela pulled away from him, feeling the return of her habitual caution. "*Surprise* is a tricky word, in the way it can mean either good or bad."

"Good is the default meaning. You'll like this."

He had made his platform in sight of the ocean. He took her

there, and it looked different than she remembered, bigger, with a white tower rising from one corner like a steep-walled tepee, or like a giant cone shell, eight feet high, with its point in the air. A light swell drew parallel lines of foam on the ocean, but nestled behind the sheltering wall of a levee, the water around the platform remained calm.

Ela stepped onto the mud-stained deck, while Virgil took the flying saucer down to the water, where he would moor it. She looked around, not so much because she was curious, but because if she didn't divert her mind the subliminal raving of Auntie Dread might turn into words.

An olive drab canvas that looked as if it had been cut from the abandoned medical tent was stretched over a low frame of arched ribs, so that it made a mini Quonset hut. Mosquito netting covered both ends. Ela knelt to examine the interior and was not surprised to see that the ribs were made of structural LOVs.

Beside the Quonset hut were several stacked crates of watertight plastic that looked as if they had been rescued from the medical tent along with the canvas. Behind them, young sweet potato vines trailed from a trough on the edge of the platform.

She turned, to find Virgil watching with an approving smile as she nosed about. He glanced meaningfully at the cone-shell tepee. She could smell the smoke of a citronella candle, and she wondered if someone was in there. "This is a large space for one person," she observed.

Virgil shrugged. "I'm an American."

Ela nodded. Her heart was beating faster now, though she could not say why. She took off her farsights and slipped them into the pocket of her pants, wanting to keep this surprise for herself. Then she circled around the back side of the cone-shell tepee until she found the door. Or the entrance, anyway. It was a narrow slit, formed as the wall wrapped around itself like the closing spiral of a seashell. A panel of mosquito netting draped the opening. Ela lifted the cloth and stepped through into a tiny alcove, where a citronella candle burned in a waist-high niche. Her shoulders scraped the walls. It seemed dark there, but only in contrast to what lay beyond. Slipping past the curve of the inner wall, she stepped into a tiny chamber brilliant with light that glittered and refracted against the white walls and white floor, playing among circular streaks of blue-green shadow.

Water trickled from overhead. Ela looked up to see crystal-clear streams dripping and twisting from the roof, like spring-water seeping from porous stone. She thought it was rain leaking in until she realized that the water splashing against her feet was *warm*. She held her hand out, and a ribbon of water pattered her palm, pooling in her hand, warm and clear.

"It's pumped up by veins of LOVs," Virgil said. She looked back, to see him standing in the slotted entrance. He watched her anxiously. His farsights were nowhere to be seen. "It's filtered, then funneled through hollow spaces in the walls where it's heated by sunlight."

"It's a shower?"

He nodded. "It's not very hot."

"I don't remember what hot is." She peeled off her poncho and dropped it on the floor. Then she stepped under the braided trickles. As the water ran through her oily hair and flowed past her closed eyes, she felt a frantic little laugh forming deep in her belly. It was a shower! A blessed, warm-water shower.

She wasn't going to shower in her clothes.

Tossing her head back, she peeled off her long-sleeved shirt and dropped the filthy wreck on top of her poncho. Now the water's fingers ran down past her gray sports bra and her mud-stained khaki pants. She unbuttoned those, and kicked them off too, watching Virgil watch her.

After a few seconds, he edged a little farther into the brilliant chamber. Then he hesitated . . . giving her a chance to scream or flee or order him out? Most gentlemanly. But when she failed to take advantage of this window of opportunity, he peeled off his own shirt and added it to her pile of things. The light wrapped across his pale skin, finding each seam between his muscles, each hollow between his ribs, glinting against the nearly invisible shafts of golden hair that sprouted in a sparse cross on his chest and belly.

He smelled of mud.

She smiled for the first time that day as the knots in her soul began to loosen. "Will you sit with me?"

She did not wait for an answer, but settled cross-legged on the floor, the warm water splashing, trickling through the candle-scented air. He hesitated, half-crouched, one hand on his knee. "You're sure?"

She nodded, smoothing her wet hair back from her forehead. "Face me," she said. "Think with me."

He was warming up to this. She could see it in his eyes, in his half smile as he sat cross-legged on the glittering floor, combing his hair back with his large hands. He had started with a scattering of solitary LOVs across his brow, but each one of those had since reproduced many times so that now his LOVs gathered in gemlike clusters along his hairline. In the scintillating rainbow light they were almost colorless. He said: "I can't hide what I'm feeling."

"I don't want you to." Desire unfolded inside her like a lotus blooming, its petals falling open to reveal a banked fire at its center blazing up at the kiss of oxygen. She gave herself up to the feeling, leading her LOVs to capture it, amplify it—

—and to *project* it.

She watched his eyes and saw lust bite down on him like a cobra's jaws. A glassy look washed over his face. When he spoke, his voice had been squeezed to a hoarse whisper as if he were on a rack and this was all pain and not pleasure. "Why now, Ela?"

"I don't know. I guess . . . in case there is no other time." Striving not to lose this link with his eyes, she wrestled her sports bra off over her head. She slipped out of her mildewed swim shorts, cursing them for a chastity belt and swearing she would never put them on again.

Everything had changed. All her life, the future had been a mass tugging at her, drawing out her desires over years. A strange attractor bending her behavior on a long curved path around it. Now her future had burst apart into a fog of particles, and she could not see even an hour ahead. *Now* was all, and everything she was or ever would be felt suspended in this moment.

So intense was the focus the LOVs gave her, that reality seemed to bend around her now, closing the two of them off in this chamber of light and candle scent and warm trickling water. She rose to her knees before him, drunk on the blush of her own body, suffused with warmth from toes to scalp.

He rose to meet her and she felt swallowed by a beast of slick warm hungers as he took her in his arms. "You're not afraid."

The words came from somewhere subterranean, rumbling beneath an Earth of blood and bone. True words. She whispered them back, as if they were a mantra. *"I'm not afraid."* Her LOVs had let her finally leave that behind.

Some untroubled time had passed—hours, maybe—when Ela awoke to an insistent drumming, a pounding rhythm that forced her back into the world. She blinked, and the sound resolved into the drumming of rain against the dark curve of olive drab canvas that roofed Virgil's Quonset hut. Gray light passing through the mosquito netting at the hut's arched ends fell across her bare shoulder, illuminating a tiny, perfect, feather-soft organic robot crouched upon her skin, feeding on her blood. She watched it, marveling at its delicate wings, its fragile legs finer than a human hair, its tiny eyes, its sharp proboscis perfectly shaped to draw the life fluids from her body. Then she pulled a hand out from under the thermal sheet that covered her and shooed the engorged mosquito away.

Virgil slept beside her, covered by only a corner of the blanket. His face was a face of ancient beauty, an alabaster Buddha that has become one with the forest, embraced in vines, hearing enlightenment in a bird's song—while along the curve of his pale hip three mosquitoes were having their way with him. She shooed them off too, then lightly kissed his lips, tasted his breath, brought her LOVs close to his and shared the tranquility of his nondreaming mind.

The rain eased, giving way to human voices drawing nearer across the water. She sat up, wondering how she had come to be in the Quonset hut anyway. Her last memory was of the world ending in a blinding meltdown, an ecstatic dissolution of time and space as some god breathed into her soul and set a new world forming there.

Perhaps such a world had been conceived in some other fold of reality . . . while she had fallen back into the same world that had always claimed her.

She found her clothes—still soggy—draped across a line, and wriggled into them. Her farsights were still tucked in the pocket of her pants.

The voices arrived, along with the thunk of a boat against the platform. The soft tread of footsteps soon followed, generating a faint vibration in the floor. Virgil stirred and touched her back. She turned to find a tired smile on his face. "Lie down with me," he whispered.

"People have come."

"Only for a minute."

"I think it's Nash . . . and another man I don't know."

Virgil sat up with a frown of sharp concern. His arm went around her shoulder. "Stay here in the tent." He mouthed the words, putting hardly any volume into them.

"Why?" Her voice was not as loud as her heartbeat. "What's wrong?"

"The new man, Steven Ho. He calls himself a research scientist, but I've seen him. He's a professional soldier."

"Then he'll already know who I am."

"I don't want him to know about us. He could use it against us."

"He already knows, Virgil. You know they're watching all the time, with their peeper balls, their surveillance drones, their robo-subs, and who knows what else. They're listening to our whispers right now. *They know.*"

He shrugged. "I still want you to stay."

He pulled on his pants and his shirt. He slipped on his farsights.

"Virgil," Nash called in a low voice. Ela could hear him shifting from foot to foot as he waited a few yards beyond the Quonset hut. "Virgil, we know what you tried to do this morning."

Virgil kissed Ela's cheek. He kissed her ear, his reluctant sigh flowing warm against her neck and shoulder. "Stay here." Then he crept out of the hut and stood, blocking the entrance so that she could not get out if she wanted to. Rainwater ran off the blue tek-fabric of his shirt as he crossed his arms over his chest. She could not see his face.

"Hello, Nash."

Nash answered, sounding querulous. "We know about the smuggling attempt, Virgil. It's over for you now. We're asking to have your asylum revoked. You and Ela Suvanatat."

"We didn't do anything."

From the back of the hut Ela heard a ripple of water, as soft and mechanically smooth as a desktop waterfall. She looked around, in time to see a tiny glass canoe slip past, only a few feet from the platform. Glass boats were not so unusual anymore. Seated in this one was a willowy girl dressed in light cotton clothes that might have once been white. A conical rain hat hid her face, but as she flashed past, Ela glimpsed her hand resting on the gunwale. It was pale, and skeletally thin . . . and it did not hold a paddle, or a pole.

So how did the boat move?

Ela scrambled to the back of the hut and looked out as the canoe rounded the end of the platform. The girl sat perfectly still, looking as if she had *willed* the canoe to turn.

Ela glanced back at Virgil. In the growing heat of argument he had apparently forgotten his resolve to blockade her inside the hut, for he had stepped away from the door. She heard him contesting with Nash about the smuggling incident: what it meant, if it had even happened. She didn't think he had seen the canoe. It rode low in the water, and it had passed so close to the elevated platform that it was unlikely either man had seen it.

So Ela slipped her farsights on, tapped them to record, and scrambled out of the hut. Virgil looked at her in sharp surprise as she skipped past him. She in turn spent only a glance on Nash Chou, draped in a yellow poncho. Then she loped across the platform. On the other side, she looked down at the water, but already the canoe was out of sight. So she cut around the shower room—and almost ran into a stranger.

He stood at least six foot six, his bronze face veiled by a

curtain of rain that ran off the brim of his canvas hat. He wore loose field pants stuffed into shiny, knee-high boots, and a green tek-fabric shirt that showed the line of every well-developed muscle in his broad shoulders. His eyes were hidden behind opaque farsights. He looked her over, before his attention returned to the water.

Virgil was right. Steven Ho did not look much like a researcher.

Ela shuffled cautiously up to the edge of the platform, not daring to take her eyes off him for more than a second or two at a time. She remembered the IBC cop who had tried to arrest her on the edge of the reservation, and how helpless she'd been in his hands. But her curiosity was stronger than her caution. She peered over the platform's edge in time to see the girl making her way out of the glass canoe and onto the ladder. She looked to be about fifteen.

Ela leaned down, one hand on her knee. "How does your boat move?" she called.

The girl looked up with a radiant smile. In the space between her eyebrows and her hat, Ela could see a solid bridge of LOVs. Never had she seen so many on one person. They gleamed like luminous skin. "The LOVs in the hull all pump water like tiny squid, pushing the boat forward," she explained, speaking in the Australian-accented English that seemed so popular among the *Roi Nuoc*. "My name is Lien."

"I'm Ela. Your boat is lovely." She said it with full sincerity as the girl climbed onto the platform.

Virgil joined them, his fingers touching Ela's arm. "Hello, Lien."

"Pleasant to see you again, Dr. Copeland." Lien nodded, at the same time loosening the sash beneath her chin that held her hat in place.

Virgil looked to Ela. "Lien transplanted my LOVs to Ky."

Nash stood behind him now, an impatient look on his face. "Virgil! This new canoe is just one more rea—" He made a little gasping sound as Lien tipped off her hat to stand bareheaded in the rain. Ela felt her own breathing stop.

Lien's head was sheathed in LOVs. She had no hair, and no

visible skin anywhere on her scalp. Only a glittering helmet of LOVs that began at her eyebrows, ran past her ears, and ended at the nape of her neck.

"*My God,*" Nash whispered.

Steven Ho spoke in a coarser voice, "Holy Christ."

Ela felt mesmerized by the glinting display; it took an effort of will to turn away. Apparently Virgil did not feel so vulnerable. He gazed at the girl while a faint, incredulous smile warmed his face. "Lien, you have been busy."

She blushed. "Solutions are not so easy to find."

"Where are your farsights?" he asked, and for the first time Ela realized the girl was not wearing any.

Lien patted the pocket of her blouse. "They are here."

"Why aren't you wearing them?"

She looked a little sad. Then she ran a hand across her glittering LOV helmet. "Mother Tiger does not approve." She slipped her hat back on, her lips pursed as if it were a small thing, like spilled tea. "I am still *Roi Nuoc.*"

Nash stepped forward, his poncho rattling. He shook his round head. "Look at her, Virgil! This *child.* What do you think will be left of her when those LOVs are removed? This is what it's come to. *This is what you've done!*"

Lien looked at Nash as if he were some strange, wild beast. Then she turned back to Virgil. "I have a design for a citadel that will offer shelter to all the *Roi Nuoc.*"

"Shelter from what?" Steven Ho asked, speaking over Ela's shoulder.

Lien took a moment to examine him. Then she smiled. "Shelter from the rain, the wind, the sea, the heat when it returns . . . but not from bombs or guns. We cannot hide from that if you finally choose to come against us."

CHAPTER 35

Summer had not been outside in days. She was afraid to go outside; afraid of the very bodyguards who had been assigned to "protect" her. Their real job was to make sure she did not talk to the wrong people, she was sure. So day after day she sat in her office, under the surveillance cameras of the IBC, and toyed with design after molecular design, projected in three dimensions on her wall screen.

She had supervised the development of six separate viral weapons to be used against the LOVs. Three were simple, organic toxins attached to a viral vector. They would act as mutagens, interfering in LOV reproduction. Three were debilitating viruses that would act directly against a LOV host. All had been designed to distinguish between a symbiotic LOV and one outside a human immune system. She still brooded over the reason behind this. Why did Daniel Simkin want to preserve the symbiotic LOVs?

Of course, Simkin denied that preservation was his goal; he cited international laws against germ warfare: *We may not be allowed to attack the symbiotic LOVs directly; we need to be prepared for whatever level of war we are allowed to wage.*

It was a sound argument. So why couldn't she believe it?

She looked up at a molecular model of her latest effort projected on the wall screen of the darkened room. It rotated slowly, glowing in colorful 3-D. Her team had not synthesized it yet, but if they could learn to fabricate it, they would have something quite different from any other project developed to date. This was a marker virus, designed to find any remnant asterids that might have been left behind in the evacuated children, when their LOVs were removed.

Perhaps though, what was really needed was a marker virus to find the evacuated children? They were being kept under a remarkable veil of secrecy. Even the tabloids, with all their money, had not found even one of them to interview. Summer had a hard time believing that everyone involved in the welfare of these children was immune to bribes.

Of course, reports had been issued on each evacuated child. Summer had received copies like everyone else, but each bulletin amounted to nothing more than a brief, vanilla description: "all signs normal; rapid recovery; a bright and healthy child." All in all, a benign portrait that could only stir suspicion. Neurological intervention was never that easy, but Simkin refused to discuss her concerns, and no one else she had cornered would admit to knowing more.

Summer cautioned herself against unwarranted speculation. No meaningful conclusion could be drawn on a mere absence of fact. Still, she could not escape a sense of unease. Were the children being kept out of sight because the procedure used to remove the LOVs had gone seriously wrong?

She dropped her farsights on the desk. Then she got up, and paced.

What if there *had* been trouble? What if the neurosurgery involved in removing the LOVs was more dangerous than anyone wanted to admit? Was it possible that some (or all?) of the children had suffered permanent brain damage?

The procedure could only grow more difficult with each successive child, as time enhanced the complexity of neural connections, and the children continued to accumulate LOVs.

Summer stopped her pacing. She clasped her hands behind her back, staring past the rotating display. Might the *Roi Nuoc* win their petition by default, if experience showed the symbiosis was impossible to undo?

Simkin would want to hide a fact like that, no matter what his personal agenda might be.

She sighed, knowing the true explanation might be completely different. *God, how I hate secrecy!*

"Refresh screen."

The display blanked to a dim gray glow that bled into the darkened room, picking out edges, wrapping around the raw shapes of things.

When Summer had first conceived the LOV project it had promised so much. Mental illness had always haunted human history. A subtle imbalance of brain chemicals could turn a loving individual into a helpless, hopeless shell of humanity, steered by a mind utterly detached from reality. Drugs and therapy and even surgery sometimes helped, but they were all crude cures, akin to setting off bombs in a city to kill the rats that spread plague. By contrast the LOVs had offered a subtle, infinitely adjustable means of balancing neurochemical signals— but nothing ever unfolds as foreseen.

Summer had conceived the LOV project as a cure for a host of mental afflictions, but now she had to wonder: Had she accomplished the destruction of these children instead?

CHAPTER 36

The Sea Palace grew on the coast, beyond the last of the sea dikes with their forests of replanted mangrove. Its foundation was an estuarine mudflat, built up by silt and sediment from the flood. When the dry season came and the river receded to its banks this would be new land, unowned by anyone. For now though, water stood knee deep over the site.

That didn't matter to the spiders. They convened around Lien as she crouched in the shallows, forty-eight of them, gathered in loose concentric circles. In the gray daylight beneath the perpetual clouds, the LOVs on Lien's skull could be seen gleaming as they communicated to the spiders the design she had conceived for the Sea Palace. Virgil stood at a respectful distance with a small crowd of *Roi Nuoc*. He hungered to know what Lien herself was feeling during this exchange. Did she have a direct awareness of the dialogue between the LOV colonies? Or was she just another kind of chassis for the LOVs to ride? Spider legs with an agile pair of hands attached, and a little extra processing power.

Mother Tiger still did not approve. The ROSA had become a

tiny icon stalking the screen of Virgil's farsights, back and forth, back and forth, anger caught within a cage. Lien did not wear her farsights.

Almost two hours passed, and then the conference of spiders broke up. Some scuttled fifty yards up or down the coast; others waded closer to the silt bars and the foaming lines of breakers that marked the estuary's intersection with the sea. An IBC platform had been anchored beyond the breaking waves. Virgil could see someone there, watching the gathering on shore while a cloud gray drone floated overhead, recording the spectacle of the spiders arranging themselves in precise ranks, defining the shape of a regular pentagon with an area as large as a city gymnasium, one point facing out to sea. The spiders crouched in place, so that their central globes disappeared beneath the shallow water; only the bend in their knees remained above the surface, leaving the estuary looking as if it had been pierced with circles of shining white sticks.

The spiders did not move again. Lien returned to her territory; the other *Roi Nuoc* scattered to their own holdings on small glass boats or flying machines. Virgil stayed until sunset, but nothing more happened that day—at least, nothing he could see.

By next morning the situation had changed. The spiders were still in place, but now a low, pentagonal foundation of LOVs grew around, beneath, and between them, like a concrete pour locking their legs in place. The day after that the spider chassis were completely buried—but the globes no longer nested within them. They had been lifted above the growing platform, each one held in a transparent cup at the top of knee-high pedestals that rose as the platform rose.

The UN scientists brought in heavy equipment to map the subterranean structure; they drilled test cores and what they found surprised no one: The Sea Palace grew from roots extending deep into the mud of the delta. Ten thousand years of mud. Ela tried to imagine the archaeology being done down there as the roots dissected the remains of animist cultures, of Chinese and Viet and French kingdoms, of twentieth-century war.

When Lien first shared her plans, Ky had worried about the wisdom of the project: "It's too big. It will be seen as a fortress. It will look as if we are *daring* the IBC to attack." The *Roi Nuoc* had listened politely while the project advanced with the same unalterable momentum that seemed always to surround the LOVs. It was as if they generated a cultural gravity that pulled everything around them faster and faster into an unknowable future.

The foundation grew for a week, fed by its invisible root system. It was the trick of LOVs that they would program most of their structural members to die off, so that the mass of the project grew rapidly while the number of living LOVs requiring metabolic support increased at a much slower rate. Most structural LOVs survived only long enough to deposit one more scant layer of limestone, before they were buried by the progeny that would form the next.

The root system expanded in a similar fashion: Its network of fragile veins grew far faster than the number of living LOVs requiring nutritional support, so that as the days passed, more and more material was transported to the Sea Palace, allowing it to grow at an ever-increasing rate, until oxygen became the limiting factor. No one realized how thoroughly the LOVs' frantic metabolism had scoured the air around the platform until Ky made the mistake of taking two reporters on a tour of the project, on a day when the rain had stopped and the wind did not stir. Within minutes they were dizzy from lack of oxygen. Ky guessed what was happening and made it to the platform's edge with one of the reporters in tow, but the other had to be rescued by a UN helicopter.

After that, the *Roi Nuoc* would inspect the platform only on windy afternoons, but the UN scientists would go out anytime, wearing oxygen tanks while they gathered air samples at different heights above the project.

Within a week the foundation grew into a solid block of pseudolimestone eight feet high, its sides hung with lovely filigrees of living pipe. At that point the pattern of growth changed as walls began to form. On the seaward side of the palace the walls were eight feet thick, breakwaters built to withstand the pounding waves of Class IV storms. The interior walls, at a mere three feet in width, were almost petite by comparison.

The platform was divided into two huge rooms that were eventually enclosed with vaulted ceilings so that they looked like coral caves in an undersea palace. The chamber on the inland side had a wide, arched doorway, numerous window slits, and a band of frosted glass at the top of the outer walls. The ocean room at the building's massive prow was darker, a shelter built to withstand foul weather and waves. It had no windows. Air was pumped in through the walls by capillaries of living LOVs, while columns of brightly luminous LOVs cast an eerie glow against the darkness. Two stairways led to the roof, where the walls of a lighter second story were just beginning to form.

Ela climbed the stairs one windy evening to stand beside a parapet three feet high. Globes floated in troughs at the top of the growing walls, casting a gleaming light upward against her face. She stood at the point of the pentagon that faced the sea—the prow—and leaned over, looking down at the building's gleaming foot. There the geometrical perfection of the Sea Palace failed. The LOVs at the seaward point had never stopped reproducing. They laid down layer upon irregular layer of limestone, building a miniature headland as a buffer against the pounding waves of future storms. As the building eroded, it would be rebuilt again.

It would last longer than the people it had been made to shelter.

She wondered if this was why the UN had put off its decision for so long: Did they hope to claim what was left when the *Roi Nuoc* were gone? What was the market value of the knowledge evolving here?

"*Ela?*"

She started at the sound of Virgil's voice, emanating from her farsights. Then she answered softly, "I'm here."

His image appeared onscreen. She could see candlelight behind him, and the dusky blue of the twilight sky. His LOVs gleamed blue-green across his forehead, casting a wan light that emphasized the gaunt lines of his face. "Thuyen has dysentery," he said. "She'll be taken out tonight."

Ela nodded, unsurprised. Unless something changed, it was only a matter of days for all of them. She could see their future in Virgil's face, as the hard outlines of his skull emerged from beneath his thinning skin. He looked as if he were melting away. They all looked that way. Ela could feel her own teeth loosening in her gums. When Thuyen was gone, only nineteen *Roi Nuoc* would remain on the reservation. Each one of them was determined to stay, but they could not hold out forever.

Virgil looked uneasy with her silence. "Ky and I will take Thuyen to the research station."

"You'll talk to Nash again?"

"I'll try."

"Maybe there will be some vitamins you can steal."

"I'll do what I can."

The link closed. Voices floated up the stairwell from the lower rooms; smoke from the flash grill on the landing thickened the air. No matter what the UN finally decided, Ela knew they truly had become a tribe, sharing what fish they could catch. There was nothing else but fish.

She leaned on the parapet, her folded arms resting on the lip of the trough. The ocean was a dusky blue even darker than the sky. Lights gleamed on the IBC barges, and in merry outline on the observational blimps anchored up and down the coast. Closer, colder, was the light of the globes in the trough. Their chill blue-green glow brightened as night descended. They were aware of her. Ela watched the closest globe migrate toward her, producing a petite swirl and distortion of water behind it as it moved. The familiar sense of recognition and greeting touched her. Mother Tiger stirred, and all around the edge of Ela's screen a crust of blue-green ice began to build.

"We must hold out as long as we can," she whispered into the nascent cognitive circle. They must survive until the UN made its decision. The lawyer had promised it would not be much longer. He'd been more positive lately about their chances. He thought that maybe the remaining *Roi Nuoc* would be allowed to negotiate to keep their Lovs . . . but at the same time he warned that no matter what, she and Virgil and Ky would face prosecution in an international court.

The uncoupling of their fates from that of the children had come as a relief to her. She did not want to give up, but it was easier to believe in a future for the children alone. To hope for their reprieve.

"We have to survive until the decision," she whispered.

Then relief supplies would be flown in, even over the objections of the IBC, and their society would go on for a while longer.

Mother Tiger stalked the base of her screen, while the blue-green field expanded. Ela felt herself falling forward along a slow arc, deeper and deeper into the mesmerizing pull of the Lovs.

"Survival depends on our supply of food and medicine. We have no way to get medicine . . . and the only food left is fish."

The tiger sat, twitching its tail, waiting for her to find the path she wished to walk.

"We can survive on fish. For a while anyway. We could . . . if there was enough."

"Fish are abundant," Mother Tiger said, its low voice soft and warm and soothing as candlelight.

"We are not so good at hunting them," Ela conceded. In fact, they were getting worse. "We have no energy to go after them, and nothing to replace our damaged nets." She smiled wistfully. "It would be easy if the fish swam to us! If they swam into pens or ponds. If we had them in ponds, like before the flood, then it would be easy to take them. How could we get them into the ponds? How could we get them to swim to us? This is silly, right? But I heard whales can be driven to beach themselves. It's a brain infection, or something. A virus or bacteria that drives them to do it?"

Mother Tiger said, "That is a dominant theory."

Ela nodded. "Everything we do—everything any creature does—depends on brain chemistry, on the electrochemical interactions in our brains. And we know how to affect that. Yes, I mean the Lovs. They link to neural tissue. Could they form a symbiosis with a fish brain? Probably not. But a symbiosis is not really what we need. We want to drive the fish to our pens, to our nets. Could the Lovs do that? Suppose they could. Then they would be a parasite that controls the behavior of its host. We could send them out to hunt for us, the way we might have sent out the men of the village to hunt for meat.

"But how could LOVs catch fish? We know it's the other way around. Fish eat LOVs. They are shining, glimmering prey, and they don't survive in the fish stomach. LOVs find new hosts only when we move them. We are voluntary hosts. Transplanting the LOVs is part of our role in the symbiosis. But fish won't volunteer. So how to get the LOVs to the fish? They might be shot at the fish, attaching when they hit. But they are so tiny and light they could not go far. Perhaps they should have a way of moving, some sort of flagellum. A chain of LOVs could form a flagellum. Like a delicate sea snake. It wouldn't have to swim long distances. Mostly it would drift, until a victim drew near, probably wanting to eat the shiny tendril. Then it could whip into action, driving its leading segment into the fish's head. Then the LOVs could use their chemical factories, driving the fish toward the hormones leaking from the Sea Palace . . ."

Her voice trailed off as the sound of light footfalls reached her, drawing nearer as someone mounted the stairs. "Ela?" It was Oanh's voice. "Your farsights wouldn't accept a link."

Ela turned, the blue-green field of her awareness burning away like a dream image. *Had* it been a dream?

"I would not have bothered you," Oanh said. "But we are ready to eat."

"I'll come. In a minute."

Oanh nodded, her eyes black pits beneath the light of her LOVs. "Are you all right?"

It could not have been a dream. Ela had imagined a new kind of LOV, a *predator*. There had never been predatory LOVs before.

Ela looked back at the globe, moving away now along the trough.

What have I done?

"Ela?"

Surely it would come to nothing. Idle speculation, that's all it had been. LOVs did not behave in the way she had imagined. She forced herself to look at Oanh. She forced herself to smile. "I'm all right," she said. "Just fine. Let's eat now . . . while we can."

All through the next day Ela loitered about the Palace, anxiously watching for signs that her musings were being made real. She didn't see any evidence of it. She didn't really expect to . . . after all, she had been engaged in a cognitive circle with a globe on the parapet. It would have limited communication with globes in the water . . . right? She comforted herself with this thought until near noon when a spider came down the stairs, walked through the great hall of the Sea Palace, and disappeared into the water. Did it carry *her* globe? There was no way to tell.

She schooled herself to be calm.

Two more days passed. Perhaps her scheme had been forgotten. Perhaps it had been mistranslated or misunderstood. Perhaps it would require a hundred years of experimentation to get right, or perhaps it was unworkable on some basic level. Perhaps there weren't enough fish left for the LOVs to have a fair chance of finding them. By the end of the third day she began to relax, convinced nothing would come of her ill-considered session.

Then on the fourth day, catfish began congregating in the shallow water around the Sea Palace's foundation.

Ela was sitting on the stairs just outside the arched entrance, working with Oanh to repair a net, when she noticed the dark, barbelled shapes of the fish chasing one another in water only a few inches deep. One of them broke the surface with a frothy ruffle. Oanh looked up from her work, her eyes going wide as she saw the fish. Four or five large catfish at least, stirring up swirls of mud at the foot of the algae-coated stairs. It took only a few seconds to get the net over them and haul them up. Ela eyed their glossy black bodies wrapped up in the net's white filaments. Then she looked at Oanh, and without saying a word, she removed her farsights, toggled their power switch, and slipped them into her pants pocket.

Oanh considered this. Then she too slipped her farsights off and put them away.

Ela crouched to examine their catch. The catfish lay limp and glossy within the net. She turned one over without unwrapping it, and there it was: a pale filament, trailing from a point on its head just behind the eye. Fear squeezed her by the neck. Oanh sensed it. She leaned over to look, and Ela felt the flood of her sharp concern. "What is that?" Oanh asked. "Do you know? You do."

Ela nodded. "It's a chain of LOVs."

Oanh bent closer to examine it. Then she whispered to Ela, "You expected this." It was not a question. "Did you design it?"

Ela let her gaze stray to the other dark, shining lumps of hijacked protein wrapped up in the net's white mesh. "I guess so."

"It's . . . clever," Oanh said tentatively, as if testing Ela's opinion on whether it was clever or not.

Ela said, "It was a mistake."

"How? The fish are here. That is what you planned?"

"Yes."

"The LOVs forced them here?"

"That was the design."

"It's clever."

"Yes. I guess so."

But would it stop here? Ela knew it would not. The LOVs were never static.

Oanh embraced a thoughtful silence as they removed the fish from the net. Each one trailed a LOV filament. Some had two. Ela pinched them off. She started to toss them into the water, but then she thought better of it and threw them under the archway, where they would dry out and die. She didn't want to send evidence of their experience back into the wild population.

By the time the net was empty, more catfish were circling in the shallows. A circuit of the second floor revealed them nuzzling all around the base of the Sea Palace. Ela sat down behind the parapet, thinking *Maybe this isn't so bad*. But she couldn't believe it. What would happen when the UN scientist discovered what was going on?

Delighted cries arose from below as the remaining *Roi Nuoc* discovered their good fortune. The fishing party that followed went on all afternoon, with fish after fish gutted alive and tossed over flash grills to be cooked almost before they had stopped wriggling. Everyone ate their fill and still, hundreds more catfish nosed about the base of the Sea Palace, like black tassels on the hem of a white dress. No one mentioned the LOV filaments.

But they must have noticed.

Perhaps Mother Tiger had counseled everyone to silence.

Oanh was wearing her farsights again as Ela descended the stairs. Smoke from the grills had reddened her eyes, and she looked less happy than the others. "Are you going?" she asked, as she followed Ela outside.

"Yes." She touched her stomach. "I'm so full I'm going to be sick. I need to lie down where it's quiet." Ela untied her little canoe from its mooring. "If Virgil comes back from the research station, tell him where I've gone."

Several seconds passed as Oanh studied Ela's face . . . reading the telltales? "Why are you still not wearing your farsights?"

Ela's hand jumped as if to touch the missing frame. "Oh. My eyes are tired. I-I have a headache."

"The UN decision will be announced tomorrow."

Ela turned, fear and hope spilling through her mind in equal measure. "You've heard this?"

Oanh nodded somberly. "Mother Tiger shares your concerns."

Ela nodded, and slid into the canoe. The late-afternoon rains began as she paddled back to Virgil's platform. A heavy downpour, that set the water boiling. She stopped once to bail her canoe. She stopped again just a few feet from the platform when she spied a small object floating in the water. It was hard to make out amid the pounding, splashing drops of rain, but it was dark in color, and it moved against the current like an animal, swimming. A rat. She stiffened. Her lip curled in distaste, and she gripped the paddle harder, but the rat didn't seem aware of her. All its energy was focused on reaching the platform. After a minute, it bumped up against one of the pilings. Its tiny paws scrabbled at the shiny reef of LOVs and somehow it found purchase there. It climbed, up, and out of the water.

"Scat," Ela said softly. "Go away."

The rat turned to look at her. It was a large rat, its wet fur black and bedraggled except at the head where lighter hair reflected a greenish cast from the water. A blue-green cast. Almost luminous.

Ela's eyes widened. Slowly, slowly, she let her paddle slide into the water, nudging her canoe closer. The rat watched her, its dead black eyes following her every movement. Now she could see it easily: The rat's head was covered in a helmet of LOVs that encircled its eyes and cranium, and descended halfway down its snout. Ela felt the skin on her neck tighten.

Did I do this?

The prow of the canoe nudged the piling, bringing her eye to eye with the rat. A dank sweat covered her skin. Her heart pounded harder than the rain, while the rat's LOVs glittered. Ela could see the flash and glitter of her own LOVs bright in the corner of her vision.

Abruptly, a sensation of hunger flooded her. The rat was hungry. She knew this. She could feel its hunger.

Kin.

She felt its weak call on her support.

Kin.

As if having LOVs made it more than a rat.

Her revulsion must have been coded into the millisecond flash of her own LOVs because the rat suddenly turned, scrambling frantically up the piling. Ela reacted with equal speed. She raised the paddle and swung hard, clipping the rat across the spine. It fell into the water. She hit it again, driving it under the surface. Out of sight.

CHAPTER 37

F or many days, Virgil had spent most of his waking hours working with Ky to evacuate sick and injured children. The most common afflictions were dysentery and small wounds gone septic in the filthy conditions. There was no predicting where the next case would strike—only the certainty that it would. Virgil felt like a seer with myopia, able to see disaster looming in the future, but never knowing where it would fall.

When disease did erupt, it hit hard and fast. Malnutrition had eaten away at the *Roi Nuoc*'s physical reserves, so that twelve hours of fever could reduce a child to a shell of fragile skin and delicate bone, life escaping bit by bit with every fiery exhalation.

And still none ever volunteered to leave the reservation. They knew it meant losing their LOVs, and most preferred to take their chances, even when their fever left them no chance at all. Some would go so far as to shed their farsights and disappear into half-drowned orchards infested with snakes that had gathered in the trees to escape the floodwater. Virgil and Ky were forced to become hunters. Their presence was feared. When they arrived to fetch the ill and the injured to the research station, stricken children looked upon them as if they were angels of death.

So when Virgil returned to the Sea Palace and Oanh told him of how Ela had refused to wear her farsights all afternoon and then had left, complaining of headache and nausea, Virgil suspected the worst. He stood on the steps of the palace, eyes closed, breathing deeply to stave off panic. *Why now?* he thought. *Why now?*

The UN had promised a decision on relief supplies within twenty-four hours, but if Ela had contracted dysentery, she might not last that long. He would have to bring her in for treatment now, tonight. . . .

And she would be arrested, or she would join the disappeared. In either case he would not see her again.

Not now, he thought. *Not this soon.*

They were supposed to have one more day.

He waved off Oanh's offer of help and bounded onto the back of the flying saucer, cursing its maddening, slow pace as it glided through the rain-pummeled darkness. He looked ahead to the platform, searching with his farsights for warm candlelight, but the only light came from the eerie glow of LOVs in the shower walls.

After what seemed an hour, the flying saucer bumped up against the deck. Only the rain moved, in wild, dancing splashes. He forced himself to patience, tying up the saucer and settling it against the water before he went into the hut.

Ela was there, wrapped up in their thin blanket, watching him—though he could not have been more than a glimmer of LOVs to her eyes, for she still was not wearing her farsights. He looked at her with nightvision, but even so her image was dim, blurred. This night was very dark, lit only by their LOVs. He could see well enough to know she did not smile.

He peeled off his wet shirt and left it by the door, then he dropped to his knees beside her. With his wet hands he felt her cheeks, her forehead.

Her skin was cool.

"Ela? Oanh thought you might be sick."

"I'm not sick." Her voice was flat, emotionless. Not like Ela's voice at all. "What time is it in New York?" she asked. "Has the UN made its decision yet?"

"Not yet. Ela, what's wrong?"

"Lie down with me, Virgil. Please. This one more time."

He was awakened in the morning by an emergency call from Nash. In the gray predawn light, Ela watched him as he picked up his farsights and slipped them on, her face with the same flat, hopeless expression she'd had last night. He wondered if she had slept at all.

Nash's tonsure of thinning hair was rumpled and his eyes were shadowed with fatigue, but his face looked curiously animated. "Virgil. Come to the station now. I don't want to say more."

Virgil sensed a trap. "What's up?" he asked lightly. "What do you have in mind?"

"Something you need to see. I won't say more. Come in now. This may change your mind about everything."

Ela had slipped out the back of the hut to relieve herself. When she returned he told her what Nash had said. She nodded. "I'll go with you."

"It's possible they've gotten permission to arrest me."

"I don't think that's it."

"What then?"

"Let's just go and see."

So they washed, and pulled damp clothes onto pale skin. Virgil thought of leisurely mornings in Honolulu with a full pot of coffee and sausage and pastries. Then he put on his rain gear and climbed on the back of the flying saucer. Ela was already waiting for him. She stepped on the touch pad, sending them gliding into the air.

Nash waited for them just inside the shelter of the research-station door. He led them through a short hallway to one of the labs. It looked like a fish store, with four rows of aquaria stacked to the ceiling, casting their cool light across the muddy floor. But on closer inspection Virgil decided it was not like any store he had ever seen. The tanks were too large and the water too cloudy as the soothing *brrr* of the pumps kept the silt stirred up. Besides, there were no small, colorful fish. Most of the tanks held globes, dull blue under the lights. Some had glinting carpets or crusts of structural LOVs. Only a few had fish: dull-colored carp, striped tilapia, or black catfish. Earth colors.

Nash stopped in front of the only tank in the room with clear water. Its sole resident was a small black catfish huddled in one corner. Nash bent to examine it, his hands on his knees. "This specimen was caught this morning at the Sea Palace. Look closely at its head."

Virgil glanced at Ela. She stood back a few paces, watching Nash, not the fish. Her expression was tense, frozen. A mask hiding some terrible knowledge.

He leaned forward to examine the catfish. The motion startled the creature. It wriggled, turned in a tight circle, then settled down again. Following Nash's instructions, Virgil looked at the head.

A thin white filament trailed from a point just behind its eye.

Virgil went cold. He tapped his fingers, summoning the magnification option on his farsights. Then he leaned closer. The white filament proved to be a chain of LOVs. He turned to Ela. She met his gaze with a look of wary expectation. "You're not surprised, are you?" he asked.

"No."

"Oanh told me about the fishing party yesterday. You saw these filaments?"

"All the *Roi Nuoc* saw them."

"No one said a thing."

Her shoulders rose in a defiant little shrug.

He reacted in exasperation. "Everybody knew, but you didn't tell me? Is this what's been worrying you?"

"Of course I'm worried. It may be a predator. We haven't had predators before."

But as she talked, a typed message appeared in his farsights:

→ I designed it to affect the behavior of fish so they would swim to the Sea Palace.

His brows rose. He mouthed the word *You?*

She nodded. Then her gaze slid to the catfish while her fingers tapped.

→ I requested this design. It's my fault.

Nash was watching her hand. She noticed his interest and turned to him. "Nash, you haven't changed your mind about the LOVs, have you?" she asked. She touched her forehead. "You still think this is wrong?"

He nodded, looking confused at this sudden shift in the conversation. "Yes. I do."

Ela bit her lip. "Nothing the LOVs do is ever static," she said softly. "We never want to remember that."

Virgil sensed she was still sending him private messages. He followed the direction of her gaze to Nash's round forehead. There, just on the edge of his receding hairline, two tiny LOVs gleamed.

Virgil dropped his gaze to the floor, using all his LOV-enhanced control to stay calm, but it was wasted effort: Nash had already seen his moment of alarm.

"What's going on here?" he demanded. "You two know more than you're saying. If you've got an explanation, put it forward now, because I guarantee you this *will* affect the UN decision."

Virgil edged toward the door. "I need to think about this, Nash. I'll—I'll get back to you, in an hour. Or so. Ela—" He touched her arm. "Let's go."

She moved toward the door without another glance at Nash, but Virgil did not have the same control. His gaze slid again to the pair of LOVs gleaming on Nash's brow.

Nash saw the look. A puzzled frown crossed his face, and then he raised his hand to touch his forehead. . . .

Virgil bolted for the door, shoving Ela ahead of him. They dashed down the tiny hallway, past the startled guards, then out through the swinging doors. Behind them, Nash let out a roar of rage. Ela jumped onto the flying saucer. Virgil followed, stomping hard on a touch pad. The flying saucer slipped forward, carrying them away from the jurisdiction of the guards.

Ela sat down hard, her face an emotionless mask. "It's the beginning of the end," she said.

Virgil nodded. Neither the UN nor the IBC would tolerate LOVs that preyed on other life-forms, especially human life-forms.

"I'm sorry," she said, staring ahead at nothing. "I went too far."

Virgil crouched beside her. "It's not your fault. It would have happened sooner or later anyway. It was inevitable." He put an arm around her, and felt grateful when her weight eased against him. "But we should have seen it coming."

Ela said, "Mostly you don't."

CHAPTER 38

They were halfway back to their platform when Ela stirred. "The clouds are breaking up," she said. "I can't believe it. It's been weeks since we've had so much open sky."

Virgil looked up, to see broken floes of luminous white clouds set against a pearly background. He chuckled. "Maybe we'll finally get to dry out."

"With our luck we'll get sunburn."

"The weather is changing," Mother Tiger said. "There is a danger."

An inset window opened on Virgil's farsights, displaying a satellite image of the South China Sea. Just off the coast, centered over the western half of the Spratly Islands, was the ominous white spiral and well-defined eye of a summer typhoon. He heard the catch of Ela's breath.

Mother Tiger said, "It has been upgraded to a Class IV storm. The waves are already rising."

Virgil asked, "How many hours away?"

"Twenty to twenty-four."

Ela stiffened in his arms. "Look there!" She leaned forward, her slender finger pointing to the eastern sky where the sun was just beginning to rise. Its searing light picked out a staggered line of shimmering points running from north to south, the highest no more than twenty degrees above the horizon.

"Drones?" Virgil suggested.

"I think so."

The sun slipped from behind a low cloud and all doubt evaporated as its horizontal rays glinted and shimmered over a fleet of miniature airplanes, each one trailing a misty rainbow tail. Virgil stared at the spectacle. "They're dropping something. Some liquid chemical."

"Over the Sea Palace," Ela whispered, extricating herself from his arms. She tapped her fingers. "Oanh! Everyone should be inside, under the roof, before they breathe it in."

Virgil's view shifted. He looked out of someone else's farsights; he could not tell whose. Someone at the Sea Palace. There was Oanh, grilling a breakfast of catfish on the stairs, while five other kids—all of them older kids in their middle teens, for none of the young ones were left anywhere on the reservation—lounged and chatted at the water's edge. In the next instant the scene transformed: All six were on their feet, bounding up the stairs and in through the Palace door without a cry being uttered, or a moment of discernible confusion. Two other teens were inside, still sleeping. Oanh stopped to rouse them, while four more came charging down the inside stairs. They rushed together into the windowless ocean room.

The light dimmed. The view turned back. Virgil gazed beyond a frame of two arched doorways, out to a brilliant morning through which a fine mist fell, splitting the sunlight into sprays of color.

Ela was tugging at his arm. "Get down!" His focus shifted. He glanced up to see the drones almost overhead now. Then he dropped with Ela against the saucer's deck. She pulled her rain poncho over both of them. "They're trying to poison us," she hissed. "That's what they're doing."

He could not hear the mist fall. He couldn't hear the passing drones. He stayed huddled with Ela beneath the poncho all the way to the Sea Palace, and when the saucer bumped up against the stairs they did not bother to moor it, but ran inside, not touching any surface except with their bare feet.

K y met them inside, resolving the mystery of whose farsights Virgil had been gazing through. "I saw what happened at the research station."

Virgil nodded, hearing the basso growl of waves washing against the building's prow. "Did you know before?"

Ky looked at Ela. It was not a friendly expression. "No."

She turned and walked away toward Oanh.

Virgil said, "Mother Tiger knew."

Ky did not answer this. "We are all here except Lien and her cadre," he said brusquely. "They cannot be contacted."

"None of them are wearing farsights?"

"No. I was with them yesterday evening. They don't believe they need farsights anymore." He stepped closer to a pillar wrapped in veins of gleaming LOVs. He laid his hand on it. The LOVs Lien had transplanted to his forehead had grown into tiny diamond clusters. "They may be right. They've grown beyond us, I think. Taken another path. They are no longer *Roi Nuoc*." His voice grew soft. "It's too bad we won't have more time. I would have loved to see how this all turned out."

Virgil said, "It's not over yet."

Ky nodded. Then his melancholy seemed to leave, as if he had closed a door on it and turned away. "Do you know what chemical they dropped on us?"

"No. Do you?"

"I know very little. There has been a rather severe communications problem this morning. It seems no one in Hanoi can receive my link."

Though Ela stood across the room, her voice intruded from their farsights. "So we go beyond Hanoi," she said. "And beyond the UN—"

"Ela," Ky said, "the world already knows about us. We are a popular evening entertainment—but no more than that. There will be no protest when we are canceled."

"There must be something more we can do. If we come together, if we think about it together . . ." It was their code phrase for a cognitive circle. "We might find some way—"

She was interrupted by a cry of alarm from the second floor. *Lên dây coi cái này!* Come up here! Come look!" It was Ninh's voice, shouting down the stairwell. "The Sea Palace is melting!"

Virgil was first up the stairs. He raced up from the gloom of the ocean room into a sea of blinding light. Line after parallel line of foaming waves had thrown up a mist of salt spray, saturating the air and dissolving the sun's rays, so that light seemed to ooze from everywhere at once. The edges of shadows were lost and color boundaries blurred. Ninh looked at him with wide eyes. Then he pointed at the parapet.

Virgil skidded to a stop before it. His first glance showed him nothing obviously wrong with the wall. It looked intact, undamaged. Not melted at all.

Then he peered into the trough that topped the wall, and understood the reason for Ninh's alarm. Something had gone wrong. The water that should have nourished the globes looked milky white. Virgil dipped his hand in, tipping a little of the discolored water into his palm. He whispered his farsights to magnify what he saw and the truth unfolded:

The water was filled with white structural LOVs, but they

were deformed. They had no limbs, no way to attach to one another. He ran his fingers along the top of the trough and it was the same thing: his fingertips came away sparkling with legions of unattached LOVs, like a fine dust of tiny diamonds.

He raised his gaze to the sky, seeing again in his mind the rainbow tails of mist falling from the passing drones. "It was a mutagen," he said. "That's what they dropped." He rubbed finger and thumb together, feeling the diamond dust slide between them. "These are the LOVs that have been made since then— the next layer in the wall."

All around him tentative hands rose; fingers brushed the LOVs embedded on worried brows. It was a religious gesture.

"It didn't fall on us," Ela said. "All of us here, we took shelter."

"It could still be here as a vapor in the air," Virgil pointed out, waving his hand at the salt spray. "We could be breathing it in right now."

He looked up at the sound of a helicopter. It was coming out of the north, moving low over the water and drawing swiftly nearer as it followed the coast. Some of the *Roi Nuoc* edged closer to the stairs.

Not Oanh. She dug her nails into the parapet. "This chemical won't affect old LOVs," she said firmly. "We won't lose what we have." As if pushed away by her will, the helicopter swung out to sea as it neared the Palace, passing a quarter mile offshore.

Ky watched it go by. "Even if that is so, Oanh, there will be no more like Lien. New LOVs cannot attach without their limbs."

"Don't assume anything," Ela warned. The helicopter was turning inland now, on a line for the research station. "The LOVs will mutate again. They'll adapt to this, like they've adapted to everything else."

Softly, Virgil said, "I don't think so." The helicopter hovered over the station, descending to the rooftop landing pad. The staff would be gathered there, waiting to evacuate. The reservation had gotten dangerous, now that LOVs had learned to hunt their hosts. "This is only the start. There will be more genetic weapons, or viruses, or chemical drops. They've had time to develop an arsenal. After all, they have Summer Goforth."

"And we have the LOvs!" Ela snapped. "Look what they've already done for us. Virgil, we can't give up."

"We won't give up." But he couldn't imagine what they would do.

Ky said, "The IBC will surely wait to hear of our surrender before the next plague is released"—a flurry of protest arose from the *Roi Nuoc*, as they insisted they would not surrender; Ky smiled—"so we should still have a little time."

"There is a storm coming," Virgil said as his gaze shifted to the unhappy sea.

Ky nodded. "We need to find Lien and her cadre. They know better than any of us what the LOvs can do. We can shelter together in the Sea Palace, and consider our options."

The overflights continued, but after the first pass with drones the IBC switched to helicopters, saturating the reservation and the surrounding sea with their chemical mists. For the first time in weeks the sun refused to retreat behind its veil of clouds. Its fierce rays refracted in the salt spray, and in steam rising from the muddy shallows, driving these natural vapors to mix with the chemicals released by the IBC until every breath became thick with salt and unknowable poisons. Sweat pooled on the skin and in the eyes, stinging miserably.

Despite the terrible air, Ky left to find Lien. Virgil went with him, wearing Ela's poncho in the hope it would keep some of the falling chemicals away from his skin. It was fantastically hot, and he sweated profusely beneath the waterproof garment.

They took the largest remaining wooden boat and poled toward the mangrove stand where Ky had visited Lien and her cadre just last night. Three times they had to get out and float the boat over shallow mud bars. Their feet stirred puffs of white LOvs in the silt. Once they passed a submerged dike encrusted in LOvs. Milky rivulets flowed off of it, following the current.

They had brought no drinking water. For weeks it had rained so persistently that clean water for drinking had been taken for granted. But half an hour in the sun changed that attitude. Virgil pulled off the poncho, preferring to risk poisoning over heatstroke. It hardly mattered. Sweat poured off him, even as his mouth went musty and his tongue swelled. Ky was no better off. So they changed their route, turning inland toward a cluster of platforms.

It was a ghost town on the water. The *Roi Nuoc* who had lived there were gone, evacuated to the Sea Palace, or to IBC custody beyond the reservation. Now only silence lived there; the soft plop of Virgil's pole in the water was an intrusive sound.

As they passed the first platform, Ky nodded at muddy rings on the stilts marking the highest reach of the flood. "The water has dropped at least fifteen inches."

"The typhoon could reverse that with a storm surge."

Ky looked grim. "If the storm is bad enough, this land could be lost forever. The ocean's level is rising. A little erosion, and this delta will be gone."

Virgil poled the boat toward the lowest platform. With any luck the catchment system would still be working. They might even find a few clean containers to carry water.

Ky crouched in the bow, balanced on one knee, his hands raised to catch the edge of the platform which stood at the height of his chest above the water. Virgil dragged his pole, slowing the boat so they bumped gently against the stilts. Ky grabbed the platform's edge and swung himself up.

Virgil wanted to blame his heat-addled mind for what he saw next. The platform appeared to *move*, sliding toward the boat in a slow, soundless glide.

Ky's eyes widened. He dropped flat against the deck. "It's slipping off!" he shouted. "Back the boat away!"

Virgil jabbed the pole in the mud and bore down on it, sending the boat shooting backward. He turned in time to see the deck glide off its stilts, toppling into the water where it splashed like a calving glacier. Ky jumped free just before it hit, landing several feet away in his own muddy explosion of spray. He popped back up to the surface, spluttering and treading water while Virgil strove to bring the boat around.

"Did you see that?" Ky shouted. "Nothing was holding it in place! My weight unbalanced it." He stroked back to the half-submerged platform, and climbed up on its slanted surface so that Virgil could bring the boat in and pick him up. Afterward they circled the stilts.

All the platforms had been designed to rise with the flood-waters; a living layer of LOVs at the top of every stilt continuously added to its height. But the mutagen had changed the structure of those LOVs. Without limbs to hold them in place while their shells bonded, they acted like tiny ball bearings. Ky's weight had been enough to unbalance the platform and send it sliding off into the muddy water.

They poled between the other platforms, eyeing the rain catchment systems, some with basins obviously full. "We could try again," Virgil said.

Ky shook his head. "We can't risk crushing the boat. Let's find Lien. There will be water when we get back to the Sea Palace."

It took twenty minutes more to reach the mangrove stand where Lien had built her platform. They called out as they approached. But the helicopters had returned with another load of chemical spray; if anyone answered their hails, it was impossible to hear over the droning engines.

The platform itself was hidden within the tangle of trees. They tied the boat to a trunk, then climbed out onto a six-inch-wide plank of LOVs. Rings of LOVs anchored the plank to the roots and trunks, so it didn't slide as they stepped on it.

Ky went first, while Virgil followed close behind along a path that wound through trees draped in gleaming webs of LOVs, with here and there a globe suspended in the mesh.

By the time they drew near the center of the stand, the helicopters began to move away. As the noise level dropped Ky again tried calling out, but still there was no answer. He stopped on the path, looking back at Virgil with uncertain eyes. "I was here last night and all was well. I left around midnight."

Virgil set his hand on Ky's shoulder, but he said nothing. There was nothing to say. Silence crept out from under every leaf; it steamed into the air with the evaporation of water. Even here in the shade the heat was dizzying. Virgil wiped sweat from his forehead. "Let's not record this."

Ky stiffened. He stared ahead into the canopy, where flies buzzed. Then he fumbled with his farsights, pulling them off and toggling the power switch. Virgil did the same.

They discovered Lien and her three companions a few minutes later.

They had made a platform of many levels, each one anchored with rings around the trunks and limbs. They lay together, side by side on the lowest level beneath several healthy globes suspended in a webbed canopy. Virgil felt a sick sense of déjà vu wash over him as he watched flies crawl in and out of Lien's open mouth. Her eyes stared upward through the transparent lens of farsights in power-down mode. All four of them wore farsights. The haggard expressions on their exhausted faces reminded him too much of Gabrielle.

Ky crouched at their feet, the back of his hand pressed against his mouth as he studied their faces. "I was here just last night. They were fine. They were happy." He rubbed at his eyes. "Is this what happened to your friend, Gabrielle?"

Virgil nodded, as Ky's grief resonated against his own. "It looks the same, if this *is* a cognitive circle . . ."

"It is. They did them all the time. For hours on end. Mother Tiger used to interrupt them. That's one reason they gave up their farsights. Lien especially. She didn't need them anymore. She was a natural philosopher. She didn't need Mother Tiger's help to understand the LOVs, and anyway, she didn't . . ."

His voice trailed off as he looked again at the four bodies, their helmets of LOVs dull gray in the sunlight. Virgil felt the rush of his sudden, terrible suspicion. "Ky? What is it?" He knelt beside him. "What were you going to say about Lien?"

Ky turned to him, and Virgil felt overwhelmed by his pain, his fury at some unspoken betrayal. "The other reason she gave up her farsights," he whispered. "She didn't trust the ROSA anymore."

"Mother Tiger—?" Virgil was incredulous. But Ky's suspicion had gotten inside him. His hand moved to touch the bulge of his farsights, switched off and safely tucked into his thigh pocket. The ROSA could not observe them. Virgil looked again at Lien's tortured face, and at last he saw the anomaly that had alarmed Ky. "If they didn't need farsights, why are they wearing them?"

"There is one we could ask."

"Ky . . ."

"Think about it!" Ky insisted, in a low, urgent whisper. "They must have been talking to the ROSA last night after I left. There is no other reason for them to wear farsights. But Mother Tiger said nothing about it."

"Come on, Ky. How could Mother Tiger have harmed them? Why?"

Ky raised his hand. "Be careful what you say." He nodded at a peeper ball drifting just within the tangle of mangrove trunks.

"It's the IBC," Virgil said. "We should leave. They'll be here soon."

Ky's gaze followed the peeper's flight. He gave a slight shake of his head. "The enemy is not always easy to recognize."

Virgil looked again at the peeper. What was Ky saying? That the peeper might not belong to the IBC? Then who—?

He turned to Ky, and mouthed the words *Mother Tiger?*

Ky shrugged. "The LOVs did not do this," he said, still speaking in whispers. "Not directly. I won't believe it. Lien had too much experience. She'd done hundreds of cognitive circles. She knew how to control her own trance." Then Ky tapped his temple, the universal symbol for farsights. "But if she was wearing farsights, who was in control?"

Virgil shook his head, unwilling to believe any of this. "Her farsights are powered down."

"When farsights are stolen, the resident ROSA will switch them off, no? As a matter of security. And consider this—I left here near midnight. How many hours have passed since then? Not enough for them to die. Not unless they were *led,* deliberately down into a terrified state, a hellish trance they could not break."

Virgil felt a fresh sweat break out across his chest. He could not take his eyes away from the peeper ball hovering among the globes. "Don't say any more." He started to rise. "We have to get back. All the *Roi Nuoc* are dependent on—"

"They are safe, I think. For now. Because they are still *Roi Nuoc*."

Of course they should be safe. Mother Tiger's whole existence had been written around them. "But Lien . . ."

"Didn't I say it myself this morning? She and her companions had evolved beyond us. Her purposes and Mother Tiger's were no longer the same. Perhaps Lien had some plan Mother Tiger did not approve of. I know she wanted to persuade the rest of us to follow her, and leave the ROSA behind."

Ky leaned forward, reaching beneath the web of suspended globes to lift away Lien's farsights and close her staring eyes. Then he touched the dying LOVs on her companions' heads—and froze, his lips parted, his eyes wide in wonder. Slowly, he turned his head to look at Virgil. "Can you hear their souls?"

Virgil felt the hair rise on the back of his neck.

Ky settled back on his heels, gazing up at the canopy of suspended globes. "Can you feel this sense of warning, or is it only my mind slipping away?" He touched the LOVs on his forehead. "Tell me you can hear them, Virgil."

Virgil looked up. His heartbeat quickened. He brushed his hair back from his forehead—and then he did hear something. Murmured voices inside his head, their words inaudible but their meaning clear all the same: *Run fast! Run fast!*

It was a mantra that pulled Panwar's ghost up out of an old, old well of memory, speaking words he had never spoken in life: *Our machines have almost caught us up. We need to change, before they leave us behind forever.*

Ky's hand on his arm brought him back from the dark, blood-drenched utility tunnel. Back to the present. "Do you hear them?" Ky insisted.

Virgil nodded. "It's the globes. E-3 remembered Gabrielle. It's the same."

"It's a message. You understand? We cannot fail."

CHAPTER 39

Spiders were summoned to the ocean room.

Wet blankets had been hung across the doorway to keep the pestilence out. Ela crouched beside the barrier, peeking past the edge of a blanket at the spider waiting on the other side. In her hands she held a spare pair of farsights left behind by a *Roi Nuoc* evacuated from the reservation. Her own screen winked blue-green as Mother Tiger translated her instructions. After a minute the spider raised the brittle wands of two adjacent legs, lifting the spare farsights from her hand. Then it waddled awkwardly away on its six remaining limbs, climbing the stairs to the Palace roof.

Ela glanced over at Ninh, crouched on the other side of the blanket-draped doorway, instructing another spider to carry another pair of farsights to a post outside the Sea Palace. They had four sentries now, to warn them of the approach of the IBC. She let the blanket fall back into place.

How much longer?

In the lower field of her farsights two small windows looked out on the progress of Virgil and Ky. She could see what they saw and hear their conversation. She was not the only one watching. An outcry of fear and consternation had swirled through the ocean room when Ky's weight on the abandoned platform sent it sliding into the water. Now, anxious murmurs followed them along the path that wound through the mangrove. Silence fell when Ky paused to call to Lien. Ela strained to hear a response, but only the buzzing flies answered. Virgil shifted. His hand swept in a blur across the field of his farsights. "Let's not record this," he said softly.

Seconds later, both windows closed.

Ela traded a glance with Ninh. There was no need to say what they both knew: Lien would have responded if she could.

"What can we do now?" Ninh asked.

"I don't know. Watch? Wait?" She touched the LOVs on her

forehead. Counting herself and Ninh, only thirteen of the *Roi Nuoc* remained. If Virgil and Ky made it back, they would be fifteen.

Ninh said, "We have money. There has to be something we can do."

"Hire our own army, then."

"No. We would all die."

"Ninh is right," Mother Tiger said, speaking through both their farsights. "This would never be approved."

"Approved by who?" Ela asked.

The ROSA said, "By me."

Ela felt a chill touch her neck. She wondered if the UN would find it necessary to eliminate Mother Tiger too.

She started pacing, making circuit after circuit of the room, trailing her fingers against the damp wall. The *Roi Nuoc* had gathered in a loose cluster at the center of the room. They sat cross-legged, each carrying on a separate conversation as they busied themselves with Mother Tiger or with interviews or propaganda. In the windowless room the only light came from gleaming pillars of living LOVs. The blue-green wavelength stole the color from their skin, giving them the faded look of old film, of poorly preserved photos shot in black and white. Their voices sounded distant, almost lost within the low, reverberant rumble of storm waves pounding the prow of the Sea Palace. The typhoon that had generated these swells was stalled over the Eastern Sea where it fed on the warm, shallow water, building up its strength.

Ela whispered to Mother Tiger, opening new windows within the field of her farsights.

Through a spider-sentry on the roof she watched another overflight of helicopters. A foaming breaker boomed against the Palace, throwing a fan of spray across the roof.

Another spider-sentry stood watch on the dike behind the Palace, looking inland through air heavy with mists and glints of refracted, rainbow light. Beneath it, at the foot of the dike, two ruined skaters floated amid a raft of gray foam gathered at the water's edge. Their joints had collapsed so that their legs splayed in a star pattern. Their buoyant float pads held them on the surface, but they sagged at the center so that their globes were submerged. In the strange light their blue-green color was lost, and they looked a sickly gray. A fish picked at one of them.

Ela felt her hands begin to tremble. Until now, only newly forming LOVs had been affected by the IBC's chemical rain. But these were mature skaters. A mutagen should not have been able to cripple them . . . which meant a second poison had been released, one that was toxic to existing LOVs.

"*Virgil!*" she whispered urgently. "*Ky. Come back now!*"

"Their farsights remain off," Mother Tiger told her. "They cannot be reached."

"The IBC has used a new poison."

"Yes. An analysis of light refracted by the air drops indicates at least three different toxins."

"Mature LOVs are dying."

"Yes."

A noise like popcorn bursting, or like muffled firecrackers erupted from outside. Ela hurried to the curtain of wet blankets and peeked past the edge to the arch of daylight at the outer doorway. A spider was crouched at the intersection of sun and shade. Peeper balls drifted around it like glinting soap bubbles. One had been waiting by the curtain, poised for just such an opportunity. It slipped through as Ela held the blanket open a crack.

She cursed and dropped back, swatting furiously at the peeper, but it glided up, out of reach. She let it go, knowing there were many others already ensconced in the dark corners of the ceiling.

The popping noise grew louder, more frequent. Ela scanned the windows along the lower field of her farsights until she found the view from the spider-sentry poised at the main door. It showed the flying saucer drifting over the stairs, bouncing and jerking as its hull popped in a scatter shot of tiny white explosions. Its pressure cells were bursting open, one after another, throwing tiny splinters of glass and plasma into the air.

Ela bowed her head, running her fingers through her hair as she fought a surging panic. She froze as a link icon popped up in her field of view. It was a simple symbol, a circle surrounding three letters: *IBC*. Mother Tiger had long ago been instructed to filter all but the highest-priority links. "Open it," Ela murmured, her words swallowed up by the low rumble of waves.

The symbol expanded. It held for several seconds, then Daniel Simkin appeared, leaning on a podium with a map of the local coastline behind him. He was addressing a news conference:

". . . an agreement reached with the United Nations has allowed us to operate freely within the infested territories since dawn. An evacuation of all remaining civilians is being arranged as I speak. I will not underplay the crisis we are facing. Three months of political stonewalling and corruption has allowed the evolution of the worst biological disaster in human history and the imminent approach of Typhoon Corazon threatens to spread the infestation far beyond its present boundaries. That cannot be allowed. In the hours remaining to us before the storm arrives, the IBC will be releasing a series of viruses specifically targeted at LOV physiology. None of these viruses—I repeat, *none* of these viruses—can harm any other life-form. There is no reason for concern on this point. We have chosen this multipronged strategy to counter the well-known fact of the LOV's adaptability. Any single scheme would leave a remnant population of resistant LOVs. But no LOV will be immune to every virus in our arsenal. By sundown, this crisis will have reached its long-overdue conclusion."

Ela tipped her head back. Fast, shallow breaths rushed past her lips. "Break the link." She looked around the ocean room, at twelve faces, all reflecting the shock she felt. Her hand knotted into a fist. "Where is Virgil?"

"Still no word," Mother Tiger said.

"The IBC will be coming soon." She started pacing again, her fingers trailing against the wall. The Sea Palace had roots running deep into the mud. Nutrients flowed up through insulated channels to feed the pillars of gleaming LOVs that gave them light, and to feed the LOVs in the walls that recycled their air.

The air was still fresh; the light unwavering though poisons swirled in the outside air. Spider-sentries were collapsing. Their skewed viewpoints showed living pipes turning sickly gray. Droves of flies buzzed the walls. On the roof, the globes in the troughs had begun to dissolve, but in the cool, dark shelter of the ocean room the air was fresh.

Clean.

Ela froze in midstride, staring inward at the germ of an idea. "Oanh!"

Her shout echoed against the walls, breaking cognitive circles that had just begun to re-form in the wake of Simkin's news conference. "Ninh. Phan. Everyone. Come." She glanced at the dark ceiling, where peeper balls hid among the shadows. She didn't dare express her idea aloud. "Let us all sit together."

Recognizing her excitement, her need for secrecy, they came together without questions, joining their separate circles into a loose cluster. Ela sat facing them; her fingers began to tap. Mother Tiger guessed at the words she was spelling, and wrote them out in quick sentences:

Lovs are dying everywhere but here. Ocean room sheltered. Lovs here are protected from pestilence. They are unharmed.

Ela raised her left hand to her forehead, touching the symbiotic Lovs implanted there.

Can we shelter our own Lovs?

Remember: What we call a Lov is only a shell around one end of a cluster of neural asterids. The first asterids developed by Summer Goforth had no shell. They lived entirely within the brain of their host. Could we re-create that design?

The proposal stirred a chorus of thoughtful sighs, though no one spoke a coherent word aloud. They were all aware of the peeper balls.

Ela waited for some responding message to write itself out across her screen, but none came. She looked from one puzzled face to the next until finally Ninh held up his hand, palm out, and wiggled his fingers.

No fingerpads.

Ela winced. Of course. The *Roi Nuoc* did not have fingerpads, so how could they type?

Well, on a virtual grid of course. She tapped out the proposal and within a few minutes Mother Tiger was recording their awkward finger movements, assembling the letters they "touched" into brief messages—while rearranging the virtual keys every few seconds to slow anyone trying to decrypt their words. A conversation began.

The LOVs must be redesigned, yet they could not do it themselves. No one knew how. They could only detail the problem for the LOVs to explore. Questions and answers were traded through the interface of Mother Tiger and the concept evolved as teams of LOVs created competing solutions. Ela could not follow even the coarsest details. To her it only felt as if their circle was converging.

Virgil turned his farsights back on when he and Ky reached the edge of the mangrove stand. Instantly, a link to Ela opened. "Virgil! You and Ky have to come back. Now. There's only a little time." Fear whispered in the sibilant undertones of her voice. Virgil knew better than to ask questions. He followed Ky into the boat, grabbed the pole, and began pushing for home.

At high noon the overflights stopped. Daniel Simkin spoke to them again, though this time it was a private communication as he explained in detail how they were to exit the Sea Palace one by one, walking outside into the pestilence-laden air, where they would present themselves for arrest.

"Come find us in the ocean room," Ela countered softly, determined to seize these few extra minutes for the LOVs to finish their task. "We'll be waiting for you here. We won't resist."

There was a disturbance at the curtain. She peeked past, and discovered a crippled spider trying to get through, but it was contaminated. It could not be allowed in. So she kicked it through the curtain, three times, breaking its legs. Then she crouched by the barrier, peering through a slit at the outer door.

Ninh squatted beside her. "Ky and Virgil are almost here." He sent her the screen. The image was skewed but she could see them: two small figures, Virgil poling the boat, Ky crouched in the bow, watching for snags and shoals.

"Hurry," she whispered.

Virgil nodded, his harsh breathing loud in her ear.

A helicopter lifted from an offshore platform. It swept toward shore, toward the boat, coming in fast. Virgil glanced at it. Then he shouted a warning to Ky and jammed his pole into the mud, sending the boat skidding forward. It rammed against a hidden mud bar, but both men were ready for the impact. Ela watched them leap clear; watched them splash down in knee-deep water. They broke for the Sea Palace in a stumbling run. Loudspeakers shouted at them to freeze and drop their weapons. It was a show, Ela knew. Part of the endless quest for better ratings. The IBC knew they were unarmed.

Virgil and Ky might have read the script. They ignored the warning and ran faster.

Virgil reached the stairs a step ahead of Ky. He glanced up, and through his farsights Ela saw the helicopter loom into view above the parapet. Its shadow caught him in a column of darkness, the negative image of a searchlight. The loudspeaker again commanded him to freeze. Instead he darted under the arch as shock troops in color-shifting camouflage slid out of the helicopter's belly, gliding like water drops down twin cables.

Ela's viewpoint shifted. Now she peeked past the barrier of wet blankets, watching Virgil with her own eyes. He saw her. "Ela!" His eyes were wild.

"Hurry up!" she screamed at him. Then: "There's not enough time."

Ky filled the arch of sunlight behind him. "I'll hold the door."

"You can't hold the door," Virgil said.

"Go!" Ky roared. "Go see what she wants!" He turned back to face the troops, his hands raised, palms out. Then a flash of brilliant light erupted from his farsights, a tiny lightning bolt chasing back the shadows in the palace hall. Ky cried out in pain. His hands shot up as if to grab the farsights away from his face. He never reached them.

The shock troops outside saw the sudden movement, and fired. Ky's shoulder blade exploded. A second round opened a crater in his lower back. Blood sprayed the walls, falling in heavy spatters across Virgil's shirt as he turned a stunned face toward the carnage.

"Virgil!" Ela screamed. "Come now! Now."

Outside the soldiers were shouting, conjuring explanations for the murder. It shouldn't have happened. Ky was unarmed. Anyone could see that. Anyone at all, because Ela sent the sequence to her news site while Virgil lingered wasteful seconds over this tangle of protein that used to be Ky Xuan Nguyen.

"*Virgil.*"

He looked around at her.

"Now. Please." He would have to come to her. She would not step around the curtain and risk contaminating the *Roi Nuoc*. None of them knew how long the design change would take, or if it would work at all. They needed time. She would not take a second of it away from them.

Her urgency must have burned past his shock. He ran to her. He did not slow down. "Wait! Stop!" Ela cried. She raised her hand in a warding gesture. "Don't come in. You're not clean."

Virgil stumbled, his eyes wide as a frightened dog's. He stopped himself with a hand against the wall. His chest heaved and sweat shone all across the rosy flush of his face. Great smears of blood stank across his shirt. He started to step away.

"No!" she shouted. "Don't go." She edged her shoulder past the barrier of hanging blankets, feeling the dampness licking at her skin. "Look at me. *Think* with me—"

"There's no time. My God, Ela. They—"

"*Now.*" She reached toward him. She touched his cheek; the back of his neck, drawing him closer.

"It's too late," he whispered. "Lien and her cadre—"

"I know."

"And Ky—"

"It's too late," she agreed. "Kiss me now."

His gaze sharpened. He must have caught some encoded trace of her mood. "You know something."

"Kiss me now." Her lips brushed his cheek, moved barely against his ear: *Let me teach you to retreat.*

He embraced her, his arms so tight her breath came hard. "Listen to me!" she gasped.

She drew back far enough to meet his eye; far enough for her LOVs to whisper their secrets. His mouth brushed hers. Then he froze, staring deep into her eyes. His raw shock filled her. "What have you done?"

She didn't answer. She only kissed him again lightly as silhouettes of armored soldiers gathered in the brilliant afternoon light pouring down outside the doorway. He heard them, but she would not let him turn and look. "They murdered Ky," he whispered.

"I know."

"We need to talk."

"There's no time."

"We can't give up."

"We haven't." She closed her eyes and kissed him hard, fixing the sensation of it, the scent of him in her mind. Tasting his raw shock. How had it come to this?

"Step away," a stern voice said.

She looked up into the faceless shield of a soldier's mask. What had moved her to make the choices she had made? What moved anyone? She never would have chosen this end; Virgil never would have consented to this outcome . . . except they *had*, with every decision made since the module fell.

CHAPTER 40

The evacuation went swiftly. Each *Roi Nuoc* was placed under arrest. Their farsights were confiscated. They were transported by helicopter to a converted merchant ship waiting offshore in stormy seas. After a quick march across a rolling deck, they were taken below where they were placed in separate, padded cells, seven by seven feet. There were no bars, no windows, and no furniture. A grill in the ceiling introduced air that was sterile and without scent. Ela sat on the padded floor, staring at the gray walls. Waiting.

She could not get Ky's death out of her mind. She tried hard not to think about him but every time her eyes shifted she thought she saw blood on the walls. She could not get the smell of it out of her nostrils. Why was he dead? He had not threatened anybody. She saw it all again: the way he had turned back to the door, palms raised in peace, ready to negotiate for a few more seconds, a minute or two of additional time, and they had shot him down.

Hadn't it gone that way? No. She was forgetting that strange flash of light from Ky's farsights, a burst of electronic lightning that must have seared his eyes. He'd reacted instinctively, grabbing for the farsights. The nervous soldiers had jumped just as hard and *then* Ky had died.

Killed by that one frantic gesture. He might be alive now if not for that flash of light.

Where had it come from? Ela wondered. What had caused it? Mother Tiger would know, but without farsights Ela had no way to contact the ROSA.

Maybe it had been a booby-trap message sent by the IBC. Maybe similar accidents would happen to all of them.

She could not sit still. So she went to examine the cell door, following the seam with her fingernails, but both the lock and the hinges were hidden. She looked up at the air vent. It was out of reach, even when she jumped. She sat down again.

Where was Virgil now? Where was Oanh?

Again she looked up at the air vent. "Maybe I could get a bath?" she said aloud. Then later: "I want to see a lawyer." They would probably send in a death squad instead.

But no one came.

Absently, she scratched her forehead, wondering what to do next. Later, when she looked at her fingertips, minute white specks glittered behind her nails. She sucked in a sharp breath. Then she scratched her head again. More specks appeared. Her hand started to shake, so she pressed it against the padded floor to hide her distress from any watching cameras.

Her LOVs were flaking away. Panic stirred in her belly. She had planned for this to happen; she had helped to engineer it, but how could she be sure it was only the outer shells of her LOvs that were dying? What if the asterids themselves had been poisoned by some viral weapon of the IBC?

She closed her eyes, breathing deeply, slowly, concentrating on an image of blood spattered across white walls. She would surely feel the loss of the asterids. But she felt the same. Even this fear was utterly familiar.

S ummer Goforth arrived in Saigon in late afternoon, on an IBC charter flight in the company of Daniel Simkin. They were ferried out to the ship on a helicopter that bucked and shuddered in the rising wind. Beneath them, whitecaps screamed off heaving waves. Lightning crackled on the horizon. The helicopter set down hard on the rolling ship, breaking a strut.

The storm seemed to lessen when they were inside, and could no longer see the furious weather. That was illusion, of course. The worst would come tonight.

Summer toured the holding cells with Simkin and his aides. She viewed the security arrangements. There was a surgical facility, but rough seas made it impossible to consider the delicate procedure that must be required to remove the symbiotic LOvs.

At last they were shown into a small conference room, where coffee was served with a light supper. Simkin left to take a private call. His aides had business of their own and soon Summer was alone. It was not unexpected.

She looked around the little room: six chairs and a table and maps on the wall. No doubt they hoped she would stay here and be content. Daniel had not wanted to bring her along at all, but he'd given in when she threatened to resign. Evidently there was a chance he might still need her.

She slipped her farsights on.

She had been given access to the camera feeds from each holding cell. She scrolled through them now, glimpsing youths huddled in corners, or twitching in restless sleep. Virgil's cell was empty. Someone had said he'd been taken to another room for questioning. Ela Suvanatat was present.

Summer watched her for several minutes, perplexed by her

spasmodic movement. Every few seconds her right hand would rise to scratch compulsively at the LOVs on her forehead: just one scrape of her fingernail; rarely two. Then she would yank her hand down, like a child who has just had her wrist slapped. She would slip her hand under her thigh as if to hold it there, but it never stayed for long.

Summer tapped her fingers, magnifying the image just as Ela raised her hand again to scratch. Her nail picked at a minute, gray LOV. It popped free. A tiny spot of blood welled up where the LOV had been.

Summer's heart rate jumped. Sweat prickled her skin. What she had just seen should not be. Symbiotic LOVs were fragile, yes, but they could not be removed by gentle scraping. She zoomed in closer.

Ela's LOVs had all lost their healthy blue-green color, fading to a pearly gray. Summer had seen this before. When she'd examined the LOVs on Panwar's corpse, they had looked like this. The conclusion was inescapable: Ela's LOVs were dying, flaking away beneath the compulsive scratching of her fingernails.

But how was that possible? None of the viruses released by the IBC should have affected the symbiotic LOVs. Daniel had been adamant about that, and Summer had done everything she could to ensure it. Ela's LOVs could not be dying.

Yet they were . . . and Ela knew it. See how she stared at the wall with dull, unfocused eyes, fear painted in a sheen across her smooth face? Panic lurked just beneath the surface.

"Dr. Goforth?"

The soft query startled Summer from her speculations. With a shaking hand she slipped her farsights off, turning to see a crew member in cream coveralls leaning past the door to peer into the conference room. "A package for you, Dr. Goforth, to be delivered upon arrival." He opened the door wider, presenting her with a small carry-case, twelve by six by four inches high, perforated with air holes all around its upper half. Something scurried and scratched within it as he set it on the table. She signed his pad and he withdrew, while she read the specimen tag fixed to the handle. Nothing had been written on the line describing the contents of the box; only time and place of collection had been recorded. On the back of the tag though, scrawled in indelible pen, was an additional note: *LOVs on fish surviving too.*

Summer peered through the air holes, but it was dark inside the box. All she could see was the blue-green glow of a patch of healthy LOVs.

Virgil's forehead itched madly as the outer shells of his LOVs flaked away one by one. He didn't want to call attention to it. He didn't want to give anything away. So he refused to scratch. Instead he sat hunched in a hard steel chair at one end of a small table in an equally small room, his hands tucked under his armpits and tears of agony standing in his eyes, trying to follow the endless questions of the two IBC officers assigned to interview him. They kept asking him about the LOVs: how he controlled them (if he did control them); what his long-term plans had been; what potential he saw in the LOVs; how he felt now. It always came back to that: How do you feel?

I'm frightened and angry. Why did you murder Ky?

How do you feel?

I'm tired. I want to sleep.

He was hungry too, but then he was used to being hungry, so he didn't bother to mention it.

How do you feel?

I'm tired. I don't want to talk anymore.

After a while he lost the thread of the conversation. His focus shifted inward. He searched his mind, looking for blank spaces, for some sign that the LOV asterids were dying along with their outer shells. He had lived with the LOVs so long, he thought he would know if even one failed. But he could find no blank spaces. Calmness continued to flow on command and when he returned his attention to his interrogators, he could discern in their faces the subtle telltales that let him see through to the emotions behind their professionally expressionless pose.

How do you feel?

The door of the conference room slammed open with criminal force. Summer jumped. Then she tapped her fingers to clear her farsights, before turning an angry gaze on Daniel Simkin.

He stepped into the room and closed the door behind him. "You fucked up. Their LOVs are dying." His farsights were opaque silver. His face was stony.

Summer could remember when seeing the LOVs die had been his goal. When had that changed? And why? "It's not my doing."

"Like hell it's not. We introduce your viruses, and within hours their symbiotic LOVs are dead. That's a pretty clear cause and effect."

She stood up. She had persuaded a crew member to bring her a large plastic box with tall, smooth sides. She'd set it on the table, and released the live specimen into it. Now she gazed down at the gray rat as it shivered in a corner, its helmet of LOVs gleaming healthy blue-green. "Why aren't you worried about the rats, Daniel? And the parasitized fish? None of my viruses did any harm to them."

He glanced into the box. Then he looked back at her. "Where did you get that?"

"Someone with the UN sent it to me. You haven't controlled these wild LOVs, Daniel."

He smiled. But it was a reptilian smile, without a hint of warmth. "We didn't know LOVs were living symbiotically with wildlife until this morning."

She gestured at the rat. "These LOVs weren't harmed by my viruses."

He snorted. "So the rat-symbionts are safe. Congratulations. But it was the humans I wanted to protect."

She crossed her arms over her chest. "My viruses did not do this. I suggest you look elsewhere for a cause."

"Elsewhere? What are you implying? The UN—?"

"No, of course not. What does the UN know? But have you bothered to ask Copeland what's going on?"

Virgil was escorted to a conference room, one big enough to hold an oval table and six chairs. A twilight illumination came from a trough of indirect lights around the ceiling. As his eyes adjusted to the gloom, he was startled to discover Summer Goforth present, seated beneath a wall clock identifying the time in Hanoi as just past midnight. He was less surprised to see Daniel Simkin.

The rest of the chairs were empty, but on the table itself was a large plastic box. "Go ahead," Simkin said, gesturing him forward. "Have a look inside."

A rat scuttled around the bottom of the box. In the dusky light its head glowed bright with a blue-green skullcap of LOVs. Virgil looked from Summer, to Simkin, then back again to the rat, fascinated by the creature. "Is it supposed to simulate one of us?"

Simkin shrugged. "Not exactly."

"How long ago did you implant the LOVs?"

"We didn't implant them. This specimen was found on the reservation this morning. You're not familiar with the phenomenon?"

"No."

"It's LOVs are healthy," Summer said.

Virgil felt the hard clutch of fear. The deck lifted and rolled beneath his feet, swayed by typhoon winds as he turned to meet her gaze. No professional mask of detachment hid *her* emotions. The suspicion in her eyes was easy to read. "Your LOVs are dying," she went on. "We'd like to know why."

He forced himself to look away. Had she guessed? No. How could she? He closed his eyes, calling on a state of calm. "You ask me why? When the poisons you released this morning—"

"No," Simkin said. "We didn't want to expose any of you to unknown risks, so we made sure that nothing we dropped could harm any LOV protected by a mammalian immune system."

They waited on his answer, the only sound the scrabbling of the rat. Virgil touched his flaking LOVs. "I don't think your testing was adequate." He said it calmly, softly. So it startled him when Summer reacted in alarm. Her eyes widened. She sat up a little straighter, while the telltales of astonishment bloomed across her face. It was like reading one of those downtown neon church signs, flashing in postmidnight darkness: *Repent, for the end is near.*

She knew. He could not doubt it now. Somehow she had guessed about his LOvs. Despite their dead white color, she knew what was hiding inside him. Virgil thought back over the last minute. He must have made a mistake, done something to give himself away. But what? But what?

He breathed deeply, willing away the panic that wanted to flood his brain. . . .

But that was it, wasn't it? That was what she had seen. He did not have the bearing of a broken man.

Simkin asked, "How did you destroy your LOvs?"

It was a wholly unexpected question. Virgil stared at him in mute surprise. Then his gaze cut to Summer, and he caught an almost imperceptible nod. So Simkin did not know. But Summer did . . . and she hadn't told him. Not yet. Why not? "I didn't destroy them," Virgil said. It was so easy to speak the truth. "That's something I would never do."

Ela had been let out of her cell twice to use the bathroom and once to shower. The female guards who escorted her to the toilet refused to answer any questions and would not respond at all to Ela's repeated demands for a lawyer. Maybe she didn't have a right to a lawyer. The IBC was not constrained to operate under American law when it was not in America, after all.

She had been dozing, but she came immediately awake when her cell door swung open for a fourth time on its silent hinges. She had no way to know the time, but some inner sense told her it was close to 2 A.M. Summer Goforth looked in on her. Ela recognized her from news accounts. She sat up, rubbing at her forehead, feeling the tiny pockmark scars where her LOvs had been. "Where's Virgil?"

"Asleep," Summer said. "His cell is watched more closely than yours. Come out here, away from the cameras."

Ela's eyes widened. She glanced over her shoulder, then she stepped out of the cell. Summer closed the door.

The brig was dimly lit and wrapped up in silence. No one was in sight: not guards, or prisoners. No windows looked into the other cells. Ela surveyed the blank doors, wondering which one hid Oanh and Ninh and all the other *Roi Nuoc*.

Summer said, "The IBC is corrupt. I don't believe Daniel Simkin is interested any longer in destroying the LOVs. I believe that he and his allies—whoever they might be—have moved on to exploiting them."

Ela answered experimentally. "Our LOVs are dead."

No smile softened Summer's stern gaze as she spoke in a fast, low voice. "You decoupled the asterids from their shells, didn't you? You thought they could live in your brain tissue and we would never know the difference—but that's how I originally designed them to live. It wasn't hard to guess. So far, I'm the only one who knows, but that can't last. Look at me. You can tell I'm not lying . . . can't you?"

Ela nodded, seeing a hard-edged honesty in Summer's face. "Why are you talking to me?"

"Because Daniel has no intention of destroying the symbiotic LOVs. Maybe he never did. I would do it myself if I could, but it's too late. His people have had weeks with all those children who were evacuated before you. So much knowledge must have escaped by now that it will never be possible to put the genie back in the bottle."

"I don't understand. The other *Roi Nuoc*, their LOVs were removed—"

"Do you know that?"

"It's what they told us."

"It's what they told me, but I don't believe it anymore."

A creeping dread came over Ela. "You think they're dead."

"I don't know. I just don't."

"We trusted your humanity," Ela whispered.

"There is too much money involved. I think—I'm just guessing—what's been found inside the brain tissue of those kids is going to make a lot of people very, very rich and long-lived."

"Medical applications?"

"Try an on-ramp to nanotech."

"Oh, God."

"I think they're being farmed," Summer concluded.

Ela leaned against the wall, forcing herself to be calm, to think. "We have to get out of here."

"That would be nice," Summer agreed. "But how? We're at sea. There's a typhoon outside and cameras in every cell. I might be able to get one or two of you to the deck, but—"

"No. We all go together, or not at all."

Summer shook her head. "Then I don't think it's possible to escape."

Ela froze, hearing a resonance in these words. She nodded slowly. "Of course you're right. We can't escape. We have to arrange for them to let us go."

"Uh-huh. And how will you do that?"

"I don't know yet! Let me think. Let me—" The answer came while she was still protesting. "They would have to take us out if the ship was sinking, don't you think?"

"It's not sinking."

"Then I'll sink it."

"Will you?"

Ela smiled. It was easy to see that Summer had begun to suspect her sanity. "I did an article once on the disappearance of a merchant ship. It was sunk by pirates. Speculation said the owners hired them to do it, so they could collect the insurance."

"You want to hire pirates? How would you pay them?"

"That won't be a problem." Ela's account had grown to over $250 million the last time she'd checked.

"But how will you broker a deal? You need an ally on the outside."

"I have an ally. May I use your farsights?"

Summer hesitated, but only for a moment. She had already committed herself, just by talking to Ela. There was no going back now. Her focus shifted to the screen of her farsights. She ran through a quick sequence of finger taps, then she slipped them off and handed them to Ela. "They'll work for you now."

It took a few minutes to contact Mother Tiger because Ela did not know the codes, and had to use a search engine to establish a link. But moments later the tiger goddess's great luminous eyes were gazing from the screen. Her growl trembled with restrained fury. "Where have my *Roi Nuoc* gone?"

• • •

Summer returned to the conference room after the scheme was set in motion. No one was there. Even the rat had been removed.

She sat in one of the bolted-down chairs, clutching at the table every time the ship plunged in heavy seas. The storm was growing worse. It seemed almost enough to sink the ship without help from outside agents.

She had little doubt that Ela's ROSA would find a willing mercenary. The master of an old Soviet vessel, perhaps, or a decommissioned American frigate. The route between Hong Kong and Singapore had been notorious for centuries, its endless islands and inlets and desperate governments offering haven to enterprising pirates. But even if an agreement was made, could any ship find them in such weather? Could the children safely transfer?

Did it matter?

For these children, the alternative was too grim to contemplate.

Near dawn she heard a muffled explosion. The deck shivered, and a fire alarm kicked in. A second explosion followed, this one louder, closer. Summer rose and went to the door. The corridor outside was empty, but she could hear running footsteps on the deck overhead. She sent a link to Daniel Simkin, but he did not pick up. She sent a link with an emergency tag. Still he did not answer. Then, somewhere overhead, she heard a door slam shut, followed by the steel shot of a closing lock. Terror lanced through her. "Daniel?"

She remembered seeing stairs on her tour of the ship. She ran for them.

The engines had stopped. The ship rolled freely in the waves, tossing her from wall to wall as she made her way forward. She found the stairs and hauled herself up. She tried the door. It would not open. It was locked, from the outside. She pounded on it, but no one came. Was this the only way out?

Think!

Maybe this was some kind of emergency procedure. Seal the doors, contain the damage. So there had to be another way out. Right?

No. It didn't make sense. The brig was on this deck, but no one had come to evacuate the kids. . . .

Because they were useless now, weren't they? With their LOVs gone. Or so Daniel would believe. It would be more convenient to let them drown, and Summer with them. Already the deck was beginning to tilt, the stern descending. "Daniel!" she screamed, clutching at the railing to keep her balance.

No. Don't panic. Think!

He was letting them drown because he thought they had no value. But he was mistaken in that. The *Roi Nuoc* had lost only their LOV shells. They still had their LOV asterids twining through their brains. Daniel could still find some use for them. Summer composed a brief text message explaining this fact, then she sent it to Simkin with an emergency tag.

Ela had been dozing when the first torpedo hit. She huddled on the floor, counting down the time until the second impact. Two million dollars for two carefully placed torpedoes.

A deep *boom* told her the bargain was fulfilled. The walls shivered. And then she was on her feet, ready to evacuate.

But minutes passed, and no one came.

The floor began to tilt.

Ela pressed her ear against the door. She could hear a distant, arrhythmic drumming . . . like fists against padded walls? Cries of terror teased at her mind, so faint they might have been imagination.

Then the cell door burst open, spilling her into the brig. She landed on hands and knees. Looking up, she expected to see one of the guards, but it was Summer Goforth. Her expression was wild, frightened and furious as she slammed the cell door back into its stays. "There are life jackets in the closet at the end of the hall!" she shouted gesturing toward the brig's open door. "Get them out. Bring them here." Then she stepped over to the next cell, and hammered in a code.

Ela scrambled to her feet. "Where are the guards?"

"Simkin forgot to tell them to take us out." She slammed the cell door open.

"So we're on our own?"

Summer punched in another code. "For now."

"There's something you're not telling me," Ela said, reading the telltales on her face.

"Just get the life jackets."

Roi Nuoc were emerging from their cells, looking around with wary eyes. "Tell me," Ela insisted.

Summer threw her a hard glance. "We're locked in down here, on the lower deck. Daniel means for us to go down with the ship." Another door slammed open.

"You said he wanted our LOVs!"

"So far as he knows, you don't have any!" Another door. "I've sent him a note clarifying that."

"So we live or die depending on if he reads it?"

Another door. "Get the life jackets! Now. Get them on these kids while there's still time."

Ela grimaced. She wanted to stay and argue more, but Summer was right. They had to be ready to go . . . if they were to go at all. She crooked a finger at Phan and Oanh, and together they ducked out into the hall, sliding down the slanting deck to the closet, where they gathered as many life jackets as they could carry. "We're going over the side," Ela told them. "Be ready."

Phan returned first up the passage. Oanh followed. Ela took the rest of the jackets and scrambled behind them up the sloping floor. By the time she returned to the brig, all the cells were open and half the kids already had their life jackets on. Summer was nowhere to be seen. "Where's Summer?" Ela shouted. "The foreign woman."

Ninh answered as he buckled a life jacket on. "She went with Virgil to see about the door. Take life jackets for them—and put one on yourself!"

A victorious yelp greeted Ela as she started up the passage. "They've opened the door!" Virgil yelled, his voice booming back down to the brig. Ela could see the foot of the stairs, but she could not see him. "Everybody out, *now*."

"Everybody out!" Ela echoed, waving the kids past her. She stayed at the brig, making sure no one slid back down the passage. They were fourteen in number, fifteen counting Summer.

No one panicked. They moved quickly, calmly up the corridor, like brave young soldiers from Marxist posters. Doubt was not allowed to intrude.

Oanh was last out of the brig. Ela followed her up the passage, catching her elbow as they neared the top. "Don't wait too long," she said. "We must go over the side as soon as possible. Make sure everyone knows."

They reached the stairs. Ela looked up, to see the door standing open. The ship was listing so badly she and Oanh had to use the handrail to haul themselves up. Virgil waited at the top, a helping hand extended. "Summer said you planned this; that we're to go over the side of the ship."

Ela looped a life jacket over his head and helped him buckle it on. "Yes. We'll be picked up in the water. Mother Tiger has it all arranged."

He caught her wrist. "Mother Tiger?" Raw fear looked out of his eyes. "You've talked with Mother Tiger?"

An old panic stirred, and she tried to wrench her hand away. "Why are you holding me like that? Let go. What's wrong with you?"

He released her wrist. He touched her face. "Ela, listen to me. We can't depend on Mother Tiger anymore. Ky believed Mother Tiger caused Lien to die."

"No. That's crazy. You can't believe that, Virgil. Don't talk that way. Mother Tiger is our tool, our ally. It exists for us. Ky made it that way."

"It's changed."

"Everything has changed! But it doesn't matter. It's too late. Stop talking nonsense, because this is our only way out. Virgil, we have no other choice."

CHAPTER 41

Virgil hesitated at the weather door, wrapped up in a sense of doom. Their lives depended now on a ROSA he could no longer trust...unless the very fact of dependence meant safety? Mother Tiger existed to serve the *Roi Nuoc*. Surely they would be all right so long as they played that role? It's what Ky had believed.

Ela glanced back at him, her eyes warning against any more crazy talk. Then she slipped out past the weather door. Virgil followed. The wind hit, slamming them both back against a wall. Two crew members were there, their shoulders hunched against the sheets of rain stomping across the deck. One of them clipped a lifeline to Virgil's jacket, then shoved him toward the boats where the *Roi Nuoc* were being seated among a skeleton crew.

Dawn had not yet arrived. Clutching the line, Virgil glanced around at a dark gray sea raging beneath a sky of the same color. The bronze light of a setting half moon leaked past a veil of clouds. Visibility was hardly a quarter mile even when the ship rose to the top of a swell. He could not see the vessel that would pick them up. He turned to look for Ela.

She held on to the line, a few steps behind him. Her wet hair whipped around her face, her dark eyes were stern. Her yellow life jacket looked so bright in the gloom it seemed to have an illumination of its own. He watched her hands busily unclipping her lifeline. She nodded at him to do the same.

Instead he leaned close, shouting to be heard over the wind. "Where is the other ship?"

"Gone! We couldn't trust mercenaries to pick us up."

"Then how—?"

There was a cry from the boats, barely audible over the screaming gale. Virgil turned to see a peppering of yellow life jackets going over the side, pulled down by the white water of a clutching wave. He held the image in his mind and counted quickly. Nine. No, ten figures escaping into the black sea.

Ela's hands scrabbled at his vest, fighting to unclip his tether. "Come on, come on!" she screamed. "Before they try to stop us. I have talked to Mother Tiger, Virgil. There is *nothing wrong.*"

Water sloshed across the rolling deck. The crew fell back from the boats in terror. Two smaller, slighter figures extracted themselves from the knot of panicked seamen and ran for the rail, pitching themselves over, headfirst into the storm.

Virgil felt his lifeline snap free. He stumbled backward, Ela's weight propelling him toward the water. His mind was filled with horror. The kids were already gone, over the side with only their life jackets to keep them from drowning. *But there was no ship to pick them up.*

"Ela, we can't do this! This is crazy."

"Yes!" She tugged on him, pushed on him. "Yes, we were all driven insane by our LOvs. They drove us to suicide. Now Virgil, over the side!"

Another wave washed the deck. Virgil fought against the retreating flood of white water as it curled around his legs, tugging on him. Then he looked up. Across the draining deck he saw Simkin returning to the rail to reclaim a half-flooded boat. Their eyes met, and in that glimpse Virgil knew that all the suspicions Summer had whispered to him as they crouched at the top of the stairs were true. Simkin had become a different kind of enemy; a hidden player in an invisible war. They would find no refuge with him in the boats.

The wave pulled away. He looked for Summer, but he could not see her. Then Ela tugged on his hand one more time. He turned. He put one foot on the railing, and as the side of the ship began to rise from the water he launched himself together with Ela over the side.

The lash of rain had not prepared him for the shocking splash of the sea. Cold enfolded him as Ela's hand vanished from his grip. He thrashed, trying to find her again, but everything had disappeared—the sky, the freighter, the bright yellow wink of her life jacket—erased by the liquid gray solvent of the sea.

Virgil did not go under, but it felt like he did as the wind drove salt water down his throat. Spume howled past his face as he crested a swell. He glimpsed the setting moon low in the sky, and then he spun half-around and went sliding down into a trough between waves, submerging at the bottom, only to be bumped up by something smooth and hard.

Stories of sharks were legion in the South China Sea. He thrashed and lashed out, but a mountainous swell was carrying him up again, and the phantom object was gone. He turned his back to the wind and told himself it could not have been a shark. Sharks were extinct, or nearly so.

The top of the swell blew off and wrapped around his head in a choking veil of white foam. Then he was sliding down again, and this time he saw it before he hit: a dark, oblong object just below the heaving surface of the moonlit water. He struck against it; felt the same smooth, unyielding texture beneath his hands. A hull? A blue hull.

He recognized it then. It was the *Marathon*. Had Mother Tiger brought it here? Was this the rescue Ela had planned?

His questions fled as he saw the low mound that contained the hatch. He lunged for it as it went sliding past, and managed to catch the rim. But instead of the hard hatch plate, his fingers found a taut membrane stretched across the entryway. The hatch was already open.

As the *Marathon*'s bow slid toward the swell's crest he hauled himself over the rim. The membrane irised under his weight, opening just enough to let him wriggle headfirst into the little chamber, accompanied by a cascade of seawater. *"Iris!"*

He screamed the name of his ROSA, but it was Mother Tiger that answered. "You must bring my *Roi Nuoc* aboard."

He lay still for a moment, stunned into silence by this simple command. It was exactly what the ROSA should have said, what he would have expected it to say if Ky had not sown doubt in his mind. "You saved me," he whispered.

"That is what I am for."

"But you didn't save Lien."

"Help my *Roi Nuoc*, before they drown."

An ally or an enemy? There was no way Virgil could decide that now.

He sat up, slamming against the chair as the *Marathon* rocketed down a swell. "Is this our only vessel?" he asked through gritted teeth.

"It is," Mother Tiger affirmed.

Virgil could not imagine how they would fit fourteen *Roi Nuoc* inside the Marathon's tiny cabin. All by himself he filled up the minuscule floor space.

Mother Tiger said: "Phan is outside now. Show him how to come in."

Virgil looked up at the little hatch as the marathon churned in a trough. The membrane pulsed under the pressure of wind like an arrhythmic heart machine. A stream of water dripped through its center. Phan was drowning out there, along with all the other *Roi Nuoc*.

Moving quickly now, he opened a floor level cabinet and pulled out a rope he remembered seeing there. He secured one end to the chair mount, then he stripped off his life jacket and tied that to the other end. "Is Phan still close?"

"Yes."

Virgil stood, his feet splayed, using the chair and then the wall to steady himself. He held on to the life jacket with one hand; with the other he grabbed a rung of the hatch ladder and pulled himself up far enough to shove the life jacket through the membrane. The wind took it away, but he caught the rope and held on to that, then followed it through until he stood balanced on the lowest rung of the ladder, the membrane clutching tight around his ribs.

He could see Phan in the moon's bronze light, gliding up the face of a wave. He was downwind, so Virgil let the life jacket pay out. There was no use shouting. His voice would never carry over the gale. But it didn't matter—Phan had already seen the jacket skipping along the surface of the water. His eyes grew wide and white as they fixed on Virgil. For a moment Virgil thought sure he was going to turn and lunge away from this apparition, half-a-man standing above the wild sea.

But the *Roi Nuoc* had not been raised to superstitions. Phan lunged for the vest, catching it on his second try. Virgil hauled on the rope as the marathon accelerated over the crest of a swell, sliding down again in dizzy acceleration to splash against the trough. In the quiet interval as they rose on the next swell, Phan reached the marathon. Virgil grabbed him by both hands, then ducked through the membrane, dragging Phan after. They tumbled together to the floor, Phan choking, and gasping for breath.

"There are storage vaults here, and here," Virgil said, slapping the walls. "Start emptying them. Get ready to throw the stuff out because we are going to need the room."

Phan nodded, while Mother Tiger announced, "Ninh is outside."

Virgil lunged for the ladder, resolving to accept the ROSA as an ally, at least for now.

Now and then as she bobbed at the crest of some great swell Ela would glimpse a bronze half-moon persisting a few degrees above the horizon. Once, its dirty light sparkled across the dark shape of a distant lifeboat cresting on a swell. The boat's storm canopy was buttoned down tight. It faced the waves as it properly should. Such modern lifeboats were supposed to be unsinkable, so whoever was aboard would certainly survive. She hoped Summer Goforth was among them.

She spun around as the next wave rolled under her. Wind blew spray in her eyes. More fell from the sky. Every half minute or so a great explosion of spray roared upward from somewhere just beyond her short horizon. The next swell carried her even closer to the foaming explosions. From the wave's summit she looked down to see the foundering ship, lying like a black shoal just beneath the surface, the swells erupting against it in torrents of white foam. In that glimpse she saw something else: a bit of golden brown flotsam. It was caught in the windblown tracks of foam that swirled around the ship. She saw it for only a moment before it disappeared beneath the surface. But as she started to slip down the backside of the swell she thought she saw it appear again, a few meters away from where it had been.

As she crested the next wave she looked for the *Roi Nuoc*;

she hadn't seen any of them since going into the water. It was as if she had leaped into a different ocean . . . one much closer to the arctic circle. How could it be so cold?

And why was the dying ship taking so long to seek the bottom? Each swell was carrying her closer to it. Already she could feel the tug of its vortices against her feet. A torrent of salty rain pelted her as another swell burst against the hulk. She choked and slid round, and then she saw the bit of golden brown flotsam again, much closer now, sliding down the face of a foam-addled wave. A ghost white hand emerged from the water beside it, then the object turned. The moon shone over a pale human face draped in sodden hair that gleamed golden in the brassy light. A cry reached Ela's ears, like the high-pitched call of a seabird. Then she dropped behind the next swell, and the apparition was gone from sight.

But she could not banish it from her mind. That had been Summer Goforth in the water, and without the yellow blaze of a life jacket to hold her up! But why wasn't she on the lifeboat? She had reached the deck ahead of Virgil. She should be safe with the crew, locked in under the lifeboat's storm canopy.

Ela waited for the next swell to lift her up—and there was Summer, swimming toward her though it meant fighting the direction of the waves and the downward tug of the sinking ship. Ela felt her own exhaustion, and wondered that Summer had survived this long without a life jacket. But the same currents that she fought went to work for Ela. Kicking hard, Ela went rocketing down the face of a swell. The distance between the two of them closed. They reached for each other with outstretched hands. Ela felt cold skin, and then she had her arms around Summer as a monstrous swell lifted them through an explosion of foam, up over the unseen hulk of the dying ship and suddenly the fountains of foam were receding behind them.

Summer leaned back against Ela, letting her weight rest on the life jacket as she raised her left hand as high as she could above the water. She clutched a set of farsights in her wrinkled white fingers. Her right hand emerged next and she began tapping, no doubt sending an emergency signal to some satellite far overhead.

Ela felt a rush of horror. They must not call for help. They must not give their existence away. If it was known that any of them had survived, the hunt for them would never end.

She grabbed Summer's arm and dragged it back down again, prying at her fingers until she felt the farsights fall away.

Virgil ducked back into the submersible, pulling Lam in behind him. Ninh caught her limp body, drawing her down into his lap, supporting her as she leaned over to retch seawater onto the floor. There was six inches of standing water there already, warmed by the dwindling body heat of the *Roi Nuoc*.

Virgil glanced up sharply as a *whir* and a metallic *click* announced the closing of the hatch. The membrane withdrew, and the drip of water ceased. "Are we done?" he asked as he clung to the ladder, surveying the cramped cabin. Kids were sitting on the console, and on the arms of the chair. Some had slipped into the bulk storage bins. To make room for them all, the life jackets had been cast out, along with the blankets, spare electronic modules, and most of the food. "Is this all of us?"

Oanh had been keeping count. Now she answered from her perch on a shelf just behind him. "This is only thirteen."

The air was hot and foul, the filters pushed far beyond capacity by the presence of so many. Virgil turned to Oanh, frowning, unsure if he was thinking clearly anymore, or if she was. "But we should be fourteen . . . right?"

The *Marathon* steadied. Its nasty rolling sprints among the swells ceased so that Virgil knew they must be diving.

Oanh nodded. "It's Ela who's still missing."

"Then why are we diving?"

Oanh couldn't answer him. Virgil glanced forward at the screens, but he could not see them past the kids crowded on the console. "Mother Tiger? Where is Ela? Can't you find her?"

The ROSA's soothing voice purred. "That one cannot be recovered. An emergency beacon has marked her position. If this craft returns for her, it will be seen. Then it will be known that some of you survived."

"I don't care," Virgil said. "Go back."

Oanh repeated this command, and then several others around the cramped cabin, but Mother Tiger did not to respond.

W here was the *Marathon*? Ela held Summer Goforth in the snug circle of her arms and wondered. When would Mother Tiger come to pick them up? Let it be soon.

Summer had fought hard to keep the farsights, but after they had fallen away she seemed to give up. Now she lay limp in Ela's arms, her only motion an occasional spasm of retching when the wind drove water into her mouth.

Ela dreaded her stillness, fearing each time that she would never move again. She must not lose her grip on Summer. Her life jacket was all that held them up.

She blinked salt from her burning eyes. The sky was brightening. Its light touched new bruises forming against the pale skin of Summer's face. Ela knew she had been given a life jacket on the ship, but here she was in the water without one. With bruises. No doubt someone had meant for her to die.

It wasn't hard to guess who.

How long had they been in the water? A long time.

It seemed long anyway.

She glimpsed the half-moon again. No longer did it hang suspended above the horizon. It had sunk, to become the tip of a golden nail protruding from the endless ocean. Time was passing. Her time, and Summer's. And maybe, all the lifetimes of the *Roi Nuoc* who had gone ahead of her into the water. Why had the *Marathon* failed to come?

Because Virgil was right, and Mother Tiger had betrayed them.

"*No!*" Ela refused to believe it. To believe it was to give up.

M other Tiger!" Virgil shouted, though there was so little oxygen in the marathon's packed cabin that he could hardly breathe. "If Ela's alive we have to go back for her. *Now.*" He wanted to say more, but there was no air. Maybe they would drown, all of them, in a sea of their own exhalations.

"Be calm," the ROSA warned. "There are no resources for this."

"I'll be calm when she's here." But Virgil felt dizzy now, drenched in his own unhealthy sweat. Very soon the bad air would force him to be calm. "Go back up," he pleaded. "Go now."

Oanh laid a hand on his shoulder. "We will vote," she said. "If we go back for Ela, we risk discovery. Who will go back?" She repeated this in Vietnamese and everyone raised a hand, though it was easy to see they were afraid.

"So it's decided," Oanh said. "We all will take the risk of going back."

But the *Marathon*'s course still did not shift. The ROSA did not respond.

"Is our link bad?" someone asked.

"That's it," Virgil said. "Of course. We're underwater now. Mother Tiger can't have left more than a shell of itself here. We have to get the antenna up, or—"

"Even a shell of Mother Tiger would be able to respond," Oanh said.

Virgil rubbed his eyes. "Okay then. Okay. Maybe we can take manual control?"

"Do you know how?" Ninh asked.

One of the kids spoke from the console. "There are key sequences here."

Mother Tiger said, "Don't use them. None of you knows how to pilot the *Marathon*."

Oanh scowled. "We'll learn."

Ninh nodded. "Use them," he urged.

"Use them," Virgil echoed, and then everyone was saying it.

"No," Mother Tiger said. "I will do as you ask."

After the moon set, the sky grew brighter, taking on a pearly gray luminescence. Ela felt warmer. Dreams dodged through her mind. In one of them she felt Summer begin to slip from her arms. She woke abruptly, and tightened her grip. How long had it been since Summer coughed?

Ela tried to raise her higher but the sea slapped her face, driving salt water into her lungs and nasal membranes, setting her coughing again.

She was too tired for this. Much too tired. She no longer had the strength to hold the world together and so it began to dissolve, breaking down into dreamspace.

She tried to blink, to awaken herself just once more, but her eyes were seared with salt and she could see only a nonsensical vision: a dark silhouette sliding down the face of a gray swell. A dream image coming for her. Some part of her laughed in scorn. All the modern people had said this last vision would be a plain white light, but they were wrong. Either that, or Ela could not even manage to die correctly, for this was a black sea god, half man, half serpent. She slid into the trough between two giant swells, and felt herself slide under—

—into a hot, steamy world, low lights shimmering on sweat-covered limbs, stinking breath flowing past her ear and the smell of vomit. Fresh water trickled across her swollen lips, flowed into the salt-inflamed tissue of her mouth, feeling holy. Swallowing was agony. She turned her head and threw up.

CHAPTER 42

The air was cooler. Ela's eyes were closed, her head resting against Virgil's chest as she listened to the soft beat of his heart, the slow tide of his breathing. For a long time those sounds defined her world. It was a peaceful world now.

When she'd first come aboard the *Marathon* the air had been unbreathable. Panic had set in as she felt herself suffocating but Virgil had held her close, whispering calming words in her ear, urging her to look inward to a deeper level of awareness, a trance state that would require only a little oxygen to sustain her.

With the help of her hidden LOVs she had done it.

But now she stirred; her breathing deepened. Some sense she could not name warned of something amiss. She opened her eyes, and looked up into Virgil's sleeping face, shiny with sweat and framed in a tangle of hideous dreadlocks. A stubble of beard had broken past the hormone-treated follicles of his face, while on his forehead blue-green flecks of LOVs were already re-emerging. She raised a hand to touch them. "Virgil"—her voice an ugly croak escaping from a throat made raw by salt water—"wake up. Wake up please. We have gone too far south."

His eyes opened. His gaze fixed on her briefly, a remote glance as he returned from his trance state. Next he looked about the cabin, at the *Roi Nuoc* occupying every surface, every niche. Their eyes were closed, their breathing shallow, their faces all wearing the sublime expressions of youth deities on an ancient temple frieze. Only Summer Goforth suffered a troubled sleep. She lay in the pilot's chair, shivering and muttering in some fevered dream. Virgil frowned at her as if she were something inexplicably out of place. Then his gaze returned to Ela. His eyes warmed. "Can you really tell where we are?"

Ela nodded, touching her own budding LOVs, hard and real on her forehead. Some new sense had awakened inside her and she knew, as if a map of the world glowed inside her head, exactly where they were. "We've gone too far south. Who decided we should go this way?"

The *Roi Nuoc* began to open their eyes.

"Nothing was decided," Virgil said. "There wasn't enough air to speak or think, before." He sniffed, as if measuring the oxygen content. "It's better now."

"It won't be for long. Not when we all wake up. We should be on shore by now. We *are* going back . . . right?" They had to go back. Too much had been left behind.

Low voices rustled through the packed cabin as many among the *Roi Nuoc* voiced their support, but Virgil frowned. His palm brushed Ela's forehead as if to check for fever. "You want to go back? But there's nothing to go back to. It's all gone."

"No." Oanh spoke from her perch upon a shelf. Her pink T-shirt was stiff and wrinkled. "The other *Roi Nuoc* are still in the delta—the ones that never were on the reservation. And maybe the disappeared too. We need to find them."

"We have to find them," Ela said. "We can't let them find us first. They are not free, and most of them are so young. If they are alive, it will not take much to turn them into enemies."

"But they won't look for us," Ninh said. "We must be dead. That's what will be said about us. No one will look for us to come back from the sea."

Ela scanned the faces of the *Roi Nuoc*. They were packed across the floor and up the walls of the marathon's tiny cabin, but they had their LOVs to keep them calm. She made her confession: "In the water Summer Goforth was using her far-sights to call for help. I took them away from her, but maybe someone saw me do it. They will wonder why, no? Why did I do such a crazy thing?"

"Because we *are* crazy," Virgil said, touching the tiny specks of his new LOVs. "You said it on the ship. Our LOVs have driven us mad."

Summer must have been awake, listening to their debate, because she spoke up now in a hoarse, whispery voice. "The disappeared won't believe that—*if* they're still alive. They know you. They'll think the same way you do."

Mother Tiger's voice purred from the speakers, overriding all other talk. "They will know you would choose to return. That is why you will not return."

With an arm around Virgil for support, Ela sat up a little straighter. "A ROSA is telling us what we must do?"

"It's not the first time," Virgil said. He told her why she had been in the water so long. "Mother Tiger didn't want to bring you and Summer aboard—because of Summer's farsights, I think."

Ela looked from him to Oanh, too stunned to speak, feeling as if she were drowning again.

"It's true," Oanh said. "We were going to switch this sub to manual control. That's when Mother Tiger gave in and started to help."

Ela did not want to believe it. "But Mother Tiger is our ally."

"Ela, listen to me!" Virgil said. "I tried to tell you before. Even Ky had doubts." Then he told them all of Ky's suspicions. "He thought Lien's death might be more than a tragic accident."

"So if anyone follows Lien, that one isn't *Roi Nuoc* anymore?" Ninh asked. "Is it our link with Mother Tiger that makes us *Roi Nuoc*?"

There was a brief debate about it, mostly in Vietnamese. The air was getting stuffy again, and Ela was remembering. "I saw something when Ky died," she said softly. Only Oanh and Virgil heard her, but Oanh quickly signaled the others to listen while Ela described the blinding flash of light that had erupted from Ky's farsights. "He jumped to pull them off, and they shot him."

She wanted to show them a vid to prove what she was saying, but the *Marathon* was too far underwater, and Mother Tiger's partial persona would not or could not respond. But Summer offered herself as a witness. "I saw it too. I wondered about it. I thought maybe it was Daniel's work, or a government official who wanted to close the books."

"Mother Tiger would have filtered those inputs," Virgil said.

The partial persona remained silent. Perhaps it did not have the complexity to respond to these accusations, or perhaps it saw no need.

"We should vote now," Oanh said. "Who wants to go back?"

All around the marathon, hands rose. There was no dissent.

"Then change course," Virgil said to the ROSA shell that had charge of navigation. "Take us back to the delta."

They listened intently, but none could sense the marathon changing direction.

Summer sat up a little straighter, twisting around to look at the console. "It's a question of psychology," she said, her voice still hoarse, hardly more than a whisper. "Products like the *Marathon* are made for people who like adventure. People who like adventure don't like depending on a ROSA. When I was in Australia last summer I rented a *Marathon*. It wasn't hard at all to handle it on manual."

Summer was able to pilot the marathon to within a few miles of the delta coast. There they surfaced, hoping for a news update. Instead they received a full link with Mother Tiger. Virgil had expected keen argument from the ROSA, but its intelligence was more subtle than that, and it did not have human pride or human peevishness. It had only a goal: to keep the *Roi Nuoc* safe. So when it calculated that it could not stop them from going ashore, it offered to guide them instead.

Virgil urged the others to accept the ROSA's help. "We'll be safe, so long as our goal and the ROSA's is the same."

They waited until evening. Then Mother Tiger steered them to an unguarded river mouth far south of the reservation. Debris thrown down by the hurricane clogged the waterway, forcing the marathon to surface. It glided silently upstream, sending a V of ripples out across the moon-spangled water. Ela squeezed out of the hatch and watched the ripples unfolding, rolling outward until they tangled in the drowning vegetation. Streamers of clouds snaked in a high-elevation wind, but along the river the air was still.

Ela was keenly aware of the *Marathon* moving through her own inner map of the world. She felt more aware of everything: the soft voices from below, and dashing shapes of fish in the river, hurtling satellites, and the rumble of ancient generators reverberating over the water, the smell of night blossoms and of mud, and the count of each soft beat of her heart.

The *Roi Nuoc*, from beyond the reservation had been alerted to their coming. Mother Tiger had instructed them to gather farsights and cash cards, and to hide these things beneath a concrete pier that served a shrimp-packing company set up along an otherwise empty stretch of waterfront. The kids themselves were long gone by the time the marathon pulled up to the moonlit pier.

Ela was first out. She scrambled under the pier to retrieve the stashed bundle, passing it up to Ninh. There were clothes wrapped around the farsights: clean white tek-fabric shirts and slacks. Cash cards were abundant. Cash, at least, was no longer a problem for any of the *Roi Nuoc*, thanks to Ela's income.

Ela put on the new garments. Then she threw her old clothes into the swollen river. Moonlight glittered on the water as the marathon slipped away from the pier, a dark shadow gliding downstream, faster than the current. Ela watched it go.

She still held her new farsights in one hand, reluctant to put them on. She was not the only one who hesitated: Oanh stood beside her, looking undecided. "You don't trust Mother Tiger anymore, do you?" she asked, glancing nervously at the other *Roi Nuoc*. Most of them had slipped their farsights on even before changing clothes.

Ela turned her own set over in her hands, watching moonlight play across the lens. "I am thinking of what *Roi Nuoc* means. 'Water puppets.' Little doll figures that perform on a stage of water. Whose puppets have we been? I used to think Ky Xuan Nguyen was the puppet master, but I know now that was never true. It was always Mother Tiger."

Ky had once asked her about Sawong, the old transvestite who had cared for her until he had gone away with his lover, leaving her alone in Bangkok. *You could have looked for Sawong, or waited for him to return, but you didn't. Why not?* Ela finally had an answer for him: "I don't need a master." She drew back her arm, and cast her farsights out across the water.

Oanh saw what she was doing and jumped to stop her, too late. She made a little cry as the farsights disappeared with a splash. The other *Roi Nuoc* gathered around, murmuring in shock: "Why did you do that, Ela? Did you mean to do it? You are angry with Mother Tiger, aren't you?"

Oanh looked mournful. "It will be hard to live without the ROSA."

"We have the LOVs now," Ela reminded her. "We don't need Mother Tiger anymore."

Phan's grin flashed from beneath his farsights. "Mother Tiger is saying you were never really one of us anyway."

"More lies," Oanh said.

Ela shrugged.

Lam spoke now, in Vietnamese. Ela had picked up enough of that language to gather the meaning: *"Mother Tiger asks What is Roi Nuoc? How can we be Roi Nuoc without our farsights?"*

Ninh nodded vigorously, his forehead wrinkled in a worried frown. "How can we find each other without them?"

Even Virgil was ready to compromise. "We can't just throw an advantage away, Ela. We won't know what's going on if we can't see through other lenses. We won't know if one of us is in trouble, or what's happening in the world."

"But with them, we will always be under Mother Tiger's eyes," Ela countered. "Have you already forgotten Ky? And Lien? And me?" She shook her head. "We escaped the IBC. Now we have a chance to create the life we want, without asking anyone's permission. *Anyone's*. We are not little children anymore."

Oanh bowed her head. She held her farsights for a second, her gaze lingering regretfully on their beautiful silver frame. Then she sighed and, looking up, she hurled them into the river, watching them through their long spinning flight, until they splashed down in a little geyser of spray. "I am no longer a water puppet," she said. "Ela and I have become something else now . . . something different. Water fairies. *Tien Nuoc*. Without masters, we find our own way."

Summer Goforth had been standing on the edge of their circle. Like the rest of them she was dressed in white, but unlike them she did not have farsights. Now she met Ela's gaze and asked, "Aren't the LOVs your master now?"

Ela shook her head sadly. "You don't understand it. The LOVs are part of us. They *are* us. Their fate and ours is the same."

Summer had helped them escape the ship, but it was clear she still did not approve what they did. "What are your plans for me?"

Ela frowned over this. "My plans? I don't have plans for you. It's your life. Your choice."

"Mother Tiger doesn't agree," Ninh said softly.

Ela threw him a sharp look. "I can guess what the ROSA has to say!"

"I can too," Summer said. "Does it explain that I could betray you? That I could bring authorities after you and that you must do whatever is necessary to prevent this?"

Ninh admitted that was the essence of it. "Mother Tiger has never asked such a thing of us before." He sighed and slipped off his farsights. Then he looked at Oanh. "I cannot be *Tien Nuoc*," he said. "Not a lady-spirit. Let us be *Tiên Thân Nuoc*, instead. A spirit of the river; one that cannot be seen." Oanh smiled, bowing her head in approval.

Tiên Thân Nuoc. Ninh stepped to the river's edge and tossed his farsights spinning into the moonlight.

Virgil looked grim, but he joined Ninh, casting his own farsights away into the water. The others followed. One by one they severed their link with Mother Tiger, becoming *Tiên Thân Nuoc*. Becoming free.

When the last of the farsights was gone, Virgil turned to Summer. "Will you betray us?" he asked. "Or will you join us? You made this thing—maybe just in time . . ."

Summer shook her head in firm denial. "What Simkin wanted to do to you—that was worse than anything you've done. But this . . ." Her gaze swept their circle. "It's out of control. Can't you see that? Can't you see how dangerous this is?"

Ela slipped her arm around Virgil's waist. "Yes. We can see it. We have the LOVs. We see both sides."

The delta myths had not been wrong. They were an alien generation. Ela had known it about herself ever since she'd been a child in Bangkok, telling the fortunes of humble people who looked on her and her affinity for unknown things and were afraid. Such people would try to hold the world still, but for that it was much too late.

"*Will* you betray us?" Ela asked.

Summer glanced around at the anxious faces waiting on her reply. "It's not me you need to worry about."

"The disappeared," Oanh said. "If they're alive, they'll be looking for us."

Ela nodded. "I think they're alive." Too much had been invested in them to let them die. She glanced over her shoulder, dreading to see a peeper ball drifting out of the vegetation. There was nothing. Not yet, but her uneasiness spread to Virgil, and then to Oanh, who said, "We should go."

So they parted, scattering in twos and threes into the countryside. Virgil was anxious to be off, but after a few steps Ela hesitated, and turned back. Summer eyed her warily. "You have no trust of us," Ela said. "Maybe it must be that way. But in time I think you will come to see this is not wrong." She raised a quick hand before Summer could argue. "We are not changing our minds. You know this."

"It's something I'm learning," Summer admitted.

"That's good. Learning is a skill most people forget."

"Ela," Virgil said, "we should go."

Ela nodded, but still she did not leave. "I did not get to tell you about my ROSA, Summer. I think Mother Tiger has found it by now, but when it was mine, it was good at telling fortunes. For you, I think Kathang would say something like 'This one cannot close her eyes. Even when she turns away, she will always see through to the heart.'"

Summer responded with a skeptical laugh. "Your ROSA must have been out of practice, Ela, because I can't even see through to my own heart. I can't see past this night."

"Still, I think you will not betray us."

Summer wasn't so sure. Long after Virgil and Ela were gone, she stood alone on the pier, watching the muddy water run past. Insects called, an airliner growled far overhead, and somewhere, a bird spoke. Could the LOVs still be contained? It was possible. Certainly new weapons could be designed . . . but how could they be deployed against the disappeared? Daniel had made control immeasurably more difficult so that Summer found herself considering failure:

Would it be better to live in a world created by the *Roi Nuoc* or by Daniel Simkin?

That was the heart of it.

"I will come after you, Ela," Summer promised, speaking softly to the night, to the flowing river. "But only after I bring Daniel down."

She waited on the pier for three more hours, until a district police officer chanced past on his motorcycle. Summer convinced him to take her to the police station. From there she called her ROSA, and after that she opened a confidential link to the United Nations. Some there still knew her name.